Emma Fraser emigrated to Africa with her Gaelic-speaking parents when she was nine years old and remembers lying in bed and listening to the sound of her father playing the bagpipes drifting across the veld. She returned to the Western Isles of Scotland years later and went on to qualify as a nurse and worked in Edinburgh and Glasgow before going on to study English Literature at Aberdeen University. Emma began writing when her daughters started school and she has published three historical novels, two of which were shortlisted for the Romantic Novel of the Year Award. Her third book, *The Shipbuilder's Daughter,* was inspired by, as always, true events – this time by the Glasgow shipyards where her grandfather once worked. *Greyfriars House* is her fourth novel.

Keep up to date with Emma by following her on Twitter (@EmmaFraserBooks) or becoming her friend on Facebook (www.facebook.com/emmafraserauthor).

Also by Emma Fraser

When the Dawn Breaks
We Shall Remember
The Shipbuilder's Daughter

EMMA FRASER

GREYFRIARS HOUSE

sphere

SPHERE

First published in Great Britain in 2018 by Sphere

13 5 7 9 10 8 6 4 2

A CIP catalogue record for this book
is available from the British Library.

ISBN 978-0-7515-6611-6

Typeset in Bembo by M Rules
Printed and bound in Great Britain by
Clays Ltd, St Ives plc

Papers used by Sphere are from well-managed forests
and other responsible sources.

MIX
Paper from
responsible sources
FSC® C104740

Sphere
An imprint of
Little, Brown Book Group
Carmelite House
50 Victoria Embankment
London EC4Y 0DZ

An Hachette UK Company
www.hachette.co.uk

www.littlebrown.co.uk

Dedicated to the nurses who served during WW2.
Your bravery humbles me.

Do not stand at my grave and weep
I am not there; I do not sleep.
I am a thousand winds that blow,
I am the diamond glints on snow,
I am the sunlight on ripened grain,
I am the gentle autumn rain.
When you awake in the morning's hush
I am the swift uplifting rush
Of quiet birds in circled flight.
I am the soft star-shine at night.
Do not stand at my grave and cry;
I am not there; I did not die.

MARY ELIZABETH FRYE,
1932, BALTIMORE, USA

Prologue

Charlotte

October 1984

The house looms behind me, grey and forbidding in the moonlight. From the turret window a light flickers so briefly I can't be sure I saw it. Ever since I arrived on the island I have had the sensation I am being watched, that someone wants me gone. But I no longer trust my senses. There is so much that is strange about Greyfriars.

It is very still. As if the island is holding its breath. I move towards the shore. What my great-aunt has told me so far has shaken me. And there is more to come. More secrets to be revealed. I am not sure I can bear to hear them.

As I pick my way along the rough path I think regretfully of the torch left behind in the porch. But I persevere, wanting to put distance between me and the house. The moon and stars provide just enough light although every now and again scudding clouds obscure them and I am momentarily plunged into darkness.

I continue through the trees, innocuous in the daytime, but in the shifting darkness as sinister as watching sentinels. Then at last I am in the open again, the sea, glittering in the moonlight, stretching in front of me. I suck in lungfuls of salty air and my pulse slows.

A rustle comes from the copse behind me and my heart kicks as I whirl around. Something has moved within the

1

shadows. I think of the ghostly presences my mother told me about, then immediately dismiss the thought with an impatient click of my tongue. The only ghosts are the ones in my head. Some placed there by Georgina, others of my own making.

Tiger has run off and I can hear the cracking of branches as she sniffs amongst the piles of rotting leaves. A shape swoops over my head and I smother a cry. A flutter and a flash. It is just the owl that roosts in the eaves, returning with a mouse trapped in its beak.

It isn't just the house that unsettles me, or the two women within, it is me, the way I feel inside. Untethered and adrift. A boat without an anchor at the mercy of the wind and tide.

I'd told myself I'd come here to find answers although I knew, deep down, I was fleeing from the world, my grief, my guilt, from having to make a decision about the rest of my life.

Tiger growls. She has emerged from the bushes and is standing in front of the copse of trees, her ears up, her tail rigid behind her. The hair on the back of my neck stands on end. I know she is there before I see her. The figure emerges from the shadows, her face hidden. I have seen her before. Edith sleepwalking, I've been told. I no longer believe it.

Chapter One

Charlotte

Eight weeks earlier

I stood on the narrow pavement in front of the Old Bailey as cameras pointed in my direction, their flashes almost blinding me. The questions came thick and fast.

'Miss Friel, how does it feel to have won your first murder trial?'

'Look this way, Miss Friel, and smile!'

'Did you know you'd be creating a precedent when you agreed to take on this case?'

'I didn't win on my own, gentlemen,' I said with a nod in the direction of Giles who was standing next to me, his hand on my back, uncomfortably close to my backside. I shifted slightly, not enough so anyone would notice, but enough to ensure Giles had to remove his hand.

But the win *was* truly all mine. Even if I was only junior counsel, it was me who'd established Mrs Curtis had called 999 no fewer than thirty-four times, not one call of which resulted in any action by the police. Not even so much as a caution. It was me who harassed the hospitals, ferreting out each report of Susan Curtis's repeated attendances. It was me who presented the jury with enough evidence to bring in a not-guilty verdict.

Giles hadn't wanted to take the case. Not just because he didn't care about the Mrs Curtises of this world and it was

3

pro bono, but also because he was sure we would lose and he didn't like to lose.

Neither did I.

But the moment I'd met Susan Curtis, and seen how down-trodden and defeated she was, I'd cared. And when I'd heard her story, I'd seen a chink – a possible line of defence – and I had known I could get Susan off.

'Miss Friel, how does it feel to know that someone is guilty but yet do everything in your power to have them released back into society? Do you not think people should pay for their crimes?'

All eyes turned towards the speaker of the last question; a journalist from the *News of the World* whom I loathed. As soon as the trial was over we'd hustled Susan into a taxi – understandably she'd no desire to face the journalists – and now thwarted of their prey they were determined to get their tuppence worth from me.

'Happily the jury agreed with me that if Mrs Curtis hadn't defended herself with the only means available to her, her husband would have almost certainly killed her and quite possibly their son.'

But the journalist wasn't finished. 'Don't you think you might have just given any woman unhappy with her marital situation carte blanche to do away with her husband, knowing that she has every chance of walking away scot-free?'

I held his gaze, trying not to reveal my contempt. 'I hardly think Mrs Curtis has walked away scot-free, as you put it. She's spent over a year in prison, separated from her son. And I doubt the events of that night – or the months and years before, when she was beaten on a regular basis, terrified every time she wouldn't survive – will ever leave her.'

'Now, gentlemen,' Giles said, stepping forward before I could say any more, and he knew me well enough to know I had a great deal more to say. Furthermore, he had let me have the limelight long enough. 'This, as you know, was an unusual case . . .'

As the reporters turned their attention to the great Giles Hardy, I slipped back inside and went to the robing room where I removed my robe and wig. Despite eyes gritty from lack of sleep after weeks of poring over evidence and witness statements into the early hours, I was still buzzing. When I was confident that the reporters had gone I left the Old Bailey and headed back to Chambers.

I hurried along Fleet Street passing the offices of the major newspapers, weaving my way through the tourists irritatingly blocking the pavement as they stopped to take photographs of the Old Cock Tavern, before turning right into Chancery Lane.

Even after ten years I still got a thrill walking through the Inns of Court. Off the main tourist route it was a rarefied, separate part of London – almost a little village in itself. I loved the sense of history in each stone, knowing I was walking in the footsteps of the Knights Templar, Oliver Cromwell and Thomas More. I had worked hard to earn the right to be part of it, and now, with the success of the Curtis trial, everything I had ever wanted was within my grasp.

I was smiling to myself as I crossed the quad in front of the offices of Lambert and Lambert. A man stepped in front of me, blocking my path. There was only time for the briefest moment of recognition, the tiniest shiver of fear, before he pulled back his fist and slammed it into my face. My spine jolted as I hit the pavement.

My head spinning, I scrambled to my feet. All I could think of was that no one must see me. But it was too late. A crowd had already gathered, a barrister I knew restraining the man who'd hit me. A woman clutched my arm.

'Are you all right?' she asked. 'Shall I call an ambulance?'

I raised my hand to my cheek and winced. To my relief it didn't seem to be bleeding. 'No. I'll be okay.'

'How can you do what you do and still live with yourself?' My attacker was struggling to release himself from the grip in which he was held. I recognised him now. It was Alfred

Corrigle. He'd been in court all through Simon's trial. Simon had been accused of raping Alfred Corrigle's daughter, Lucy, and against my better judgement I had defended him. Successfully.

'Do you know my daughter tried to kill herself?' Alfred's face was contorted, droplets of spittle flying from his mouth. He looked a far cry from the neatly dressed man who'd been in court. He lunged towards me. Instinctively I stepped back.

'Is she okay?'

'No thanks to you, you bitch! How would you like it if it had been your sister or your daughter on the stand?'

'I was only doing my job.' Even to my own ears, my words sounded feeble.

'Your job! Letting people go free so that they can rape again. I don't know who is worse – the monster who raped my daughter or you for what you did to her on the stand. He did it to some-one else, you know. She told Lucy. She was trying to decide whether to take it to court but there isn't a chance in hell of that now. Not after what you did to my Lucy.' His voice caught and he began to sob, awful wrenching heaves that shook his shoulders. It was one of the most terrible sounds I'd ever heard.

'I think I should call the police,' someone said from the crowd that had gathered.

'No. Please. Let him go.' All I wanted to do was get away. Besides, I could see he was no longer a threat. He was a broken man. Moreover, he had a point. I'd gone after Lucy with a ruthlessness that had surprised even me.

As Alfred Corrigle stumbled away I lifted my briefcase from the ground, gave the crowd a weak smile and with as much dignity as I could muster, headed towards Bloomsbury.

I had never been so glad to close the door of my small flat behind me. I was still shaking so badly it had taken me several attempts to fit my key into the lock. Not bothering for once to remove my shoes so they wouldn't spoil the cream carpet, I collapsed into an armchair.

I sat for a while thinking about what Lucy's father had said. Had Simon really raped before? There had been no mention of it in the evidence the Crown had passed to me before the trial. But then if the woman had withdrawn her complaint, it could easily have slipped them by. Or the woman had been lying. Although I couldn't think of a reason why.

I stood to get myself a glass of water and noticed the red light on the answerphone was blinking, telling me I had a message. It was probably Giles or John checking I was all right. No doubt they'd heard. News travelled fast around the Inns of Court. Although I had no wish to speak to anyone I pressed play. But it was Mum who'd left a message.

'Charlotte. It's me, Mum. You were on the television. Well done, darling! I'm so glad you managed to get Mrs Curtis off.' There was a long pause and I thought she'd rung off but just as I was about to put the phone down, she spoke again. Her voice more hesitant now. 'Charlotte, could you come home? As soon as you can? There is something I need to tell you.'

There was nothing more. I stared stupidly at the receiver in my hand. Mum had never asked me to come home – let alone as soon as I could. Something was clearly badly wrong. But what? I took a deep breath to slow my pounding heart. There was no point in speculating. I glanced at my watch. If I hurried I could make the last flight from Heathrow to Scotland.

It was after eight when, with a fist-sized bruise on my cheek and a tightness in my chest, the taxi dropped me outside Mum's house in Edinburgh. I hadn't phoned Mum to let her know I was coming. There had only been time to pack a suitcase, take a shower and change, before the taxi tooted to let me know it was waiting. As it was I'd only just made the flight to Edinburgh by the skin of my teeth.

I let myself in and called out to Mum, but there was no

7

reply. The house was eerily quiet. Mum usually kept the radio on.

Tiger, Mum's latest rescue dog – a mix of terrier and other unidentifiable breeds – flung herself at me, running around in circles, barking, her tail wagging so fiercely her whole body swayed from side to side. I went to the kitchen to look for Mum. It was the place she spent most of her time.

Everything in the kitchen was as it had always been. The same grey flagstones on the floor, the same kitchen units, the same familiar blend of Handy Andy, lavender furniture polish, and tea. But there was no sign of Mum at her usual position at the kitchen table, a book or crossword in front of her.

The band of tension around my chest tightened.

I retraced my steps into the hall and to the sitting room. I opened the door. Mum was curled up on the sofa, fast asleep and covered by a throw. I sucked in a breath. She'd always been petite but now she looked tiny, child-sized in her make-shift bed. Her skin, almost ashen in colour, was stretched over her cheekbones, her hair sticking up in tufts. There was an unnatural flush on her cheeks and her breaths came in small, shallow, rapid puffs. Although it was the middle of summer, the gas fire was on and the room was suffocatingly hot. A carafe of water and a glass, together with a bottle of tablets, sat on the small table that had been moved from its usual position and placed within easy reach. A musty aroma – a mixture of perspiration, stale air, and alcohol rub, along with the dusty smell of pills, permeated the room. Despite the cloying heat, a chill swept across my skin. Mum had always been a fresh air fiend, so fastidious about her appearance.

Tiger slipped in behind me and before I could stop her, jumped on top of Mum and lay down in the space behind her legs.

Mum's eyes flickered open. When they focused on me, the sweetest smile crossed her face.

'Charlotte! I didn't expect you to come tonight!' She stretched as if nothing was wrong. 'I must have nodded off. What time is it?'

'Almost nine.'

'That late!' She tossed aside the throw covering her and pushed herself into a sitting position, not quite managing to hide a grimace of pain as she did. Very gingerly she lowered her legs to the ground and straightened her back.

Tiger, roused from her position, rearranged herself on Mum's lap. Mum rubbed her under the chin and took a sip of water from the glass on the table. She peered at me over the rim, her gaze sharpening. 'What have you done to your cheek?'

I had forgotten about the large bruise just below my eye. I'd thought I'd covered it with make-up but at some point I must have rubbed the foundation off.

'I hit myself with my racquet playing tennis.' Thinking on my feet came easily to me. Experience defending abused women had taught me the 'walked into the door' excuse was only ever believed by those who chose to believe it.

Although Mum didn't look convinced, she didn't challenge me. 'Have you had tea? Something to eat? You are much too thin ...'

'Never mind me. What's wrong, Mum? I can see you're not well. Why didn't you tell me?'

She had tried to, I realised. I thought of the blinking light of my answerphone, the missed calls from her I'd meant to get around to returning but hadn't and a tsunami of guilt washed over me.

'I didn't tell you because I knew you were in the middle of an important case. But you're here now and that's all that matters.'

'Have you seen a doctor?'

Mum patted the sofa. 'Come sit next to me, Charlotte.'

I lifted the tossed aside throw from the sofa and folded it, placing it back within easy reach for her. Mum wasn't quite

9

quick enough to hide her smile. My obsession with tidiness had always bemused her. When I sat down next to her, Mum took my hand. 'I have seen a doctor. Several actually.' Her voice wobbled and she waited a beat or two. 'You're going to have to be brave, we both are.'

The creeping dread I'd been feeling since I'd listened to her message on the answerphone solidified and the tight band across my chest became a physical pain. 'How bad, Mum?' I whispered, my mouth dry.

Mum took a deep breath and tightened her grip on my fingers. 'I'm dying, Charlotte. I wish I wasn't but I am and there isn't a damn thing I can do about it.'

Mum had cancer. She'd found a lump in her breast months ago but had done nothing about it until Agnes, her old friend, alarmed at how much weight Mum was losing and how exhausted she seemed all the time, had insisted she go to the doctor. Even then it had taken Mum several more weeks to make an appointment. Tests had followed, taking more time, until, when finally a diagnosis of cancer had been made, it had already spread to Mum's lungs and her bones. I knew enough to realise that when cancer had spread to other organs the prognosis wasn't good.

Even as I was trying to absorb what Mum was saying my mind had been racing ahead.

'There must be something they can do. '

'Oh, Charlotte! Believe me when I say there isn't. '

'Why didn't you see a doctor earlier? What's the name of the consultant you saw? Have you had a second opinion?'

'Charlotte! I'm not a witness on a stand.' For a moment, the Mum I knew was back. Her voice softened. 'A second opinion would make no difference. No amount of treatment will change the outcome. You're quite right. I should have seen a doctor earlier, but I didn't.' The pain in her eyes, I knew, was for me.

'But enough about me. How are *you*?' She folded her hands

in her lap. 'You must be thrilled with the result of the trial! I'm so proud of you.'

Proud of me? Proud of her only child who didn't return her calls, who hadn't come to see her mother in months? If I'd visited more often I might have noticed she was unwell and forced her to go to the doctor sooner. Then there might have been no need for this conversation.

'Mum, we haven't finished talking about you . . . '

'Not tonight, Charlotte. There are things we need to discuss, things I have to tell you, but that can wait until tomorrow. Tonight I want to enjoy having my daughter home.'

'But . . . '

She gave me a look, one I knew well. Once Mum had made up her mind there was no shifting her.

'You look exhausted,' she continued, frowning.

'It's just that I've been impossibly busy. Nothing a holiday won't fix. Now that's an idea! You and I could go to the coast for a couple of weeks – to a hotel – or a cottage if you prefer?' As if taking her away for a few days could make up for all the times I hadn't spend with her.

'It's a lovely thought, but if you don't mind I'd rather stay here. I don't have much energy these days.'

'I'll do everything. I'll book us somewhere lovely, pack for you, I'll even hire a more comfortable car.' Mum disapproved of my BMW roadster. 'We'll take Tiger. You won't have to do a thing. I'll take care of it all.'

Mum squeezed my hands. 'Perhaps in a while, when I feel a little stronger. Now, please, just for tonight, let's talk about other things.'

Mum refused to say any more about her health. Instead she asked about my journey and whether I'd seen Princess Di and if I thought her second child would be a boy or a girl. Princess Diana dispensed with, she asked me about work.

I lied and told her it was all good.

*

Later, back in my old room which remained exactly the same as it had been the day I left for university, I lay awake, my thoughts whirling as I tried to absorb what Mum had told me. She was only fifty-four. It was impossible that she could be dying. Images spooled through my head; Mum and me in London, Mum applauding when I graduated, us in the library where Mum worked, me reading a book, looking up to find her eyes on me. Her quick smile, how she'd always put me first, made me the centre of her world.

Another childhood memory popped into my mind. Mum reading to me from Winnie-the-Pooh, a favourite when I was very small. I couldn't remember the title but I did remember one particular quote. Winnie asks Piglet what day it is and when Piglet replies, *It's today, Winnie!*, Winnie-the-Pooh tells him today is his favourite day. I made her read that story to me over and over again. Then as I grew up, I forgot about it. Tomorrow became my mantra. I'd do it all tomorrow. See Mum, take a holiday, treat her.

I had been too busy thinking about the next day to make the most of the one I was living, and along the way, I'd forgotten what was really important.

Now there would be too few tomorrows. Not enough todays.

The next morning, having barely slept, I was up as soon as it was light. I showered quickly, peeked in Mum's bedroom to find her still sleeping so tiptoed downstairs. Tiger fetched her lead and looked at me imploringly. I took my Sony Walkman from my handbag, put my headphones on and took her out and into the grounds of the Astley Ainslie Hospital. When we returned I made some toast and spread it with marmalade before setting a tray with a china cup and saucer and a pot of Mum's favourite Earl Grey.

Mum was awake but still in bed when I entered her room. 'I was just going to get up and dressed,' she said when she saw I had brought her breakfast.

'I thought I'd spoil you for a change.' I set the tray on her dresser and moved to help her sit up, but she rebuffed me with an exasperated shake of her head. I waited until she'd settled herself against the pillows, before placing the tray on her lap.

'But what about you, have you had breakfast, Charlotte?'

'I'll get mine in a little while.' Not that I felt like eating.

'In that case, why don't you keep me company while I eat,' she said as I hovered over her.

'Will I open your curtains?' I knew I was fussing, but couldn't help myself.

Mum nodded, popping a tiny morsel of toast into her mouth.

'Right,' she said briskly, pushing aside her tray. 'I've made a start sorting out my affairs.'

'Mum! That can wait.'

'No, Charlotte. I have to do it while I still have the strength. I'll feel better knowing everything is in order. Now sit down. Your pacing about is unnerving.'

Obediently I perched on the end of her bed.

'There is so much I need to tell you. I hardly know where to begin.'

'What sort of things?'

Mum sighed. 'I received a letter. Perhaps that's as good a place as any to start. Open the drawer in my bedside table and get it out for me. It's right on top.'

I did as she asked.

'I think it's best if you read it yourself,' she said, when I held it out to her.

Mum's name and address was written in fountain pen in the sort of elegant writing that used to be taught in school. I smoothed out the good quality sheet of paper inside.

It was headed Greyfriars House.

Dear Olivia

No doubt you will be surprised to hear from me after all these years. You may well be equally surprised to

13

learn that I have thought of you often. As has Edith.

We would like you to come to Greyfriars House as soon as you can. We have a great favour to ask of you. I shall explain everything when we see you as it is not something that can be put in a letter.

I imagine that you will be reluctant to come and I should not blame you. But do. I beg of you. Before it is too late.

We have no phone so telegram your reply. Greyfriars is still only accessible by boat therefore I shall have to arrange for someone to bring you across.

Your aunt,

Georgina.

I read it twice more before I looked up. 'Aunt Georgina, Mum? You have an aunt?' I'd always believed that I was Mum's only living relative. Her parents had died during the war and Mum, like me, was an only child. 'And who is Edith?'

'Edith and Georgina were my mother's sisters.'

'How come you've never talked about them?'

Her brow knotted and for a moment she seemed far away. 'I've not seen or heard from them in years. Not since you were a baby.'

'What do you think they want from you now?'

Mum sank against the pillows and I was struck anew at how pale and thin she was. 'That's just it! I can't imagine what they want, after all this time. It's not as if either of them have ever shown any desire to have anything to do with me – or you. Although at one time I believed them fond of me . . . or at least I believed Georgina fond of me.'

'I don't understand, Mum. What is Greyfriars? A nursing home?'

She shook her head. 'Greyfriars House has been in our family for generations. My grandfather bought it as his hunting lodge.' She closed her eyes and smiled. 'We used to go there

14

every summer when I was a child – right up until the war. I wish you could have seen Greyfriars and how it was back then.' When her eyes flickered open, they were shining. 'I've never forgotten a moment of that last summer, perhaps because it was the last time I remember being truly happy as a child.' She took a shaky breath and the light in her eyes dimmed. 'The war changed everything – people, places. Nothing, and no one, was ever the same afterwards.' Mum looked so sad I ached for her.

Although I had been born only a few years after the war had finished, it had always seemed so far away – almost inconceivable – and nothing to do with my generation. We were much more concerned with the cold war and the prospect of being nuked into oblivion by twitchy-fingered politicians. Mum had never spoken about her experience during the war, and to my shame, I had never asked.

'We've never really talked about so many things, have we, Charlotte?' Mum said, reading my mind. She sighed. 'So much I never told you.'

'Tell me now, Mum,' I urged her.

That was when I learned about Greyfriars.

Chapter Two

Olivia

July 1939

Olivia gave a loud whoop as she jumped from the boat and turned to take in her first sight of Greyfriars. It was every bit as wonderful as she remembered. Almost three times the size of their London house, and with a turret, which was to be her bedroom this summer, its pale sandstone glowed in the sunlight.

Too excited to wait for Mother and Father, she ran through the arch in the rhododendrons that shielded the garden from the nearby mainland and across the springy, clover-scented manicured lawn, past the summer roses and towards the front door where the servants were waiting to greet them. Stopping just long enough to say a quick hello, she scampered past them, across the polished floorboards of the hall and up the wide jewel-blue-carpeted mahogany staircase. She couldn't wait to see the turret room again and make it her own. They'd been coming for the summer for as long as she could remember, which, given she was only nine, wasn't really that long when she thought about it. But she'd always loved the turret room and, finally, Mother had decided she was old enough to have it.

She raced along the first-floor corridor to the end and then up the narrow windy steps to the turret room. Her room! For the whole summer!

It was circular, with one half of the circle taken up by windows. Father had told her they'd once been tiny but his father had replaced them when he'd built the house, with these big ones that let the light in and allowed anyone looking out to see almost the entire front and side of the island. She gazed with delight around the room, noticing the pink-flowered quilt on the enormous four-poster bed and the tiny posy of pale pink peonies in a crystal vase on the dark wood bedside cabinet. Once she had her books and puzzles on the shelves, it would be truly perfect. Especially since she wouldn't have Nanny breathing down her neck morning, noon and night telling her what a young lady could and couldn't do.

This year, Nanny wasn't with them. Olivia was to go to school after the long holiday and Nanny had gone to another family to take care of their children. She was supposed to have come to Greyfriars before going to the other family but her mother had become unwell and Mother had given her some time off to visit her. It was difficult imagining that Nanny's mother could still be alive – Nanny surely wasn't that far off going to join God herself. Olivia couldn't help but be glad Nanny wasn't here – even if it wasn't nice to wish someone's mother unwell.

She had a whole week before the first guests, Aunt Georgina and a few friends, were to arrive. Kerista might be an island but there was so much to do; miles and miles of it to explore, croquet on the lawn, or bathing on their private beach. There was even a yacht to take them to Oban or to the other islands and Mother had promised they would go for a sail on her once Aunt Georgina and the others arrived. Then, later on in the summer, more guests were expected and with everyone gathered, there was to be a party.

Eager to re-explore the island, Olivia ran down the narrow, curling steps that led from the tower to the first floor, and along the corridor, passing her old nursery and the ballroom where the final dance of the summer would be held. She scooted down the next flight of stairs and into the morning room where Mother, Father and Edith were taking tea.

'Might I go outside?' she asked Mother.

'As long as you are back in time for dinner.' Mother barely glanced up from her conversation with Aunt Edith, but Father smiled at her and nodded. Mother and Father were different at Greyfriars. The London Father was usually sombre and distant but the Greyfriars Father laughed and swam with her and seemed to cast off his mournful air along with the smog they'd left behind in London, and usually, freed from her charitable obligations, Mother spent more time with Olivia.

If only Aunt Edith hadn't been there then Olivia would have had Mother and Father all to herself. Aunt Edith was nice enough, if a little bossy. She was always telling Olivia to tidy her hair or change her dress when it only had a tiny stain on it, but then Aunt Edith was a nurse and Mother said nurses had to be bossy.

Grabbing a slice of cake, Olivia scooted back into the entrance hall, narrowly avoiding a servant carrying a tray, and let herself out into the bright sunshine – and freedom.

Over the next few days, she would spring out of bed as soon as she heard the servants moving around the house, pull on her skirt and blouse, and, stopping just long enough to thrust her feet into wellington boots, would leave the house, returning only when she was hungry or when she'd had enough of her own company. But for most of the time the island was her kingdom.

With no one else to play with she'd become adept at creating her own games. Last summer she'd imagined herself a member of the Jacobite army as they'd marched south towards England. Alternatively she'd been Flora MacDonald, hiding Prince Charles from would-be captors, at other times she was the Lady of the House, whose husband had gone off to fight alongside the Pretender and who would watch for him from

18

her bedroom window. (The latter game had lasted only the tiniest part of an afternoon. There was little fun to be had staring out of a window, no matter how forlornly.)

Today she'd gone down to the west side of the island. Here, although there were as many trees as on the other sides of the house, they grew oddly, not as strongly as the others and leaning in one direction as if they were a corps of ballet dancers bending at the waist. Donald, the ghillie, said they grew like that because of the prevailing wind coming from the direction of Balcreen, which was just across the water.

On this side of the island, Kerista was quite wild; the sea always more turbulent and the shore barren, with fat, glistening rocks instead of sand. Olivia far preferred it to the other side.

There was a small farm a little distance away, with a row of cottages where Donald lived with his wife. The other cottages were used by the extra staff who were employed for the summer. The miniature farm had a hen house and a couple of cows which one of the maids milked twice a day, sometimes letting Olivia help.

The hens wandered freely down here and suddenly Olivia had an idea. What if she could teach them to swim? She caught one and waded out, laying her in the water. But she flapped her feathers in Olivia's face and squawked back to the shore.

'What are you doing?'

Olivia looked up to find a girl, of about ten or eleven, with long curly hair and wide brown eyes looking down at her.

'I'm teaching the hens to swim.'

'Hens can't swim,' the girl scoffed. 'Everyone knows that.'

'Maybe because they haven't been taught!' Olivia fired back. She stood up. 'I'm Olivia Friel. Who are you?'

'Agnes MacKay. My mother's your summer cook. Usually I stay with my grandmother in Balcreen when Mam's working, but Granny's not feeling well, so I've come here for the day.'

'Do you want to play?'

Agnes nodded.

'Let's pretend the hens are our navy. I'm the admiral and you are my sailor.'

'I should be the admiral,' Agnes protested. 'I'm older than you.'

Olivia thought about arguing but then Agnes might not play with her. 'In that case,' she said, 'we'll both be admirals.'

They got to work. Agnes was quick on her feet, stronger than Olivia, and more used to catching hens. Agnes showed Olivia how to tuck her dress into her knickers and persuaded her to take off her shoes, telling Olivia that her bare feet would grip the rocks better. They did but not much. The girls kept slipping on the seaweed-covered rocks and soon they were both drenched. Neither of them cared. Olivia couldn't remember the last time she'd had so much fun, although sadly Agnes was no more successful than Olivia at creating a navy out of the hens.

They had been chasing after a hen that would not, no matter how hard they tried to persuade her, stay in the sea, when Olivia felt a shadow fall over her. She looked up, shading her eyes against the sun, to find Donald, his gun cracked open and over his arm, towering over her. Surprised, her grip on the hen slackened and her reluctant sailor flapped away, squawking with indignation.

'What are you doing, miss? Agnes?' The ghillie had a furrow between his brows Olivia could have slipped a pencil between.

She stood up, and, although she only reached as far as his hip, decided to brazen it out. She stared up at him, doing her best to mimic the haughty look she imagined a lady would give her subject – the same one Mother gave her whenever she was in the wrong.

'We are trying to teach the hens to swim, but they are being very disobedient.'

His mouth turned up at the corners. 'It's clear you've spent too much time in the city, Miss Olivia. Hens can't swim.

Never have been able to and never will. It's lucky for them you never drowned them. Best to leave them be.'

'They are our subjects and our navy,' Olivia insisted. 'We are their commanders. How will they go into battle if they can't swim?'

Donald laughed and to her annoyance ruffled her hair. When he turned to Agnes he looked much more disapproving. 'Agnes! You should know better. The last place the pair of you should be is down at the shore on this side. There is a nasty riptide and you could drown, just like the little girl, and then what will your mothers do? They'll mourn you forever and into eternity. Is that what you want?'

'What little girl?' Olivia asked.

'Why, the little girl who drowned in this very spot a good many years ago. Some folk believe that she's lonely and wants company so whenever someone comes down to these rocks she reaches out her arms and tries to pull them in so they will stay with her. I imagine that the company she'd like best would be another little girl around her age. So, mark my words, stay away from this bit of the island. If you want to play in the water, go down to where the ladies and gents swim. There's a nice slope to the shore there.'

When he started back towards Greyfriars Olivia and Agnes scurried after him and fell into step beside him, Olivia doing a little hop skip and jump to keep up.

'Tell me about the little girl,' Olivia demanded. 'What was her name? Did she live here all the time or did she only come in the summer like me? Does she come into the house? Her ghost, I mean? Or does she stay in the water? Is she a mermaid now?'

Donald rubbed a hand across the greying stubble on his chin. 'All right then, I'll tell you, but don't go repeating what I say to anyone else – especially the grown-ups.'

Agnes nodded so energetically Olivia thought her head might come loose from her neck.

21

'We promise.' Olivia spoke for them both.

Donald waited until they were all perched on rocks before he began.

'It was many, many years ago, long before I was born or even my father or his grandfather. The house as you see it wasn't built yet. There was only the tower. It was in 1745 – the family were supporters of Prince Charlie. Do you know who he was?'

'Of course. He was the rightful King of Scotland – or so many people believed. My governess told me about him. She said he was called the Young Pretender because he had no right to the throne,' Olivia said.

'Aye, well, all that is in the past. All that matters is that the family who lived here supported him. But to do so was against the law. Even worse it was treason!' He smacked his lips together as if the very thought of treason thrilled him. 'Any how, that doesn't have much to do with my story except to say, the family was hiding out here. The clan chief who owned Stryker Castle over on the mainland supported the Jacobite cause as did many of the highland Scots. Now Lord Farquhar's estates were in the borders but Lord Farquhar thought it unwise to leave his wife, Lady Elizabeth, and their daughter, Lady Sarah – they only had one child – there alone while he went off to fight alongside Prince Charlie. All this happened just before the battle of Culloden.'

In her head Olivia was conjuring up images of a lady dressed in plaid – her long hair which, when worn loose, would come almost to her bottom. Just like the lady she'd pretended to be!

'Lady Elizabeth would have gone with him if she could,' Donald continued, 'but she knew if her husband was captured the King's army would ransack their home in the borders – perhaps even torch it and burn it to the ground – and she loved her little girl more than her own life and didn't want to take the chance anything might happen to her. And her husband, Lord Farquhar, loved Lady Elizabeth above all else. So he was happy that she agreed to stay here until the battle was won and Charles took his rightful place on the throne.'

Olivia was scared to speak, or even to nod, in case she broke the spell. Agnes was quiet too, although, until now, she'd chatted all the time.

'Lady Elizabeth used to stand on the ramparts, at the top of the tower and watch for him coming back. Some say she loved her lord too much. That she spent so much time watching and waiting for him to return, she forgot to take care of her little girl. However then, like now, she had many servants and there should have been plenty of folk to keep an eye on little Sarah. But it's a fact of life, the more people there are to do a thing, the more people think that someone else is doing that thing.

'And this Sarah was a very curious girl, like the pair of you. She became bored with being in the turret, waiting for her mother to come down to keep her company, so she decided to go and play outside. Now she knew she wasn't supposed to, not on her own, so she waited until her governess was having tea with Cook – they were great friends – before she sneaked outside.'

A sense of dread wrapped itself around Olivia like a thick morning mist. She knew what was going to happen, yet she still hoped that in the telling, something would change and that little girl would still be all right.

'Anyways,' Donald went on, 'she got outside and she came to that same place where I just found you. She could probably see it from the nursery window as the trees and bushes hadn't been planted back then. Maybe it was a particularly hot day like today and she thought she might paddle. Certainly she had taken off her stockings – they were found on the rock, all neatly rolled up.

'It was almost lunch time before anyone realised she was missing. Naturally they searched the house from top to bottom first, including the servants' rooms, the turret and the cellars. Lady Elizabeth was beside herself with terror, as was the governess who well knew it had been her fault. Only once they were certain that Lady Sarah wasn't in the house did they search outside. When they found Lady Sarah's stockings on the rock they knew they would never find her, at least not alive. Two hooded crows – bigger and blacker than anyone had seen before – were circling over the house and everyone knows that they are announcers of death.'

Olivia did her best to hide a shudder, but couldn't help an involuntary look up at the sky. To her relief there were no crows, only seagulls. But the sky had darkened and the breeze had picked up, brushing across her arms like a giant's fingertips.

'Two days later Lady Sarah's little broken body was washed up on the rocks. They picked her up and wrapped her in plaid and brought her back to the house. They laid the poor wee mite's body in her bedroom and Lady Elizabeth stayed with her for seven days and seven nights. She might never have let them bury her only child if Lord Farquhar hadn't returned from battle.

'He was, as you can imagine, heartbroken to learn of the death of his only child, his precious Sarah. But he knew she had to be buried. And eventually after pleading and going down on his knees to his wife, she agreed. You'll know that Prince Charles was defeated – but Lord Farquhar was fortunate in that he didn't lose his lands. They'd taken pity on him and left his estates in the borders intact. With their daughter buried, he wanted Lady Elizabeth to go back with him to their estate in the Borders where they would live out the rest of their lives as best they could, but Lady Elizabeth wouldn't go. Her mind had turned. She wouldn't accept that it was her daughter they had buried, choosing instead to believe that someone had taken Lady Sarah and that one day she'd find her again.' Donald lowered his voice to a whisper. 'They say that at night, Lady Elizabeth still walks Greyfriars and the grounds looking for her daughter. And that Sarah does come back for a week or two every year and that mother and daughter are happy for that short while, until it is time for Sarah to return to the other world again. Others say that Lady Elizabeth believes that if she can find another little girl and drown her by the rocks, then her daughter will be restored to her and they can be together all the time.'

Olivia shivered. She exchanged a glance with Agnes who looked riveted and terrified in equal measure.

Donald stood. 'That's why you must never play down at that shore. Not unless you want to join Lady Sarah's ghost – or replace her. Now, Agnes, away you go back to the farm and dry off. I'll be taking you back to Balcreen shortly. And, Miss Olivia, you'd better do the same.'

That night alone in her room, her parents having kissed her goodnight and with the candle blown out, the story Donald had told her and Agnes played in Olivia's mind. She imagined she could hear the doorknob turning, as Lady Elizabeth crept into her room to look for her daughter. No matter how hard she stared and tried to make out shapes in the darkness, or strained her ears for any sounds of ghostly footsteps, all she could hear was the sea and the wind. Did ghosts make a sound? Would the first she knew be when she felt an icy cold hand touch her face?

Olivia burrowed deeper under the blankets, willing her eyes to stay open and alert but after a while her lids started getting heavier and heavier. And then she was wide awake, with the terrifying sensation she was not alone. She didn't dare breathe, and her heart was hammering so loud she could no longer hear the sea. She tried to shout for her mother but no words would come.

A woman stood only a couple of feet from her bed, her face, partly covered by the hood of her cloak, pale in the moonlight, her eyes two dark hollows. Behind her, Olivia's rocking horse moved gently on its rockers.

25

'Have you seen Lady Sarah?' the woman asked.

Olivia shook her head, too frightened to speak, knowing with a horrible but absolute certainty it was the ghost of Lady Elizabeth standing in front of her.

'I don't know where she can be! I heard her calling for me but I can't find her!' Lady Elizabeth held out a mottled blue hand. 'Will you help me find her?'

Olivia shook her head again. She didn't want to go anywhere with Lady Elizabeth. But then – Olivia couldn't think how – they were down at the shore, on the wild side where Donald had said they mustn't play, surrounded by a thick mist that made the familiar unfamiliar. Lady Elizabeth was tugging at her hand, hauling her along, and Olivia was powerless to resist.

When they reached the rocks Lady Elizabeth knelt by Olivia's side, her dark eyes full of entreaty. 'Lady Sarah will be so lonely. Won't you play with her for a while? All you have to do is go into the water. She'll come to you then.'

'I don't want to!' Olivia finally found her voice but it sounded small in the darkness and mist. 'Please don't make me.' She tried to pull away but Lady Elizabeth's grip was too strong and she was being dragged ever closer to the water.

Then a little girl with strands of seaweed caught in her long blonde hair rose from the sea and waded ashore. Olivia thought her heart would stop. 'No, Mother,' the girl said, coming to stand next to them. 'Leave her .... her mother would be too sad. And I have you to play with.'

Suddenly Olivia was back in her bed, her heart banging so hard she thought it might jump out of her chest. She lay in the semi-darkness too petrified to move. A bad dream, it had only been a bad dream, she told herself. But there was a faint smell of wax from a candle that had recently been extinguished and overlaying that, a tang of damp and seaweed and Olivia was convinced if she looked hard she would see wet footprints on the floor. For once she wished she was back in the nursery, Nanny in the room next door.

26

She thought of running along the corridors to Mother's room. But that would mean venturing into the dark and the possibility of coming across Lady Elizabeth. It was only a nightmare, she repeated to herself over and over. She huddled deeper under her blankets and squeezed her eyes shut. It took a long time, but eventually she did fall asleep and this time her sleep was dreamless.

When she opened her eyes again sunshine was streaming in through her window and last night's nightmare seemed exactly that. As she bounded out of bed, she told herself that even if Lady Elizabeth did walk Greyfriars, Lady Sarah would never allow her to hurt Olivia. Nevertheless, Olivia never played down at that part of the shore again and sadly neither did Agnes return to Kerista.

Chapter Three

Even if Agnes had come back to Greyfriars, Olivia wouldn't have been able to play with her. Her freedom was to be curtailed for a while. Today, the first guests were to arrive although there were to be only four: Mother's friends, Agatha and her husband, Gordon, who were regular visitors to their house in London, Aunt Georgina and someone called Findlay.

With their arrival, summer would start properly. There had been no activities so far. No croquet or board games, no trips to Oban. With Aunt Edith being there, most of the time Mother normally spent with Olivia when they were at Greyfriars had been taken up with her. Mother and Aunt Edith spent hours, just the two of them, their heads close together as they whispered and laughed, or studied pictures in magazines, or retreated to the morning room, only emerging for tea, or lunch on the lawn, or dinner. Whenever Mother found Olivia dawdling in the house, trying to listen to what they were talking about, she would shoo her outside and tell her to go and play. Olivia didn't really mind. She would have liked a little more of Mother's attention but there would be time for that once the guests had gone.

Preparations for the guests' arrival had been going on since the day the Friels had arrived and had become more frantic with every passing day. Cook had been in a frenzy all week, shooing Olivia from the kitchen whenever she went in search of something to eat, even snapping at her once 'that didn't she realise she was getting under everyone's feet and couldn't she wait until proper mealtimes?'

Earlier she'd hung out of her bedroom window, watching Donald's boat approach the small pier, squinting to catch her first sight of the new arrivals.

Aunt Georgina had been in Paris, modelling, for the last couple of years so Olivia had only a distant, vague memory of her.

Georgina stepped ashore first. She was dressed in wide, cream palazzo trousers and a silk blouse, her hair tied up in an emerald green bandana. Her laughter rippled across the still air as she used Donald's outstretched hand to steady herself. 'Really, one would have thought Peter would have built a bridge across by now. Already I feel like Robinson Crusoe.'

Aunt Edith and Mother hurried down to greet the new arrivals, Father following at a more dignified pace behind.

Agatha and Gordon joined Georgina on the pier. A tall, well-built man with short, dark hair, leapt out after them.

Leaving her spot by the window, Olivia scurried downstairs and, almost bowling over a maid in her haste, hurtled towards the door, skidding to a halt just in time to compose herself. She might only be nine, but Mother would be livid if she didn't greet their guests like a young lady.

Checking no one was looking, she spat in her hand and smoothed down her hair, tucking a stray lock into the ribbon that held her hair back and flapped her hand in front of her face in an attempt to cool her flushed cheeks.

They had started back towards the house by the time she stepped outside. Mother and Edith were on either side of Georgina, their arms tucked into hers, while Father walked with the stranger and Agatha and Gordon a few paces behind. Through the arch in the rhododendrons, Olivia saw the little boat was already heading back over to the mainland – no doubt to collect the luggage. It had taken Donald four trips to bring theirs across.

Miss Chivers, the housekeeper, was waiting on the steps and she frowned down at Olivia, tucking a lock of hair Olivia had missed under her ribbon.

Olivia ducked away from her reach and hurried towards the guests, meeting them on the other side of the rhododendrons.

'You remember Olivia?' Mother said to Georgina as they stopped to greet her.

Georgina bent and placed the tip of her finger under Olivia's chin. 'I'm not going to say that you've grown or any of that nonsense,' she said. 'I am very pleased to see you again.'

When her aunt smiled, Olivia was struck speechless by her beauty. All the sisters were beautiful but Georgina was especially so with her milk-white skin, lightly sprinkled with freckles, her thick, rich red hair and her lovely mouth shiny with lipstick. She had the same blue eyes as Mother and Aunt Edith, but where Aunt Edith's were a pale blue, Georgina's were almost indigo and twinkled, as if she had a secret she was just bursting to tell. Everything about her fizzed and bubbled. Like a light. Olivia just wanted to look and look at her. No wonder she was a model!

'Mr Armstrong, this is my daughter, Olivia.'

Olivia held out her hand and the stranger shook it. He wasn't good-looking in the way that Olivia's father was, his nose was too big, his mouth too wide, but he had the same buzzing energy as Georgina had.

'I've brought something for you, Olivia. It's in one of my cases. Why don't you come up to my room after tea and I'll see if I can find it?' Georgina said. She took Mother's and Edith's arms again. 'Come on, you two. I'm simply dying to hear your news!'

The adults walked through the arch Donald had carved in the rhododendrons, appearing to have immediately forgotten about her. All except for Mr Armstrong. He held out his arm for her to take – just as if she were all grown up.

She fell a little in love with him right at that moment.

After tea, Olivia ran up to Georgina's room and knocked on the door. Georgina opened the door and smiled.

'Oh, there you are, Olivia! Come in! Come in! I'm still looking for your present, can you believe it?'

Georgina opened the doors of her massive over-packed oak wardrobe and started sifting through the garments hanging on padded wooden hangers. 'I can't think where the maid has put it . . .'

Georgina's clothes were a riot of colours and textures: shiny silks in emerald, ruby, cream; muslins and lace in white; fine wool in forest green, diesel blue, peat brown; velvets; cotton in florals, polka dots and other patterns. Olivia wondered if her aunt wasn't perhaps looking too quickly as the hangers were slammed impatiently against each other.

Several hats lay on the bed, tossed there as if Georgina couldn't decide which one she liked best. Olivia picked up one in forest green with a felt thistle on its side brim and tried it on.

Georgina stopped what she was doing and studied Olivia, her head tipped to the side. 'That colour is perfect on you.' She lifted the hat from Olivia's head and tossed it on the bed. 'But we don't wear hats on Greyfriars! Hats are for the city. Just wait until you see what I brought you all the way from Paris. Now where on earth could it be?'

She started rummaging through her drawers; intimate undergarments, petticoats and camisoles in silk and lace spilled onto the floor or got caught in the drawers as they were hastily closed.

'It wouldn't be in here . . .' Georgina murmured as her long fingers probed the back of the next drawer. She looked up and smiled. 'It has to be somewhere.'

'Could it be this?' Olivia suggested, picking up a flimsy,

31

tissue-wrapped package she found on the seat of the velvet-covered chaise longue beneath Georgina's bedroom window.

Georgina clapped her hands together. 'Clever girl! You found it!' As Olivia continued to hold it out to her, Georgina gleefully plonked herself onto the quilted covers of her four-poster bed and said, 'Well then, open it!'

Her hands trembling with excitement, Olivia peeled away the wrapping to reveal a thin-strapped silk camisole top in the palest shell pink. 'It's beautiful,' she gasped, holding it up. Its hem was embedded with a row of tiny pink diamantés. She'd never owned anything so beautiful or so grown up; Mother insisted on cotton vests in the summer, itchy woollen ones in the winter.

Georgina grinned. 'Do you like it?'

Olivia hugged it against her. 'I love it. Thank you, Aunt Georgina.'

'I've never understood why one can't have beautiful things, regardless of how old one is. Even when I'm ancient, I'm going to buy all my clothes from Paris.'

Just then there was a knock on the door and Aunt Edith stepped into the room.

'Look what Aunt Georgina brought me.' Olivia held out her new camisole top for Aunt Edith to inspect. 'Isn't it beautiful?'

'That's what you bought her, Georgina?' Aunt Edith said lightly, but Olivia could tell she didn't really approve. 'I guess a boring old jigsaw puzzle could never compete.'

'I did like it,' Olivia protested. 'But a hundred pieces is too easy.'

'I'm just teasing,' Edith said, ruffling her hair. 'Now would you mind excusing us? Your Aunt Georgina and I have lots to chat about.'

That evening Olivia was to join the guests for dinner, although as soon as it was over and the men and women separated – the men to the study and their cigars, the women to the smaller of the two sittings rooms – she was expected to excuse herself and go to her room.

In years to come, what she remembered most about that evening was how everything and everyone glittered. Flowers had been sent up from London and placed in vases all over the house until it was impossible to be anywhere without their scent filling the air. The maids had been busy too, dusting and polishing until Greyfriars, that to Olivia's eyes shone anyway, sparkled and reeked of beeswax as well as the scented flowers. Usually there was only a boat from the village across the water on a Monday and a Friday, but lately it had being coming with provisions every day.

Olivia had changed quickly and run downstairs even before the first gong sounded. Although the day had been warm and the sun wasn't due to go down for hours yet, the fire in the hall had been lit, candelabra placed on every available surface so that everything was bathed in a golden light and she sat on the fender to get the best view of the staircase.

Mother and Father were first; Mother in blue taffeta and Father in evening dress. Next came Edith who was wearing a full-length, blue velvet dress with a thin belt and pearls at her throat. Then came Findlay, looking distinguished and handsome in his dinner jacket and bow tie. Agatha and Gordon followed a few minutes later. Agatha was wearing cream silk and wore a tiara in her hair. As each adult reached the foot of the stairs they took a drink from the tray the manservant held before disappearing into the drawing room. Finally, a good ten minutes after everyone else, came the person Olivia had been waiting for. When Georgina appeared at the top of the first flight of stairs, Olivia caught her breath. Her aunt's hair had been waved and parted at the side, so it hung over one eye before falling to her shoulders like a sheet of molten fire. Georgina's ruby red dress clung to her like a second skin, hugging her hips and flaring as it fell to the ground. It was cut low at the front, and with the tiniest of straps. As Georgina glided down the stairs, Olivia could clearly see the shape of her long legs through the thin material of her gown and when she passed by, Olivia saw it was cut even lower at the back. An inch or two more and surely her bottom would be exposed!

She followed Georgina into the drawing room and immediately the chatter and laughter came to an abrupt stop. There was a collective gasp as everyone took in how beautiful Georgina looked. It was as if she was the sun, and everyone else, with the exception of Findlay, the planets revolving around her. He was the only one who hadn't gasped when she'd come in. Instead he'd just looked at her with his dark eyes, his lips pressed into a hard line.

Georgina walked over to the gramophone and put a record on. As the music swirled around the room, whatever spell she had cast was broken and the adults started talking again.

Chapter Four

Later that evening, banished to her room and just as Olivia was wondering whether she dare risk getting out of bed to sit on the stairs so she could at least listen to what the adults were saying even if she couldn't see them, there was a soft tap on the door and Georgina came in. She was carrying a glass of champagne in one hand and holding a cigarette in the other. There were spots of colour on her pale, almost alabaster, cheeks and her eyes were glittering.

'I thought I'd slip away for a bit,' she said, 'and come and see you.' She looked around the room and smiled. 'Do you know this used to be my bedroom when I was a child?'

Olivia smiled back. Of course Aunt Georgina would have slept here!

'None of the adults are ever given it because of the steps,' Georgina continued. 'If at all squiffy, we wouldn't be able to manage.'

The narrow, windy stone steps, hollowed at the centre by the thousands of feet that had trod them, was one of the things Olivia liked best about the turret.

Georgina selected a book from one of the bookshelves, studied the spine and placed it back on the shelf. Yet, Olivia had the distinct impression that if she asked Georgina to tell her the title of the book she wouldn't have been able to.

'Edith and I used to share. You'd imagine with all these

rooms that we would have had one each, but when we were girls we liked to be together all the time. Isn't it wonderful when sisters are friends too?'

Olivia wished *she* had a sister. If only Agnes had come back . . .

'It's not much fun on your own, is it?' Georgina said, as if reading Olivia's mind.

'I wish Mother and Father would have a baby,' Olivia blurted. There was something about Aunt Georgina that made a person feel they could confide in her.

Georgina raised an eyebrow. 'Did you tell your mother that?'

'I did. She said she was happy just to have me. But she looked sad when she said it.'

'Mmm.' Georgina leaned over and ruffled her hair. 'Then you should believe her.' She stood and drifted around the room as if she were looking for something but didn't know what.

'What is Paris like? Have you been to the Eiffel Tower?' Olivia asked. She was genuinely curious but more than that she wanted Georgina to stay and keep her company a little longer.

'There and everywhere.' Georgina sank down on the bed and propped herself up on her elbows. 'Paris is the best city in the world. At least . . . ' Her face clouded. 'It was until recently.'

'Why? What do you mean?'

But Georgina just shook her head and jumped to her feet again. 'You simply must visit one day. When you are older. Take a boat down the Seine, visit all the galleries and museums. Do you know the French have cafes where you can sit outside and have your coffee while watching the world go by?'

'Couldn't I come and stay with you? Perhaps before the summer is over. Mother could come too.'

'That would have been wonderful but I don't live there any more. In a few weeks I'll be in Singapore.'

Olivia was dismayed. Singapore was thousands of miles

away. It might be years before she saw Georgina again.

'Why are you going to *there*?' Olivia asked. 'When you said you like Paris so much?'

A shadow crossed Georgina's face. 'Sometimes one just has to move on. Nothing ever stays the same, no matter how much one wishes it could.' She gave her head a tiny shake. 'Singapore will be just as much fun as Paris, I'm sure.'

'But it's so far away!'

'Yes it is. And that might not be a bad thing.' The last was said almost to herself. Before Olivia could ask what she meant, Georgina's expression brightened. 'It will take almost six weeks to get there on a steamship! Can you imagine that? Perhaps when you are older you could come and visit me there? With your mother and father.'

The prospect cheered Olivia enormously. As long as it wasn't too long a wait.

Georgina sat down on the edge of the bed. 'Do you know that once this part of the house was a defensive tower? That's why this room is shaped as it is and why the steps are so narrow and worn. The family of the people who owned the castle over on the mainland, the one that's in ruins now, used this tower so they could hide if they had to. They were Jacobites. You have heard of the Jacobites, haven't you?'

Olivia nodded. 'Donald said this bit was part of a castle a long, long time ago, back when Bonnie Prince Charlie was trying to get his crown back.'

'That's right. Before that, during the reformation in the sixteenth century, the room below this was the priest's room, the one that's the nursery now. I'm assuming you know where the secret staircase is?'

'A secret staircase! Where?' How could she not have known?

Georgina walked across the room and pulled back a thick length of cloth to reveal a door. She tugged the wrought-iron handle but it wouldn't budge. 'Dash! It's always kept locked. No one knows where the key is. I imagine Miss Chivers has it on her bunch if it hasn't been lost. There's a double wall all the way around the turret and that's where the staircase runs. It goes from here up to the ramparts and down all the way to the outside – right past the nursery – there's another secret door that leads into there.'

'No, there isn't! You're teasing me. I would have seen it.'

'Unless you knew it was there, you'd never find it. You know the cupboard in the nursery? Well right at the back is another door. It looks like part of the wall but there's a hidden catch which opens it onto the outside stairs.'

Olivia stared at the door with horrified fascination. If there were ghosts that was the way they'd come. Her skin prickled. What if Lady Elizabeth *had* been in her room? What if it hadn't been a nightmare after all? What if she came back? But that was silly. Ghosts could walk through walls. They didn't need doors. No. It had been a nightmare. That was all. She'd gone to sleep thinking of Lady Sarah and Elizabeth – no wonder she'd had a nightmare about them. But still . . .

'Is that how Lady Sarah got outside without anyone seeing her? Is that why it's kept locked? Because she escaped from the nursery and drowned?'

Georgina came back to sit on her bed again. 'So you know about Lady Elizabeth and Lady Sarah?'

'Donald told me and Agnes about them.'

'Who on earth is Agnes?'

'She's the summer cook's daughter. She came to Kerista for the day when her grandmother was ill. We were down at the west shore trying to teach the hens to swim when Donald discovered us.'

'You were trying to teach the hens to swim? My dear, how very imaginative.'

'I know better now,' Olivia mumbled. She wished she hadn't mentioned the hens. It made her seem very silly.

Georgina took a long sip of her champagne. 'What did Donald tell you?'

Georgina listened intently, her lips slightly parted as Olivia repeated what Donald had said, revelling in being the centre of Georgina's attention. She didn't tell Aunt Georgina that she might actually have been visited by Lady Elizabeth. The hen story had made her look enough of a baby.

'Do you know he told Edith and me that exact same story when we were children? I'd forgotten until now. It's why we call that bit of the island Sarah's Rocks.' She laughed. 'For the longest time Edith believed Lady Sarah was real and used to insist she join in our games, much to the annoyance of your mother and I.'

So Aunt Edith had seen Lady Sarah too? What about Lady Elizabeth? Had she also seen her? It was odd to have something in common with Aunt Edith.

'So they do walk Greyfriars!'

Aunt Georgina laughed. Then she must have seen that Olivia was serious and a small frown puckered her brow. 'They did live here once but I imagine Donald told you that story for the same reason he told us – to keep children away from that part of the island. Even the adults don't risk swimming there. Apart from the riptide, there are nasty sharp rocks so you really mustn't paddle there again.' She tilted her head. 'Tell me, were you frightened when he told you the story?'

'No!' Olivia lied. She wanted Aunt Georgina to see her as too grown up to be frightened by stories of ghosts. 'Besides, I don't think ghosts can hurt you.' Not child ghosts anyway. Lady Elizabeth she wasn't so sure about.

'You are so very like Edith! Nothing ever frightens her either.'

Olivia didn't want to be like Aunt Edith, she wanted to be like Aunt Georgina! She glanced over at the locked door. 'Do you think it might be true? That Lady Elizabeth does walk the castle's corridors looking for Lady Sarah and that Lady Sarah comes back once a year to be with her mother? Donald said Lady Elizabeth loved Lady Sarah too much and

39

that's why she can't rest in peace. Do you think someone *can* love too much?'

Georgina twirled the champagne glass between her fingers and the light from the paraffin lamps caught on the crystal, casting shards of light on the walls. 'I imagine with its long history Greyfriars has seen its share of tragedy, but I don't think it has any more ghosts than anywhere else.'

Olivia held her breath. 'You do believe in ghosts then?'

Georgina was silent for a long moment as if giving Olivia's question full and serious consideration. 'I think the only ghosts that exist are those in our heads,' she said eventually. 'Our guilty conscience. I think when we put right any wrong we might have done those ghosts disappear. Perhaps Lady Elizabeth didn't love Lady Sarah enough to take care of her properly. Maybe if she forgave herself for losing her child, she'd be able to stop looking for her and rest in peace.'

Once more Olivia thought she saw a shadow cross Georgina's face but when her aunt smiled again, Olivia knew she must have been mistaken. What did Aunt Georgina have to be sad about?

Georgina gave her head a little shake. 'Hark at me! All philosophical. I can't imagine you have anything to fear from ghosts inside or outside your head. You're a good girl – one who is much loved.' She took another long sip of her champagne, stood and ruffled Olivia's hair. 'I suppose I should get back. They'll have noticed I'm gone by now.' A mischievous expression crossed her face. 'On the other hand, perhaps I'll take a turn in the garden. Don't tell them you've seen me. Pity the door to the secret stairway won't open or I could have snuck out that way. I'm going to make it my mission to find that key.'

'*Don't!*' Olivia wanted to cry. She still hadn't made up her mind about whether ghosts were real or not and didn't want to take any chances. She'd much rather the door remained locked.

When, with a last smile and a quick kiss on Olivia's cheek, Georgina slipped away, Olivia felt as if she'd taken some of the light with her.

Olivia checked the door Georgina had shown her again, just to make sure it was locked, which of course it was. Perhaps she should ask Mother whether she could sleep in another room. One without hidden doors and secret staircases? But she loved the turret! And although she didn't care at all for Lady Elizabeth she wouldn't mind if Lady Sarah came back looking to play. Lady Sarah wouldn't hurt her regardless of what Donald said. As long as she kept away from her rocks. Furthermore, if Aunt Edith wasn't scared of ghosts then neither would she be. Feeling much better for having decided that, Olivia took her atlas from her shelf, located the correct map and traced the outline of Singapore with her finger. Aunt Georgina had invited her to stay! She couldn't wait to go.

She sat in front of her dressing table and studied her reflection in the mirror, practising Georgina's smile and the way she lifted one eyebrow.

The tinkle of Georgina's laugh drifted through her open window and Olivia hurried across to look out. On the far side of the lawn, almost hidden by the shadows, champagne glass in hand, Georgina was spinning around as if dancing to music no one else could hear.

A flicker of movement from one of the windows on the ground floor caught Olivia's attention. She wasn't the only one watching Georgina. Standing at the library window, looking out, was Findlay.

Chapter Five

In the days that followed, the adults swam and picnicked, sailed and went out on shoots. There was an odd atmosphere about everyone, as if they were charged with electricity. Olivia kept hearing snatches of conversation, most of which she couldn't follow, and whenever the adults spotted her, they would stop mid-sentence and start speaking of the hot weather or some excursion they had planned. They were definitely keeping something from her.

Olivia would loiter, trying to hear what they were saying, but the adults rarely stayed still long enough for her to catch more than the odd word or phrase. On one occasion, Agatha and Gordon had strolled past Olivia as she was sitting reading a book under the shade of a beech tree, Agatha muttering something about a scandal in Paris, and 'how she had the nerve to show her face in polite society she had no idea!' but, to Olivia's frustration, she couldn't work out who they were talking about as no name was mentioned.

This afternoon, the adults, with the exception of Findlay, had gathered on the lawn for lunch. So that she could watch them unobserved and listen to whatever secrets they were hiding from her, Olivia had hidden behind a tree – making herself as small and unobtrusive as possible, which wasn't difficult as she wasn't very big to begin with – and especially if she pretended she was a statue and stayed absolutely still.

Chairs and tables had been brought out and arranged under the shade of a tree, a picnic blanket spread on the ground. Mother was sitting with her legs neatly together as she'd repeatedly told Olivia was the only way for ladies to sit. Father was next to her smoking a pipe. Georgina sprawled on the blanket, her face lifted towards the sun, in exactly the way Mother disapproved of, while Edith sat in one of the other wicker armchairs, her feet propped up on a stool.

Olivia wasn't sure where Findlay was, out with his rifle probably. If she wanted to be Aunt Georgina, she also wanted to marry someone exactly like Findlay although she wasn't altogether sure why. He wasn't very talkative and always had to be coaxed to join in when, after dinner, the adults would dance in the drawing room to records they played on the gramophone, but he liked to sail and had taken the yacht out almost every day, either with company, or on his own, and once with Olivia. He rarely stayed still for longer than a few minutes, hence the reason he wasn't here, preferring to go out with Donald and his gun. But when you were in Findlay's company you felt as if you were the only person that mattered, even if, like Olivia, you were only nine.

But, as Olivia had overheard Miss Chivers say once, he liked his whisky rather too much for his own good. Whatever that meant.

The thing about Georgina was that only she could lounge in a manner that suggested she was about to fall asleep, yet the next moment spring to her feet with the speed of a cat. Today, she was wearing pale green silk pyjamas, the top cut low, revealing her long slim neck, and her long hair, the colour of the sky just before the sun went down, hanging loose around her shoulders.

Edith's voice drifted across the still air. 'If war is coming, I want us to face it together. If anything happens . . .'

They were all quiet for a while. A thrill ran up Olivia's spine. War! What could be more exciting? She held her breath.

'We don't know for certain that there will be a war,' Mother said. 'There's still a chance ...' She glanced at Olivia's father who reached across and took her hand.

'It's inevitable, my darling. We should accept that.'

The servants had appeared with trays of sandwiches and tea so Mother let go of Father's hand. Mother thought public demonstrations of any sort were vulgar.

Aunt Georgina sat up and lit a cigarette. 'I think war might be rather exciting,' she said.

'You only think war will be exciting, Georgina,' Mother retorted, 'because you will be thousands of miles away from it all.'

'I'll still be doing my bit,' Georgina replied. She ground out her cigarette on the grass and accepted a cup of tea from Aunt Edith. 'I don't blame you for not wanting to wait, Eadie. If I were you, I'd snap him up before someone else does. I can just see you, leading the life of a wife and mother, becoming all matronly, holding luncheons and attending to the less fortunate – you'll be a force to be reckoned with – just like Harriet. When *I* marry, I still intend to have fun.'

Mottled red suffused Mother's neck when Georgina said this, but Mother 'didn't deign to reply' as Olivia heard her tell Father later. Olivia knew the sisters liked each other really. They were always together, walking arm in arm, chatting and laughing and teasing one another.

Georgina lowered her voice and Olivia couldn't hear the rest of what she said, but she heard Findlay's name being mentioned and something more about war.

Edith smiled dreamily. 'Even if there is a war, it might not last very long.'

Mother was still frowning. 'I can't accept there is going to be a war, Peter. Not after everything Chamberlain has done to keep us out of it.'

'He's nothing but a fool if he thinks Hitler will be satisfied for long,' Father retorted. 'We've betrayed Czechoslovakia – didn't keep our part of the bargain – damned dishonourable if you ask me.'

Father worked in Whitehall – something to do with the government, although Olivia wasn't sure exactly what – only that he seemed to know things no one else did.

'There will be a war,' Father repeated quietly. 'You can be sure of it. And it will last for years. Millions will be killed, just like last time.'

'Oh, let's not talk of war and people dying,' Aunt Georgina said, lying back and placing her hands under her head. 'It's far too beautiful a day. Let's talk about what we are going to do tomorrow instead.'

At that moment Findlay arrived back, his shotgun broken and held against his side, the barrel pointing down, the gun dogs running ahead. Laddie, Olivia's favourite, immediately sought her out, his excited yelps exposing her to the adults.

Mother's lips pursed and she beckoned Olivia over.

'Olivia, I do hope you haven't been listening in to the adults' conversation?' she said.

'No, Mother!' She pretended indignation, but when Aunt Georgina winked at her behind Mother's back, Olivia realised she'd known she'd been there all along. She gave her aunt a grateful smile. 'I only came in search of tea.' She helped herself to a scone from a gold-rimmed plate and bit into it.

'Darling, don't stand and eat,' Mother said. 'Do sit down. And put your food on a side plate. What everyone will think of your manners when you go to school, I shudder to think!'

Olivia sank into one of the empty chairs. Findlay was standing with his hands in his pockets. Donald, who'd been out with him, had taken away the partridges he'd shot.

Mother shook her head. 'There's no point in worrying about something that might never happen.' She stood. 'Now if you'll excuse me, I should go and discuss Saturday's menu with Cook.'

*

That evening Olivia had begged and been allowed to sit in her mother's bedroom as she changed for dinner. She'd helped Mother fasten her necklace, watching in awe as her maid did something to her hair, her fingers moving so quickly and so dexterously Olivia couldn't ever quite see how she managed to make Mother's thick, dark blonde hair look exactly like one of the models in the magazines Georgina liked to flick through.

Mother was already dressed in an evening gown that clung to her and showed off the deep blue of her eyes. Apart from Aunt Georgina (and the thought brought with it a shiver of disquiet – as if she were being disloyal), Olivia thought no woman quite as beautiful.

Father came into the room then and Mother dismissed the maid with a smile and a flick of her fingers.

'You look as lovely as ever, my darling,' Father said, taking Mother's hand and turning it over so he could kiss the inside of her wrist.

Mother sighed at her reflection in the mirror. 'Do you think we'll ever come back here? I mean afterwards. If there is a war?'

Father looked at her, his forehead crinkling. 'You're very pensive tonight.'

Mother grasped his hand and laid it against her cheek. 'I have the dreadful feeling something has come to an end. That things will never be the same.' She smiled up at him but her eyes stayed bleak. 'That we'll never be as happy again.'

Her words made Olivia feel hollow in the pit of her stomach.

'Chin up, old thing. It may not come to war. There's still a chance, however small, that Hitler will back off. Regardless of what I said earlier, we must keep on hoping.'

Mother gave him a small, shaky smile. 'Don't mind me. It's the black dog, that's all. You know how it visits me sometimes. It will be all right. It has to be.'

Father noticed Olivia then, although she was trying to do

her statue thing. 'Olivia, shouldn't you have changed? Off with you. Dinner, as you are well aware, is on the stroke of seven-thirty and you mustn't be late.' Although his voice was stern she knew he didn't really mean it. Father never raised his voice to her. When his eyes flickered back to Mother, the hollow feeling in Olivia's stomach got worse. She knew neither he nor Mother really believed that everything was going to be all right.

Chapter Six

In the Highlands during summer, night fell only for a few hours. Even then, it barely got dark before the sun rose again. Olivia knew this because she'd taken to creeping out at night when everyone was asleep. The island belonged only to her then and she wandered freely. She had come to know the island like the back of her hand and there was nothing on it to be frightened of, apart from the ghosts of Lady Elizabeth and Lady Sarah, and if she did come across them – well she'd deal with that if it happened. Thankfully she'd had no more nightmares about either of them.

As always during that long, hot summer, she'd left her bedroom window open. Dinner had been subdued. Findlay was to leave early the next morning to join his regiment and his imminent departure had cast a cloud over everyone and everything.

She was reading in bed – with the curtains left undrawn it was light enough to see without having to light her paraffin lamp – when she'd heard the sound of crunching steps on the stone outside her window and a muffled giggle. She slipped out of bed and, careful not to stand too close, even though she was certain she couldn't be seen, peered out of the window. As her eyes adjusted to the half-light, she saw Aunt Georgina walking towards the side of the island where it was safe to swim, a towel around her neck, glasses in one hand and a bottle dangling from the other. It seemed Georgina was going for a midnight dip. In which case she might let Olivia join her. Careful not to stand on a creaky floorboard, she exchanged her pyjamas for her swimming costume, slid her arms into her dressing gown and pulled thick socks over her bare feet. Although she was quick, Aunt Georgina was out of sight by the time Olivia had crept down the stairs and opened the heavy front door, holding her breath when it creaked. When the sound didn't alert anyone she slipped outside into the balmy air.

Treading lightly, Olivia ran across the lawn, praying that Mother or Father wouldn't choose that moment to look out of the window. If they did, they would spot her easily and would be very angry with her for being out of bed when she was supposed to be sleeping. They might even prevent her from joining in the weekend activities – an intolerable thought although not sufficient to turn her from her course. She hurried on, noting as she did, a discarded towel on the rocks.

Laughter drifted across the still night air, followed by the deep rumble of a man's voice Olivia recognised immediately as belonging to Findlay. She came to a halt. Findlay might not be pleased to have a child join in with the adults. On the other hand he'd always been kind to her. Just then she heard a rustle from the bushes and she thought she saw something move within its depths. Her heart pounding, she slipped behind a tree. She couldn't help it. No matter what she told herself she didn't want to come across the ghost of Lady Elizabeth. For a moment she considered turning around, back to the safety of Greyfriars. She looked back towards the house – a dark grey shape in the semi-darkness. It was further away than the beach and she couldn't be certain what lay between her and it. Far better to stay near the adults.

She peeked out from behind the tree. Findlay was already in the sea, only his chest visible above the rim of the water.

Georgina was on the shore, a few feet away. She lifted her arms and pulled the kaftan she was wearing over her head, letting it float to the ground. Underneath her kaftan she was wearing her costume – an emerald-green one-piece. Her long limbs were pale in the half-light. She'd loosened her hair and it tumbled down her back. For some reason seeing her in a state of near undress unnerved Olivia.

Findlay didn't say anything, just turned to watch her, standing stock-still.

Georgina poured whatever was in the bottle into two glasses. Knowing Aunt Georgina it had to be champagne – she never drank anything else. Still holding the bottle in one hand and the glasses in the other, she picked her way carefully over the pebbles, almost stumbling once. Olivia nearly called out then. Didn't she realise if she slipped and fell the glasses would smash and she could hurt herself? She thought Findlay would come out of the water and take the glasses from her but he stayed where he was, just watching.

Olivia could hear the murmur of their voices, not what they were saying. Georgina sounded as if she were laughing, he sounded a little cross.

Georgina waded out to him until the water came up to her shoulders. Her hair was floating behind her as if she were some sea creature.

When she was no more than a few inches away from him she handed him one of the glasses. Instead of drinking, he flung the glass away.

Georgina drank from hers then did the same, her glass joining Findlay's at the bottom of the sea. Then, Olivia almost stopped breathing. Georgina ran her fingertips along Findlay's bare chest before winding her arms around his neck. He gripped her wrists and dipped his head towards her saying something in a low, urgent tone.

Olivia spun away – all thoughts of joining them having disappeared. She dared not stay and watch any more. If they saw

50

her, they would be furious, might even accuse her of spying on them and she couldn't bear either of them to think badly of her. Her heart still racing, she ran as fast as she dared back to the house, sprinted to her tower room and threw herself under her bed covers.

When she woke up the next morning Findlay had gone.

Chapter Seven

Olivia sat in front of the dressing table trying not to yelp every time Edith ran the brush through her tangled hair.

'Do you like being a nurse?' Olivia asked her aunt. 'Will you look after the injured soldiers if there is a war?'

'Why are you so certain there will be a war?'

'I'm not silly. Or stupid. I've heard what the adults are saying. I hope the war lasts long enough so I can join the army and help shoot the enemy. I think it's silly women can't be soldiers.'

Edith's reflection smiled condescendingly. 'Quite the blood-thirsty little thing, aren't you?'

Her comment stung. Olivia wasn't a silly little child. She knew things. A lot of things.

'Will Georgina still go to Singapore after she marries Findlay?'

Edith laughed. 'What an odd thing to say. What on earth makes you think Georgina is going to marry Findlay?'

'I saw them kissing. That's what people do and then they get married, don't they? That's how babies are made,' she blurted, then immediately wished she could swallow her tongue. Aunt Edith was bound to ask her how she knew and then she would find out that she'd been creeping about late at night and tell Mother and Olivia would get into terrible trouble.

Edith gasped and the brush fell out of her hand. She spun

Olivia round, her fingers digging into her shoulders so hard Olivia had to bite her lip to stop herself from crying out with the pain and shock of it. 'You'd better explain yourself, young lady. It's one thing making up stories that can't harm anyone, quite another—'

'I'm not making it up!' Olivia tried to wriggle from Aunt Edith's grasp but her grip was too strong. 'I know the difference between made-up stories and things that really happened. I saw them!'

'When did you see them?' Aunt Edith hissed, shaking her even harder. 'Do you know what happens to little girls who lie?'

She was *not* a liar, she was not! Lying was a mortal sin, or so the Bible said. Olivia's vision blurred with tears. She knew she was in trouble whatever she said now. 'I did see them! The other night. In the sea. Why don't you ask Aunt Georgina yourself?'

The colour drained from Edith's face and she dropped her arms to her side. Olivia rubbed her shoulders where her aunt's fingers had pinched her skin.

Why was Aunt Edith going on so? People who loved each other kissed. She'd seen Mother and Father do it once when they thought she wasn't looking. 'If they are going to get married, what does it matter?'

To her bewilderment, Edith gave a strangled cry and ran from the room.

Later that evening, when Olivia was in bed, Mother knocked on her door. She looked pale and upset, her hair coming undone from her pins, her face not made up, and Olivia immediately knew Edith had told her what she'd said.

Mother sat down on Olivia's bed with a heavy sigh. 'Why on earth did you tell Aunt Edith you saw Aunt Georgina and Mr Armstrong kissing?' she demanded.

'I didn't mean to cause any trouble.' Olivia's voice wobbled. She hated it when Mother was disappointed in her.

Mother took Olivia's chin between her fingers and tipped her face so she was forced to look into her eyes. 'Did you really see Aunt Georgina with Mr Armstrong? It's very important that you tell me the truth. I know how you like to make up stories!'

'It's not a story,' Olivia protested. 'I really saw them. I don't understand why Aunt Edith was so angry with me.'

Mother paused as if deciding what to say. 'Because Aunt Edith was hoping to marry Mr Armstrong. They were supposed to announce their engagement at the party here at the end of the summer.'

'Aunt Edith and Mr Armstrong!' It couldn't be true.

Mother pursed her lips. 'What were you doing outside at that time of night, anyway?'

Olivia explained about following Georgina down to the shore thinking she wouldn't mind if Olivia joined her for a swim, and how she hadn't known that Edith loved Findlay. 'I never saw Aunt Edith and Mr Armstrong kissing!' she cried.

'My dear child, grown-ups don't kiss in public, not unless they are vulgar.'

'I didn't mean to cause trouble,' Olivia repeated, furious that tears had sprung to her eyes.

Mother took her hand and squeezed it. 'Your Aunt Georgina can be very naughty. She did something – they both did – that was very wrong.'

Olivia kept quiet. It hadn't seemed wrong to her.

'We are going to leave the day after tomorrow with Aunt Edith. Father has been recalled to London and I have decided that we should go with him. Edith needs me.'

Olivia didn't want to leave Greyfriars but she knew she had spoilt everything. Leaving Greyfriars would be her punishment.

'What about the party? And the other guests that were coming?'

Mother sighed and shook her head. 'There can be no party

now. Or guests. The servants have started closing up the house. In the meantime you are to stay in your room until I say you can come out. You shouldn't have been out of bed and you must be punished. One of the maids will bring you your meals.'

Olivia thought she'd been punished enough. Mother and Edith were angry with her, there were to be no more guests, no party and she was to be taken from Greyfriars more than a month early! But she knew no amount of pleading would change Mother's mind.

The next day passed in slow motion, each boring minute feeling like an hour. One of the maids brought her a boiled egg and a glass of milk, before scurrying away again. Lunch was fish paste sandwiches and more milk.

It was another blisteringly hot afternoon and Olivia was reading *Robinson Crusoe*, when through her open window, voices drifted up. She peered out of the window to find Georgina and Edith outside facing each other. Georgina was wearing a summer dress, fully made-up, her lips painted a deep red. Edith was in a white blouse and skirt and was pale apart from her flushed cheeks.

'You mustn't blame Findlay. It was all my fault. I was squiffy – you know how I am when I drink too much,' Georgina said.

'Do you really think that is any sort of excuse? How could you? You knew we planned to become engaged! Do you grudge me my happiness so much you had to spoil it the way you spoil everything? You could have had anyone you wanted – why take him?'

'I didn't take him,' Georgina said with a wry smile. 'No one *takes* another person.'

'You've always left a trail of destruction in your wake. Never given the least bit thought to the people whose lives you've wrecked. It wasn't enough that you ruined that woman's life in Paris – you had to ruin mine.'

'Whatever people are saying about me, it isn't true,' Georgina said quietly. 'And I haven't ruined your life. There's no reason you and Findlay can't still get married.'

'Marry him? After he made love to you?'

'I keep telling you he didn't. He quite rightly rejected my advances. When he returns you can ask him yourself.'

A morsel of doubt crept through Olivia. She thought back to what she'd seen; Georgina's hands around Findlay's neck, her face lifted to his, his arms on her wrists. Now she thought about it, she hadn't actually seen them kiss. Although they'd been about to. She was sure of it. But the doubt wouldn't go away. If she were honest she wasn't really sure. Not at all. Perhaps she should run downstairs and say so?

'It's you he loves. And if you really loved him you'd fight for him.' Georgina's voice softened. 'I would if I were in your shoes.'

'What could you possibly know about love? The only person you care about is yourself. You take lovers as other women drink tea,' Edith retorted.

Georgina twisted the large ruby ring she wore on her right hand around and around and raised an eyebrow. 'One lover – perhaps two – I hardly think it's the equivalent of drinking tea. Everyone in Paris has lovers. And that was a long time ago.'

'One lover – three – what does it matter? You're used goods.'

Georgina's eyes flashed. 'Don't be so utterly middle class. How can anyone ever match up to your high ideals? It's quite impossible. My God, Edith, you can be such a prig!'

'And they have names for women like you!'

There was a stunned silence.

Olivia waited for Edith to say she was sorry, that she didn't mean it.

Aunt Edith's face flushed a deep crimson. 'I don't want to see either of you again.'

'You can't mean that.'

'Oh, but I do. I'm going to go back with Agatha and Gordon. I'll stay in the house in Edinburgh until I decide what to do with my life now you've ruined it. I'd prefer it if you stayed away.'

Georgina was even paler than Edith. 'Don't go, Eadie. Not like this!' She reached out for Edith's hand, but Edith pulled hers away as if Georgina's touch would contaminate her.

For a long moment they stood, still facing each other, both breathing deeply. Olivia held hers.

'If anyone should leave it is me,' Georgina said softly.

'You think I'm going to stay here? Lick my wounds? As if I've got something to be ashamed of? And you forget, there are people who have to be informed that there is to be no engagement – a party to be cancelled.'

Georgina reached out to her again but Edith stepped back and shook her head. 'I will never forgive you for this. Never! As far as I'm concerned, you are dead to me. Dead!'

Chapter Eight

Edith, Agatha and Gordon left later that afternoon. Georgina stood on the steps as if still hoping Edith would say goodbye, but Edith barely glanced at her. When Mother returned from seeing them off she squeezed Aunt Georgina's shoulder as she passed but didn't say anything to her. Georgina looked so sad, Olivia thought again about telling the truth – that she hadn't actually seen Georgina and Findlay kiss. But it was too late now. Anyway, Aunt Edith was horrible! The things she'd said to Aunt Georgina. She deserved to be unhappy. Besides, anyone could see that it was Georgina and Findlay who were supposed to be together. How she wished Georgina would look up so she could give her a friendly wave. She wanted Georgina to know she was on her side.

With all the guests apart from Georgina gone, the house seemed bereft – even the servants were subdued. When Olivia was released from the confines of her bedroom, she tried to find Georgina but she was either in her own room, or closeted with Mother in the morning room.

Acutely aware it was her last day, Olivia tried to find pleasure in her usual pursuits, poking around the shore in search of treasure tossed up by the sea, visiting the cows and ponies on the farm, but she couldn't capture the joy of the previous weeks. Eventually she gave up trying and trudged back to the house. She wanted to say something to Aunt Georgina — to apologise for all the trouble she'd caused.

She found her alone in the library, sitting in front of the window, a book in her lap. She looked up and smiled when she saw Olivia. 'Looks like you and I have caused a spot of bother, Livvy.'

Olivia ran over and flung her arms around her. 'I'm sorry. I didn't mean to get you into trouble.'

'Oh, darling girl, you didn't get me into trouble. I did that all by myself.' She held Olivia at arm's length and studied her face. 'Actions have consequences. We should never forget that.' She drew her thumb across Olivia's cheek. 'Now, don't you cry or you'll make me cry too.'

'I heard what Aunt Edith said. She's horrible. She should never have said those things to you. I think you're far nicer than she is and I'm glad Mr Armstrong prefers you to her.'

'That's not true, Olivia. He loves your Aunt Edith and he's quite right to do so.'

'But—'

Aunt Georgina hugged Olivia again, pressing her against her chest so closely Olivia could smell her perfume and her shampoo. 'You mustn't admire me, Livvy. I'm not the sort of woman you should look up to. Your Aunt Edith is a far better person than I'll ever be. If you want to be like anyone, be like her.'

Leaving Georgina at Greyfriars, they returned to London the way they'd come. The boat first, then a car to the station, a train to Inverness and finally the Royal Scotsman. But where the journey up had been filled with gleeful anticipation, they were a subdued trio on the way back and Olivia knew it was all her fault.

By the time they got to London, the capital was already preparing for war. Sandbags were being brought in trucks before being piled up outside public buildings. Windows were being taped, air raid shelters prepared and a blackout had been ordered.

War was declared two weeks later. Shortly afterwards, protesting furiously, but to no avail, Olivia was packed off to Fife to stay with Agatha and her husband, where she was to remain until it was time for term to start. Instead of going to school in London, she'd been enrolled at St Michael's – Mother's old school. Father wanted Mother to go and stay with Agatha too, Olivia heard him pleading with her, but Mother refused to be persuaded.

'I'll visit Olivia whenever I can, but I'm staying here with you,' she said, tears in her voice. 'They are going to need people in London to help and I'm a good organiser. And if it's more practical help that's needed, I can roll up my sleeves with the best of them.'

That made Father smile, although briefly.

'If only this trouble between Georgina and Findlay hadn't happened, then Edith would be living in Edinburgh and Olivia could have stayed with her,' Mother continued. 'Now Edith has applied to join the QAs and goodness knows where they'll send her!'

'Trouble always follows Georgina. I'm beginning to regret organising that posting in Singapore for her. What if she embarrasses us further? Forlorn lovers in Paris, attempts to seduce her sister's fiancé, engagements called off, really, Harriet!'

'There was no ditched lover in Paris,' Mother said quietly. 'People thought it, and I admit it is easy to see why they might, but it was quite untrue that she encouraged him. Georgina might be naughty, very naughty, and more than a little wayward, but she didn't do what they said she did.'

'How can you believe a word she says? And do you deny that she tried to seduce Findlay? Having a few too many drinks is no excuse. God knows what else she got up to in Paris. Living the life of a bohemian, drinking in clubs and bars, consorting with all sorts. It is one thing being flighty, quite another ignoring the rules of decent society.' Father picked up his newspaper – a sure sign he considered a topic over.

A few days later Agatha came to fetch Olivia in her motor car.

Saying goodbye to Mother and Father was difficult, but Olivia tried her best to be brave and not cry. She kept telling herself she would see them soon. Mother had promised to come to visit whenever she could, with Father if he had leave.

But Olivia knew, deep down inside, that nothing would ever be the same again.

Chapter Nine

Charlotte

1984

Mum trailed off, looking drained.

'So Findlay was Edith's boyfriend?' I almost wanted to say 'beau'. Boyfriend didn't seem right.

'I didn't know! It never crossed my mind! Georgina and Findlay arrived together and I just assumed they were with each other. All I saw was the way Georgina looked at him. Edith was quieter, more reserved. I never guessed that it was *her* Findlay was supposed to be in love with. Everything fell apart after that summer. Nothing was ever the same. And for years I believed it was all my fault.' She took a shaky breath. 'Maybe it was. I should have told someone I might have been mistaken – that I never saw them actually kiss.'

'It wasn't your fault, Mum. It's ridiculous to even think that. You were a child and quite frankly, Georgina sounds a bit of a bitch. What was she thinking of, going after the man her sister hoped to marry? What kind of woman would do that? And what sort of man would respond? Sounds to me as if Edith was better off without him.'

Mum massaged the crease between her brow. 'I've thought about it a great deal over the years. Findlay could have just as easily been telling Georgina to leave him alone as about to kiss her. He was a gentleman, after all. And even if he had been about to kiss her . . . it might not have meant anything.

And to be fair no one could have blamed him. If you'd known Georgina, it wouldn't have surprised you. Even my father seemed to be under her spell. Everyone wanted to be near her, to have her smile at them. The closest I can describe it is that it was like being in the presence of a movie star.'

'A singularly selfish, self-absorbed movie star. One with particularly loose morals even by today's standards.'

'But that was only one side of her. She was kind and fun – at least as far as I was concerned.' Mum rummaged around in her drawer of her bedside cabinet and brought out a photograph. 'That's us. That last summer.'

It was a group photo in black and white. There were three women and one man. The woman in the chair I recognised as my grandmother and the man standing behind her, his hand resting on her shoulder, eyes squinting against the sun, my grandfather. There were two other women, the aunts I was sure. One lay on a hammock that had been strung between two trees, a long, bare leg hanging over the side, in a posture of abandonment that looked out of place next to my grand-parents' formality. A cigarette hung from between her fingers. Her hair was loose around her shoulders, her teeth small and even, and a smile played around her full lips. The other woman was sitting on a picnic blanket, her legs tucked underneath her. She was smiling at the camera, a look of adoration on her face. Mum was next to her.

'I imagine the woman in the hammock is Georgina and the one on the blanket, Edith?'

'Yes.' Mum's voice was barely above a whisper. 'You can see how beautiful the sisters were – especially Georgina.'

'Who took the photograph?' I asked.

'I think it was Findlay. It was him who gave it to me.' She smiled. 'I kept it along with the camisole Georgina bought for me. I found both the other day when I was sorting things. One day when you marry and have children, your daughter might wear the camisole.'

I'd always suspected Mum wondered if I would ever marry. She'd been so pleased when I started going out with Christopher, an A&E registrar, and clearly disappointed when we'd broken up. Not that she'd ever said – or asked – anything.

Mum glanced at the clock. 'Good grief! Look at the time! I need to get up.'

Leaving Mum to get dressed in privacy, I went downstairs, the photo still in my hand, my head filled with images of a bygone age, of beautiful women in evening dresses and a large house on an island.

Until this morning, I hadn't appreciated the sort of family my mother had been born into. She'd never given any inkling. I knew little about my grandparents except they had been killed during the war and until now, had never thought much about them. Yet the way Mum had described Greyfriars it seemed her family had once been wealthy. Although I'd never been aware of us being short of money – Mum had given me a generous allowance while I was at university and more when I was a pupil at Lambert and Lambert – Mum had always been thrifty; the central heating was only used in the depths of winter and we'd never been on holiday overseas.

In the kitchen I switched on the kettle and while waiting for it to boil, I studied the photograph again. Mum was right. All the sisters had been beautiful, but Georgina's beauty had been remarkable. She did have the sort of face that made you want to keep on looking at.

Placing the photo down, I spooned coffee into a mug. Why had Mum not told me about them before? Why had I never met them? The aunts, Georgina in particular, appeared to have been fond of Mum, and Edith couldn't possibly have held a grudge against a child who'd blurted out what she thought she had seen in all innocence – even if she had been mistaken.

As I'd lain awake last night I'd run through my schedule in my head. The Curtis murder trial had only recently been concluded and, as there was no way of predicting how long it would run for, I hadn't accepted any other big cases. Therefore all I had on my calendar was a high-profile divorce, a breaking and entering, and a banker who put far too much of his obscene salary up his nose, and had been accused of attacking a policeman who'd stopped him for driving erratically. These could either be passed on to someone else within Lambert and Lambert or the cases returned.

Taking the telephone from the hall into the kitchen and closing the door, I phoned the office and asked to be put through to John. In theory I should have spoken to Giles, given he was Head of Chambers, and told him about Mum and what I intended, but I had been at Lambert and Lambert long enough to know where the true power lay – with its senior clerk, John Woods. He more or less ran the firm. And he was very good at it. In order to get the pick of the cases for Lambert and Lambert, he schmoozed with solicitors and insisted that we did too. He was the decision maker, the one with the power to hand the most prestigious, the most lucrative cases to the barrister of his choice.

'Where are you, miss?' John asked as soon as he came on the phone.

'At my mother's. In Edinburgh.'

'I hope you are planning to press charges against Corrigle,' John said. 'We can't let people think they can get away with attacking barristers, miss. Especially not those of a feminine leaning.'

He always spoke as if he'd been raised in Victorian times. At least to me.

'Forget about it, John. I have no intention of pressing charges. His daughter tried to kill herself. I think he has enough to worry about.'

'If you're sure, miss,' he said dubiously.

'I am.'

His voice brightened. 'The Curtis case will make your name,

65

miss. Mark my words.' I visualised John behind his desk, one expensively suited leg crossed over the other as he twirled a pen between his fingers.' It's already all over the news. All those years of hard graft finally paying off, eh? They'll be beating a path to your door.' He lowered his voice to a confidential whisper. 'Perhaps it's time for you to go after silk?'

I wanted nothing more. It was what I'd been working towards for years.

Giles was as yet the only member to have been given silk, and I intended to be next. In big murder trials, the client was represented by two barristers, one a QC, the other, the junior, his second. It was junior counsel who usually did most of the work but the QC who received the credit. I didn't mind too much – that was the way things worked. Besides, in law circles everyone who counted – those who considered applications for silk – would know it was me, not Giles, who'd won the case. 'I've had solicitors on the phone all morning, wanting you to represent their clients,' John continued. 'There's one in particular—'

'That's what I wanted to speak to you about,' I interrupted. 'I can't accept any new cases. I need to take some time off.'

'What? Now?'

I hadn't taken a holiday in the last five years. Come to think of it, I couldn't remember the last time I had taken more than a couple of days. And to take time off now, when I had just won the most important case of my career – no wonder John sounded incredulous.

'If you need a break, and I can see you might, can't it wait?' he said.

'No. My mother is unwell. That's why I'm in Edinburgh.'

'When will you be back?'

I swallowed. It was getting more and more difficult to keep my voice steady. 'I'm not sure. Not for some time.'

'What about the Littlejohn divorce? You're due to represent her in court.'

'Sophie should – will – be able to handle it. She's in her second six. I've done all the background. It should be a rollover.'

About half of my work came from representing women who had been married to rich, powerful men who, not content with dumping them for a younger, prettier model, also wished to leave them if not penniless, then pretty close to it. It never ceased to amaze me how many of these women were unaware of their rights and even when they were, how few wished to fight for what was only their fair share. It was only usually when the penny dropped that they might spend the rest of their lives in rented accommodation, without any of the comforts they had been used to that they instructed a solicitor to instruct me. I had taken my first high-profile divorce case four years ago, won a tidy settlement for the wife, and ever since had been in demand. There was nothing vindictive about it, I got no pleasure from witnessing the end of a marriage, but fair was fair. It was what I was paid to do.

'And your fee? You know you'll have to give a large chunk to your pupil?'

'I do.' Money had never seemed less important.

'And the Griffin case?' he continued, referring to the cocaine abusing banker who'd assaulted the policeman.

'Give it to one of the others or return it.'

There was a long pause on the other end of the phone. 'He won't be happy. His solicitor asked for you especially.' John hated returning cases. And I knew he'd worked hard to get Griffin's solicitor to send us more work.

'I'm sorry, John.'

'This is the worst time for you to be away, you do know that?' John continued. 'You have to grab the iron while it's hot. You might be barrister of the moment now but people, especially solicitors, have short memories.' The threat wasn't so much veiled as stripped naked and doing a little pirouette. Either I return soon to the fold or he'd pass the cases he'd earmarked for me to someone else. Tenancies with Lambert and Lambert were highly sought after and chambers there breathtakingly expensive. Several hundred pounds a month. My recent successes meant I was on the brink of being able to cover my expenses several times over, but even so, if I wasn't working it meant I wasn't making money and if I wasn't making money, neither was John, who took a percentage of my earnings. Lambert and Lambert couldn't evict me, but although John and I had known each other for almost ten years, I knew without a shadow of a doubt that he would find a way to get me out if he thought I was no longer pulling my weight.

'I'll take my chances, John,' I said, striving to keep my voice even. 'Now, could you put me through to Sophie, please?'

'I'll see if she's in.'

Of course Sophie would be in. No matter how early I came to the office, Sophie always managed to be there before me. I was her pupil master, a term that made me wince or smile, depending on my mood. The term they used in Scotland was even more bizarre, where pupils 'devilled' for their masters.

A small brunette, with an Asian mother and an English father, Sophie was different to most of the pupils at the Inns of Court and pretty much an exception. Although pupils no longer had to pay to be taken on by a set, competition for places was still high and, more often than not, the result of an introduction. When less than ten per cent of women were self-employed barristers, who you knew still got you places rather than ability and Sophie hadn't gone to Oxford or Cambridge, but to Liverpool. As if that wasn't enough of a disadvantage, her mother was a housewife and her father a bus driver. Despite having everything against her, I had no doubt she would make it. She was one of the brightest pupils I had ever mastered. She had graduated not only with a first but with the medal for the year, and I had argued long and hard to persuade my colleagues to take her on as a pupil at Lambert and Lambert. She hadn't let me down. She intended to work for the Crown Prosecution Service when she was called to the bar. Defence lawyers I was sure would learn to fear her.

'Charlotte. How are you?' Her quiet voice, that disguised a steel-like resolve, came over the line.

'I've been better. My mother is ill and I need to take some time off.'

'Of course. If she is unwell, you must be with her. Is there anything I can do?'

Perhaps it was the way her voice softened, or perhaps because it was the first time I felt I didn't need to defend my decision, but unexpectedly my throat tightened and I was unable to speak for a moment.

'I'll need you to take on the Littlejohn case,' I said when I thought I could trust my voice again.

'Do you think I am ready?' she asked, although she couldn't hide the flare of excitement in her voice. 'More importantly, will Mrs Littlejohn accept me in your place?'

'I'll see that she does. She might take a little persuading but she'd be a fool to go with anyone else. I know you'd prefer something meatier the first time on your own in court, but once John sees how competent you are, I'm sure he and the others will give you more briefs.'

She didn't waste time trying to get extra reassurance, instead she quizzed me on the case. She'd been working with me on it so knew most of the detail, but was keen to know what line I would take were it me in court.

'You have to find your own angle,' I said. 'Be yourself. That's what will make people sit up and take notice. John has my mother's home number, if you want to talk anything over. Not that I think you'll need to.' I hesitated. 'There's something else I need you to do for me. You can say no, but I hope you won't.'

There was a long silence on the other end of the line when I told her what it was. I knew I was asking a great deal.

'You don't have to do it if you don't want to,' I added. 'I'll find another way.'

'I'll do it.'

'Thank you, Sophie. Ring me if you find out anything.' Hopefully there would be nothing to discover, then I could put Lucy Corrigle to one side and concentrate on Mum.

'I will be thinking of you,' Sophie said in her quiet, serious voice. 'And your mother.'

While I'd been on the phone, Mum had come downstairs and was in the sitting room. The windows had been opened, letting in the sounds of the birds outside and the sweet-smelling scent of roses. Her tablets had been tidied away.

She glanced up from the sofa and smiled. Her eyes were bright, her hair neatly brushed and she'd even put on some lipstick. It took every ounce of self-control I could muster not to weep.

'When do you have to leave for London?' she asked.

My chest tightened. So she'd gone to all this effort hoping to make it easier for me to go back to work.

'I'm not going anywhere, I'm here for as long as you need me.'

'No, Charlotte! I don't want you putting your life on hold for me!'

'It's non-negotiable, Mum. I haven't taken a holiday for years. I'm more than due time off.' I dipped my head so she wouldn't see the pain in my eyes, how frightened I was that this was the last time we'd have together. I couldn't even bear to think it.

She took my hand and squeezed it. 'In that case, I'll just have to make the most of you while you're here.'

'How about some lunch?' I asked, returning the pressure of her fingers. She'd barely eaten any of her breakfast. 'I could rustle us up some scrambled eggs if you'd like?'

Mum grimaced. 'I'm not terribly hungry, Charlotte.'

'You need to eat!'

Mum arched her eyebrows and I bit back a sigh of frustration. Who was I to talk? Engrossed in work I'd often skip meals, most days grabbing a sandwich from a supermarket for my supper.

'You're not the best cook in the world, you never were.' Mum laughed and the tension that had quivered for a split second between us vanished.

The eggs turned out better than my mother feared and after lunch, cups of tea in hand, I helped her sort through some of her financial papers. There was so much she wanted to do; write to her bank, call her lawyer to update her will, pass over Power of Attorney to me.

It wasn't long before Mum was too exhausted to do any more. She slumped back and I looked over at her in alarm.

'Why don't you have a nap?' I jumped up, ready to help her. 'Can I get you a glass of water? Do you need some painkillers?'

'Stop fussing, Charlotte,' Mum said softly. Nevertheless she let me ease her legs up onto the sofa, Tiger shuffling out the way until I had covered my mother with a blanket.

'I'll leave you to rest,' I said, tucking her in.

She reached out her hand and grabbed my wrist. 'Stay and talk to me, Charlotte.' She managed a small smile. 'There will be plenty of time later for me to rest. But right now there is so much more I need to tell you.'

The ache in my chest blossomed. I wished we could pretend that everything was just the same – us in our separate chairs, books open, looking up occasionally to discuss and argue about what we'd been reading. But we had so little time to get to know each other again and if Mum had things to tell me, I wanted to hear them. I sat back down and smiled to let her know I was listening.

'Talking about Greyfriars has brought it all back.' When she looked at me I saw her eyes were shimmering with unshed tears. 'Nothing was the same after that summer. Everything changed. Perhaps if the war hadn't happened. Or if my parents hadn't died . . .'

71

Chapter Ten

Olivia

1941

Despite it being May, the dining room was cold and bleak, the curtains pulled closed to shut out the sun.

A wireless played classical music softly in the background above which could be heard the scratching of fountain pens on paper, escaping sighs and the occasional muffled sob. As on every Sunday evening, the girls, twenty of them, were composing the obligatory weekly letter home.

Olivia sighed and looked up, thinking of what she should write. She'd given up pleading to come home after Father had told her that the Friels put their best foot forward, lifted their chin, and made the best of things. Everyone was suffering, he said, and she had to be brave too.

She didn't feel brave, she felt utterly miserable. Boarding school was nothing like Mother had promised it would be. It wasn't fun at all. Perhaps because the St Michael's Mother, Aunt Georgina and Edith had attended in Fife had been requisitioned for a hospital and the school decanted to a castle in Perthshire.

Under any other circumstances, Olivia would have been delighted to have finally got her wish to live in a proper castle, but this one was a disappointment and nothing like Greyfriars. Where Greyfriars had been light and sunshine and happiness – until the last few days of that holiday anyway – the castle was gloomy and forbidding and she hated it.

Her dorm, shared with nineteen other girls, was in the original ballroom. All the paintings that had once hung there had been taken down, as if the schoolgirls' grubby hands might defile them, and twenty cast-iron single beds set out in a row, ten on either side. Each girl had a locker and a narrow cupboard for her belongings, every item marked with their name.

Boarding school simply didn't suit her. It wasn't just living cheek by jowl with the other girls, or even the gloomy, freezing cold castle – it was the lack of freedom. Every moment of every day was accounted for and followed a strict pattern. There was no kindly matron to soothe the girls' homesickness in the absence of mothers – quite the opposite. Matron's entire *raison d'être*, or so it seemed, was to make the girls' lives as miserable as possible. No sergeant major in the army could have been more of a stickler for following rules. And there were oodles of them. No talking once they had gone upstairs, no getting out of bed after lights out, no talking to boys on the way to church, prep after school, hockey every Saturday, every last thing on their plates to be eaten no matter how vile – and most of it was vile.

She should be getting used to it after almost two years, but she just wanted to be at home with Mother and Father. It had been ages since she'd seen them.

A tear slipped down her cheek and she used the cuff of her school cardigan to wipe it away. It was almost impossible to imagine Britain was at war. Although many of the girls had fathers fighting abroad or had come from homes in London, they never spoke of it. Far away from it all, it was easier to imagine that nothing terrible was going on. But in London it was different, and it was all the more exciting for it.

The first Christmas when, because the bombing they'd expected hadn't happened, she'd been allowed home, had been lovely. Enormous balloons hung over the city, the front of most of the buildings were partly covered with sandbags, the windows criss-crossed with black tape and there were soldiers and army trucks and cars everywhere.

Despite the rationing, Cook had squirrelled away enough to produce a feast on Christmas Day. There had been a tree and presents too. Father had a desk job in a ministry in London so he was there in the evenings. During the day, Olivia and Mother had walked through Regent's Park, or visited some of Mother's friends. Once they had had tea at the Lyon's tea room in Piccadilly, just the two of them, and Mother had talked to her, as if she were quite grown up.

Mother told her Aunt Edith had been accepted by the Queen Alexandra's Imperial Nursing Service and was in Peebles undergoing some sort of extra training and that she hoped to be sent abroad. Aunt Georgina had written from Singapore and Mother read Olivia snippets from her letters. Everything Georgina wrote made Olivia want to go there more. No one mentioned Findlay and Olivia knew better than to ask.

It was almost worse going back to boarding school the second time. Especially when it was so difficult to find out what was going on in the rest of the world. They were allowed to listen to the wireless once a week when they wrote their letters home, but never to the news bulletins. The only news they had of the war was the occasional smattering of gossip from a letter, but it was impossible to keep everything from them. When, last September, the Germans started bombing London and kept on bombing it, everyone knew about it.

Mother made light of the bombing in her letters. She told Olivia that London was determined to carry on as normal. She and Father still went to the cinema and out for dinner. Mother even made it sound like fun. Everyone was certain that Hitler would give up soon.

But it had meant Olivia couldn't go to London last Christmas. Instead Mother and Father had come to stay with Agatha and Gordon. It had been almost as much fun as the Christmas before, although Father had only been able to manage a few days. They'd gone for long walks, muffled up in coats and scarves, returning to hot chocolate in front of the fire. Best of all, Mother said that she and Father hoped to go to Greyfriars for two weeks in the summer, taking Olivia with them. It would just be the three of them but, Mother had said with a big smile, it would be perfect.

The wireless was playing Mozart now. She mustn't feel sad. In just over a month she'd be on her way to Greyfriars.

Catching the eye of the housemistress she bent her head to her task and picked up her pen again. It was difficult to think of things to write about. Perhaps she should tell Mother one of her stories? She seemed to quite enjoy them.

'Miss Friel!' Olivia jumped as her name rang out and everyone turned to look at her. 'You are to go with Miss MacDonald here,' the housemistress said. 'Miss Walpole wishes to see you in her office.'

Olivia's heart thudded. She hadn't even noticed that Melanie MacDonald, one of the prefects, had come in. She'd been too absorbed in deciding which story to write in her letter. Being called to the headmistress's office was not a good thing.

Melanie didn't even look at her as she followed her out of the room and along the deserted corridors. Olivia racked her brains trying to think what rule she might have broken. It was easy to break the rules, without even knowing you had. The only one she knew for certain that she *had* broken was going out through the sash window at the far end of the dormitory and onto the flat roof where she'd hide behind one of the chimneys and read. One of the other girls, Brenda Smith, had seen her climbing back in after rest period and had probably told on her. Brenda Smith thought the more she tittle-tattled the more the teachers would like her. She was wrong.

Melanie stopped outside the headmistress's office and knocked. Olivia took a deep breath. So what if she was in trouble? The worst they could do was make her stay downstairs after prep without a book to read or homework to do.

When the headmistress's voice bade them enter, Melanie opened the door and gave Olivia a little shove before closing the door behind her.

Olivia had never been in Miss Walpole's office before and she looked around with interest. It was large, more like a sitting room than an office, with a fireplace, a leather armchair, a bureau with a tray holding a crystal decanter and matching glasses on it, as well as ornaments – including a ballerina in a long dress with the toe of a blue slipper peeking out. There were landscape paintings on the wall, mostly of the sea but one or two of sombre-looking people staring grimly into the middle distance. All this Olivia took in in a moment. It was only when the headmistress glanced towards the window that Olivia noticed that someone else was in the room. Backlit by the sun streaming through the window their features were obscured. When the figure turned and stepped out of the light and Olivia saw it was Agatha, her heart stopped. Olivia never forgot what Agatha was wearing; a black dress and a matching hat with a small veil that hid her eyes. When Agatha took off her hat Olivia saw that her eyeliner had run. It was that that almost shocked her most. Agatha was never anything but immaculate.

Something terrible must have happened. No one was allowed visitors or even phone calls, except for one Sunday every month. The only exception to this rule was when a relative or family friend came to break bad news.

She guessed it had to be her father. But deep down inside she knew if it had just been Daddy, Mother would be standing there and not Agatha. She scrabbled around for an explanation that might still offer hope. Perhaps Father had been injured and Mother had to stay by his bedside. Perhaps Agatha had been sent to fetch Olivia to them?

When Miss Walpole told Olivia to take a seat and handed her a handkerchief, she wanted to run from that room and keep on running.

'Is it Father?' Olivia's lips felt frozen and she could hardly form the words.

Agatha nodded. 'I am so sorry, my dear child. There was a raid. A bad one. The night before last. I would have come sooner but I only found out for certain . . . ' She dabbed at her eyes with her handkerchief.

'Is he going to be all right?' Olivia asked. She still clung to the last faint remnants of hope that he'd only been injured.

When Agatha came over to her and crouched by her side, Olivia saw her eyes were drenched.

'I'm so sorry,' Agatha whispered, 'but your dear father is dead.'

It was as if someone had taken a bucket of freezing water and flung it over Olivia.

'And Mother?' She didn't want to hear the answer. She wanted to get up and leave. She wanted to turn the clock back, imagine herself anywhere except there, in the headmistress's study with the two women looking at her with unbearable pity in their eyes. An image of that last summer in Greyfriars came rushing back. Mummy in the bedroom, telling Daddy about the black dog and how she was worried they'd never be as happy again. Olivia knew then that if Father was dead Mother would never survive his loss. But even as those thoughts were rushing through her head she was telling herself that she would care for Mummy. With Olivia beside her, Mummy might not miss Father quite so much.

Agatha just looked at her and uttered a cry.

'You are going to have to be a very brave girl,' Miss Walpole said. 'I'm so very sorry, Olivia, but your mother was killed too. They were in the house together when the bomb struck. I know this must be a dreadful shock.'

'Mummy *and* Daddy?'

To have lost one of them was bad enough – but both. She would remember the horror of that day, the disbelief, for the rest of her life.

The room was going in and out of focus and she thought she might faint. 'Can I go to them?' If she could see them for herself . . . It might still be some sort of ghastly mistake.

'You're to come home with me,' Agatha said gently. 'For a few days.'

Olivia could only stare at her. She didn't want to go anywhere, except to London to Mother and Father.

'I've written to your aunts to tell them,' Agatha continued, 'although I can't be sure when, or if, they'll get the letters. I understand that Edith is abroad too. As soon as they hear the news I'm certain they will write to you, perhaps even come for you. In the meantime you must try to be strong. Your dear mother and father would want that.'

'What about the funeral? When will it be?'

Agatha's fingers fluttered to her throat. 'Oh, my dear, there can't be a funeral.' She bit her lip and looked over to Miss Walpole in desperation.

'The house in London was destroyed. Most of the street was,' Miss Walpole said. She and Agatha exchanged a look. 'I'm afraid . . . the bodies . . . ' Miss Walpole cleared her throat. 'Your parents' home took a direct hit. When your aunts return I am sure they will organise a memorial service. You will be able to say your goodbyes then.' Miss Walpole stood, making it clear there was nothing more to say. 'Now, Olivia, go and ask Matron to help you pack a bag.'

Olivia remembered little of the next few days. Agatha was kind, treated Olivia as if she had the flu, keeping her in bed and bringing her tea and toast. But after a week she said she thought it best that Olivia returned to school. She said of course Olivia must stay with them on all her out weekends and holidays too – until such time one of her aunts was able to take over. She would write again and ask what they wanted done with her.

If Olivia found boarding school difficult before, it was so much harder afterwards. Nothing seemed to have anything to do with her. It was as if there was a glass bubble around her, separating her from everyone else. She spent more and more time in an imaginary world, either the one she read about in books or the one she created in her head. She decided that her parents weren't dead and wove one of her stories around why they couldn't come for her. Father was working in secret for the government and had to go somewhere, taking Mother with him. They couldn't tell anyone – not even Aunt Agatha – because it was top secret and of course they couldn't tell Olivia in case she let it slip. They would return when the war was over, explain they'd had no choice and she would forgive them because they were together again. She'd imagine them some-where exotic – America was her favourite choice – because there they would be safe. But, of course, Mother and Father never came. And as the years passed, she gave up the fantasy.

Chapter Eleven

Olivia

1947

Olivia was in her final year at school before anyone mentioned her aunts again.

She was staying with Agatha and Gordon for the weekend when one night she came downstairs to make herself a hot drink and overheard Agatha talking to Gordon in the sitting room.

'It's simply too bad,' Agatha was saying. 'No matter how fond we are of her, Olivia should be with family. When we agreed to act as her guardians it was with the understanding that Georgina and Edith would take over after the war. I never thought we'd still be doing it seven years later!'

'She'll be eighteen soon and legally an adult. It's not as if she's our child. It was one thing acting as her guardians during the war, when there was no one else, but to expect us to continue to take responsibility when she's an adult, that really takes the biscuit,' Gordon agreed with an annoyed rustle of his newspaper.

'But how can we go and leave her all alone? She might be almost eighteen but she's still very much a child.'

Gordon's reply was indistinct.

'I appreciate they had a difficult war,' Agatha continued. 'Life as a prisoner of the Japanese couldn't have been easy, but the war's been over for almost three years and they have a duty towards that child. A duty towards poor, dead Harriet. They wouldn't even have Olivia at Greyfriars for the summer breaks. Apparently it was quite impossible. Can you believe that! Now they say that Olivia is settled and they see no need to unsettle her.'

Hearing the creak of Gordon's chair as he stood, Olivia backed away from the door. Her aunts had been prisoners of war! Why had no one told her? No wonder they hadn't sent for her. But what about after the war? They could have written and left it up to her to decide whether she wanted to go to Greyfriars. Clearly they had no interest in her. Tears burning behind her lids, she crept upstairs without her Horlicks and went to bed.

The next morning Agatha told Olivia that she and Gordon were planning to emigrate to Australia.

'It is so dreadfully miserable in Britain at the moment. Gordon's hip aches whenever it rains and I long for the sunshine. We would both be very happy if you would come with us.'

It was very sweet of Agatha to invite her, and perhaps, if she hadn't overheard them talking last night, or if she hadn't had plans of her own, Olivia might have given it serious consideration.

'If possible I'd like to stay here. I've applied to Edinburgh University to study History and if I get the marks I expect, I think they'll accept me.'

'Of course they will. But are you sure, dear? I hate to think of you here on your own.' Agatha placed a bowl of porridge in front of Olivia.

'I'll be all right. I'll need to find a job, one I could do in the evenings or weekends, but I'm sure I can find something. I don't care what I do.'

'But, my dear, there's no need to get a job! Your aunts have being sending me money for you every month.'

'They have?' She'd always felt dreadful that Agatha and

Gordon had had to support her. All Father's money had been tied up in the bombed London house.

'Oh yes. Shortly after the war was over they returned to Greyfriars.' Colour suffused Agatha's face. 'I wasn't sure what to tell you! I expected them to write to you themselves and when they didn't, I thought . . .'

'It better not to tell me they had no interest in contacting me,' Olivia finished for her. Agatha nodded, looking mortified.

'I'm so sorry, Agatha, that must have been difficult for you.'

'More difficult for you. They should have come to see you. At the very least they should have invited you to visit them at Greyfriars. You were Harriet's only child. Their only niece!'

'Why didn't you tell me my aunts were prisoners of war?' Olivia asked.

Agatha flushed. 'How do you know that?'

'I heard you and Gordon talking about it once.' She didn't mention it was last night. Agatha would be mortified if she knew Olivia had overheard her and Gordon's discussion.

'We didn't tell you when we first heard because we didn't know for sure what had happened to them after Singapore fell – even if they were alive or dead. We didn't want to say anything until we were sure either way. It was all so confused and almost impossible to get information about anything or anyone. We only knew for certain they had survived when Georgina wrote to us from Greyfriars to ask if we could continue to keep an eye on you.' She shook her head. 'Whatever difficulties they experienced as prisoners it was no excuse for not arranging to see you.'

'I can't imagine being prisoners of war was a pleasant experience,' Olivia said, although she silently agreed with Agatha. Her aunts could have got in touch after the war was over. They'd never even tried to organise a memorial service for Mother and Father. 'But they did send you an allowance for me. That was something.'

'It's Harriet's share of the house in Edinburgh and yours by right. Your aunts have been renting it out.'

'Would it be enough, do you think, to help me through university?'

'More than enough I should imagine. My dear, I was going to wait until your birthday to tell you, however I see no reason not to tell you now, you own, or, to be more exact, will own, a third of the house in Edinburgh as well as a third of Greyfriars when you turn twenty-one. You will need to decide what to do when you inherit. In the meantime, I have put the allowance that Edith and Georgina have been sending these last years into an account for you. Gordon and I didn't want anything for looking after you.' Agatha mentioned the sum she had put aside as well as the monthly allowance. 'As long as you are careful, it should be more than enough to cover your university fees along with room and board, with some left over to clothe yourself and buy books.'

Olivia had worried about how she was going to be able to afford university. Now she wouldn't have to worry about any of that. It was a huge relief. She couldn't have borne to ask Agatha and Gordon to help out when they'd already done so much and for far longer than either of them had expected. Of course, she would have much rather her parents had still been alive and there had been no money to inherit. A lump rose in her throat. She still missed them every day. It was as if there was a big empty space inside her that nothing could fill.

Chapter Twelve

Charlotte

1984

A tear slipped down Mum's cheek and my chest constricted. I'd never seen her cry. I took her hand and squeezed it.

'Oh, Mum, how horrible for you. To lose both your parents when you were so young! And to overhear what you did. You must have felt so rejected!'

She dabbed away her tears and sighed. 'Agatha and Gordon were terribly kind to me but they weren't family and I always felt a little like a cuckoo in a nest. I didn't spend much time with them – holidays, of course, and the odd weekend – and my time at boarding school made me pretty self-reliant. In those days it toughened you up. It was the same for most of us. Tears and homesickness weren't tolerated, one had to put a face on things.'

Whatever she said, my heart ached for the girl my mother had been.

Mum knotted her hands together, clearly struggling to get her emotions under control. 'When I found out that my aunts had been prisoners of war, I understood why they hadn't sent for me during the war. I wish Agatha had told me at the time! It would have made it easier to understand why they didn't come.'

'They could have made more of an effort to see you when the war was over.'

'I've always wondered why they didn't but in time I gave up thinking about it, but by the time Agatha told me they were back at Greyfriars it had been eight years since I'd last them and I'd got used to being on my own and depending on myself.'

Mum was a whole lot more forgiving towards her aunts than I would have been. For them to know Mum was orphaned but not to have taken her in, or at the very least kept in touch was, in my view, unforgivable.

'But if you had a share in the house – it was as much your home as theirs!'

'It was clear they didn't want me at Greyfriars.' Her voice hitched.

'You don't have to talk about it any more, Mum. Not if you don't want to,' I said, giving her hand another squeeze.

'I do. I haven't spoken about it before. Besides, the next part's important – for you.'

'In what way?'

'Because of what will happen after I'm gone. I still have my share in Greyfriars and it will come to you when I die.'

I wasn't interested in a share of a house I'd never seen and even less prepared to think about a future without Mum in it.

'And there's more, I'm afraid, Charlotte. This house – the aunts still own two thirds,' Mum went on, her fingers fidgeting nervously with the pearls around her neck.

Now that was a shock. 'What do you mean?'

'We came to an arrangement. Years ago. I thought I had swapped my share in Greyfriars for their share in this house but when I started sorting out my affairs I realised that wasn't the case.' Mum shook her head. 'It was all so complicated.'

'Didn't you get anything in writing?'

'We didn't think like that. Not back then.'

'Do you think that's the reason the aunts want to see you now?'

'I don't know. It might be. But why not before?'

'Whatever they want now, try not to worry about it, Mum.

Conveyancing isn't my area of expertise, but I can easily find someone. It can all be sorted without you seeing them.' My dislike of my great-aunts was deepening with every new revelation. 'Oh, Mum, all the people you lost. Your parents, your aunts, Agatha and Gordon – then Dad.' I couldn't bear to think of how lonely she'd been for most of her life. 'You must have felt so abandoned – so alone.' But she wasn't alone now. She had me. And I wasn't going anywhere.

Mum's eyes blazed. 'I'm not telling you this so you can feel sorry for me! You talk to me as if I am some kind of saint. Everybody makes mistakes, Charlotte, and I'm no different.'

I was taken aback by the vehemence in her voice. 'I didn't mean . . .'

But Mum wouldn't say any more, declaring suddenly she was too tired and needed a nap. Looking at the greyness of her face, I had no option but to believe her.

Over the next few days, Mum and I discussed and argued about books, still our fallback position when it came to conversation. When we'd exhausted that, I'd read to her or we'd listen to the radio together. The news always seemed to be grim; the miners' continuing desperate strike, the rising unemployment figures, famine in Africa, and Aids was becoming an epidemic. When we'd had enough dispiriting news we'd change the station to Radio Three and listen to that while reading instead. She hadn't said anything more about Greyfriars and I didn't press her. Recalling her childhood clearly upset her. I should have guessed there was more to the story than what I already knew.

I'd been home almost a week before she mentioned her past again. She was on the sofa and I was sitting in the armchair, pulled up close to her, reading from Evelyn Waugh's *Decline and Fall* and making us both chuckle when, after I finished the chapter, she placed her hand on my arm.

'Charlotte, we need to talk,' she said. 'I've put it off long enough.'

I closed the novel and marked our place with a bookmark. 'Fire away.'

'There's something I have to tell you. Something I know you'll find hard to accept and particularly hard to forgive. I should have told you a long time ago.' She smiled faintly. 'There is nothing quite like being close to death to make one realise how much one wants to unburden one's self.'

I felt a ripple of unease. What else, apart from her childhood, hadn't she told me about?

'Your father isn't dead. At least not as far as I know.'

I gaped at her in stunned silence. I'd been eight or nine when I'd asked Mum why she and I had the same surname when everyone else I knew had the same surname as their fathers. All Mum had told me about Dad up until that point was that he'd been a university lecturer in history and had died before I was born. Whenever I tried to find out more about him she'd simply say he'd been wonderful, that she wished Dad and I could have known each other and how sorry she was she didn't have a single photograph of him to show me. It had never crossed my mind they hadn't been married. She'd told me then that they had been planning to, but my father had died before they could.

I'd felt the shame of it then, and had never told anyone. Now it seemed that even then my mother hadn't told me the whole truth. My father might still be alive.

'Why did you tell me he'd died?'

'Because I didn't want to tell you the whole truth.' Her eyes filled with tears and she lowered her voice to a whisper. 'Because I was ashamed and I didn't want to diminish myself in your eyes.' She raised her head and looked me in the eye. 'I need to tell you everything now. I only hope, when you hear what I have to say, you'll find it in your heart to forgive me.'

Chapter Thirteen

Olivia

1950

To Olivia's gratification and delight, she did get in to Edinburgh University. Agatha waited until term started before she sailed to join Gordon who had left a few weeks earlier. It was hard saying goodbye, to Agatha in particular, but Olivia's sadness was tempered by the excitement of being independent and starting a new life.

University was everything Olivia had hoped for. She found a room in a house in Nicholson Street. Mrs Linklater, the landlady, was strict, but her rules – no male visitors after six, in for the night by ten, no cooking in the bedrooms, except to make a cup of tea – were easy after boarding school. There were two other women students in the house who shared a twin room. They were in their final year and Olivia saw little of them. They were either at the library or out with friends. But when they did meet over breakfast and supper, meals provided by Mrs Linklater, they were friendly enough.

There were many similar to Olivia at university – young women with sheltered upbringings who were away from home for the first time, or who, like her, had spent their childhoods in boarding school. Many had lost brothers and fathers during the war and even a few like her, who had lost everyone. She threw herself into her new life. She joined the Celtic society, had the occasional meal out with her fellow students and went for long walks. Above all else she loved the intellectual demands of her course. She'd taken History and English Literature to begin with, and enjoyed both of them, but when it came time to decide what subject to take to honours she'd plumped for History. She had a notion that after senior honours she might go on to do a Bachelor of Laws.

She was in the penultimate year when she met him and, almost immediately, she knew he was the one.

As always, she was sitting in the third row, determined not to miss a word, not to be distracted by the students making paper aeroplanes in the back row, or snoozing, snoring softly. She didn't ever take the front row – that made her too conspicuous, but here in the third, she was sufficiently inconspicuous while able to concentrate on the lecture.

He was American; a Ph.D. student standing in for the term for their usual lecturer who had had to take some time off to care for his wife who was ill. Ethan – he told them to call him by his first name – was considerably more casual than their usual lecturers. Instead of standing he perched on a chair, speaking directly to his audience without the need for notes, or even a blackboard. He was good-looking although she suspected not everyone would find him so. He was tall, with a beaked nose and a mouth that turned up at the corners as if his lips were either just beginning or just finishing a smile. His suit was cheap, she had a good eye for that sort of thing, but his shoes were polished to a high shine, his shirt freshly laundered, his tie neatly knotted. But despite this there was something faintly exotic, even dangerous about him. In many ways, he reminded her of Findlay.

He was giving a lecture on Scottish heroes of the past and had everyone in the lecture theatre hanging on his every word.

'Some might think Rob Roy McGregor a romantic figure – indeed that is how he is often depicted – a man of the people for the people – but I would argue that he was probably little more than a thief. History often imbues figures of the past with motives and behaviour for which there is no evidence. But does it really matter? Is oral history as important as written, documented original sources? Can it ever – should it ever – become part of history? I'll leave you to pick your own figure from the past and to write an essay comparing and contrasting original sources with oral history. Papers due in advance of your next tutorial. Any questions, come and see me.'

He kept looking at her as he spoke and she had to try hard to resist turning around to see if there was another, better-looking girl behind her, but no, it was definitely her he was looking at. Every now and again he would flash a devastating smile and she prayed she wouldn't humiliate herself by blushing. She wished she'd worn her new blue dress instead of the plain skirt and blouse she had on and that she'd taken more time with her hair.

That afternoon, she spent ages in the library deciding who to write about. She wanted to find the right person – someone where the oral history was important if not critical to the way history viewed them.

Immediately she thought of Bonnie Prince Charlie, his supporters and their connection with Greyfriars. The Jacobites had passed into history as the most romantic of rebels – but how much of their history was fact and how much romanticised?

The remainder of the week she worked on her essay, refusing to question herself as to why she was so determined to impress Ethan. She'd other essays to write, reading to do, but this particular essay was all she worked on.

She finished her paper the day before it was due and was about to slip it under his door when unexpectedly it was flung open. She was bending down and had almost fallen over.

He'd looked almost as surprised to see her there as she was to find him looking down at her.

'Do you normally crouch like that outside your tutors' doors?' he asked with a grin.

She'd blushed, perfectly aware her skin now matched her hair.

'I was – my essay,' she stuttered, gesturing to the sheets of papers half in and half out of the doorway. 'I didn't want to disturb you in case you were in a meeting with another student – so I . . . ' She nodded mutely at the papers and made a scrambling attempt to gather them together.

When he knelt beside her to help, she caught a whiff of his aftershave and more faintly, toothpaste on his breath.

When her essay was back in a neat pile, he asked her to come in and made her wait while he read through it. When he'd finished he set it down on the desk and grinned again. Her heart did a little pirouette inside her chest. 'Not bad. Not bad at all. I do have a couple of questions however.' He glanced at his watch. 'Have you eaten? I was too busy to grab lunch and I get grouchy when I'm hungry.'

'No, I—'

'Come on then. There's a cafe nearby that's not bad. I hate eating on my own. Won't you join me? We can talk about your essay then.'

She should have said no; it was an unwritten rule that students and tutors didn't have relationships but she was flattered and so told herself that as he was a Ph.D. student it didn't really count. Who was to know? He was the first man ever to ask her out.

They went to a little cafe not far from the university. It was fuggy with smoke and crowded. They talked about the Jacobites, argued whether Mary, Queen of Scots was guilty of treason or whether she was simply badly advised and at the mercy of men who used her to serve their own ambition, before moving on to King James the VI and his belief in witchcraft and subsequent penchant for burning women at the stake. When they'd finished discussing the pros and cons of

91

James the VI's rule, Ethan asked her what she intended to do once she'd graduated. Perhaps it was the way he hung on her every word, his eyes never leaving her face, making her feel that everything she said was fascinating, that made her confide her secret dream about going in for law.

'So no plans to become an historian then?'

'I don't imagine it will be too dissimilar. The law relies on history, as well as the ability to assimilate and consider many facts,' she shot back. 'Taking different accounts from different sources and sifting through them to establish what is true and what isn't.'

He leaned forward, looking impressed. 'Do you know I believe you're right! I've never thought about it like that before. So tell me, do you think Mary, Queen of Scots had anything to do with Lord Darnley's death? And if not, why not? And what about Rizzio? Is there any evidence her courtiers had him murdered?'

They argued back and forth, both taking one viewpoint and then arguing another. Eventually she'd glanced at her watch only to find it was after nine. She'd had no idea it was so late. She stood and gathered up her bag. 'I should go. My landlady likes us to be in by ten.'

'Where do you live? I'll escort you home,' he said.

As they walked he told her that he was married and had two children, a boy and a girl, and that he was looking forward to returning to America to see them. He was at Edinburgh only for a term, and would be going back to Boston just before Christmas. It hadn't crossed her mind he might be married – let alone have children. She did her best to hide her disappointment and embarrassment. Thankfully it wasn't far to her flat. When they reached her door she held out her hand and thanked him coolly for the meal and walking her home. She desperately hoped he'd had no inkling she'd thought they were on a date.

She avoided his lectures after that although she always found out from a fellow student what the essay topics were and always ensured they were well written and submitted on time. Every time she caught a glimpse of him on campus, usually striding along deep in conversation with a student or one of the other lecturers, her heart would somersault. Why, oh why, did the first man she fell for have to be married?

One Saturday she was visiting Holyrood Palace and was peering at a copy of Mary, Queen of Scot's death warrant when she glanced up to find him studying a number of gruesome-looking weapons on the wall.

He looked as taken aback to see her as she was to see him. He came to stand next to her and looked down at the document she'd been examining.

'Thought you'd check up on Mary, Queen of Scots? Still think she was an innocent?'

So he'd remembered their conversation. A guilty but delicious thrill ran through her.

'I keep thinking how it must have been for her. So far away from everything that was familiar. Queen of a country when she could barely speak its language, never mind understand its culture. She must have felt so alone.'

He slid her a puzzled look. 'Not something I imagine you've ever experienced.'

She refused to admit it was a feeling she knew only too well. Far rather he think her too popular and busy to ever feel lonely.

'I haven't seen you at my lectures recently,' he continued. 'I hope it's not because you find them boring.'

'Not at all.' She was pleased to find she sounded cool. 'And I have turned all the necessary essays in. You've given me an A for every one, so I'm assuming you aren't going to put in a complaint about my absences.'

He looked perplexed but didn't reply. It was then she noticed that somehow they had both made their way to the Queen's antechamber.

'See that dark spot on the floor.' Olivia pointed to a bit

near the window. 'That's supposed to be the stain of Rizzio's blood.'

'Do you think it was his baby she had?'

'Not enough evidence to convict her, I would suggest.'

Ethan laughed. 'She certainly got around. I've never come across a woman who slept under so many roofs. I'm making it my mission to visit as many as possible. Hey, I don't suppose you want to come with me?'

Her heart hammered against her ribs. 'Wouldn't your wife mind?'

'Eunice doesn't mind much. She and the kids could have come with me to Edinburgh, but Eunice wasn't keen to uproot them. They've just started school. 'Sides, she has plenty to keep her busy in Boston.'

By unspoken consent they had left the Queen's antechamber and started towards the exit. As they walked he told her he'd joined the army in '44 when he was eighteen, postponing his studies so he could. He'd met Eunice during his first leave and married her on his second.

'People did crazy stuff like that back then. After the war was finished – we'd already had our son by then – I realised we hardly knew each other. Jeez, it sounds like such a line.' He gave her a sideways look. 'Our daughter was born just over a year later.' He stopped, placed a hand on her arm, turned her gently to face him and looked her in the eyes. 'I love Eunice but I'm not in love with her. I want to be straight with you.' He hesitated. 'I know I have no right to ask you to keep me company – but I'd very much like you to come with me to visit all these cool castles Scotland has.' This time it was he who flushed, he who seemed uncertain. 'If you say no, I'll never bother you again, I promise.'

It was on the tip of her tongue to say no, instead she found herself nodding.

Over the following weekends they visited Edinburgh Castle, took a bus to Inchmahome in the Lake of Menteith and a boat to the castle on Loch Leven, and all the other places within a day's journey of Edinburgh where Mary Stuart had either stayed or been imprisoned. Although they both pretended that all they shared was a love of history Olivia knew he was falling in love with her as she was with him. It was the happiest time of her life.

Chapter Fourteen

Charlotte

1984

Mum stuttered to a stop. 'I fell in love. With my heart and soul – and I use the last word deliberately. It felt as if I'd found a missing part of me. If you'd ever been in love you would know how it feels. To have someone understand you so well they could finish your sentences, to feel the world was a brighter place when they were in the room. In the years after Mother and Father died I'd felt small and unimportant. He made me feel as if I was a star in a movie, or rather my own life. As if I mattered. I was happier than I'd been in years – since that last summer at Greyfriars.

'Although we had to be discreet, we spent every moment we could of the remainder of the term together.' Her cheeks were two high spots of colour in her pale face. 'During those weeks I thought a great deal about that last summer at Greyfriars and in particular, Edith. If she'd felt for Findlay a tenth of what I felt for Ethan, how could she have let him go? And as for Georgina, whatever wrong she'd done was nothing compared to the wrong I was doing. I tried not to think of Eunice – or the children she and Ethan had together.

'I knew I could never have Ethan, but all I – we – could think about was the moment. I could no more have stopped being with him than I could have stopped breathing. It's not something I'm proud of and I can't expect you to understand but you have the right to know.

'He talked about divorcing Eunice, but I wouldn't let him. He would have lost his children, and very likely his position with his American university. The loss of his job we could have lived with but breaking up his family? In those days people rarely got divorced – except for film stars. For most it was considered a scandal, something to be terribly ashamed of. What we had already done was bad enough.

'He returned to America for good just before Thanksgiving. It broke my heart to say goodbye and I know it broke his too.

'I realise you must be shocked,' Mum continued after a pause, her troubled eyes never having left my face. 'Your mother having an affair with a married man. I was shocked at myself. I knew it was unforgivable but I couldn't help myself.'

Shocked was one way of putting it. She'd had an affair with a man when she'd known he was married. I couldn't imagine anyone less likely to do what she had. All my life she had been the person I looked up to – my lodestone – the person I most wanted to be like – the person whose approval I most wanted. Now to find out that she had only been human made my world tilt. My father could be alive! And I had a half-brother and sister! That she'd omitted to share something so fundamental shook me to the core.

'I didn't realise I was pregnant until he'd been gone a month,' Mum went on. 'I put my nausea down to a combination of feeling miserable and flu. Sex wasn't much discussed in those days – Agatha had told me very little. When I started my periods she gave me a pack of pads, but that was pretty much it. I knew there were ways a woman could prevent pregnancy, but one had to be married before a doctor would prescribe a diaphragm and the pill was still way off in the future. I thought if we were careful . . . ' The flush on her cheeks deepened. 'To be honest I didn't let myself think of what might happen.

'I thought about whether I should tell him about the baby

but I knew if I did, he would be forced to choose between me and his family. I just couldn't do it. He adored his children and got on well with his wife – even if he wasn't in love with her. I know you're finding this difficult to understand, but you must believe me when I tell you, those weeks with your father were worth all the years I spent without him.'

I didn't care what Mum said. Ethan, my father, had to have taken advantage of her. He'd been married, with children and in a position of authority. Mum was younger than him and naïve for her age. There was no excuse. To put it in a nutshell, my father had been a smarmy creep.

The sun was shining through the open window, and I could hear the footsteps of people going about their business; the world outside continuing as normal whilst mine was shifting on its axis. Mum was still watching me apprehensively, waiting for my response.

'Although we'd agreed not to write to each other, he promised he'd come back for me when his children were grown up,' she continued when I didn't say anything. 'When you were sixteen, I sent him this address – just that on a piece of paper. I trusted he'd know it was me who sent it. He would need it if he was ever to come to me.' A look of immeasurable sadness crossed her face. 'He never did.'

The swine, I thought, furious on Mum's behalf. 'Why didn't you tell him about me then? Didn't he have a right to know?'

'Because I was frightened someone – Eunice – would open the letter. All I sent was this address. And, Charlotte, I have no right to ask you this, but please, think carefully before you try to find your half-brother and -sister. One thing that kept me going through the years was that his children would never find out about us.'

Still reeling, I tried to imagine how it must have been for Mum all those years ago. She'd been so alone. Her parents dead; the woman who was the closest thing to a mother she'd had since the death of her own mother, thousands of miles away, her aunts having nothing to do with her, the man she loved, out of reach. If she hadn't been so alone would she ever have fallen for a married man? I felt a hot surge of anger against my two great-aunts and the man who was my father.

'Maybe spending the rest of my life apart from him was the price I had to pay for what I did,' Mum continued softly, 'but if it was, it was worth it. I hope you'll feel like that one day.' She smiled ruefully. 'Although I fervently hope he won't be married. No mother wants her child to repeat her mistakes. Not that I can imagine it. You've always been –' she was quiet for a moment as if picking her words '- so in control. Sometimes I wish you would let yourself go – do something outrageous. Oh, Charlotte, I wonder if you're happy.'

I stiffened. 'Of course I'm happy, or I would be if . . .' I couldn't bring myself to finish the sentence.

'I wasn't dying,' Mum said, doing it for me.

I could only nod.

'I'm not frightened of dying. I don't think people truly ever die. Maybe I'm still that girl who believed in ghosts. How can all that energy – that love – just disappear? And if I won't be around in physical form I'll still be with you in spirit. I'll be in your memories.' She smiled slightly. "I'll be the thousand winds that blow . . ."'

I would have given anything to believe that.

'I wish I had longer, much longer, but only because I can't bear the thought of leaving you.' She sighed. 'If only you would meet someone who can make you feel the way your father made me feel. Then I could die knowing you weren't on your own.'

'Mum, it's the eighties. Women don't need to be married to live happy, fulfilling lives. And you were on your own! You made a wonderful life for me. No daughter could have asked for more.' What did it matter what she'd done in the past? She was still my lodestone.

Mum gave a slight, dismissive shake of her head but I could tell my words pleased her.

99

'You were – are – everything to me. From the moment you were born, encouraging you to be the woman I couldn't be was all that mattered. Looking back I wonder if I pushed you too hard. No mother has the right to expect their child to live the life they wanted for themselves. But look at you now! I haven't told you enough how proud I am of you.'

An embarrassed silence fell. Mum hadn't ever been one for heaping praise.

'I should have told you that more often. My generation were brought up not to praise, not to discuss feelings – not the way you see it on American television where people are always hugging and talking about their emotions in great detail. It wasn't done. I regret that now. The Americans could teach us a thing or two.'

'I've always known you loved me, Mum,' I said awkwardly. 'You didn't have to say it.'

'I will say it. I love you. Oh, Charlotte, come here.'

It was only then I realised that tears were running down my cheeks.

Mum shuffled over to the other side of the sofa and patted the space beside her and, feeling like a little girl again, I sat down next to her. She passed me a handkerchief and I blew my nose.

'Do you remember when you were a little girl and you used to cuddle up beside me while I read you a story?'

I nodded. I leaned into her, drinking in her familiar warmth, the mumness of her. The knot of tension that had been holding me in its thrall since I'd learned of Mum's illness eased just a little.

'When you realised you were pregnant, what did you do?'

'By then I was almost three months. I was thrilled. At least I was once I got over the shock. I would have something of Ethan. But unmarried mothers in those days were scandalous. Far worse than divorcees.

'I didn't know what to do or where to turn. I almost broke

and wrote to Ethan but almost immediately dismissed the thought. It would put him in an impossible situation. We had made our decision. We couldn't be together. That I was pregnant with his child couldn't be allowed to change anything. To tell him when he wouldn't be able to see his child, would be cruel and make him question his decision to go back to his wife all over again.

'It was a bitterly cold winter that year and I was able, with the help of bulky sweaters and coats, to hide my growing tummy. But I knew I couldn't keep it a secret for much longer. So I went to my tutor and admitted I was pregnant. To say she was disappointed and shocked was an understatement. She told me I had to leave, that the university had an obligation to its other female undergraduates. As if being in the vicinity of an unmarried mother would corrupt them. She did say I might be able to come back when it was all over – pick up my studies again and sit my finals – which I was scheduled to sit shortly after your birth, but only if I came back as a married woman. And that wasn't going to happen.

'A few days after I'd spoken to my tutor, I returned to my lodgings to find my landlady waiting for me in the hall. She demanded to know if I was in the family way and when I admitted I was, she told me I had until the end of the week to vacate my room.'

'Oh, Mum. How awful for you. Why didn't you get in touch with Ethan then? He had an obligation to help, at least financially. You should have told him about me.'

'He would have come back. I know he would have! But it wasn't as if I needed money, I still had my monthly allowance. I could have found other lodgings somewhere out of Edinburgh – pretended I was a widow and started afresh – but I wanted to go somewhere to hide. I was so ashamed, so very ashamed. I'd let everyone down and my dreams were in tatters. I was glad for the first time that Mother and Father were dead so they would never learn of my shame.'

'What about Agatha? Wouldn't she have helped you?'

'She was in Australia, remember? But I could have gone to her. She would have taken me in. But after everything she had done for me, and even if I wished to go and live on the other side of the world, I just couldn't. I was embarrassed and would have been an embarrassment to her and Gordon. They deserved better.

'My life, the clear, untroubled path I thought I had set out for me had all gone wrong.' She paused. 'That was when I told myself "no more". I knew I had to pull myself together for your sake. Whatever mess I had made of my life couldn't affect yours. You would have the life I could no longer lead.' Her dry, almost translucent hand reached out for mine and squeezed it. 'There was really only one place I could think of to go. And as soon as I thought of it, I knew it was where I needed to be.'

She closed her eyes.

'Greyfriars?' I asked.

Chapter Fifteen

Olivia

1950

Olivia stepped out of the train and onto the platform, clutching her suitcase. It was dark and cold and the headache she'd had almost constantly over the last few days pounded unmercifully, making her feel nauseous and dizzy. She'd written to her aunts informing them of her arrival but couldn't put a return address as she no longer had one. She'd said nothing of her pregnancy as it wasn't the kind of thing she felt she could put in a letter. She'd bought herself a cheap ring, looked up timetables, purchased her ticket and packed a bag, leaving anything that wasn't essential behind. All she owned now was in the suitcase she was carrying.

The train journey north couldn't have been more different to the one she'd taken almost eleven years earlier. Back then it had been summer and she'd been happy, now it was midwinter, dark just after three, snowing heavily and she felt as miserable as the weather.

The journey seemed interminable. The train was bone-chillingly cold and kept stopping. It would sit on the tracks, releasing the occasional sigh of steam, while gusts of wind rattled the carriage, blowing more icy flakes through gaps in the door.

She was the only person in the compartment and the snow muffled any sound, making her wonder whether the driver and the few other passengers who'd boarded with her at Waverley had abandoned the train. She huddled deeper into her coat, frozen to the marrow and wondering what lay in store. Her feet were still damp, muddy slush having soaked through the leather of her shoes. Boots or even wellingtons would have been so much more practical but she'd wanted to make a good impression, or at least as good an impression as an unmarried, pregnant woman might hope to make. She twisted the ring she wore on her left hand. It was too tight. She should have bought a bigger size. She had decided to tell her aunts the truth – they would find out soon enough anyway, but in the meantime there was no need for anyone else to know she was pregnant and single. Tears pricked her lids as she thought about all the mistakes she'd made. But loving Ethan was not a mistake, she told herself fiercely. Neither was having his child. She simply must stop feeling sorry for herself and think of her baby.

With all the delays it was far later than she'd anticipated when the train had eventually arrived at Connel Station.

Only one other passenger alighted along with her and he or she – it was difficult to tell in the dim light – was soon swallowed up by the sleet and darkness.

As the wind whipped around her legs, she wondered what she would do if her aunts refused to take her in. She couldn't face returning to Edinburgh – not when she didn't even have her studies to distract her from thinking of Ethan. And where would she go anyway? From bed & breakfast to bed & breakfast? Besides, she reminded herself, Greyfriars belonged to her as much as to her aunts, or would do in a few months. She had an equal right to live there. If they didn't want her at the house she could stay in one of the farm cottages, supposing one was empty. For all she knew they were all occupied.

It might only be for a few weeks. She just needed a place where she could lick her wounds for a while before deciding what to do.

But first she needed to get to Greyfriars.

She looked around, expecting to see others waiting for the train to Balcreen, but there was only the station master who was already locking up the ticket office and preparing, it seemed, to leave for home.

'Excuse me,' she said, her voice sounding small. 'When does the train for Balcreen leave?'

'Train to Balcreen? There's not been one for years now. They ripped up the tracks during the war and never put them back. No need, you see. Most folk drive these days or take a taxi.'

It hadn't occurred to her the train to Balcreen would no longer exist. 'In that case, do you know how I can find a taxi to take me there?'

He looked at her as if she'd lost her mind. 'A taxi? Now? Didn't you arrange for one in advance?'

She shook her head. If only she didn't feel so unwell . . .

'There's only Duncan and Angus that do the taxis, but I doubt you'll find either of them willing to take you out there at this time of night, what with the snow. They are probably already tucked up in bed or down the pub having a dram. These roads are treacherous enough in the daytime in good weather. In the dark, with the snow almost blocking them, they're nearly impossible.'

'But I have to get to Greyfriars!'

He pushed his cap up his forehead. 'It's out of the question. Not tonight.'

'Is there a hotel nearby then?'

'Yes, but it closes for the winter. Folk that own it take themselves off to Glasgow to spend time with their children and grandchildren, you see. Not many tourists visit here at this time of year. You'd have been better continuing on to Oban.'

Olivia felt like crying. What was she to do? Knock on a door of a nearby house and ask them to take her in? She couldn't imagine anything worse than knocking on a stranger's door – apart from spending the night at a deserted railway station. She would have knocked on half a dozen doors before doing that.

'There's the inn at Balcreen,' the station master said. 'They stay open because of the bar, you see. They'd probably manage a room.' He tutted. 'I'll have to take you. You can't stay here.'

'Would you? I'd be so very grateful.'

'You stand under the canopy and out of the snow while I finish up here. I won't be more than a few minutes.'

She waited, her teeth chattering while he locked up the waiting room. She could barely feel her feet when eventually he nodded for her to follow him.

His car was cold, but at least she was out of the snow. Her head was buzzing, making her feel dizzy. She couldn't remember the last time she'd eaten. She had to do better. For the baby's sake.

'I'm so sorry to take you out of your way,' she said once they were on the road.

'Och, it's no trouble really. Could hardly leave a young girl in the snow, could I?'

Silence lapsed as he concentrated on navigating the narrow, pot-holed, single-track road, each bump of the car sending jolts of pain through her throbbing head. Her nausea was getting worse and she prayed she wouldn't be sick all over the back seat of his car.

Thankfully she managed to hold on and less than half an hour later he drew up outside a low-slung, white washed inn partly obscured by the swirling snow. Lights burned brightly within and as she got out of the car, the rumble of laughter filtered through the still night air along with the pungent reek of a peat fire.

The station master took her suitcase from the back of the car. 'I'll come in with you,' he said. 'Just to make sure you'll be all right. Not that Mrs MacKay would ever turn a young

106

woman in need of a bed away. If she doesn't have an empty room more than likely she'll give you hers.'

As soon as they stepped inside, the sight of a warm fire lifted her spirits.

The few other people in the bar looked at her curiously before politely turning away. A plump woman with permed grey hair and wearing an overall over a short-sleeved dress, came out from behind the bar and hurried over to them.

'Do you have a spare room for this lady, Mrs MacKay?' the station master asked. 'She was hoping to get across to Kerista tonight but I explained it's impossible. Not with the snow and it being dark.'

Mrs MacKay exchanged a surprised look with the station master before taking Olivia's hands in hers. 'Och, you wee soul, you're frozen. We need to get you warmed up. Come on upstairs and get you into bed. I'll have someone put the fire on in there and as soon as you're tucked up I'll arrange to have some soup brought up.'

In the face of her kindness, it was all Olivia could do to stop herself bursting into tears. She had no doubt, if she'd done so, Mrs MacKay would have wrapped her in her arms and hugged her.

She had only just enough time to thank the station master before she was bundled upstairs, Mrs MacKay carrying her suitcase, and into a small room with a double bed set under the eaves.

'Now you get yourself into bed while I organise that soup. The room won't take long to warm up once the fire is going.'

Still shivering, but feeling the nausea and tension that had beset her during the day begin to ease, Olivia hurried into her nightie and slipped between the cold sheets.

At that moment there was a knock and when Olivia called 'enter', the door opened and a woman holding a pail of peat entered. They recognised the other at the same instant.

'Goodness, Miss Olivia,' the woman said. 'What on earth are you doing here?'

Olivia sat up and pulled the bedclothes to her chin. She hadn't seen Agnes in years. Not since she'd come to play with her that day at Greyfriars and Donald had told them the ghost story. Now Agnes, a more grown-up Agnes, but still clearly recognisable by her curly hair and twinkly eyes, was standing in front of her.

'I was on my way to Greyfriars. I hoped to get there tonight, but the train was delayed and there was no one to take me. The station master told me that the inn still took people in for a night or two and he drove me here.'

'You are going to stay at Greyfriars?' Agnes's mouth dropped open. 'Goodness!'

'Yes. With my aunts.'

Agnes set down the pail by the fire and started screwing up paper before placing some twigs and peat on top. Within moments it was burning brightly.

'I'll be back in a sec,' she said, turning towards the door. 'Mum's setting a tray for you.'

It was only ten or so minutes when Agnes returned, bearing a tray with a steaming bowl of soup and some bread.

'I didn't expect to ever see you again,' Olivia said, as Agnes placed the tray on her lap. 'What are you doing here? I mean obviously you're employed . . .' she stumbled over the words. The difference in class hadn't been so obvious when they were children, but now with Agnes waiting on her in her nylon overall, her red and chapped hands, it was marked enough to embarrass them both.

'I'm maid of all sorts,' Agnes muttered, colour rushing to her cheeks.

Olivia wanted to put Agnes at her ease. To let her know she was the same Olivia she had played and giggled with, but she was so tired, the warmth of the room making her drowsy, a sense of lassitude overtaking her limbs and spreading upwards until it seemed almost too much of an effort to speak.

Agnes set the tray on her knees. 'You've to eat it all up. I'll collect your tray later. I have to get back to the kitchen but we can catch up tomorrow.'

As Agnes closed the door softly behind her, Olivia took a sip of soup and although her stomach revolted initially, knowing she had to eat for the baby's sake, she was able to force down most of the mutton broth along with half a slice of the bread. She immediately felt better. Her headache was still there but some of the queasiness had gone. Tomorrow the storm would have died down and she could complete her journey to Greyfriars. She was a little worried her aunts might be waiting up for her but there was little she could do about it; it wasn't as if she had a telephone number to call them. Warmed and comforted she placed the tray on the nightstand, went back to bed and, for the first time since she'd discovered she was going to have a baby, slept soundly.

The next morning her headache had returned as had her sense of unease about foisting herself on her aunts. Pushing aside the covers she crossed over to the window and drew the curtains back. The snow had turned to heavy rain that lashed against the window with such force it was as if tiny pebbles were being thrown against the panes. But the room was so warm and cosy – the fire had been replenished at some point during the night – so that despite her headache, Olivia felt better than she'd done in weeks.

There was a soft tap on the door and Agnes came in carrying a large jug in one hand and the clothes Olivia had been wearing the night before, freshly laundered in the other.

'I'll just leave the water for your wash on your dressing table, miss,' Agnes said, placing Olivia's clothes on the chair. 'I'll come and fetch it later. When I bring up your breakfast.' Her eyes strayed to Olivia's stomach. 'Oh! You're in the family way. In that case it's better you stay in bed and rest. For the wee one's sake.'

Too late, Olivia covered her stomach with her hands. She

wished Agnes hadn't seen. No doubt her pregnancy would be around the village in no time. However there was nothing she could do about it now.

'You can call me Olivia, Agnes,' Olivia said, slipping back into bed and under the sheets.

Agnes looked pleased. 'So when did you get married?' She placed the jug on the dressing table, before adding lumps of peat to the fire making it hiss and spit. 'And how come he's not with you?'

'He . . .' Olivia hesitated. 'He died.' It was the first thing that popped into her head.

Agnes turned to face her, her laughing eyes full of distress. 'I'm sorry. Me and my big mouth.' She grimaced. 'It always did get me into trouble.'

Under the bedclothes, Olivia squirmed. She hated lying to Agnes, but what else could she do? It wasn't just because of her own reputation, she had her aunts and their feelings to consider.

'Is that why you're here? To stay with your aunts? Didn't your husband have family that could take you in?'

'They live in America. I have no desire to go so far away.' She wished Agnes would stop asking difficult questions. 'And Greyfriars is my home, after all.'

'We heard your poor parents died in the war. You have been through it, haven't you?'

The kindness in her voice made tears burn behind Olivia's eyes. She blinked them away. Agnes's sympathy, at least in part, was undeserved.

'What about you?' Olivia asked, eager to turn the conversation from herself. 'Are you married?'

'Och, no. Not found anyone yet. No one I can imagine spending the rest of my days with at any rate.' She covered her mouth with her hand. 'There I go again. Putting my big foot in it.'

'How is your mother?' Olivia remembered Agnes's mother had been the summer cook at Greyfriars that last holiday.

'Didn't you recognise her? That was her who showed you to

your room last night. Not that she recognised you either – you being grown up and all.' Agnes perched on the side of Olivia's bed. 'Mum and Dad took the inn over after the war. I've always helped them out. And as soon as I left school, I started working here full time. I do the rooms when we have people staying and anything else that's required. But to tell you the truth, I'm dying to get away from Balcreen. I've known all the boys here since I was a wee girl and they hold no interest for me – not in that way. No, I'd like to go and work in Edinburgh or Glasgow. In a boarding house or one of the hotels. Bound to meet someone more interesting then.'

How could Agnes bear to leave her parents? Olivia would have given anything to have hers alive and nearby. The thought was followed by a deep stab of shame. But then they would have known that she'd let them down.

'Your mother and father would miss you if you left.'

'No, they won't. They're getting too old to run the inn so they've sold it and are going to Canada to live with my sister. I have no wish to stay on here. I met the new landlady when she came to see the place. She's a bossy boots, that one. She'd have me running around doing all the donkey work while she queened it over me and painted her nails. Besides, this place won't be the same without Mam and Dad. Mam and I have our moments but she's not bad at heart.' The look of love in Agnes's eyes told Olivia she minded more than she was letting on and Olivia felt a pang of empathy for her.

'Why don't you go with them? To Canada, I mean?'

'My sister and I have never really got on. Anyway, it's time I made my own way in life.' She grinned and her eyes lit up. 'There's a whole world out there just waiting for Agnes MacKay!'

Olivia smiled back. This was more like the Agnes she remembered. Agnes didn't seem to have changed at all. She was still the same girl looking for adventure. 'I should get up and dressed. I need to get to Greyfriars.'

'Och, you'll not be getting anyone to take you across there until the wind dies down. Some time this afternoon, I expect. I can telephone Duncan the taxi and put him on standby if you like. He'll come and fetch you in his car when it calms down. In the meantime, you stay in bed. I'll bring up your breakfast. Mum does a great fry-up.'

Olivia's stomach clenched and she clamped her hand over her mouth. Suddenly, she didn't know how, Agnes had one hand holding her hair out of her face, while at the same time she held a wash basin under her chin. Agnes waited patiently, whispering soothing words of comfort until Olivia stopped being sick. When Agnes was certain Olivia had nothing left to bring up, she wiped her face with a facecloth and towelled it dry.

'Perhaps not a fry-up then. Some porridge and dry toast instead and a big pot of tea. You lie back and try and nap while I see to it.'

A short while later, Olivia had closed her eyes but had been too on edge to go back to sleep. Agnes knocked and bumped open the door with her hip. She put the tray she was carrying on the chest of drawers.

'I telephoned Duncan. He says he'll be along when the weather improves. But are you sure you shouldn't stay here with us for a night or two longer? We could have a right old natter. I could ask Duncan to take a message to your aunts to let them know where you are and that you've been delayed. I would have telephoned them but they don't have a phone. Not many people here do, apart from us.'

'They are at Greyfriars though?' Olivia asked. It was only now that it occurred to her that they might not be. They could be holidaying for all she knew. Might not even be in the country. But even if they weren't and the house had been shut up, someone would have a key.

'Oh, aye. Where else would they be? Not left that place in years, neither they have.'

So they *were* still at Greyfriars. Olivia wasn't altogether sure if she were relieved or disappointed.

'I'd like to see the look on their faces when you turn up,' Agnes continued, straightening and tidying the already neat room and hanging Olivia's clothes in the wardrobe. 'You must be the first visitor they've had at Greyfriars since they came back from the war.'

It was only then that Olivia realised what Agnes had said earlier. About her aunts not having left Greyfriars in years. That couldn't be right! She remembered the dances and parties, the days out on the yacht. Georgina was the most sociable person Olivia had ever met. And Edith, although she was quieter, had also appeared to enjoy company. She couldn't imagine two women less likely to live alone on an island.

'I can't imagine they won't be pleased to see you,' Agnes continued, before Olivia had a chance to say anything, 'although . . .'

'Although what?' Olivia prompted when Agnes faltered.

'Nothing. Don't mind me. I have no idea what they might think. No one's talked to them since they came back to Kerista after the war. They didn't even tell Mum they were coming back there to live. She would have gone over with me and a couple of other girls from the village to get Greyfriars ready for them. That house had been empty for years. Must have needed a good dusting and airing. When Mum heard that they were there, she did go over to ask them if they needed help – there are always folk looking for work around these parts – but Miss Edith acted most strangely. She told Mum that she and the other Miss Guthrie would manage perfectly well, that they had become used to managing on their own during the war, and preferred to live simply. She then went on to say that they weren't receiving visitors – of any sort. Well I can tell you Mum's nose was fair put out of joint. She'd taken on the inn by then, so she was only doing them a favour offering to get help because she'd worked there every summer up until the war started. They didn't even invite her in! Folk thought that the war would change the way some folk looked down their noses at others because they had bigger houses or more money, but not in the Misses Guthrie's case, oh no!' Agnes hurried on, barely stopping to draw breath. 'They were snobbier than they'd ever been. Mum was mortified the way they treated her that day.' Agnes sniffed. 'She couldn't understand it. Good manners never cost anything and the Misses Guthrie always had beautiful manners – at least that's what Mum said. She said Miss Georgina could be flighty, but she'd never treated the servants as if they were of no importance. Miss Edith was always more reserved, but she always spoke kindly to the people who worked at the house. Miss Edith never even asked after Mum's family. She would have known Mum's brothers had been in the war. It was as if she couldn't wait to get rid of Mum.'

Her aunts' treatment of her mother still clearly rankled with Agnes. It certainly was very odd. Olivia couldn't imagine how they'd manage Greyfriars without help.

'They've never even stepped a foot off the island since they arrived,' Agnes continued, shaking her head and making her curls bounce.

'What? Never?'

'Not as far as anyone knows. They have all their shopping delivered by Lovatt's the shop. And they never got around to employing a daily, even though they must know there's plenty who would be grateful for the work and that house is too big for two ladies to manage on their own. Folk think they've gone a bit queer in the head.' Agnes flushed. 'Sorry. I shouldn't have said that. Them being your aunts . . . '

There had to be an explanation for their behaviour, although what, Olivia couldn't imagine. A shiver of disquiet ran up her spine. What if they turned her away too?

Chapter Sixteen

It was late afternoon before Agnes told Olivia that Duncan, the driver, had come for her. The heavy rain had eased to a fine drizzle but it was still very cold and Olivia's headache had returned, worse than ever.

Duncan had a mop of curly brown hair and kind eyes. When she gave the address, his eyebrows rose.

'Greyfriars House, eh? Well, well. Can't remember the last time anyone visited there. Never taken anyone over myself, at any road.'

So everyone appeared to take great pains to tell her.

'You know Greyfriars?' she asked.

'My Uncle Donald was a ghillie there before the war. He spoke of it often.'

'Donald! Is he still alive?'

'No, he passed away a couple of years ago. It was very sudden.'

'I am sorry. I remember him from when I was a child. He was very kind to me.'

'Even if he hadn't told me, a family like that was bound to stick out in these parts. Place was empty during the war, but after – can't mind how long after – the Misses Guthrie came back to live there. We were all surprised. The family only ever used it during the summer. Now you've turned up. We didn't even know there were any family left. Thought it was just the Misses Guthrie.'

Olivia stared out of the window. It was all very odd but there was no point in pondering the change in her aunts. Her headache continued to pound and she felt nauseous again. It had to be the anxiety of being turned away. But surely they wouldn't. They might not have kept in touch but they were still her aunts. Her mother's sisters. That had to mean something. She massaged her temples. Once that first meeting was over, she'd feel a lot better.

'I'm surprised they didn't let me know there was a visitor needing taking across. You see it's me who takes their groceries over once a week on the wee boat and they would have left me a note.'

Olivia's heart plummeted. Her letter couldn't have reached them. Well, it was too late now. She was here. There were no trains back to Edinburgh. Not until Monday. If necessary she could go back to the inn. But what then? She couldn't think. Her headache was so bad, her vision was blurring.

'But you'll take me now?' she asked.

Duncan rubbed his chin. 'Dare say I could. Wouldn't take long. Don't know how else you'd manage.'

'Thank you. I'm sorry to put you out. It's not a very nice day, is it?'

He caught her eyes in the rear-view mirror. 'It's as good as we get here at this time of year. Wait you until the real storms start. We've been lucky to have missed them so far. But on a good day, there's nowhere like it. Just you wait and see.'

As if to belie his words, heavy rain started to fall again, obscuring the limited view she'd had from the car window with a sheet of water.

They had only gone a few yards when he came to a stop. 'You stay inside where it's nice and dry. I just need to pop into the shop to let them know I'll be a while yet. Unless you'd care to come in and have a cup of tea? The wife would be happy to oblige, I'm sure.'

'No, thank you.' The last thing she wanted was to face

a barrage of questions she couldn't answer without lying. Besides, she wasn't sure that if she did manage to swallow even a tiny sip of tea that it wouldn't come straight back up.

While she waited for Duncan to return she wound down the window. Although cold rain blew in, stinging her face, the fresh air eased her nausea a bit. She only had to hold on a little longer. When Duncan returned a few minutes later he was carrying something. More cold air rushed in with him as he settled himself in front of the wheel. He set a pair of orange oilskins down on the passenger seat.

'They might be a little big for you but they'll be better than nothing. Wife wanted to come out to ask you in but I told her you'd already said no. That you were keen to get to your destination. She says I'm to tell you to make sure you stop by if you're in the village.'

The car pulled away with a jerk, sending a flash of pain through her head as if her brain was bouncing around inside her skull. Happily, it was only a short time later when Duncan pulled over again. The rain had stopped and as the sun slid out from behind a cloud, a final hurrah before disappearing again, it bathed the land in a warm golden glow.

'Now that's the west coast weather for you,' Duncan said cheerfully. 'Still, I suggest you put on the oilskins I brought for you. Just as likely to rain again before I've got you to the house.'

Olivia eyed the garments he was holding out to her. Duncan wasn't a large man but they'd still swamp her. It was bad enough appearing on her aunts' doorstep, having invited herself, without looking like a waif and stray.

'If it rains again I'll put them on,' she said. 'But if I remember correctly it only takes a few minutes on the boat to get across.'

'Ten in fine weather, fifteen when there's a swell like there is today.' He grinned through tobacco-stained teeth. 'At the very least use the trousers to sit on, it'll keep your bottom dry.

And sling the jacket over your shoulders. You're so wee it'll probably cover most of you anyway.'

As he'd predicted, the rain began to fall again, heavier than before. She put the oilskin jacket on and placed the trousers over the seat nearest the prow. Duncan stepped in after her and pushed the small boat away from the pier.

Something flew past her head – a bat or a bird – and she ducked, smothering a cry behind her hand. Her heart missed a beat, making her feel more light-headed than ever. All she wanted was to get indoors, out of the rain and lie down until the dreadful feeling of nausea and the pain in her head had passed. Clutching the oilskin jacket closed with one hand and the side of the boat with the other, she tried to stop shivering. As she huddled deeper into Duncan's jacket, she made herself imagine she was already in Greyfriars, tucked up in bed, sipping a cup of tea, a hot water bottle at her feet, her aunts smiling down at her.

They must have been in their early to mid-twenties when she'd last seen them, so what did that make them now? In their early to mid-thirties. Far too young to be living so far away from anyone and anything.

She summoned up a picture of her aunts that last summer – Georgina in her long, tight-fitting ruby red dress, and Edith in blue velvet. She couldn't imagine either woman being anything else but still glamorous and beautiful. Her chest tightened. Mother had been beautiful too.

The oars clunked with each dip in the water, the dull lap, lap of the sea against the boat, the harsh cry of seagulls circling above; each sound a painful stab to her head, the rise and fall of the boat exacerbating her queasiness.

Mercifully, it wasn't long before Duncan drew up beside the pier and leapt out to tie the boat to the post. Even in the poor light she could see that it was rotting and should be replaced. He reached out a hand to help her from the boat and, as she waited for him to retrieve her suitcase, she shrugged out of the borrowed oilskin and peered towards the house. At one time she would have had a decent view of Greyfriars from where she stood, but now, if she hadn't known the house was there she might never have guessed. When she was here last, there was a distinct path but now it was barely visible, overgrown as it was by rhododendrons, their branches, thick with leaves, obscuring the house. As she walked through the tunnel in the hedge the wind whipped at the branches so that they moved and swayed, reaching out to her like gnarled, skeleton hands, catching at her clothes like witches' fingers. Behind her, she could hear Duncan's laboured breathing and stifled expletives and was glad he hadn't left her on the pier to make her own way.

Suddenly the path through the rhododendrons came to an end and she stopped, shocked. There it was, Greyfriars! But a far cry from the way she remembered.

Admittedly she'd only ever been here in the summer and it was bound to be different in the winter – but this different?

The once manicured lawn was overgrown and covered in weeds. A shutter hung off one of the second-floor windows, banging forlornly in the wind. Ivy, brown and stringy, clambered up the front of the house, almost obscuring the downstairs windows. Water streamed from one of the gutters.

She'd expected the house to be lit up the way she remembered from her childhood, but it was in darkness, apart from a single light flickering from one of the upstairs rooms. She had an eerie, creepy sense of unwelcome and, for a moment, she was tempted to ask Duncan to take her back to the Balcreen Inn. Then she remembered the words her father had written all those years ago. People like them did not – and never would – run away.

She took a deep breath, continued through the ankle-high grass and up to the front door, tugged on the round brass knob and heard it jangle. At least the bell still worked.

She turned to Duncan. 'I'll be all right now. How much do I owe you?'

The sum he named seemed ridiculously low but she hadn't the wherewithal to argue. She was shivering and the dizziness and nausea had come back with a vengeance. She reached into her purse and counted out the pennies, pressing them into his hand when he appeared reluctant to take them. Out of the corner of her eye she thought she saw a shadow move behind the window that when she was a child was used as the morning room – as if someone had peeked out, then stepped back into the shadows.

'I'd best wait until someone answers the door,' Duncan said, looking around with avid curiosity. 'Perhaps you should just go in? They could be at the back of the house and not have heard the bell. I never come this far. They insist I leave their groceries down at the pier for them to collect.'

Olivia hesitated, before ringing the bell again. Someone had seen them arrive. Shouldn't there still be at least one live-in servant? This house was far too large for two women to manage without help. But both Duncan and Agnes had been adamant that her aunts lived here on their own without so much as a daily.

Should she do as Duncan suggested? Try the door and if it wasn't locked, walk straight in? Still she hesitated. Aunts or not, she just couldn't bring herself to do it. On the other hand she couldn't stand here all day. She reached for the door handle, but as her fingers closed around the brass knob, finally, the door swung open.

She didn't immediately recognise Georgina. It wasn't just that she was older, her once luxurious russet red hair streaked with grey, it was the expression on her face that threw Olivia. One of utter shock. There wasn't a spark of welcome, or of the mischief that had always danced in the depths of her eyes.

Behind her, hovering at Georgina's shoulder, was Edith. She too had changed. Her once neat appearance was almost dishevelled, her hair short and badly cut and she seemed so much smaller and thinner than Olivia remembered, almost bird-like. But what really shook Olivia was the look of terror on Edith's face.

They were fading in and out of focus – as if they weren't real – only ghostly approximations of the aunts she remembered.

'Yes? Can I help you?' Georgina said. 'Goodness me! Is that you, Duncan?'

Olivia held out her hand. She couldn't think what else to do. 'It's Olivia. Your niece?' she added when her aunt gave no sign of recognition. 'I wrote to you, asking' – dash, that was the wrong word – 'to let you know I was coming to stay.'

Edith shook her head slightly as if by doing so could make her disappear. 'Olivia? Coming to stay?' she echoed.

'Didn't you get my letter?' Olivia said desperately. She was terrified her aunts would deny knowing who she was and close the door in her face.

'Let the poor lass in,' Duncan said from behind her. She'd almost forgotten he was there. 'Can't you see she's almost dead on her feet?'

'It's Olivia, Edith, Harriet's daughter. That's who it is!' Georgina exclaimed. 'Can't you see, Edith? It's little Olivia all grown up.'

'You'd better let her in,' Edith muttered from behind Georgina's shoulder.

Georgina stepped back and opened the door just wide enough for Olivia, followed closely by Duncan, to squeeze through. There hadn't been any electricity when she was last here and it seemed there still wasn't. As there were no windows in the hall it was mostly in darkness, lit only by the oil lamp Georgina held in her hand.

'We didn't get a letter,' Georgina murmured.

Donald plonked Olivia's suitcase on the hall floor, as if by doing so he could force her aunts to take her in. She should have waited until morning. Or moved in to a bed and breakfast in Edinburgh and waited for a letter back. Or sent a telegram from the inn and waited there until she'd received a reply.

'I arrived last night, but the train was late and there was no way of getting here. I stayed at the inn ... ' Her voice felt as if it were coming from a long distance away.

The light from Georgina's lamp cast ghostly, elongated shadows on the wall, the figures of her aunts wavering and dissolving. Everything started to spin and the floor came rushing towards her. And then nothing.

When Olivia came to, she was lying in the large, four-poster bed in the room her parents had used when they were at Greyfriars. Her shoes had been removed and she'd been covered with an eiderdown. Olivia fancied she could smell the faint tang of roses of the scent her mother had always worn. As a wave of grief washed over her, she grabbed a handful of the quilt, brought it up to her face and inhaled deeply.

Weak sunshine filtered in through the window, in front of which stood two people, Edith and a man, their heads bent close together. The man was dressed in a woollen suit and white shirt and had a stethoscope in his hand. She must have made a sound as they turned around. The man smiled. Her aunt did not.

'Come back to join us, then?' the doctor said, with that forced joviality her albeit limited experience with medical men recognised. 'You gave your aunts quite a scare.'

He walked towards the bed and lifted her wrist, feeling for her pulse. He frowned. 'Now then, I would like you to give me a specimen of urine. I have a container you can use.' He turned away and rummaged in a battered leather bag and retrieved a pot with a flourish. 'Ah! I thought I'd one with me. Otherwise I would have had to send the nurse across with it.'

Was it Olivia's imagination or did Edith blanch at his words?

'The sooner I can get a specimen tested for albumin the better,' the doctor continued, 'although I am already almost certain what is wrong with you.' He turned back to Edith. 'Would you mind leaving us for a few minutes?' he asked.

Clearly reluctant, yet without saying a word – she hadn't spoken at all – her aunt left the room.

'Now then,' the doctor said, perching on the end of the bed. 'Am I correct in thinking you are going to have a baby?'

Olivia nodded, tears rushing to her eyes. Since she'd fallen pregnant she seemed to cry at the drop of a hat.

'There, there,' he said, patting her shoulder as if she were four instead of almost twenty-one. 'Nothing to cry about. You and baby should be fine, although you'll have to stay in bed until baby is born.'

Stay in bed! Olivia was horrified. When she'd made up her mind to come to Greyfriars it wasn't with the expectation she'd be cared for by her aunts. She struggled into a sitting position. 'I can't do that for over three months!'

He frowned down at her. 'You need to understand that complete bed rest is essential if we are going to keep you and baby healthy.'

A chill swept across her skin. 'What's wrong with me?'

'I believe, although I can't be sure, that you have a condition called toxaemia. Have you been having headaches? Dizzy spells?'

She nodded. 'They started about two weeks ago. I thought it was because ... things have been difficult.'

'Difficult times don't help, but I don't think it's that alone. When I checked your blood pressure I found it to be on the high side. Nothing too alarming,' he hurried on, 'but enough to cause concern. I had a look at your ankles and both are swollen as are your fingers. Didn't you notice?'

She hadn't, although now she thought of it, the ring she had bought to wear on her left hand was uncomfortably tight. She'd just thought she was putting on weight with the baby.

'All your symptoms, taken together, is enough for me to be pretty certain you have toxaemia,' the doctor continued. 'I'll

123

be able to confirm my diagnosis once I've tested a sample of your urine.'

'What exactly is toxaemia?'

'It's a disease that sometimes happens in pregnancy. It can elevate the blood pressure, affect the kidneys.' He stood, looking down at her, smiling as if to reassure her. 'It almost always goes away when the baby is born.'

'Isn't there something else you can do about it? Give me a pill?'

'The only treatment is complete bed rest.' He paused. 'And even then it's not a cure. We will have to keep a close eye on you. If we can't keep your blood pressure down then we might have to deliver baby early.' She must have looked as stricken as she felt, as he added quickly, 'But let's not get ahead of ourselves. You do as I say, young lady, and all should be well. Your Aunt Edith used to be a nurse, I understand. In which case she can keep an eye on you.'

'I'll go back to Edinburgh then.' But where would she go?

'You can't travel, my dear. It is out of the question. You can get up to use the lavatory, but for no other reason. We must be clear on that. Now what about your husband? Where is he?'

'There is no husband,' she mumbled, unable to meet his eye. 'He died.'

'My dear. I am so sorry.' He stood and returned his stethoscope to his bag. 'However, I suggest you remove your ring, in case your hands become more swollen.'

Olivia tugged it off, glad to have a reason to dispense with it.

'Now for that urine specimen. Do you feel you can manage the bathroom on your own? Or should I ask your aunt to take you?'

She shook her head, appalled at the thought of her aunt having to take her to use the WC as if she were a child. 'The bathroom is only a short way along the hall.' She threw back the quilt and was about to put her feet on the floor when a wave of dizziness washed over her. She swayed. Happily the doctor had his back to her and hadn't noticed. Otherwise no doubt he would have insisted on calling one of her aunts.

Her suitcase had been unpacked and her dressing gown laid across the foot of her bed. The dizziness passed after a few moments and she eased herself out of bed. She reached for her dressing gown and slid her arms into the sleeves, grateful for its warmth.

'While you're producing the specimen for me, I'll have a word with the Misses Guthrie. Just leave it next to the bed when you're finished,' the doctor said. 'I'll come for it before I leave.' He glanced at his watch. No doubt he had other patients to see.

'Thank you for coming, Doctor,' Olivia said, belatedly remembering her manners. 'I'm sorry to have taken up so much of your time.'

'Not at all. Not at all. Have to say I've always been intrigued to see this place close up.'

She followed him out of the room and onto the landing. She wasn't altogether surprised to find Edith and Georgina standing there. They spun around, looking as if they'd been caught in the act of something. Olivia smiled weakly in their direction, knowing her cheeks were burning. This was not how she'd intended her reunion with Edith and Georgina to go.

Chapter Seventeen

Charlotte

1984

Mum's eyes flickered, as if recalling the journey had exhausted her as much as the trip had all those years ago.

'What happened then?' I asked.

'That's the bit I think about a great deal. It was all so strange. I know I wasn't well and I was very sad. I missed Ethan so much and being at Greyfriars again brought so many memories back, particularly of Mother and Father. I'd tried hard not to think of them while I was growing up – it hurt too much – but being back at Greyfriars . . . ' She stopped and took a deep breath. 'I know you'll think this is crazy but I started to believe that someone else was there apart from my aunts – an unseen presence. Sometimes I thought it was Lady Sarah, or Lady Elizabeth, maybe even my mother's spirit – whatever you want to call it – but it wasn't at all comforting – at least I didn't find it so. I don't think I could have been in my right mind, but it all felt so real.' Her voice had dropped to a whisper.

'You don't have to think about it if you don't want to,' I said quickly. Although Mum had always had a vivid imagination – when I was a child, she could make up stories to tell me at the drop of a hat – I couldn't imagine her believing in ghosts.

'No. I do. If you are going to go there, you should know everything.'

I had no plans to go, but I didn't tell Mum that. Whatever the aunts wanted could be dealt with by letter.

'Why don't you have a nap and you can finish your story later?' I suggested.

'I need to tell you.' She was becoming increasingly agitated. Spots of colour suffused her pale cheeks and her eyes glittered as her restless hands pulled at a loose thread on her cardigan until it came free with a snap.

'There's time enough, Mum. I'm not going anywhere.' I smoothed the hair from her forehead and she smiled slightly. Moments later her eyes closed and her breathing deepened. I draped a throw over her and, not wanting to leave her, picked up my book. But I couldn't concentrate enough to read. Instead I mulled over what Mum had told me, trying to put myself in her shoes. She'd been so young, younger than I was now, and by her own admission much more naïve and protected than I had been at the same age. She must have been so frightened, must have felt so alone, so worried about the child she was carrying and what would happen to them both. She'd arrived mid-winter, when the sun barely rose before it disappeared, when the wind was cold and threatening, not knowing what reception she'd receive from two women she'd not seen in years and had shown no interest in her during that time. Then to find out she was ill, to sense that she wasn't welcome, that she would have to stay at Greyfriars whether she wished to or not, must have been another huge stress.

But something about her stay at Greyfriars had upset her – still upset her.

Poor Mum. I felt a fresh wave of fury at the man who had fathered me, at my great-aunts – at myself, with the whole bloody world.

*

127

While Mum was napping, I spoke to Sophie on the phone. The Littlejohn case had gone according to plan and she'd won a decent and fair settlement for our client.

'She didn't want anything beyond what she felt she was entitled to,' Sophie said, 'which made it pretty easy. And it went so well, John passed the Griffin case to me.'

'Are you going to persuade him to plead guilty?' I asked. 'He'll lose his licence but might just get away with a suspended sentence on the assault.'

'No. I'm going for a not-guilty plea – on the basis he was pulled over without reason.'

'I don't think that's likely to work.' Sophie's approach worried me. It seemed over-confident. If she failed to convince the court that Griffin shouldn't have been stopped, the judge would take a dim view of a not-guilty plea. Or was it my own anxiety, my need to have control over my cases that made me think like that? The feeling that Lambert and Lambert was moving on without me? On the other hand I wouldn't cry any tears if Griffin did go down.

'What about the other matter?'

An uneasy note crept into Sophie's voice. 'You were right when you said there had been another case. It took a while but we found it. Annette Riley. Like Lucy she was a student but working as a barmaid to help fund her course when she had the misfortune to come across Simon. Apparently Simon invited Annette out for dinner, but made up some story about forgetting his wallet at his flat and needing to stop there. Annette reported the alleged attack to the police and they forwarded the report to the Crown. For some reason, it never made it to the prosecutor's file prior to Simon standing trial for Lucy's rape – probably because Annette changed her mind and withdrew her complaint.' She paused. 'I don't see what else we can do. I've already crossed more professional boundaries than I'd like. Especially as Simon's father is one of our biggest clients.'

That he was, was the only reason I'd agreed to take on

Simon's defence. Normally I wouldn't have touched a rape case with a bargepole. I should have stuck to my guns. And now, with this other woman — it was impossible to imagine they were both making false accusations against the same man. I wasn't naïve enough to think that everyone I defended was innocent, but I couldn't bear to think I might have helped a rapist get off. 'Do you have a copy of the original police report?'

Sophie hesitated. 'Apparently there's a tenancy at Lambert and Lambert coming up. I'm thinking of applying.'

I was astonished on two counts. Firstly, I hadn't known Lambert and Lambert had space for another barrister, and secondly, more worryingly, that Sophie was no longer thinking of joining the Crown Prosecution Service.

'I can't afford to rock the boat, Charlotte. Not if I want to be considered. You do understand?'

I did. I had no right to ask any more of Sophie. Asking her to approach her prosecutor friend in the Crown's office had been bad enough. Perhaps I should just let the Lucy Corrigle case go? Didn't I have enough to worry about with Mum? But I couldn't leave it. Lucy had tried to kill herself. Perhaps if Simon had been found guilty she would have found a measure of peace. And if he had raped two women there was a chance he could rape again. I couldn't have that on my conscience too. I had to find a way to check out Annette's story even if it meant putting my career on the line.

'Do you have Annette's address on you?'

Paper rustled as she flicked through her diary. '24a Howth Gardens.'

I wrote it down. 'Thanks, Sophie. I'll take it from here.'

But almost immediately Lucy was put to the back of my mind. That afternoon Dr Goldsmith, Mum's GP, came on one of his regular visits. When he suggested we go into the kitchen and closed the door behind us, I knew I wouldn't want to hear what he had to say.

'Your mother is failing. You should prepare yourself.'

'How long?'

'It's difficult to say with any certainty. A couple of weeks – a month perhaps – if we're lucky.'

The crushing pain in my chest made it difficult to speak. 'Isn't there anything more you can do?'

'All we can do now is make her as comfortable as possible. I've increased her morphine. It will help with the pain but will make her more sleepy. Have you talked to her about hospice care?'

'No! Mum would hate that. I'll look after her here.'

'In which case I'll arrange for nurses to come in.'

'Thank you. Just tell me what I need to do and I'll do it.'

The nurses came in twice a day but it was me who washed her hair, soaping the thinning locks between my palms, gently massaging her bony scalp, me who helped her on and off the commode the nurses had supplied, both Mum and I initially rigid with embarrassment at this unexpected and unwished for intimacy, but sooner than either of us would have expected becoming deft at it, occasionally giggling when Mum tooted unexpectedly. Despite everything, there was a joy to our days. As Mum's life drew to an end we discovered a closeness we'd hitherto been unable to find and the time before Mum got really bad was bittersweet. I read to her and we talked more than we had done before. We reminisced about Mum's boss at the library, Miss Walker, about places we'd visited together, we discussed books we'd both loved, and we laughed and argued as we hadn't done in years. I told her again about how I'd won the Curtis case and she listened, her eyes shining as I described how I'd felt when the not-guilty verdict had come in. I didn't tell her about Lucy Corrigle or that, with every week that passed, my career was slowly withering on the vine.

As Dr Goldsmith had warned, the increase to her morphine made her sleep for hours at a stretch although it did seem to ease her pain. As the days passed, her breathing became more laboured, and she was growing ever weaker, eating little, rarely managing more than a mouthful or two before she'd push her plate away. One afternoon, after I'd helped her sit up in bed, she patted the empty space beside her.

'Time's running out, Charlotte. I need to tell you what happened after I arrived at Greyfriars.'

Chapter Eighteen

Olivia

1950

Time slipped by as if she were living in a fog. To begin with she slept for long periods of time, rousing only when one of her aunts came into her room. She was dimly aware of being washed gently and being fed sips of chicken broth before she would slump back gratefully into a dreamless sleep.

If it weren't for the meals that appeared at regular intervals, Olivia wouldn't have been able to guess the time of day, or even if it were day or night. Edith kept the curtains closed, insisting Olivia needed the darkness to help her rest. A small lamp had been left by her bed, should she need it, but otherwise the only light was from the flickering fire kept lit in her hearth or from the oil lamp Edith carried with her.

But as the days passed, eventually the headaches came less often and with less severity and Olivia spent longer periods awake. It was then that the pain of being apart from Ethan would rip her in two. Sometimes when her spirits were at their lowest, most often in the darkest part of the night, she would decide to write to him, to tell him she had changed her mind – that she was going to have his baby and he should divorce his wife and marry her instead. Then morning would come, the cold light bringing reason with it. She could never be happy with Ethan knowing she had deprived two children of their father.

But yet, an insistent, niggling voice said, aren't you depriving the child you are carrying? Doesn't he, or she, deserve to know their father? How did one weigh up the happiness of one family against that of another? In the end, it always came down to this – Ethan was already married.

Lying in bed, trying not to think of Ethan, and staring into darkness, she listened to the familiar creaks and groans of the house as it settled down for the night, recognising the banging of a shutter that never did catch properly. There were other noises too – unfamiliar and, at times, unsettling. She put it down to the fact that every time she'd been at Greyfriars in the past it had been summer and winter was bound to bring with it different sounds – the wind fiercer than she remembered – moaning and shrieking down the chimney breast in her room. But it wasn't just that. Sometimes she thought she heard the sound of light pittering and pattering from the floorboards above her, and several times she was certain she'd heard footsteps stop outside her door, before they'd move away. Once she was sure she heard the sound of childish laughter and, recalling the story of the drowned Lady Sarah, began to wonder whether Lady Elizabeth's ghost really did walk Greyfriars searching for her child. By morning she'd dismissed her overheated imaginings of the night before – the scurrying sounds above her were bound to be mice or rats. Greyfriars, being surrounded by the sea, had always been a haven for rodents and without Donald the ghillie to keep them under control, no doubt they'd multiplied. And as for the footsteps, why, her aunts were bound to pass her room from time to time.

It was almost always Aunt Edith who tended to her. Three times a day she would bring Olivia meals. She'd plump her pillows and help her sit up, placing another pillow on her lap so that she could rest the tray. Olivia had almost no appetite, and the food wasn't very appetising; lumpy porridge for breakfast, soup for lunch and tinned meat with boiled potatoes for supper, but Edith would stand over her until Olivia had eaten

133

sufficient to satisfy her aunt. Then she would help her out of bed and onto the commode which had been retrieved from somewhere and placed in Olivia's room. It was mortifying. Olivia couldn't see why she couldn't walk the short distance to use the lavatory but Edith insisted that bed rest meant bed rest and besides she'd been a nurse and was well used to emptying bed pans. Olivia didn't have the strength to argue. The business with the commode dispensed with, Edith helped her back into bed, and washed her tenderly, almost as if she were a little girl. Next Edith checked her blood pressure and ankles and hands for swelling before tucking her up again and leaving her to sleep.

As her aunt moved around the room, Olivia studied her from under her eyelashes. It wasn't just her physical appearance that had changed, but also her manner, and she seemed a far cry from the brusque, down-to-earth aunt of her childhood. Aunt Edith had always been quieter, more serene than her two sisters, but this was different. There was no serenity about her now. Her eyes had an odd blankness to them and she seemed nervous and ill at ease, often starting at the slightest noise.

She was efficient and kind when she was looking after Olivia but she said very little and as soon as she'd finished her nursing tasks, she'd leave, as if she couldn't bear to spend time in the room with her niece. Inconceivable though it was, Olivia wondered whether she still blamed Olivia for what had happened that last summer. She longed to ask if Findlay had survived the war, and if he had, whether he and Edith had made up. But nothing about her aunt suggested she'd welcome that sort – or any sort – of personal question.

Georgina popped her head around the door occasionally to ask how she was feeling, but she too rarely stayed to talk. She too had changed.

She was still beautiful, her thick hair although dashed with strands of grey, still burnished copper, her skin still porcelain white, although with more freckles than Olivia remembered, and there were lines on her face that hadn't been there before. All that was only to be expected – a natural part of getting older. But it was the change in her personality that perplexed Olivia. It was as if all the joy had gone out of her. It was almost impossible to believe that Georgina was the same woman who'd lit up Greyfriars all those years ago. As if once she'd been a chandelier and now she was a single, guttering candle.

As the weeks passed, and the headaches and nausea continued to ease, Edith brought Olivia jugs of water so she could wash herself; a small, but welcome act of independence. Although Olivia might have been feeling better physically, mentally she was lethargic and miserable and the darkened room didn't help her spirits. With nothing but the regular visits from Edith and the sporadic ones from Georgina there was little to distract her from thinking about Ethan. She needed something to keep herself occupied, or else she would surely go mad.

The next time Edith came to her room she broached the subject.

'Do you think I might get up today and sit in the armchair? I haven't had a headache for days now. That must be a good sign.'

Edith crossed over to the window and opened the curtains a crack as if scanning the outside for an answer.

'I don't see why not,' she said finally. 'I'd like to take your blood pressure first though. And check your hands and ankles.' When Edith was in nursing mode, she was confident and certain, reminding Olivia of the woman she'd been when Olivia was a child.

Olivia dutifully held out her hands for inspection. They were still swollen but not nearly as badly as they had been. Edith gave a little grunt. 'And your ankles?'

'I think they're better too.'

Edith lifted the blanket covering Olivia's feet, letting in a freezing draught of air. She prodded Olivia's ankles gently with her fingers. 'Still swollen but very much better. Very well, you can get out of bed and sit up but only for an hour or two after lunch and you have to promise me that you'll keep your legs raised.'

'I promise,' Olivia said meekly, feeling like the nine-year-old child she'd been when she'd last seen Edith.

Her aunt helped her out of bed and into her dressing gown. She settled her into the armchair next to the window and, retrieving a blanket from the bottom of the large wardrobe, covered Olivia until only her chin was exposed to the chilly air.

Olivia looked out of the window. It was grey but not raining, the sky low, and the trees and rhododendrons obscured the view in the way they hadn't when she'd been a child. A cockerel crowed, followed later by the mooing of a cow. It was then Olivia realised that she had heard no footsteps crunching on the gravel outside the house, no chiming doorbell, no knock on the door. Who milked the cow? Kept the buildings in repair? Agnes had said that her aunts didn't have a daily and never went to the village but until this moment it hadn't occurred to Olivia that they had no help at all.

Were her aunts now so poor that they couldn't afford a lad to come from the village to cut back the bushes? And others to help in the house even for a few hours a day. As Agnes had said, there were bound to be several villagers who would be glad of the chance to earn some extra money when money was still so tight for so many. Someone like Agnes herself, for example? Her aunts couldn't enjoy running up and down stairs countless times to see to her and the house could do with a good paint – a good clean, even more necessary. The Guthries had been wealthy once and all that money couldn't possibly have disappeared. After all, they could afford to send her an allowance every month – the one that had enabled her to go to university and pay for her lodgings, food and clothes as well as the occasional treat. She'd even managed to save a little and

136

had subsequently opened a savings account with the post office. The thought that they might be doing without to ensure she was taken care of financially simultaneously worried and warmed her. Perhaps she could use some of her savings to help them? It was her house too, or would be soon, and the subject needed to be broached at some point. And if she were going to be here for the foreseeable future – the future after the baby was born was still a closed book – shouldn't she make a contribution to her keep?

Her head began to throb. But one didn't ask about money and she didn't feel strong enough to raise the subject of the house or her future here. No doubt one, or both, of her aunts would at some point. Life would be so much easier if one could only say what was on one's mind. In the meantime, perhaps she could suggest employing Agnes? Edith was making up Olivia's bed with fresh linen, folding the corners of the bottom sheet into precise envelope shapes.

'Aunt Edith, I can't remember if I told you that the night I arrived, the train was late and I spent the night at the inn in Balcreen?'

Edith gave the blankets one final smooth and turned. A little frown puckered the skin between her eyes. 'Why didn't you write earlier? Your letter only arrived a few days after you did. If we'd had more notice we would have arranged for someone to meet you.'

Olivia doubted that. Despite their care of her she still believed they would have found a way of preventing her from coming.

'I'm sorry. I should have. But what I was about to say was that while I was at the inn, I met Agnes again. I played with her when I was a child. She's about my age. Perhaps you remember her?'

Edith shook her head, eyeing Olivia warily.

'Agnes's parents have sold the inn and are planning to go and live in Canada with their other daughter,' Olivia continued.

Edith's expression hadn't changed but she had begun to tap the side of her leg as if impatient to be gone.

'Anyway, Agnes wants to go to Edinburgh or Glasgow to find a job in domestic service,' Olivia hurried on, 'and I wondered, if it was all right with you and Aunt Georgina, if while Agnes is applying for posts whether she might come here for a few hours every day? If she'd like to. She could help look after me, keep me company – perhaps do a bit of light housework and cooking.'

Olivia was about to continue when Edith interrupted her.

'Absolutely not! I hope you didn't say anything to her to suggest it might even be a possibility. Georgina and I manage fine by ourselves. We like it like that.'

'It wouldn't cost very much—' Oh dear now she was travelling down the very road she had promised herself she wouldn't go, 'and I would be happy to pay for her time.'

Edith picked up the soiled bed linen from the floor. 'It is not a matter of money. I'm sorry, but it's completely out of the question.'

'Then might I invite her to visit me?' Olivia hated the plaintive note that had crept into her voice. She was no longer a child and she mustn't let Aunt Edith intimidate her. 'She would be company for me.'

Edith picked up the lunch tray and pursed her lips. 'Georgina and I do not welcome visitors. I'm sorry, I know you must find it lonely here, but Georgina and I like the solitude. *And we didn't invite you to come.* The words weren't spoken out loud but they hung in the air as clearly as if they had been.

'It was just a thought,' Olivia finished lamely. 'I didn't mean to cause offence.'

Edith's smile seemed forced. 'No offence. You weren't to know. Georgina and I had rather too much company during the war. We like it here on our own.'

But what did they do to entertain themselves? Read? Listen to music on the wind-up gramophone? How could that possibly be enough? For these two women who had once had such active social lives? What had changed them so? It had to have something to do with what had happened to them when they were prisoners. Or had Edith's break-up with Findlay broken her heart?

'What was the war like for you?' It wasn't just that she wanted to have someone to talk to, she truly wanted to know.

The dishes on the tray rattled and Edith gripped the tray so tightly, her knuckles turned white. 'Neither Georgina nor I have any wish to remember that time.'

'I'm sorry. Of course, if you don't wish to speak of it.' Every attempt to create a bond with her aunts seemed doomed to end in dismal failure. Was it because of what had happened in 1939 and her part in it? Or did Edith suspect Olivia wasn't married and disapproved? She'd certainly never once asked about the baby's father.

'Might I go down to the library and select something to read?'

'No! Absolutely not. Dr Morton was very clear that you must have complete bed rest.'

Dr Morton hadn't returned. Edith had said that, as a trained nurse, she was more than capable of monitoring Olivia.

Edith's voice softened. 'But I can select some books for you and bring them upstairs. Although I don't want you reading for more than an hour or two at a time.'

'That would be kind. Thank you.'

As Olivia waited for Edith to return she stared out of the window, remembering the lunches and games on the once manicured lawn. What would Mother and Father think if they knew the predicament in which she'd found herself? She stifled a sob. She knew how they'd feel. Appalled and bitterly disappointed.

But once their shock had worn off they would have welcomed her home, looked after her, protected her, perhaps even agreed to look after the baby while she finished her studies.

A vision of a baby sleeping under an apple tree outside the house in London, her parents looking down proudly – because no matter how disappointed they might have been to begin with they would fall in love with her baby as soon as it was born. In the vision, her child was cosseted and cared for by his grandparents – along the way she had decided it would be a boy. She'd finish her degree, do a postgraduate law degree, then her articles – perhaps in the firm her grandfather had established – before deciding what area of law to practice in. No. There was no decision required. She'd work as a prosecuting counsel – defending the poor, the disenfranchised, the inarticulate. She would be their voice, their salvation.

Her heart gave a dull thump. It was just more fantasising. Whatever her future was going to be, it wouldn't be that. She'd be a mother soon, responsible for another soul and it was time she grew up and faced reality. She returned her attention to the view. At one time she was certain she could have seen all the way to the pier from here. Now her line of sight was restricted by the height of the unpruned rhododendrons. She thought longingly of the bedroom she'd had the last time she was at Greyfriars. The one in the turret. Being at the very top of the house and with its many windows, it would have a much better view. She could watch the birds perhaps, look out to the sea and watch how it changed with the light. It would be brighter up there too.

It was Georgina who brought the books a short while later.

'Edith told me you were up and looking for something to read.' She placed the leather-bound volumes on the table beside the bed. 'There's the Brontes and Robert Louis Stevenson as well as some Dickens. I'm sorry but we don't have anything more modern.' She turned back to Olivia. 'Goodness me, you look like a baby in a blanket the way Edith has you all wrapped up.' Unexpectedly she laughed and so did Olivia, the shared laughter making her feel lighter than she had felt in days.

Emboldened, she asked Georgina whether it was possible to move into the tower room.

The amusement immediately drained from Georgina's eyes. 'It's quite impossible, I'm afraid. Surely you remember the stone steps leading up there? How narrow and worn they were? It would be too risky for you to manage them and Edith and I would find it difficult to get up and down those stairs with trays.'

Olivia did remember. Georgina's words brought Olivia back to her aunt laughing with her in that very room, Olivia asking Georgina why she didn't sleep there, Georgina's reply that adults wouldn't be able to manage the stairs if they were squiffy. Georgina swirling the champagne in her glass, the invitation to Singapore – clearly not truly meant, Georgina dancing on her own in the garden, with complete abandonment. Olivia following her down to the shore, watching as she slipped her arms around Findlay's neck. Whatever trouble her aunt had caused she'd been so alive back then. What horrible things had happened that had sucked all the joy from her?

'Aunt Georgina, did Findlay survive the war?'

Georgina's cheeks paled and she swayed slightly, grasping on to the bedstead, as if she needed support. 'Yes, he did.'

'Did he and Edith ever make up?'

'We don't talk about Findlay – he belongs to the past.'

It seemed there was no topic that wasn't off limits.

Georgina released her grip on the bedstead and smiled too brightly. 'Now, I'm afraid I must leave you. I have chores to do.'

Chapter Nineteen

As her health improved and Olivia stayed out of bed for longer and longer periods, so the hours between sleep dragged and stretched. Edith permitted Olivia to sit in the armchair in her room as long as she was well wrapped and kept her feet propped up. Her aunts brought her more books from the library, but she could only read for short periods, especially by the flickering light of the oil lamp, before her vision began to blur. When Olivia was tired of reading, she would lay her book down and stare out of the window, thinking of Ethan and watching as the leaves began to appear on the trees and the birds returned from their winter sojourns.

Once a week one of her aunts would appear from the tunnel through the rhododendrons pushing a wheelbarrow laden with food and sometimes fuel. At other times Olivia would see them outside, returning to the house with a pail of milk or a basket of vegetables or eggs.

As everyone had said, it seemed they never left the island to shop for themselves.

'We have no need to,' Georgina had said when she'd asked her. 'The store has a limited amount of foodstuffs so we order what we need and have it delivered. Eggs, milk and vegetables we provide for ourselves.'

'But don't you miss having company?' Olivia pressed. She was so bored with her own company and wished Georgina would spend more time with her. It was one thing to believe Edith content with such a dull existence but impossible to imagine the Georgina of her childhood being happy to live like a hermit.

'We had enough of living in close quarters with others during the war to last us a lifetime.'

It was the first time her aunt had referred to the war with more than a passing remark and Olivia seized her chance. 'What happened to you during the war? Agatha said you and Aunt Edith were captured by the Japanese? Was it very awful?'

'You could say that,' Georgina said with a twist to her lips, 'but neither Edith nor I have any wish to speak of that time.' Her expression softened. 'What's done is done. There's no point regretting what can't be changed, and no point dwelling on the past.'

The old Georgina would never have spoken in such clichéd terms. Nevertheless, it was good advice. Advice Olivia would do well to heed. She needed to stop dwelling on the past and start looking to the future. 'Of course. I'm sorry. I shouldn't have asked.'

Georgina sat down on the edge of the bed and took Olivia's hand. 'I didn't mean to snap.' She gave Olivia one of the brilliant smiles she remembered from the past. 'I do have regrets; not least that I couldn't have done more for you after Harriet died. I wish I could have come to see you after the war or had you to stay – but Edith and I – we needed time to recover. We were barely able to look after ourselves let alone you. All we wanted was to stay here and lick our wounds. Let the peace and solitude of Greyfriars heal us.'

Olivia could have pointed out that they had had years to heal themselves – and there was nothing preventing them from writing to her. But to confront her aunts in that way was unthinkable, especially when she'd accepted a long time ago that neither had felt any filial duty towards her and still didn't. Although one third of Greyfriars was hers, she was essentially dependent on them, treated like a guest in a country house who simply refuses to go rather than a member of their family. Her aunts never failed to ask how she was feeling and always appeared most solicitous of her comfort, ensuring she was well wrapped and her fire was kept lit. However, Olivia couldn't get over the feeling she wasn't welcome or even wanted at Greyfriars. They rarely stayed to talk to her and never, once she thought about it, visited her together. It was as if she were a chore they divided between them. She understood she'd disrupted their lives by coming and once the baby was born would disrupt it further. But she was their only living relative, the only child of a sister they'd loved. And she was here, in her family home. Really! They might make more of an effort!

She still intended that she and her child would stay there for a while, although her aunts' guarded manner whenever they were with her prevented Olivia from raising the matter with either of them and neither did they raise it with her.

One late afternoon she awoke with a start, every hair on her body standing on end, her heart beating in terror. She wasn't sure what had woken her.

She'd been reading and must have dozed off and while she'd been sleeping the room had darkened, the furniture little more than shadowed outlines.

She listened, her heart thudding sickeningly against her ribs, straining her eyes in the semi-darkness. Had the noise that had woken her been the wailing of the wind down the chimney breast, or the scratch of the branches of the unpruned rowan tree against her window? The cry of a fox perhaps? There were a few on the island, their high-pitched screams sounding so human it always chilled her.

But she knew it had been none of those. She'd had a sense of a breath against her face, that someone was in the room or had just left it. She tried to call out but the words stuck in

144

her throat. Then, with an immense effort she managed. 'Aunt Edith? Aunt Georgina? Is that you?'

There was no reply. She must have been dreaming. It was impossible to believe that either of her aunts were, or had been, in the room, heard her call out and not answered. Unless they'd left just before she'd woken?

The fire was almost out and her limbs had stiffened. The cold wind snuck between the old window frames and she stood to close the curtains to keep in what little warmth remained. But it wasn't the sun setting that had cast her room in darkness. Whilst she'd been sleeping a heavy mist had fallen. As she reached to draw the curtains, she saw Edith walking towards the house carrying a basket. Behind her aunt, in the shadows of the trees, Olivia thought she saw something move, although it was so misty she couldn't be certain. Georgina returning from the evening milking? But both her aunts couldn't be outside, not if one of them had been in her room. A deer or fox then? However, no animal moved like that, nor was it the right shape.

She shivered. Was it the ghost of Lady Sarah? She shook her head at her flights of fancy. It was being back here, amongst the ghostly presences she'd always imagined that was making her see and imagine things. Anyway, she told herself with an impatient click of her tongue, she almost wouldn't mind if it was the ghost of Lady Sarah. At least she'd have company.

Deriding herself for her bout of self-pity she climbed back into bed, the lump in her stomach making it awkward, and pulled the blankets up to her chin. Of course there was no such thing as ghosts!

Just as she was settled, there was a knock on the door and Georgina came in carrying her supper tray. It was neatly laid, a napkin under the plate and another one on the side, a silver salt and pepper pot, and as always there was a cup of the noxious stuff they liked her to drink, Bovril or something like it. The food was pretty much the same too. A slab of corned beef, some boiled potatoes and carrots on the side, kept warm with one of the cloches that always covered the dinner plates to stop the food getting cold when they were brought up from the kitchen. If it had been Georgina she'd seen, surely there had been no time for her to have come in and made up a tray for her?

'I feel terrible that you have to wait on me like this,' Olivia murmured.

Georgina reached behind her and plumped up her pillows. 'It isn't as if you can do anything about it,' she said, not unkindly, setting the tray down on Olivia's lap, before crossing over to the window.

'Did you look in on me just now?' Olivia asked.

Georgina had her back towards her but Olivia was certain her aunt stiffened. It was several minutes before she turned around. 'No. What makes you ask?'

'I fell asleep in the chair and I was sure someone was in the room, but when I called out, no one replied.'

'It must have been Edith. She couldn't have heard you. We do check up on every now and again.'

'But I just saw Edith outside.'

'Then you must have imagined it.'

Maybe she had. Sometimes, when her headaches were bad, her vision blurred. Olivia took a forkful of corned beef. Unusually Georgina took a chair beside the bed while Olivia ate.

'What will you do when the baby is born?' Georgina asked gently.

'Couldn't we stay here? We won't be any trouble.'

Her aunt looked away. 'What about the father?'

Olivia's heart thumped. She had a sudden image of Georgina in the sea, her fingers trailing up Findlay's torso, him grasping her wrists as she looked up at him, Georgina, she felt certain, knew what it was like to fall in love with the wrong person. Surely she, of all people, wouldn't judge? Olivia took a deep a breath and summoned her courage. 'There is no father – I

146

mean there is, but we can't be together.' She felt her colour rise. 'He's married. With a family. He's gone back to live with them in America.'

'I see.' The words were quietly spoken. 'Does he know about the baby?'

Olivia shook her head. 'You must think badly of me and I don't blame you.'

'Oh, my dear, I'm the last person to think badly of anyone. We all make mistakes. The best we can hope for is to be allowed to make restitution for them. If we ever truly can,' Georgina said, a wistful look on her face. 'I suspect by being apart from him, you are making yours.'

Her words brought back the conversation they'd had that last summer – when Georgina had said that the only ghosts that existed were those of a guilty conscience. It made sense then that whatever ghostly presences she felt were inside her head – the result of her own misery and guilt.

It was only when Georgina had left the room that Olivia realised her aunt hadn't said that she and the baby were welcome to stay.

Chapter Twenty

As the weeks passed, Olivia's sense she was being watched, that there was someone roaming the corridors and grounds of Greyfriars, grew. Sometimes she'd wake in the night convinced someone was in her room, certain she heard breathing, light footsteps, a smothered giggle. But there was never anyone there and no reply to her strangled demands for the person to reveal themselves and although she never saw Lady Sarah or Lady Elizabeth, she wondered. Perhaps spirits did stay around places where they were once very sad – or very happy. In which case maybe it was her mother's spirit she sensed? If so, it brought no comfort. She shook her head at her silliness. She wasn't a child any longer to believe such nonsense. Far more likely that it was just fantasies of a mind with little to occupy it. In an old house like this she was bound to think of past lives.

She kept telling herself that all these feelings would disappear along with her toxaemia as soon as her baby was born.

The baby, despite her ever-growing bump, did not yet seem real to her. She simply could not imagine a being, both separate from her yet part of her and Ethan, a child who would grow up to be a man or a woman. But she needed to make plans for its arrival, and their future.

One morning she woke before it was light, the luminous hands of the clock by her bed, when she held a burning match to it, showing the time to be ten to six. Her aunts wouldn't come with breakfast until seven. Unable to get back to sleep and fed up with the four walls of her room, she lit her oil lamp and with it casting larger than life shadows on the wall, carried it in front of her, and tiptoed downstairs. The sudden creaks and noises of the house added to the feeling that someone was following her, that there were other presences in the darkness. Gathering her courage, she told herself not to be ridiculous – ghosts didn't exist and, even if they did, they couldn't hurt her.

In the kitchen she set her lamp down on the large pine table she remembered so well. A pang of longing tore through her at the memories of childhood summers spent at that table watching Cook as she rolled pastry, or slipped Olivia a still-warm scone or a slice of newly baked bread, spread thickly with butter. Perhaps her child would sit here too? Be fed baking still warm from the oven by a caring, benevolent cook. She allowed herself a few moments to imagine Greyfriars the way it had once been and could be again. Filled with laughter and people. But as quickly as it came the image vanished. Who would wish to associate with an unmarried mother?

She took a saucepan from the shelf and milk from the larder. It was crammed with row upon row of tins: evaporated milk, bully beef, Heinz tomato soup, baked beans – enough surely to last the aunts until the end of their lives.

Once her milk was boiled she took it up to her room to drink. When she'd finished it she lay down on the bed and tried to go back to sleep for an hour or two, but instead of the hot drink making her sleepy, she was refreshed, more wide awake than she'd felt for a while. Probably down to her short walk to the kitchen. It was then that she heard it. A sort of squeak squeak, like a rocking chair or, more probably, another loose shutter hanging on its hinges. She visualised the house, trying to remember which room was above this one. It didn't take too long. It was the nursery, of course.

She had a sudden longing to see it again; to establish what needed to be done to make it ready for her and the baby. When

Olivia had used the nursery, back when she was a child, Nanny had had a room that led immediately off. Olivia could sleep there and the baby in the nursery. Remembering that the east-wing staircase the servants had used led from one of the back corridors to almost just outside the nursery, she decided to investigate. She could go there, have a look and be back in bed, and her aunts wouldn't even know she'd left her room.

Throwing on her dressing gown again she thrust her feet back into her slippers. She opened her door cautiously and peeked along the corridor, straining her ears for her aunts' footsteps, but all was still. Keeping close to the wall, lest she inadvertently stepped on a loose floorboard, she crept along the main corridor to the servants' staircase. She took the narrow uncarpeted stairs to the top where she turned right, glad of the light her small lamp afforded. It was very dark as there were no windows along the length of this corridor.

When she reached the door of the nursery, she opened it very carefully, her heart beating a tattoo against her ribs. When had she become so fearful? There was absolutely no need to feel so anxious. She had the perfect right to wander where she pleased. Nevertheless, her self-admonitions weren't enough to calm her racing heart.

The room was smaller than she recalled but even so the flickering light from her lamp couldn't quite reach the corners. The squeaking sound was still audible but slower now as if the wind had quietened down and whatever it had been blowing was coming to rest.

She lifted her lamp higher, taking in with an ache of nostalgia the doll-sized cradle that had once belonged to her, the single bed against the near wall in which she'd once slept, the shelves of children's books and the small table with chairs that was placed against the window. She crossed over to the other side of the room. In the corner was a blackboard on an easel. She held the lamp up to it, and was just able to make out faint traces of words that had been erased, insufficient remaining for her to decipher even a part. Beneath the blackboard was a painted spinning top, lying tipped on its side. She had no recollection of either the blackboard or the toy. Perhaps a child of one of the servants who had stayed to close Greyfriars once that fateful holiday in 1939 had come to an abrupt end had played here? In any case, if she were to stay at Greyfriars after her baby was born the nursery was halfway furnished. All that was required was a cot – the one she'd used as an infant would surely still be stored somewhere – a fresh coat of paint, some new curtains, a good scrub, and the windows polished. She tiptoed over to the window, expecting to find a shutter blowing gently on rusty hinges in the wind, but all were closed and fastened tight.

There it was again – the creaking sound. Her skin prickled. Once more, she had the terrifying sensation that someone was there in the room with her, or had, only in the last few moments, left. She had seen no one, heard nothing. She had simply the absolute certain sense of someone having passed close to her. A nameless dread filled her as she thought of the drowned Lady Sarah. Had this been her nursery too?

Her light tracked the noise. It wasn't coming from either of the windows that graced the room. It was coming from the other side of the room; a corner she hadn't explored.

Almost too terrified to breathe, she forced herself forward. There, in the furthest corner, was a rocking horse, still moving gently on its rockers as if an unseen hand had set it in motion. The hair all over her body stood on end as the air in the room appeared to shift. Her hand that held the lamp was trembling so much the flame of her lamp wavered, casting a giant-like shadow of her on the wall almost as if it were a malevolent being about to reach out and pull Olivia towards it.

She wanted nothing more than to be back in her room. She spun away but her legs felt leaden, as if they were glued to the floor. It took all the energy she could muster to place one foot in front of the other. Yet, even as she walked towards it, the door seemed to move away from her. It was as if she were in one of those terrifying dreams when one tries to run, but one cannot make one's limbs respond. Her heart was beating so fast she felt it could jump out of her chest. She took rapid, shallow breaths, trying to calm her racing heart but only succeeded in making herself light-headed. A tight band of pain was crushing her forehead. All she could think of was that she had to get out of the nursery and back to the safety of her room. She tried to cry out but her vocal cords wouldn't respond. The room spun and then there was the sickening sensation of the ground rushing towards her – and blackness.

When Olivia came round it was to find herself back in bed and Georgina standing over her, a worried look in her eyes, her face pale in the early morning light.

'How are you feeling?' Georgina asked.

'Not very well.' Her head felt as if it were filled with cotton wool and she ran a tongue over her lips in an attempt to moisten her mouth. Fragments of her visit to the nursery came back to her: the movement of the rocking horse, the certain feeling someone had been in the nursery, either with her or only moments before, the horrible shadows pressing in on her. The certainty that whoever – or whatever – it had been had meant her harm.

She lifted her hand and touched the back of her head, feeling a tender lump under her fingertips. 'I must have fainted.'

'You most definitely did. I heard a loud bang coming from the nursery. I found you lying on the floor, the lamp beside you. What on earth were you thinking? You could lose the baby – or might have set the house on fire. Anything could have happened!'

'I just wanted to look at the nursery.' She didn't want to tell her aunt how she'd felt up there. She lifted a hand to touch her forehead and felt something cold and damp beneath her fingers. Georgina or Edith had placed a flannel there.

Her headache had returned, more intense than ever.

'Perhaps it's best you go to the cottage hospital in Oban. You'll be forced to rest then,' Georgina said.

Her aunts had no right to try and make her leave. Whatever terrors Greyfriars held for her it was the only home she had and she had the absolute conviction that if she left, her aunts would prevent her returning. Olivia pressed her hands to her forehead in an attempt to still her thumping headache. Her head felt as if it would split in two. 'A third of Greyfriars will belong to me soon. I am entitled to stay here.'

Georgina stiffened. 'Very well,' she conceded reluctantly, 'but no more wandering about. Do you understand?'

Olivia nodded. If her acquiescence was what was required then her aunt would have it. She had no desire to revisit the nursery. Not in the foreseeable future anyway.

That night, when she got up to use the bathroom, her door wouldn't open. She pulled and pushed, thinking it must be stuck, but to no avail. The next morning when Edith brought her breakfast Olivia distinctly heard the sound of a key turning in the lock.

'Was I locked in last night?' she asked, unable to trust her hearing.

Edith appeared unperturbed. 'I thought you and Georgina agreed there was to be no more wandering about. I am responsible for you and the baby's safety. The only way we can be sure of that is by keeping your door locked.'

'Am I a prisoner?' she demanded, incredulous.

'Don't be ridiculous! You are free to leave whenever you wish. Georgina told me she suggested you'd be better off at the cottage hospital in Oban but that you refused to go. You can't have it both ways, Olivia. Either you agree to let us take good care of you, keep you safe, by whatever means we feel necessary, or you leave. Now, which is it to be?'

Chapter Twenty-One

Olivia stayed in bed most days. She read when her headaches allowed but they were coming with increasing frequency and intensity and sometimes she vomited. The days grew longer and warmer, and very occasionally, when the weather was sunny and she wasn't feeling so ill, one of the aunts would help her into the chair and open the window and she would breathe deeply, sucking in lungfuls of the sea-scented air. The trees that had been bare when she'd first arrived were now covered in leaves, blocking her already limited view of the sea. Occasionally she thought she heard the sound of girlish laughter and wondered again about Lady Sarah. She'd almost resigned herself to her presence – as long as she kept her distance.

She was only permitted to sit up for a while before one of her aunts would come in and insist she return to bed. Her ankles and hands were always puffy and her belly had become so large it was difficult to move.

A month before her twenty-first birthday she went into labour. She wasn't sure if it was the right time for the baby to come, but whether she liked it or not, it was on its way. During the night there had been a terrible storm and the rain and wind still lashed against the window panes making them rattle. Edith tried to reassure her that everything would be all right, but Georgina took one look at her and hustled Edith out of the room.

Outside her door Olivia could hear a heated exchange although not everything they were saying. Only snatches of words carried across to her but they were enough to send a chill through her. ' . . . made her leave . . . long before now! Too risky . . . doctor.' It was Edith who was talking.

'What if something goes wrong? What if she dies? It's entirely possible! Think of Harriet!' Georgina was almost shouting.

Their words filled her with terror. Was she that ill? She didn't want to die! Who would look after her baby if she did? Why hadn't she listened to Aunt Georgina and gone to Oban when there was still time?

A few moments later a flushed-looking Edith came back into the room.

'Am I going to die?' Olivia cried through the awful, clenching pains in her stomach.

'We have no intention of letting that happen.'

'I heard you . . .'

'Georgina wanted to send for Dr Morton, but I've told her it's too risky to chance taking the boat across in this storm. Anyway, there is no need to be anxious. I've delivered more than my fair share of babies.' She squeezed Olivia's hand. 'Everything is going to be fine.'

Olivia didn't believe her but she had no choice but to put herself and her baby in her aunts' hands.

As the contractions grew ever more intense she became submerged in a world of pain. She was dimly aware of the storm outside, of Aunt Edith wiping her brow and encouraging her when Olivia thought she could bear it no longer. It was a side to her Olivia had hitherto only caught glimpses of.

In the end, her baby was born rather more quickly and easily than she anticipated. She went into labour about seven in the morning and her daughter was born just after midday. Edith wrapped her in a towel and placed her gently in Olivia's arms. Olivia gazed down at her tiny, perfect daughter, overwhelmed with love. She had Ethan's nose and mouth. How she wished he could be here – how she wished he could see his daughter and get to know her. But it wasn't to be. It was up to Olivia to love, care for and protect their daughter and she swore to herself that she would do whatever it took to ensure her child's happiness. She named her Charlotte after her favourite female author.

Those early weeks with her daughter were perfect, mirroring the happiness she'd last felt with Ethan. Her headaches and nausea disappeared as if they'd never been, along with the feeling someone wished her harm. She still heard the pitter patter of mice or rats on the floorboards above her room, but apart from that there were no other noises, or strange visitations to alarm her. Only once did she wake from a nap to feel certain that someone had been looking down at her. If it *was* Lady Sarah than she clearly meant no harm. For the first time it felt as if the house was wrapping its arms around her. Edith no longer locked her door but Olivia was content to stay in her room, feeding her baby and caring for her. Edith brought nappies she had found in a linen cupboard, showing Olivia how to fold and pin them. Georgina visited too, smiling down at the baby and agreeing that yes, Charlotte was the most beautiful baby she'd ever seen.

On her twenty-first birthday Georgina brought up a cake she'd made herself. It wasn't much of one, being lop sided and hardly risen, but Olivia was touched her aunt had made an effort.

While Olivia ate, Georgina held Charlotte, gazing down at the infant in her arms with a tender smile.

'Now she's here,' Georgina said, 'you'll be wanting to make plans for the future.'

'I'd like us to stay at Greyfriars,' Olivia replied. 'Wouldn't that be all right?'

'Greyfriars isn't a place for a young woman. We are very isolated.'

'I don't mind,' Olivia said, taking a large bite of cake. Now her headaches and nausea had completely disappeared her appetite had returned with a vengeance. 'I have my daughter to care for and more books than I could ever read. When I'm back on my feet I could go into Oban if I wanted a change of scenery. There must be a bus we can take.' She smiled across at her peacefully sleeping child. 'She'll probably need all my attention for the first few months anyway.'

Georgina had seemed deep in thought while Olivia had been speaking. 'You do know that you have a part share of the house in Edinburgh, don't you? And that now you are twenty-one you come into your inheritance?'

'As I'm due to inherit a share of Greyfriars,' she reminded her aunt. Being a mother had brought back her courage.

'Edith and I have talked it over and this is what we suggest. The tenants in Edinburgh moved out a couple of months ago and Edith and I had thought of selling – with your agreement, of course. But if you are agreeable then we think it would be a lovely home for you and Olivia. In return we only wish you to sign over your share of Greyfriars to us.'

It was an astonishing proposal. Olivia had no idea what the relative worth of either property would be, but that wasn't what mattered. She didn't wish to give up Greyfriars. She still believed she and Charlotte could be happy here. The house in Edinburgh could be sold and the proceeds used to bring Greyfriars back to life. If her aunts were uncomfortable sharing the house, then she and the baby could move into one of the cottages. Although in a house this size they could easily live together while all having their own part. She told Georgina her thoughts.

When her aunt frowned, Olivia noticed the anxious lines on her forehead had deepened. Having Olivia to stay and being forced to look after her had clearly been a strain.

'Of course you should be able to stay here, but with Edith the way she is . . . She really does need peace and quiet. She finds the sound of the baby crying quite upsetting.'

What precisely did Georgina mean with Edith being the

way she was? Her aunt was different, sadder and more aloof than Olivia remembered but Georgina seemed to be implying there was more to it. Olivia didn't believe the story about Charlotte's crying upsetting Edith. Greyfriars was so large, its walls so thick, Edith could hardly be disturbed by Charlotte. But she couldn't shake the feeling that Edith – *or something* – wanted her gone.

'If we lived in one of the cottages, we wouldn't bother her.' Quite frankly, Olivia would far rather not share the house with Aunt Edith either.

Georgina shook her head. 'The cottages will require a great deal of work to make them habitable. They've rather fallen into a state of disrepair.' She hesitated. 'Didn't you say that Agnes was looking for work in one of the cities? Why don't you write to her to ask whether she would be prepared to go to Edinburgh with you? She could help you and Charlotte in exchange for room and board until such time she finds a post. Don't you think it's the perfect solution?'

In many ways it was. Olivia had enough saved up to support them all for a while – until she decided whether to sell the house in Edinburgh and buy a smaller one. Nevertheless, she was hurt. She was the only living relative her aunts had, apart from Charlotte, yet even Georgina seemed eager to have her and Charlotte leave.

'May I think about it?' she asked.

'Of course, but don't take too much time. We need to make a decision about the house in Edinburgh. We shouldn't leave it empty too long.'

Then something else happened that changed everything. One morning Olivia woke to find Charlotte gone. Her aunts had brought down a cradle from the attic and Charlotte slept in it, right next to Olivia's bed. Now it was empty.

Olivia threw aside the covers and searched every corner of the room. She was beside herself, and couldn't help the horrid imagery that leapt to her brain. Aunt Edith had tired of Charlotte's crying and decided to do something about it. Lady Elizabeth had come for Olivia's child when she couldn't find her own . . .

Olivia took a deep breath to calm herself. That was nonsense. Far more likely Charlotte had been crying and one of her aunts had heard her and crept in to take her before Charlotte woke Olivia. But she never slept through Charlotte's crying! Even a snuffle was enough to put Olivia on full alert.

At that moment she heard the sound of footsteps above her head and coming from the nursery. If someone had taken Olivia, that's where they'd be. She threw on her dressing gown and rushed upstairs, her breath catching in her throat, almost sobbing with fear and the need to find her child.

She flung open the nursery door to find Edith, a wild look on her face, holding Charlotte, pressed tightly, too tightly against her.

'Aunt Edith! What are you doing?'

Her aunt looked through her as if she wasn't there. Before Olivia could reach for her child, Georgina appeared at Olivia's elbow, panting as if she too had been running.

She placed a hand on Olivia's arm and stepped towards her sister. 'Let me have the baby, Eadie,' Georgina said softly.

Edith said nothing, just hugged Charlotte closer. Olivia's daughter began to wail.

Still speaking quietly, Georgina gently removed Charlotte from Edith's arms and passed her over to Olivia. 'Take her back to your room. I'll see to Edith.'

Olivia knew then she had no choice but to leave Greyfriars.

Chapter Twenty-Two

Charlotte

1984

The sun was sinking, casting the room in shadow, by the time Mum finished speaking.

'I was really frightened,' she whispered. 'After the episode in the nursery I became more convinced than ever that there were ghosts, or spirits – call it what you will – haunting Greyfriars and that whoever it was wanted me gone. It all seems so unlikely now. It seemed unlikely then but I couldn't convince myself it was just a feeling no matter how much I tried. Sometimes I thought I was losing my mind. And then when I found Edith with you – the look on her face – the way she clutched you – I was more scared than ever. It was easier in the end to leave . . . '

It was almost impossible to imagine Mum being so scared. She'd always appeared fearless to me.

'Of course I wasn't myself back then,' Mum continued. 'I was down. I loved your father and I'd made a terrible mess of things. I was worried about you too. You were all I had left of Ethan and I couldn't bear for anything to happen to you.' She twisted the bedcover between her hands. 'All I do know is that I had to leave and that I felt a huge sense of relief when it was time for us to go. There were too many memories, too many ghosts – real or in my head. If I *were* going mad, I knew I could trust Agnes to protect you.

'I wrote to Agnes and gave the letter to Georgina to post. Agnes wrote back by return. She would very much like come to live with me in Edinburgh. And so it was settled.'

Her voice dropped and I could tell she was tiring.

'It was strange leaving Greyfriars again, this time with a baby in my arms, and in many ways I was sad to be going. But there was no time to brood, not with Agnes travelling with us.

'She was beside herself with excitement. She'd never left Balcreen village, never been to Glasgow or Edinburgh – or even to Inverness. The furthest away she'd been was to Oban.

'I remembered the house – this house – only vaguely from when I was a child. But at least it was familiar and I decided not to sell it if I could avoid doing so. It was far too large for three people but given I wouldn't have to pay any rent, and because I still had some savings I thought we could manage for a while.

'On the journey down, Agnes and I made plans. We would shut the rooms we didn't need, heat the few we did. Agnes would look after you and take care of the house, while I tried to find a job. However much I wished I could pick up my studies where I had left off I knew it was impossible. Pretending to be married by wearing a ring was one thing, applying to university and having to prove it with a marriage certificate, quite another. Of course I'd no choice but to tell Agnes the truth and that I'd never been married. She was shocked and surprised but otherwise said it didn't matter to her one way or another.

'Although there wasn't rent to pay, I still had to find the money for food, heating, for clothes for you, for myself and, despite Agnes's protestations, she had to be given some sort of a wage. My allowance had stopped as soon as I'd come into my inheritance and my savings wouldn't last for long.

'I wasn't qualified for anything. Agnes said I could stay at home while she looked for work but I knew she would never be able to bring in enough to keep us all.

'Finding a job wasn't as easy as I had hoped. They'd ask if I had children and whether my husband was happy for me to work and when I admitted I wasn't married, they'd look at me in disgust before shaking their head. Then my luck changed. Every day I used to leave you with Agnes and go to the library to look through the job adverts in the newspapers. I couldn't afford to buy them. One day, the head librarian, Miss Walker, approached me. She had just lost an assistant who had left to get married and she wondered if I'd consider the position.

'I told her I was a single mother, but luckily Miss Walker was always ahead of the rest of the world in the way she thought. She said we could keep that to ourselves and as long as I continued to wear my ring, no one, as far as she was concerned, need be any the wiser. We both owe Miss Walker a great deal. The pay was poor and it was a good thirty-minute walk away, but I had access to all the books I could ever want to read and the salary was enough, if I were very careful, to support us all.

'They were happy years. Initially I regretted I couldn't send you to St Michael's until I remembered how unhappy I'd been there, so I sent you to the local school. When you got older, Agnes used to bring you to the library and you would sit there, engrossed in a book, until it was time to go. By the time you were eight your general knowledge was phenomenal.'

Those days came back to me in a heady rush. The silence, apart from the ticking of the clock on the wall or the whispered discussions between librarian and customer.

I loved the order. All the books with their spines facing out and always in the right place. When I'd had enough of reading, I'd prowl the shelves making sure each book was in the correct position. I was so good at it, it became my job. Was that where my obsession with order had begun?

Above all, I loved the books, their smell, the joy of having so many to choose from. Each book a new world to step in to. I read indiscriminately, Mum never vetoing my choice.

162

Whether it was Enid Blyton, Dickens, Dostoevsky or reference books, I read them all with equal enjoyment. I'd sit at the large table in the centre of the room, occasionally glancing up at Mum at the desk as she dealt with a query. She'd give me a quick smile before going back to helping the customer.

'It was the best place in the world.'

'Your appetite for reading was always voracious. Miss Walker noticed it too. She'd read English at Cambridge and thought it was exactly the right place for you. Between us we decided you would go. We agreed I would give you extra lessons in history and philosophy and discussed the literary greats with you, while she would tutor you in mathematics and science. We didn't know what you would do, we only knew you were destined for great things.

'Sometimes I worry that we – I – you were my responsibility after all – pushed you too hard.' She gave me a rueful look. 'With hindsight I realise I wanted you to have the future that I couldn't. I expect I'm not the only mother who tries to live out her broken dreams through her child. I often wondered, especially lately, if I did the right thing?' She looked at me anxiously, seeking reassurance.

'I'm very grateful you did push me, Mum. I don't think I've ever thanked you for all the time and effort you put into educating me.' I was horribly aware of how stiff I sounded. I took her hand. 'Thank you.'

Mum's too-pale face coloured. 'You are very welcome.'

An awkward silence fell. I should tell Mum I was sorry and that I loved her, but the words stuck in my throat. Habits of a lifetime were difficult to change. Three little words and I couldn't say them – no matter how much I felt them. I blinked away the tears that burned behind my lids and swallowed to ease my aching throat.

But Mum wasn't finished. 'I think something's troubling you – and not just what's happening with me – am I right?'

I shook my head.

'Please, Charlotte, tell me. I want to know.'

Mum had shared so much with me, was it fair that I didn't share some of my life with her? I realised now that by keeping stuff from her I wasn't protecting her, I was shutting her out.

'I'm worried I might have got someone off I shouldn't have,' I admitted.

'Not Mrs Curtis?'

'No. A rapist.'

'Is there anything you can do to put it right?'

I sighed. 'Not without sacrificing my career.'

'Oh, Charlotte, there's more to life than work. I wish I believed you were happier.' She held up a hand when I started to protest. 'I don't think there's much joy in your life. When did you last do something just for the sheer fun of it? Promise me when I'm gone, you'll try and find more joy. Seize life! Take risks! Let yourself go sometimes and do something crazy. Not everything has to be perfect. You don't have to be perfect.'

I wasn't sure how I felt about her words – whether I was hurt, or indignant.

'I'll do my best, Mum. I promise.'

I wasn't convinced she believed me. 'What about Georgina and Edith? Did you hear from them again?' I said, wanting to move the conversation back to Mum.

Mum looked disappointed. I knew she longed for me to confide more. 'Not until that letter. You, Agnes and I were so settled and happy here, Greyfriars and my aunts faded from my thoughts.'

'It was only when I started putting my affairs in order that I realised we'd never formalised the arrangement about the houses. I still owned a share in Greyfriars and the aunts still owned the larger share of this house.

'Since that getting that letter I've been thinking. I'd been selfish not thinking of my aunts. They were still living at Greyfriars, more than thirty years later. It didn't make sense. I regret not doing more to keep in touch. I wonder now whether Edith had — what do they call it now? Post-traumatic stress disorder — shell shock as it was called when I was young.'

It was the aunts who should feel bad, not Mum.

Everything about Greyfriars seemed so improbable — ghostly visitations, two strange aunts, one of whom might have PTSD — a house cut off from the rest of the world. It still didn't explain what help they wanted now or why they'd exchanged their share of the house in Edinburgh for Mum's share of Greyfriars. Although they had never made it official, it had clearly been their intention.

Kerista Island and Greyfriars had to be worth something. But surely relatively little compared to a large house in Edinburgh. Perhaps it was an act of great kindness to my mother — or guilt that they hadn't done more for her? In which case, why encourage her to leave Greyfriars all those years ago when Mum, on her own and with a small baby, needed them most? But to be fair, that wasn't quite right. They hadn't forced her to go and she hadn't been on her own. Agnes had been with her.

Agnes, so much more than just our housekeeper, had been part of my life for as long as I could remember. At least until I'd gone away to university at which time she'd gone to live with her married daughter in Inverness. And all these years I'd never once wondered how Agnes had come into our lives. She'd always simply been there. Neither had I ever thanked her properly for everything she'd done for Mum and me. Without her help, Mum wouldn't have been able to go out to work, I might not have spent so much time immersed in books, might not have had so much time to spend on my studies — everything that had come together to get me to Cambridge.

Agnes was one of three amazing women who had loved me and cared for me and, apart from Mum, the one who had given up the most — perhaps even more. Until now I had never thought about how fortunate I was. I might not have grown

165

up with a father, but I had been blessed to have been brought up by two women, three if I included Miss Walker, who had loved, nurtured and cared for me. There was nothing that would ever have made them turn away from me. And how had I repaid them? By becoming so wrapped up in myself, I'd barely given them a thought. I was in my thirties and I'd only realised this now. I was deeply ashamed.

'They've never asked me for anything until now and I think they might need my help. I can't go, but Charlotte, please promise you will in my place. It was such a happy house once and it could be again. I have few regrets in my life but that is one of them. Don't you think if there is a way of putting something right, we should? I can't do anything about it now, but you can – for me.'

And of course, what else could I do but agree?

In the last two weeks of her life Mum faded rapidly. In books and films when someone is dying it is usually depicted as rather beautiful; a slow, gentle slipping away, a graceful decline as the loved one gets thinner and paler until, with some last heartfelt and meaningful words, the loved one closes their eyes for the last time. It's not. It's a desperate gasping for breath, a horrible rattle, as the soul clings on. In the end she couldn't walk, barely left her bed, and even talking for more than a few minutes exhausted her. She spent more and more time asleep and all I could do for her was bathe her forehead, hold her hand, and just be there. The doctor came once a day – the nurses twice – but I never left Mum's side. I was frightened but I couldn't let her down. I had promised Mum she would die at home and I couldn't break that promise. Agnes came whenever she could and was a constant and comforting presence – a hand on my head, a squeeze of my shoulder, countless cups of tea left at my elbow.

The only time I left the house was to walk Tiger. If ever left on the wrong side of Mum's bedroom door, she would whine until I let her in. I think she knew.

166

Despite the morphia, sometimes Mum cried out with pain and time and time again I wondered whether to have her admitted to hospital – but she had loved and cared for me the whole of my life and I needed to do the same for her.

I moistened her lips with a small sponge the nurses had given me. I brushed her face with my fingertips, reciting poems I knew she loved, humming lullabies she'd once sung to me. I talked to her – remembering childhood holidays out loud: trips to the seaside, castles, villages. And when I couldn't think of anything to say, when the voice dried in my throat, I just held her hand. As Mum slipped away from me a little more each day, part of me splintered apart. She had been the one to hold me together. Soon, she was so thin it felt as if she could float away from me. She slept for longer and longer periods and when she was awake, she was reluctant to eat so I spent hours feeding her sips of milk. I needed to keep her alive and tethered to me for one more hour, one more day, one more week.

One morning I opened the window so Mum could hear the sound of the birds singing – at least I hoped she could.

"'Do not stand at my grave and weep, I am not there, I do not sleep.'" Mum's voice came from the bed, strong and true.

I whirled around to find her eyes on me, bright and clear.

'Oh Mum,' I wailed.

'It's time for me to go, Charlotte. I don't want to leave you, you know that, but please, let me go.'

'I can't, Mum. I'm not ready.' I would never be ready.

'But I am, Charlotte.' Her voice was hoarse, every word clearly an effort.

"'When you awaken in the morning's hush ...'" She whispered the lines of the poem she loved. "'I am the swift uplifting rush ...'"

"'Of quiet birds in circled flight',' I added my voice to hers and she smiled. As always we were communicating best through words others had written.

"'I am the soft stars that shine at night',' Mum continued.

In her own gentle way she was telling me that she would never truly leave me.

I stumbled over to the bed and took her hand. She squeezed mine with a strength I thought she was no longer capable of. I knew in that grasp she was trying to transmit all the love she felt for me.

'I love you too, Mum,' I said. Why had it taken me so long to say those three words? When her gaze held mine I knew what she was asking.

'It's okay, Mum. You can go. It's all right, you can go.' It would be my final gift to her.

In those last hours, when the gaps between each laboured breath grew longer and I knew it wouldn't be long, and worried that she was frightened, I lay down next to her and gathered her in my arms. Her body weighed nothing, her fragile shoulder blades like bird wings and I didn't want to hurt her. I told her that I loved her, that I promised to do more with my life, that she mustn't worry, I would be happy. That she could go.

The sun was setting in a blaze of colour and I was holding her, when she sighed and took her last breath.

I buried Mum four days later, and three days after that, I left for Greyfriars.

Chapter Twenty-Three

The leaves were falling from the trees in earnest and the evenings cooling when I drove to the west coast, Tiger upright in the passenger seat beside me, her nose poking out of the window.

At some point I'd have to decide what to do about her. Agnes had two of her own, and a London flat was no place for a dog. But I couldn't bring myself to return Tiger to the shelter. Mum would never forgive me. It was one more decision to put off until later.

Thinking of Mum brought a fresh tidal wave of grief. I thought I was prepared for her death. I was wrong. Over the last weeks I'd become accustomed to storing up anecdotes and little bits of news and gossip to tell her. Now when I thought I must tell Mum something, I'd realise she was gone and I'd be bowled over by grief again. I felt dazed as if there was a wall between me and the rest of the world.

I'd written to my great-aunts, telling them of Mum's death and saying that I would be coming in her place. Georgina had replied saying how shocked and distressed she was, they both were, to hear of Mum's passing, and how sorry they'd been not to be able to attend her funeral. But they were pleased I was coming and would arrange for someone to meet me at eleven o'clock on Friday morning, at the end of the road leading to Kerista and take me across.

To begin with, I'd intended to go to Greyfriars for a couple of nights; fulfil my promise to Mum, find out what the aunts wanted, agree what was to be done with both houses and return to London where I'd pick up my old life. But Giles had found out about my phonecall to Sophie and that had put paid to any thoughts of returning to work in the immediate future. According to Giles, I wasn't myself. If I hadn't recently lost my mother he would have taken steps to have me removed from Lambert and Lambert and, if the Law Society found out what I'd done, he'd have no choice. In the meantime, I was to take time off, keep my head down and avoid the press. More importantly I was to have nothing further to do with Lucy Corrigle or anyone else involved in her case.

The boatman was waiting for me exactly where and when I was told he would be; at eleven o'clock at the end of the dirt road, leading off from the main road that ran through Balcreen. The sun was nowhere to seen, the rain falling in a fine but unremitting drizzle, making everything appear grey and colourless. Or perhaps it was a reflection of my state of mind?

Somewhere around fifty, the boatman had an interestingly craggy face, and was wearing a thick jumper with a hole on one elbow and a peaked cap.

'Miss Friel?' he said as I got out of my car. He studied me, making no attempt to hide his curiosity.

'Yes. I hope you haven't been waiting long?'

'Not long at all. There's never any rush around here as you'll find. I'm Ian.' He bent and rubbed Tiger behind her ears. 'And who is this?'

'Tiger. I don't think she's been on a boat before.'

'She'll be fine. Keep her on your lap if you're worried. Now then, how long will you be staying? I'm only asking so I can make arrangements to come and fetch you.'

'I'm not sure. I haven't quite decided.'

He took my bag and led the way to the end of the pier where a small boat was waiting.

'And what brings you to Greyfriars?'

'I'm visiting my great-aunts.'

'Now then, that explains it.' He placed my bag in the boat. 'We didn't know they had relatives still alive. We did wonder. You see they've not had any visitors for such a long time. Not since my father took a young lass over in nineteen-fifty, or was it fifty-one?'

'But that must have been my mother!'

'Well now. Imagine that! She hasn't come with you, then?'

My chest tightened as the familiar ache took hold.

'She died.'

'I am very sorry to hear that.' He pushed his cap back on his forehead. 'Then you must be Harriet's granddaughter. Seeing as the Misses Guthrie never married.'

'You knew my grandmother?'

To my disappointment, he shook his head. 'No, I'm afraid not. But my great-uncle often spoke of the family. They were well known in these parts. The sisters were supposed to be great beauties in their day. Would you like me to lift your wee dog on board?'

'No, thank you. I'll keep a hold of her. She can be a little nervous with strangers. I've never met a dog less like her name.' I lifted Tiger and tucked her under my arm.

Ian reached out a hand and took my elbow. Although I could have easily stepped on board without his help, I let him. I found his gentle courtesy quite charming after the pushing and shoving that went on in London.

'Is there any way I can cross over without calling on you?' I asked, as he pointed the boat towards Kerista Island. 'If I wanted to go into Oban or come to the village to do some shopping?' Tiger wriggled out of my arms and stood on the seat right at the front, lifting her nose to sniff the wind. It appeared being on the boat didn't frighten her at all.

'I come over with the groceries once a week – we have the store in Balcreen – I'm due to make a delivery the day after tomorrow so if you need anything just let me know.'

171

'Then you do know my aunts.'

He lifted a shoulder. 'I wouldn't say I know them, exactly. To be honest, I can't say I've spoken to them more than once or twice. I leave the groceries on the pier. I'd be quite happy to bring them up to the front door,' he gave a small shake of his head, 'but they prefer me just to leave them so they can fetch them later. The only way I knew I was to take you across was because they left me a note along with their list.'

How very odd. There were people who liked their privacy and there were recluses. It appeared my great-aunts fell in to the latter category. Clearly nothing much had changed since Mum had last been here.

'As I said, if there is anything you want from the shop you can add it to the Misses Guthrie's list,' Ian continued, as he pushed the boat away from the pier and picked up the oars. 'They leave it for me in a jar. Keeps it dry.'

'I gathered they aren't on the phone.'

'There's the kiosk in the village, if you need one. It's usually in working order. If you want me to come fetch you, raise the flag and I'll be over eventually. If that's too much trouble, there's a small boat just like this one on the other side, in the boathouse by the pier. The Misses Guthrie never use it but I keep it in good repair just in case. You could row yourself across. Mind you, I wouldn't advise it in stormy water or when it's dark. You could get blown off course and end up on the rocks.'

'I think I can manage a bit of a swell,' I protested.

He shot me a look of alarm. 'No, indeed, you mustn't. The sea is calm now, but it can get blustery and the tide has quite a pull on this narrow bit between the island and the mainland. You wouldn't want to find yourself in the open sea now, would you? Then we'd have to get the coastguard out looking for you. They wouldn't be best pleased.' He grinned. 'Particularly seeing as one of them is me.'

'I promise I'll be careful,' I replied, with an answering smile. 'It's not far at all, is it?'

172

We were almost across already.

'You'll be fine, I'm sure. As long as you remember what I said – stick to good days, decent weather and daylight.'

We had spent long enough discussing the subject. I refused to be dependent on notes and the availability of Ian, no matter how pleasant he was, to get on and off Kerista. If I needed to use the phone in the village I could easily manage ten to fifteen minutes of rowing.

He drew up alongside a rickety pier that looked far more dangerous than any short sea crossing, and jumped out. He helped me off the boat with the same old-fashioned courtesy he'd helped me in. I half-expected him to tip his hat when I paid him.

'That's the path to Greyfriars,' he said, pointing to a wall of overgrown rhododendrons. No wonder I hadn't been able to see the house from the other side. Covered in a thick mass of leaves, with their branches curled in on each other, they created a natural wall between the pier and the house, blocking the house from view. A well-worn track led up to the tiniest gap through them which had to be the path he meant.

The dismay on my face must have been evident.

'One day that house will be swallowed up by those bushes, mark my words. They need taking out or at least cutting back. I've offered to do it but,' he shrugged, 'the Misses Guthrie would rather leave it. Now would you like me to carry your bag up to the house for you?'

'Thank you. I'll manage. '

He seemed disappointed, but with a last cheerful wave, he stepped back onto the boat, pushed it away from the pier and set off back to the other side.

As I tentatively pushed my way through the narrow path between the rhododendrons, the branches of the bushes snagged my clothes. Something rustled in their depths and I started, but it was only a bird whose nest I'd disturbed. Apart from the chirping of the small bird as it flew away and the discordant kraw kraw of a crow, it was spookily quiet.

Emerging from the bushes, I placed my bag on the ground to take in my first proper sight of Greyfriars – the house where I'd been born and that had once meant so much to Mum.

It was nothing like I'd expected and almost impossible to conjure it up the way it had been in 1939. Greyfriars House had undoubtedly been grand in its day, but any evidence of that had long gone. Although I knew that the house had changed in the years between the war and Mum's arrival in 1950, I was unprepared and dismayed for how much more it had deteriorated. I realised that when I'd visualised Greyfriars it had been lit up, filled with Bright Young Things, people, life. It had been that impression that had stayed with me. Now, in the lowering light of a rain-filled sky, all I could feel was a sense of menace. Far easier to see it how Mum must have when she'd arrived cold, miserable and desperate all those years ago.

The ground in front of me, where they'd had picnics and played croquet had once been lawn, but now the grass was almost waist high, flattened in lines where my great aunts must still walk. The house itself was almost taken over by ivy, which clambered up the walls, almost obscuring the windows on the first two floors, the rose bushes climbing up the front wall, running wild.

Shutters hung off windows, flapping disconsolately in the wind, the paint on the windows and front door peeling. The sandstone had cracked and this morning's heavy rain trickled from gutters that badly needed repairing. The window-panes were grimy, the curtains closed or half-closed.

On the right as I stood facing Greyfriars was the crenelated tower in which Mum had slept as a child, clearly a different period to the rest of the house but blending in well enough. A little below and running the length of the main house was a row of small dormer windows. That had to be the floor where the servants would have once slept. On the first floor, there were two bay windows on either side of the house with six large sash windows in between them. The ground floor was similar to the one above, but with the run of sash windows replaced by more bay windows.

I couldn't shake the impression that the house looked as if it were a living, breathing entity and not an inanimate object made of bricks and mortar. Squatting amongst the high grass, the house gave off an atmosphere of decay, ruin, hard times, even despair. It wasn't like me to be fanciful – I hadn't inherited the slightest morsel of my mother's imagination – but there was something about the landscape, the eerie half-light, the sensation that the rest of the world had disappeared like some sort of Brigadoon, that creeped me out. Even Tiger seemed affected. She huddled close to me and through the material of my jeans I could feel her body trembling. I picked her up and held her close. A frisson ran through me. I was sure I was being watched.

I looked up, scanned the front of the house and from the turret window I thought I saw a face peering down at me. Before I could be sure, the person, if indeed it had been someone, had disappeared. Thinking of my mother had no doubt conjured up that particular vision. I gave myself a mental shake. Why shouldn't there be someone watching out for me? I was an expected visitor after all. I turned my attention back to the house.

Despite the air of decay, the leaking gutters, broken shutters, damaged chimney pots, in which I was certain from the noise coming from the roof rooks were nesting, the house was still magnificent. It needed a team of gardeners and another team of workmen along with a great deal of money to restore it to what once would have been its former glory, but there was no doubt it could be done. Left any longer, though, and I suspected it would be beyond salvation.

Was this why the aunts had invited Mum to visit? Not because of any belated attempt to get to know their only niece, but rather to persuade her to sell the house in Edinburgh and use the funds to repair Greyfriars? I thought about Mum and how she must have felt arriving here, pregnant and alone, hoping for a comfort she hadn't received. I felt a fresh pulse of anger towards the two occupants.

I placed Tiger back on the ground, lifted my suitcase and strode towards the front door. I would find out what the aunts wanted, sort out the matter of the houses and get back to my life.

As I raised my hand to knock, the door was opened by a slim woman, taller than me by a couple of inches. Her grey hair was gathered in a knot on top of her head and held in place with a pencil, stray wisps falling around her face. Intense, intelligent, lively blue eyes were framed with still dark lashes. Her pale face was lined, but it wasn't difficult to see that once she had been beautiful. The phrase 'ageless beauty' leapt to mind. She was wearing a summer dress that came to just below her knees and which reminded me of those worn by heroines in movies set in the forties, and over it a thick cardigan that looked hand-knitted and a string of pearls around her neck. Her lips were outlined in perfectly applied bright red lipstick, but bizarrely she was also wearing wellingtons – as if she were about to go and work in a field. Yet somehow she carried off the look with aplomb.

'You must be Charlotte,' she said, flashing a disarmingly charming smile, and immediately I saw a glimpse of the young Georgina my mother had described so vividly. Yet despite the smile I thought I saw a flicker of anxiety in the depths of her eyes. She held out her hand. 'I'm your great-aunt Georgina.' Her voice was exactly like a BBC newscaster, low pitched and perfectly modulated. She looked down at Tiger who was at my feet.

'You brought a dog? We didn't think ... Oh, dear ... ' Her forehead furrowed.

Tiger looked up at Georgina with soulful eyes and gave an ingratiating wag of her tail.

'Tiger was Mum's dog. I had to bring her. There was no

176

one else to look after her. But she's no trouble – she's very well behaved, I promise.'

'No ... I'm afraid ... A dog! Edith doesn't like dogs. She's a little frightened of them.' She looked over my shoulder as if searching for someone to take Tiger away.

'I'll keep her with me at all times. She can sleep in my room, or the kitchen if you prefer. On the floor, of course. I brought her blanket as well as her water and food bowls.'

Georgina still looked uncertain. 'As long as you don't let her run about the house,' she conceded eventually, 'it should be all right. Please, do come in.'

She stood back and I stepped into the hall, blinking in the sudden darkness. Lit by a single pendant light it was gloomy even compared to the dull day outside and was large enough that a good proportion of my flat in Bloomsbury would have fitted into it. It was dominated by a wide, mahogany turned staircase. Facing the stair and taking up a large part of the wall was the original fireplace, the stone above it soot-stained, the grate empty apart from the charred remains of a fire. It could have done with being lit. Not just to add some cheer but because it was bone-chillingly cold. The temperature had to be several degrees below that outside. I suppressed a shiver.

'I do love big rooms, don't you? But they can be impossible to heat. I do envy those people who have central heating, although I gather it is terribly expensive. On the other hand, one doesn't really miss what one never had.' Georgina spoke with a determined cheerfulness that didn't quite ring true.

'Edith will be along in a moment,' she continued. 'Shall we go into the library? It gets the best of the sun. What little we get.' She waved her hand in the direction of the staircase. 'Leave your bag here for the time being. I'll show you to your room once we have tea.'

Without waiting for a reply, she turned, leaving me to follow her into a room to the immediate right of the front door. Thankfully it was a good deal warmer than the hall, although not a whole lot brighter. If a fire hadn't been burning in the grate, the room would have been almost as dark as the hall. I decided if I ever got the opportunity I would personally rip the ivy from the windows.

'This is the library – was once the library I should say – we use it as our drawing room now.'

The room had to have been beautiful once and, apart from its frayed, dusty look, still was. It was furnished with a sofa, several chairs, a dainty sideboard and a piano. The blue wallpaper was silk and although damp patches bloomed in places, it was easy to imagine how lovely it had once been. The ceiling was high with elegant cornicing and an intricate ceiling rose. Most striking were the floor-to-ceiling mahogany shelves that lined two out of the four walls, containing what had to be hundreds of leather-bound books and I itched to run my fingers along their spines.

A silver tray, complete with a silver tea set and china cups and saucers, was already laid out on a small side table. Also on the tray was a small plate of biscuits. Wagon Wheels.

Georgina caught my look. 'They're Edith's favourite. Just as well, as the store doesn't offer too many alternatives. Speaking of whom, where has Edith got to?'

Georgina folded her hands and glanced around the room. I was just about to tell her I'd thought I'd seen her looking out from the turret window when a voice came from the doorway.

'I'm right here. When you told me Charlotte had arrived I thought I should make the tea. You know how far away the kitchen is.'

The voice was as perfectly modulated as Georgina's, but more hesitant and barely above a whisper. Edith was a couple of inches shorter than her sister and plump, without being fat. She was wearing a skirt that once must have been part of a suit, a white blouse that had become discoloured with age and had one or two stains, recent or historical I couldn't tell, a cardigan of the palest blue, thick stockings wrinkled around the ankle, and stout, practical shoes and her grey hair looked as if she'd cut it herself with a pair of blunt scissors. Like Georgina, her face was lined, and there were age spots on the back of her hands. But it was her pale blue eyes that caught my attention. Where Georgina's were lively, hers were expressionless, almost blank, and never seemed to rest on anyone or anything for any length of time.

Edith gave her sister a small nod and almost imperceptibly Georgina relaxed.

Edith placed an old-fashioned kettle on the tray. It looked completely incongruous next to the silver tea set. 'You must be Charlotte. I am your great-aunt Edith. How do you do?' It was then she noticed Tiger. 'A dog! Oh, Georgina, a dog!'

'Charlotte brought her mother's dog, dear. But you are not to be anxious. Charlotte will keep her with her at all times.' She stressed the last three words and gave me a quick glance.

'As long as she does,' Edith replied. 'We can't have a dog running all over the house – you know we can't!'

'I will make sure she doesn't,' I promised.

Georgina waved towards an armchair. 'Please, do sit down, Charlotte.'

As soon as I sat, a cloud of dust rose from the cushions, making me sneeze. My aunts sat too, side by side on the sofa opposite me.

'We are so pleased you have come to see us,' Georgina stretched a hand towards me as if reaching for mine, but stopping short of actually taking it, 'but so very sorry to hear about your dear mother.'

Not sorry enough to have kept in touch when she was still alive. Particularly when they knew she was on her own with a small baby to care for, I thought bitterly, my antipathy towards my great-aunts rising again.

'Is Indian all right?' Georgina said, lifting the teapot. 'We rarely get visitors and I'm afraid the store doesn't run to Earl Grey.'

179

'Ordinary is what I usually drink,' I replied.

'Your mother was so young to have passed away,' Georgina continued once the tea was poured.

'Fifty-four.' I swallowed the lump in my throat.

'We adored her, didn't we, Edith? She was such a gentle soul.'

Oh, please! Really? Next they'd be saying that they'd thought about her all the time. I stayed silent. These two women had not treated my mother well. At the very best they were callous and self-absorbed, at worst, downright dishonest.

But having registered the neglect, the heavy red velvet curtains frayed at the edges, the sofas and armchairs that could have done with re-covering years ago, a niggle of doubt crept into my mind. I of all people knew how easy it was to jump to conclusions. If I were in their shoes I would have made Mum sell the house in Edinburgh, taken their share and run. Yet, despite the fact that the money would have made their lives more comfortable, they hadn't insisted on its sale. At least not so far.

'My mother spoke a great deal about Greyfriars towards the end,' I said, declining a Wagon Wheel from Edith.

Georgina eyed me speculatively over the rim of her tea cup. 'Did she? I do hope she had fond memories?'

What planet were these women on? 'As a child, yes.'

As Edith added more hot water to the teapot, her hand trembled slightly, splashing some on the table. Georgina didn't say anything, just wiped the spilled water with a napkin.

'Why don't you tell us about yourself?' Georgina asked when the table was mopped to her satisfaction. 'Do you live in Edinburgh? Are you married?'

'I live in London. And no, I'm not married.'

'A beau then?' Edith asked. It was the first time she'd spoken since she'd greeted me.

'No, I'm afraid not. Too busy.'

'Busy?'

'I'm a lawyer.'

Edith's cup rattled on its saucer and the two women exchanged a startled glance. Perhaps they were thinking that I'd use my profession to make things awkward – as far as the houses went. I hadn't quite decided how awkward I was going to be.

'Your mother must have been very proud of you,' Georgina said.

'I believe she was.' My heart gave another, wretched lurch.

Once again an awkward silence fell. Georgina and Edith sat straight-backed, their hands in their lap. I waited for them to speak. It was a technique I often used as a lawyer. People were driven to fill a silence and often ended up saying more than they meant to.

'I imagine you are wondering why we asked your mother to come and see us. We wouldn't have asked, of course, if we had known she was ill. It is good of you to come in her place.'

'I promised her I would. It sounded as if you needed her help.'

The two women exchanged another look. 'How long are you able to stay?' Georgina asked, ignoring my implied question.

'A couple of nights, I thought.' Although I had more time now and could stay longer, I wasn't sure I wanted to.

'But it will take longer than that!' Edith cried. 'Much longer. There's so much . . . '

'Edith!' Georgina said. 'Not now.' She turned back to me. 'We had hoped you would stay for a week at least. What we have to tell you,' she caught her lower lip between her teeth and paused to give her sister another sideways look, 'won't be easy. There's so much you have to know. So much that is difficult to tell, even harder to explain. And we'd like to take this opportunity to get to know Olivia's daughter.'

Get to know me when they'd shown little interest in getting to know Mum? Why? And why now? And what did they want to tell me that was difficult to explain? Why they'd neglected to sign over their share of the house in Edinburgh to Mum as they'd promised? Yet something didn't jibe with that being the reason. That could have been resolved by letter. However, there was no point in speculating when I could ask outright.

I leaned forward. 'Perhaps you could start by telling me why you wanted Mum to come and see you. Why the invitation now after so much time? I got the impression whatever help you wanted from her was urgent?' I was curious to see if they'd mention their share of the house in Edinburgh.

Now, it seemed to me my aunts were avoiding each other's eyes.

'Would you mind if we talked about all of that another time? Edith doesn't wish to be present. She has no desire to revisit the past,' Georgina said. 'And everything we need to tell you begins there.' She placed her cup and saucer back on the tray and threaded her fingers together. 'Would you like to go to your room to freshen up before lunch?' she asked, making it clear that, at least for now, the subject was closed.

I rose to my feet and with Tiger trotting behind us, Georgina led the way back into the hall. I stopped to admire the burred mahogany staircase, running my hands over the two carved lions on the newel posts. Even I could appreciate the hours and the craftsmanship that had gone into the carvings.

'My grandfather had the staircase especially made. He wanted to make a dramatic first impression on his guests,' Georgina said, stopping next to me.

He'd succeeded. But that was back then. What would he think now of the tired-looking carpets, the neglected fireplace, the chair next to it with a spring showing through the seat, the cold damp seeping through the hall, the lack of a window to allow light to break through the unremitting gloom or to warm the flagstones? From the chimney breast came the distinct sound of movement, a flutter, the call of pigeons roosting. I had been right. Birds had taken up residence in the chimneys. I wrapped my arms around my body in a futile attempt to warm myself. Since Mum's death I had been feeling cold all the time and I had to use all my willpower to stop my teeth from chattering.

I picked up my suitcase and Georgina led me up the carved staircase. The carpet that ran up the full length of the stairs must once have been beautiful too, now it was as threadbare as the others in the house, almost worn away completely on the curve of the stairs. I couldn't help but notice the bare patches on the wall where paintings had once hung. It made me a little sad and, despite everything, something softened inside me.

'We had to sell them,' Georgina said, noticing my look. 'But they've all gone to a good home. Some of them even ended up on display in a gallery.'

A stained-glass window dominated the half-landing. Now this was something that hadn't diminished with time! Made from red, blue and yellow coloured glass it displayed a shield, rampant lions on one diagonal and sheaves of corn on the other. On top of the shield was a knight's visor from which a forearm holding a sword emerged. At the bottom was a motto. 'Sto pro veritate – we stand for truth,' I translated, recalling the Latin I had taken in high school.

'It's the Guthrie family motto.' Georgina sighed. She had the same wry look I imagined I wore. 'Easy to say. Rather more difficult to live up to.'

We shared a smile. My great-aunt was proving difficult to dislike. Whatever their reasons for losing touch, their coldness with Mum, perhaps there was more to it than either of us had appreciated? Mum was willing to give them the benefit of doubt, how could I do less?

We continued up a flight of stairs to another landing. To each side a door led off and in front of us were a set of double doors. They were all closed.

'There are two wings to the house. Both are almost exact duplicates of each other, with the old ballroom running between them. Edith and I have rooms in the west wing. We keep most of the east wing closed off as well as the ballroom and what used to be the servants' rooms on the top floor. It's not as if we need the space and it's far too costly to keep the whole house heated. But we opened a room in the east wing for you. It's the room you were born in and we thought you'd prefer to stay in that wing as it's a little more private.'

She opened the door on the left. Almost immediately the dusty smell of rooms little used tickled my nostrils.

I followed her along the corridor, the floorboards creaking underfoot. I noticed the servants' staircase on my right.

'That will take you to the kitchen,' Georgina said. 'It also leads to the upper floor, but as I said those rooms are no longer in use. There are only two bathrooms, I'm afraid – one in each wing. Water can be temperamental too. The electricity still works off the generator, we've never got around to linking to the national grid, and fuel is expensive so we only run it for a few hours in the morning and evening. We tend to rely on oil lamps once we go to bed. I've put one in your room along with matches.'

'You only have electricity a few hours a day?' I couldn't keep the astonishment from my voice.

She gave me another of her brilliant smiles. 'Edith and I are used to it. We've had to cope with a lot worse. We use the back boiler of the stove in the kitchen to heat the water. It tends to be hotter in the evening when there is plenty for a bath. There's usually enough in the mornings for us to have a stand-up wash.'

A stand-up wash? I thought regretfully of my London flat and its power shower. This was not how I imagined things to be. Why hadn't they modernised? Was money such an issue? Judging by the state of the house it was.

Perhaps I should take a room at the inn in Balcreen? It was only a short drive away. I could visit the aunts from there. However, at the very least, I was here for the night. Moreover, taking a room at the inn would only drag the length of the visit out. I could cope with a little discomfort for a day or two.

Georgina stopped outside a door at the far end of the corridor.

'This bedroom faces the front,' she said, opening the door, 'which means it gets the sun in the mornings.'

The room, as faded and in need of updating as the others, was nevertheless delightful. Although the yellow wallpaper was peeling in places and the window frames swollen with damp, ivy hadn't completely covered the large windows. The sun had reappeared and light poured in. The high ceilings gave the already spacious room a sense of being bigger still. It was dominated by a four-poster bed – its curtains having being removed – with a small footstool by the side, clearly to enable the occupant to climb in without having to take a leap. The bed was carved in the same rich mahogany as the bookshelves in the library and a carpet, its colours undimmed by time, partially covered broad, dark wood floorboards. An old-fashioned washstand stood in place of a dressing table, an armchair sat to the side of a fireplace and there was a small writing table in front of the window.

Tiger ran around sniffing everything before settling herself on the rug.

'This is lovely,' I said.

Georgina seemed pleased. 'It's worn better than some of the other rooms. It's not been used since your mother stayed so we've been able to keep the curtains closed to protect it from sun damage.' She ran her fingertips down the rich fabric of the curtains.

'The bathroom is next door. No shower unit, I'm afraid, but there is a hand-held attachment. It can get a little chilly. When the generator is on, there is a wall-mounted electric heater you can use to warm up the bathroom. Like us it has seen better days.' She gave a mischievous chuckle. It was easy to see how she'd once charmed everyone. Including her sister's fiancé, I reminded myself. 'But it works well enough. I put a hot water bottle in to air your sheets and I'll refill it before you retire. I've left clean towels at the end of your bed, the chest of drawers and wardrobe are empty, so there is plenty of space to put your clothes.'

I crossed over to the windows and looked out. Although the trees and the hedge obscured most of the view, beyond them on the other side I could see tips of mountains topped with cloud and, between them and the island, a sliver of the sea. It was much easier, from here, to ignore the overgrown lawns and general shabbiness and imagine instead the charm the house once held.

If the ivy was removed from the windows, the rhododendrons cut back, the beech, rowan and oak trees pruned, the sun, when it shone, would pour in, bringing light and warmth. With a good scrub, carpets replaced or at least dry-cleaned, the windows washed, the years of dust vacuumed away, a polish to bring the wood back to life, it could be a delightful house again.

I turned back to Georgina. 'Thank you for giving me this room.'

She smiled, clearly gratified by my reaction. 'If you need us at any time, there is a bell on the table in the hall. Ring that. We should be able to hear it from wherever we are. Now, is there anything else I might have forgotten?'

'I don't believe so.' They had made an effort to make me feel welcome and I was touched.

'Lunch is at one, supper at seven-thirty and breakfast at eight. We like to keep to regular times for meals, although I have to warn you neither of us are great cooks. In the meantime I shall leave you to unpack and freshen up. I'll knock on your door about five to one if that suits?'

'Shouldn't I just come down when I'm ready?'

I could have been mistaken but I thought I saw another flicker of anxiety in the depths of her indigo eyes. 'We wouldn't want you to get lost. Much of the house is in a bad state of repair and some of the floorboards are quite rotted. I'd be happier if I could show you which rooms are in use before you go wandering about on your own.'

It was clear from the tone of her voice that I was to remain where I was until she called for me. Habits of a lifetime almost made me protest, but it was already after twelve. I would, I imagined, be doing battle with this woman and, as I well knew, picking the time and place gave the advantage. Furthermore, I was their guest. 'Five to one it is, then.'

At five to one on the dot there was a knock on my door. I'd found the bathroom which, with its original cast-iron bath, capacious sink and worn lino on the floor, was as old-fashioned and in need of refurbishment as the rest of the house. After I washed my face I reapplied my make-up and, back in my room pulled on a cashmere sweater over my blouse. I unpacked the few belongings I'd brought and laid Tiger's rug on the floor next to my bed. Then I examined my room, hoping to find a trace of Mum. To my disappointment there were no leftover books, no half-empty forgotten bottles of perfume, or a left-behind scarf – nothing to indicate that she'd lived in this room for the best part of five months.

Georgina led me down the servants' staircase to the kitchen which was at the back of the house and down a short flight of stone steps. It was several times the size of any kitchen I'd been in before, with an original flagstone floor and, like the rest of the house, seemed frozen in time. The range, in particular, looked as if it belonged in a museum. It was black, and at least twice the length and half as high again as any I'd ever seen. Above it and running the length of the wall was a shelf groaning with an assortment of pots and pans, mostly copper plated. In the centre of the room was a large, scrubbed pine table where I imagined the servants once ate and at the far end there was another door which I assumed led to a scullery or pantry.

Yet despite its size, probably because of the heat belching from the stove, the kitchen was warm and cosy. Edith was stirring something in a pot – soup, judging by the smell of lentils wafting towards me. I couldn't help but notice that Georgina was still wearing her wellington boots.

'It's just soup and sandwiches, I'm afraid,' Georgina said, indicating which chair I was to take. We might have been eating in the kitchen, but the table was laid with silver cutlery and china dishes. Beside each setting was a silver napkin ring, inside of which was a rolled-up linen napkin.

'That sounds lovely,' I said. 'I don't usually have much at lunchtime.' The truth was I rarely had time to eat when I was working. I wondered what was happening back at Lambert and Lambert. A knot formed in my stomach. Had I been reported to the Law Society? I pushed the thought away. There was no point worrying about something that might never happen.

I waited until we were all ready to start before I lifted my spoon. The soup was good. Best of all it was warming.

'I thought as the sun has come out I would show you the grounds after lunch,' Georgina said.

'Grounds is a bit of a euphemism for the jungle out there,' Edith muttered.

Georgina smiled sweetly at her sister, before turning back to me. 'Kerista Island is over a hundred hectares. Far too much land for two elderly ladies to manage. At one time there was a team of gardeners to take care of it. Without them, we've pretty much had to let it go wild. Apart from Edith's garden, that is. She grows potatoes, carrots, cabbage and turnips and makes jams and pickle from any leftover fruit from the bushes. Between that and the hens and cow – we make our own cheese – we are pretty much self-sufficient. We bake our own bread too. At least we attempt to. We also make our own clothes – they're not exactly the height of fashion, but they do. Everything else we might need we get from Lovatt's – the grocer's in Balcreen – or order from catalogues.'

It was as if she wanted to convince me she and Edith had a good life.

'Now, what do you know about the history of the house?' Georgina asked, after taking a bite of her sandwich.

'Only what my mother told me. That the original part – the tower – was built in the sixteenth century by the chief of the McQuarrie clan as a defensive tower and added on to over time. That he let a Jacobean supporter use it – to hide his family during the rebellion – and that the clan chief lost his lands and castles when the Jacobite rebellion failed. It was falling into ruin when it was bought by my great-grandfather in the late nineteenth century who rebuilt the tower and added to the house. That's about it.'

She smiled approvingly. 'It's almost everything that's known. My grandfather had the intention of creating a shooting lodge, when sharing second homes in the Highlands became fashionable after Queen Victoria's tour of the Highlands and islands. He called it Greyfriars after the church in the Old Town in Edinburgh which he attended as a boy.'

'And your father inherited Greyfriars on the death of his father?'

'Yes. It was he who added the wings and planted the rhododendrons. And then on my father's death it passed to us.'

'And to my grandmother?'

'Yes, and through your grandmother to your mother. '

'And from her to me.' I laid down my spoon and took a sandwich offered by Georgina. 'And the house in Edinburgh? It originally belonged to your mother, I believe? My mother thought that it was owned outright by her, but that wasn't the case, as I found out. Are you hoping to sell it? Or Greyfriars?'

Edith froze. There was no other word for it. She stopped eating, her spoon suspended halfway to her mouth. Suddenly she dropped it and it fell to her plate with a clatter. 'We'd never sell Greyfriars. Never! Tell her, Georgina!'

I hadn't meant to jump in quite so quickly with my questions – even to my own ears they sounded more like accusations – but I hadn't been able to let the moment pass.

189

'These are all things we need to discuss, but the sale of the house is not one of them.' Although Georgina spoke softly, there was a thread of steel running through my great-aunt's voice. She might be elderly, but she was no pushover.

Georgina dabbed her lips with her napkin. 'Edith usually has a lie-down after lunch. I normally have my nap later. In the meantime, I'll show you the grounds. Say in half an hour? We can speak more then.'

She flicked a glance in Edith's direction. Edith had her head tipped to the side, a look of concentration on her face, as if listening to something no one else could hear. 'You go on up, dear. I'll wash up.'

I stood. 'Please, let me.'

'But you're our guest.'

'I'm family,' I corrected firmly.

'Very well, if you insist. The scullery is through there.' She pointed to the door at the far end. 'I won't be long. I'll just see Edith settled.'

Was Edith ill then? Certainly she didn't seem quite 'there' in a way it was difficult to put a finger on. Did she still suffer from PTSD as Mum had suspected? Certainly she was anxious – almost fearful – and the way her eyes darted all over the place when she was speaking was very disconcerting.

I carried the plates through to the door Georgina had indicated and set them down on the sink. I looked around for a washing-up basin and a pair of rubber gloves but couldn't see either. I retraced my steps back to the kitchen, hoping to catch Georgina before she went upstairs. I was just about to open the door when I heard Edith's voice. She sounded agitated.

'She's a lawyer!'

I stood there, frozen, my hand on the doorknob.

'That might yet turn out be a good thing,' Georgina replied.

'She'll poke her nose into all our secrets. She won't be satisfied until she winkles everything out of us!'

'I thought that was rather the point,' Georgina said dryly.

'But can we trust her? We know nothing about her.'

'That's exactly what I'm going to find out. Now come on, dear . . . ' Their voices faded as they moved away and frustratingly the rest was lost.

Bemused, I headed back to the scullery. I would just have to risk chipping the fine bone china in the Belfast sink. As I ran the water, adding a few drops of washing liquid, I pondered what I had overheard. It seemed clear that despite the letter inviting me, or rather Mum, Edith didn't want me here. And what secrets was I going to ferret out? Hidden bodies? Gambling debts? Hardly. I couldn't imagine two women less likely to have deep, dark secrets. But then I hadn't imagined Mum had had secrets either. And I, of all people, should know that the most surprising people were capable of the most surprising acts. I was also slightly miffed. I thought I was good at reading people but it hadn't occurred to me that my aunts, Georgina in particular, were determined to size me up as much as I was them. She'd sucked me in, the minx. I felt a flash of admiration for her. I wouldn't underestimate her again.

One way or another, I was damned if I was going to leave before I'd discovered what it was they wanted to keep hidden from me. If nothing else it would give me something to think of apart from Mum and the hollow feeling in my heart.

A short while later, Georgina came downstairs carrying an old tweed jacket, heavily patched with leather at the elbows, over her arms. She handed it to me. 'This belonged to your grandfather. Despite the sunshine, it's chilly and it looks like it might rain again. I thought you might need it. You can keep it if you like.'

It was hardly my style but to refuse would have been rude so I slipped it on. The sleeves covered my hands by a good two inches and the hem came to halfway down my thighs. Although it smelled fustily of pipe smoke and mothballs, it was warm.

191

Georgina was wearing a grey trench coat that came past her calves and that had probably also belonged to her father at one time. On her it looked surprisingly chic. Even with the wellingtons.

Outside the door she picked up a pail. 'I'll feed the hens while we're out. I keep the feed in the byre – next door to Daisy. Our cow,' she added.

With none of her sister's apparent fragility, Georgina took long, fluid strides that I had to work hard to keep up with. We walked in silence for a while, Tiger trotting at our heels, breaking away now and again to explore, but always returning before she lost sight of us.

The rhododendrons didn't just form a barrier at the front of the house but surrounded it and we passed through another arch, this one on the west, and continued through a thick copse of oak and beech. As we passed through the trees, we emerged all at once back out into the light. I sucked in a deep breath of salty air. Now *this* was the big sky Mum had spoken of; as blue as a robin's egg, and feathered by light, white clouds, it stretched above us and in every direction there were stunning views of purple and green hills stretching into the distance as far as the eye could see. Anchored close to the mainland, small fishing boats painted in pretty whites and blues swung lazily in the breeze. On the shore, grey slabs of rock encrusted with lichen formed a natural barrier between the land and the sea.

'It's quite beautiful,' I said. 'I can see why you love it here.'

Yet, lovely though the landscape was, I could never imagine living here. The vastness, the large empty space was as intimidating to me as London would be to a villager, as was the unearthly silence, broken only by the squawking of seagulls, the sighing of the wind through the trees and the shushing of waves on the shore.

Georgina's eyes lit up. 'We do. We really do. It's the same all around the perimeter – six miles in total. I mean different views, of course, but all just as lovely. The best views are from the top of the hill in the middle of the island, although I don't advise you attempt the climb. The path is rough and badly overgrown, like all the paths on the island. It makes no difference to us, we know our way around Kerista like the backs of our hands, but you might get lost, or trip, so it's probably better you leave any walking to when you are on the mainland.' She pointed across the sea to the mainland. 'Those are the Black Hills. They have several well maintained trails.'

Half cast in shadow, they towered over the island like a brooding presence and I shivered as if a cold hand had stroked my neck.

'If you want to walk there, you'll have to take the boat to the other side, of course.'

'Ian said there was one in the boathouse I could use.'

'Yes. If you wish. I'll need to get it out for you. I'll do it later and leave it tied up at the jetty.'

'If you show me where the boathouse is, I'll get it out.'

'No. I can manage perfectly fine. I think I remember where the key is kept.' She started walking again. 'The farm is round a bit,' Georgina said. 'Along here.'

We plunged back into the woods, skirted the shore of the island until we came to another clearing, and a small cluster of houses, almost identical to each other and almost as dilapidated as Greyfriars.

'This is the farm, or I should say, used to be the farm. None of the houses are inhabited any more, of course.' She tipped her head to the side. 'They could do with some maintenance, as you can see. Everything could do with maintenance.' She sighed, then shrugged. 'We do what we can to keep the byre in decent condition of course. We wouldn't want Daisy to get wet. '

The cottages needed a bit of work but I could see the potential. They would make lovely second homes – I might even take one myself. We would have to build a bridge—

What on earth was I thinking? I had no intention of burying myself hundreds of miles from civilisation. I would get bored stiff within a couple of days. I loved living in London and hopefully soon everything would be sorted and I could return to the job I needed like an addict craved a hit. I'd find out what the aunts wanted and then, possibly the day after tomorrow, go back to London.

We went into the byre, one side of which was used as storage for bales of hay and old tea chests filled with hen food. Georgina scooped a couple of handfuls of the sweet-smelling kernels into the pail. We left the byre and walked behind the cottages. 'Could you hold on to your dog, please? I don't want her to get in amongst the hens.'

I did as she asked and picked up Tiger who settled in my arms like a baby. She loved being carried. Georgina banged a spoon on the pail and the hens rushed towards us squawking and pecking at our feet. She threw them some feed and deposited the rest in feeding bowls inside the hen house. The floor was thick with droppings so I beat a hasty retreat outside and waited for her while she collected the eggs. I really needed to buy some wellingtons or boots. As it was, my expensive pumps would never be the same again.

'Six today,' Georgina told me happily when she emerged.

She pointed to the east. 'That's part of the mainland. If you look carefully you can see Stryker Castle, once the home of the McQuarrie clan – the same people who built the tower at Greyfriars. It's a ruin now – has been for years.'

I could just about make out the top of crumbling turrets.

'Mum told me Greyfriars has a lot of history attached to it. She wasn't sure which stories were true and which made up. She particularly remembered one about a Jacobite lady and her daughter who drowned.'

'Edith and I were told that same story when we were children. I suspect it was to keep us away from the rocks. Sarah's rocks.' A shadow crossed her face. 'That's what we called them.'

194

'Mum told me that too.'

Georgina seemed to give herself a mental shake and her expression brightened. 'Fancy your mother remembering, but Olivia was a sharp little thing. As bright as a button.'

It was as if the older version of my mother hadn't existed.

The mention of Mum brought back the feelings of resentment. It seemed to me that while Georgina said one thing, her actions indicated another.

'Yet you never kept up with her. You said you adored her. She certainly adored you when she was a child. It was you she came to when she was in trouble – seeking refuge with her only living relatives.' An unbearable sadness washed over me, quickly replaced by anger. 'She needed you – especially as her own parents were dead. And undoubtedly she needed you more after I was born. At least when her parents died she had Agatha.'

'It was your mother's decision to leave Greyfriars,' Georgina replied quietly.

'Was it really? She told me she never truly felt welcome.'

Georgina looked pained. 'I know how it must seem. When you hear what I have to tell you I hope you'll understand. No one ever knows the full story – why people do what they do.' She shook her head. 'I wish I could have been more involved with your mother, more than you can know. I was very fond of her. She was Harriet's child and I loved my sister.' She caught her lip between her teeth and took a breath. 'However, you are quite right. You deserve an explanation – one we should have given Olivia many years ago. It's often easy with hindsight, don't you think, to see what one should have done?'

Her words struck a nerve. How true I knew her words to be. I should never have agreed to defend Simon. All at once, the anger drained out of me.

'I'm listening,' I said.

'Why don't we sit for a while?' Georgina indicated a rock. 'And I'll start my story?'

She waited until we were both perched on our stony seats.

'Perhaps it would be easiest if you tell me what you already know? What your mother told you?'

'It isn't a great deal. That you were once a model in Paris, but went to work in Singapore around the time war broke out. That Edith was with the QAs and that you and Edith returned to live at Greyfriars after the war. That's more or less the sum of it.'

I didn't tell her what Mum had said about her time here when she'd been pregnant with me. Perhaps it was my barrister training – never show all your cards at once. Keep what you can up your sleeve until the right time to reveal it.

'Did she tell you that there had been a falling out between Edith and I the summer before the war?'

I was taken aback. I hadn't expected Georgina to be quite as candid. I was constantly having to revise my opinion of her.

'Yes. Over a man.'

Georgina's eyes took on a faraway look. 'What a boring old cliché. But yes. We fell out over a man and because of that we didn't see each other until November 1941 when Edith ended up in Singapore.'

'Findlay?'

'Yes. How do you ... Ah, Olivia. As I said, very little escaped her.' Georgina took a deep breath. 'It's important you understand how we sisters were, what we meant to each other. So you can appreciate why what I did to Edith hurt her so much.'

There was a slight tremor in her hands, an ache in her voice. But any woman would have been hurt by her sister attempting to seduce the man she intended to marry, no matter how close they were, although I couldn't help but think that Edith had over reacted. On the other hand Mum had never admitted to anyone but me that she hadn't seen Georgina and Findlay actually kiss.

'What was my grandmother like?' I prompted Georgina

when she was silent for a while. I knew from experience that the best way to get people to open up was to start them off with questions they felt comfortable answering.

'Harriet?' Georgina's face lit up. 'She was wonderful. Our mother died when Edith was two and I was three. Harriet was quite a bit older than either of us – seven – still a child herself, but even at that tender age she took over the role of mother.'

'I'm sorry. I didn't know you were so young.'

'I barely remembered Mother, but Harriet did, of course. Apparently I inherited my red hair from my mother. Edith and Harriet looked more like my father.' She glanced at me from the corner of her eye. 'And you obviously have the gene too. Like Olivia.'

Once, especially when I was a child, I'd resented my red hair, although mine was more black than red and only in the sunshine were the copper notes obvious – I kept it short – almost cropped. The Princess Diana hairstyle was in, but unless I was prepared to spend copious time blow-drying my hair, or going to the hairdresser to have it done professionally – which I wasn't – I could never hope to achieve the look so I kept mine short, almost cropped.

'Edith, being the youngest, was my father's favourite,' Georgina continued. 'She was everyone's favourite. We all adored her. She was the one who rescued wounded birds, who made little beds for them in the nursery. With hindsight, I suppose she was always bound to be a nurse. Harriet, as the older sister, was self-assured with a quiet belief in her own worth, the one who poured oil on troubled water. I was the actress – some would say fantasist – the one who liked to imagine she was acting a role in a film that was her life – it's probably the reason I found modelling easy.

'Edith was the defender of the underdog. The only underdog I could be bothered defending was her. Even as a child I was wrapped up in my own life and became more so as an adult. I tell you this so you will judge me correctly when it comes time for you to do so. When we look back at the past, there is always a danger we reinvent it, and the parts we played in events to suit our view of ourselves. I am going to try to avoid doing that, but I know myself well enough to know it won't be easy.'

'We all went to the same boarding school in St Andrews – the same one your mother attended – and were determined to forge our own identities there. It wasn't too difficult because we were all very different. Edith loved to be outside, she played lacrosse for the school team. Harriet, your grandmother, was prefect and then head girl. Harriet was one of those people that others, particularly adults, liked. She instinctively knew how to do – or say – the right thing. I was the opposite. Harriet being head girl made me want to rebel more. It couldn't have been easy for her. You could say I was the bad sister, even from early on.' She held up a hand as if I'd contradicted her. 'I don't say that because I'm looking for sympathy. Believe me, back then, I liked being the bad sister. It had a certain cachet.

'The school expected Harriet to go to university but she met Peter, your grandfather, the son of a friend of my father, during her first season after leaving school and got engaged to him only a few weeks later. Father thought she was too young but Harriet put her foot down – said she would marry him – and that was that.'

Although I had several questions I listened without interrupting. I'd learned it was better to let people tell their stories in their own time. Besides, I was intrigued by this glimpse into my grandmother and her sisters' lives. Perhaps among it I'd find a clue to their later behaviour?

'To everyone's surprise, it was me who did best in exams, despite the constant threat of expulsion, and me who went to university to study French and History followed by a year in Paris where I went to take up a teaching position in a girls' school. I'd only been there a month or two when I was approached by a modelling agency.' She looked wistful. 'Those years were some of the happiest of my life – although modelling isn't nearly as glamorous as people think. There is a great deal of standing around being fitted.' She gave me another of her mischievous smiles. 'Nevertheless, it suited me better than teaching. As a model, I lived the life of a Bohemian, moved in literary circles, mixed with minor movie stars and when I wasn't working, I was partying. Paris was a heady place back then.' She was silent for a while, appearing lost in her memories. 'I don't mean to suggest that your grandmother and Edith were less bright – or less pretty – than I. Indeed they were both more beautiful. I was taller and slimmer though, and that was what was looked for in a model. But eventually all the partying took its toll on me. No one wanted a model who had stayed up all night drinking and looked as if she had. I began to lose work until it almost dried up. That's when I came back to Britain. I let everyone believe it was because of some illicit affair, but it wasn't.' She gave a little shake of her head as if disbelieving of her younger self. 'Can you imagine! The person I was back then preferred people to think she was easy rather than tell them she'd lost her job as a model.'

From somewhere in the distance I heard the sound of a tractor – the only reminder that elsewhere a modern world existed.

'Father passed away in thirty-six when Edith was eighteen and had just started nursing,' Georgina continued. 'I was nineteen and your grandmother twenty-three. Father had been gassed during the Great War and his chest never really recovered. I was in Paris when he died, but came home for the funeral. The three of us clung to each other during that wretched time, seeking and finding consolation in one another's company. We were friends as well as sisters back then.' She ran a tongue over her lips. 'By then Harriet was married and otherwise blissfully happy and your mother was almost six, a content, charming child. Harriet wished she could have had more children but your mother's birth was problematic and the doctors advised her against another pregnancy. I do know it was a source of sorrow to both Harriet and Peter. If they'd had more children, it would have been easier for Olivia. Peter and Harriet were always so wrapped up in each other and it made Olivia a solitary soul. I noticed how much at the time of Father's funeral. Olivia was there, not at the funeral of course, but she'd come to Edinburgh with Harriet and Peter. She was all wide-eyed and not understanding why all the adults seemed so sad. She was brought down by the nanny to say hello then returned to the nursery. It was the way things were but even so. Peter, your grandfather, was an only child, his parents having died in India when he was here at boarding school. He was brought up by a distant relative, an aunt or cousin – I forget which – and not used to physical attention but Harriet was able to reach him the way no one else could.' She smiled briefly. 'It was the way back then. Hugging and kissing in public was considered to be quite vulgar. When Olivia cried it was the nanny who comforted her better. But Olivia was loved. You should know that.'

Even this small insight into Mum's life helped me understand her better – why, until she was close to death, she'd rarely kissed and never hugged me.

'Peter was an only child and inherited the house in London from his father. It was lost, of course, during the Blitz. We inherited Greyfriars and the house in Edinburgh from our parents. My father was ahead of his time in that regard.' She broke off. A cloud scudded across the sky casting us in shadow and turning the air chilly. 'It's going to rain. We should go back inside.'

She picked up the empty pail and we made our way back the way we'd come.

The history of Greyfriars and the relationship between the sisters was all very interesting but I failed to see what it had to do with my being here or, more importantly, why my aunts had asked Mum to come. Was Georgina telling me all this now it because they were worried I would want to sell my share of Greyfriars?

'You were telling me about the fall-out with Edith?' I asked in an attempt to re-focus the conversation. 'I can see why she was hurt, given your relationship. But you've clearly made up.'

I snuck a sideways glance at her. She was looking off into the distance, a slight tremor on her lips.

'That kiss – what I did to Edith – was only the beginning. If I hadn't been the person I was, none of what happened afterwards would have happened. Edith would have been married – would have been safe and happy. It's all my fault she isn't. All my fault!'

Chapter Twenty-Four

'Forgive me,' Georgina said into the astonished silence that had fallen between us. I wasn't sure who was more embarrassed by her unexpected display of emotion – her or me. 'I've never spoken about any of this. Meeting you, talking about my sisters, your mother, it's brought it all back.'

By this time we had reached the front door and, as Georgina had predicted, fat drops of rain began to fall. She glanced anxiously at her watch. 'I should see if Edith is all right.'

Clearly she needed time to collect herself and although I was burning to know what she'd meant by her outburst, I suspected I was unlikely to get more from her right now.

'Is something wrong with Edith?' I didn't say Mum had wondered whether she had PTSD.

She slipped out of her coat and held out her hand for my jacket. Reluctantly I took it off and handed it over. Quite frankly, I would have preferred to keep it on for warmth.

'The war affected her very badly. She doesn't sleep very well. I should warn you that she is prone to sleepwalking. If you do come across her don't wake her, bring her to me.'

I nodded uneasily. I had no wish to come across a sleep-walking Edith.

'I'm afraid you are going to have to excuse me for a while. I must see Edith and then I have things I need to do. Why don't you sit in the library? Stoke up the fire if you're chilly. There's plenty to read.'

I did as she suggested, throwing some coal on the almost dead embers until they caught and flared. The rain had drained the light from the sky and the room was dark, apart from a single oil lamp on a side table. The generator must be off. I pulled an armchair over to the fire and, as Tiger settled herself in front of it with a contented sigh, I rested my head against the back of the chair and thought about everything my aunt had told me.

Which, in fact, was very little. Except that everything was her fault.

I gave up trying to imagine what she'd meant and crossed over to the bookshelves. They were filled with leather-bound books: amongst them the full works of Shakespeare, Walter Scott and Robert Louis Stevenson. There wasn't a recent paperback in sight – nothing since the 1930s. I ran my fingers across the spines until I discovered *Jane Eyre*. It had been years since I'd first devoured it, but I remembered Mum telling me that she had read it several times while she'd been confined to bed waiting for me to be born and how it was the reason she'd called me Charlotte. I turned over the book in my hand as a fresh wave of grief washed through me. *Jane Eyre* might not have been the best book for Mum to have read when she'd been so sad. Together with the gloomy atmosphere of the house it was hardly surprising she'd imagined ghosts and other malevolent forces.

I took *Jane Eyre* over to the chair to read. The wind was rising and the house groaned and creaked under its onslaught. I felt drained and lethargic, the sound of the rain on the windows, soporific. I laid the book on my lap and closed my eyes.

I was jerked awake by the sound of a woof, followed by a low growl from Tiger. She was standing at the door, her hackles raised, her nose pointing forward.

'What is it, Tiger?' I was disoriented, my head thick with sleep.

I jumped up and, scooping her up into my arms, stepped in to the hall.

I had a sense of being watched from the landing above and looked up, fully expecting to see someone coming down, or disappearing up the staircase. But there was no sign of anyone. I shivered. The hall was cool after the warmth of the library. I glanced at my watch. It was almost seven. I had to have been asleep for a couple of hours at least.

It was then I thought I heard a laugh, followed by a murmured response.

'Edith? Georgina?' I called out.

When there was no reply, I gave myself a mental shake. Like Mum had, I was letting the gloomy atmosphere of the house get to me, exacerbating the low way I'd been feeling since Mum died.

I returned to the library and put *Jane Eyre* back on the shelf.

'Are you ready for supper?' Edith's soft voice came from the door, startling me. I hadn't heard her approach. She must walk as quietly as she spoke. She'd changed out of her dress and into a long skirt and a blouse with a frilly collar. It must have been her I'd sensed earlier. Perhaps she'd come down, remembered she'd left something in her bedroom and gone back to retrieve it?

Tiger trotted over to her and wagged her tail, looking up at her with imploring eyes. To my surprise, Edith bent to pat her. I'd assumed she was frightened of dogs.

'I'll just let Tiger out. I'll join you shortly,' I said.

When I went back indoors I told Tiger to stay in the library and made my way to the kitchen. To my consternation, Georgina had also changed. The wellingtons had been replaced with heels, her oversized cardigan with a fine-knitted sweater and she'd reapplied her lipstick. I felt under dressed and at a disadvantage.

'I told Georgina we should eat in the dining room as we

have guests,' Edith said in her breathy voice. 'Instead of the kitchen as has become our habit.'

The thought of sitting at the large mahogany table in that chilly room filled me with dismay. 'I'm more a kitchen kind of girl myself. Should I have changed?'

'We usually do, for dinner,' Edith murmured. 'We like to keep up some sort of standards – especially when we have guests.'

'Charlotte doesn't have to change if she doesn't wish to, darling,' Georgina said. Nevertheless, I was aware I'd been reproved.

'So has Georgina being telling you the family secrets?' Edith said as she ladled some vegetables into a dish. The look she gave her sister was almost venomous. Pointed, at any rate.

'I've been telling Charlotte about how Greyfriars came to be in the family, I hardly think that counts as sharing the family secrets.'

'Plenty of time for that,' Edith said, giving her sister another hard stare. Despite her apparent physical frailty, like her sister, there was steel under the surface.

'I also told her about Findlay – and what I did,' Georgina added quietly. But as she unwrapped her napkin and spread it across her lap I saw her hands were trembling. 'Charlotte had heard some of it from Olivia.'

'You did? I wondered if you would.' Edith turned her pale eyes to me. 'One thing you should know about my sister is that she doesn't always tell the truth. She likes to be seen in the best light.'

The contempt in Edith's voice shook me. Was it really possible she still harboured a grudge against Georgina, even after all these years? In which case, how could these two women live together, apart from the world, when there was so much animosity still between them? At least from Edith's side. The look Georgina gave her sister, although exasperated, was loving.

'She was the beautiful one – you can still see it now if you look closely,' Edith continued with a bitter twist to her lips. 'That's why what she did with Findlay hurt so much. I wasn't much admired – but she could have had anyone. She was the one men flocked around.' Edith drew a shaky breath. 'Everything just fell into her lap. She never took anything, or anyone seriously. Did she tell you she had to leave Paris? That she had an affair there with a married man? Georgina always wanted what she couldn't have.'

So Georgina hadn't told her sister the real reason she'd left Paris. Or was it me she'd lied to? Was she, despite telling me she was going to honest, as Edith had intimated, determined to keep information from me that painted her in a less than favourable light? It would only be human.

However, there was no doubt the look of anguish on Georgina's face now was genuine.

'I didn't always get what I wanted,' she cried. She wound her fingers together and took a deep breath and when she spoke again her voice was steady. 'But you are quite correct, Edith. I had no right to do what I did. No right at all.'

The sisters fell silent and the air bubbled with tension.

'Georgina tells me you were a nurse,' I said, in an attempt to defuse the fraught atmosphere.

Edith's face softened. 'I was. And a good one too.' Her face crumpled. 'At least I was for a long time.'

'You were a great nurse all the time,' Georgina said, covering Edith's hands with her own. 'Now, shall we go ahead and eat?'

Supper was a tinned Fray Bentos steak and kidney pie served with home-grown potatoes and carrots.

'Tell us more about yourself, Charlotte,' Georgina said, as Edith divided the pie into quarters and served me a portion, along with some potatoes and carrots, before doing the same for her sister.

I gave them the bare bones of my life, leaving out the grimmer details about Mum's death. Instead I touched upon my childhood, and tried my best to describe London for them as it was now. On one hand the bankers with their Porsches and extravagant lifestyles – on the other the miners doing whatever they could to hang on to their jobs and not join the unprecedented numbers of unemployed. I also told them that apparently, in the not too distant future, people would be able to carry their phones around with them. They listened intently, as if every word was a morsel to be gobbled up.

'We try to keep up,' Georgina said, 'but it's not easy without a radio. We do get the paper delivered once a week along with the groceries. So hard to believe that we went to war again and for an island we barely knew we owned. Even harder to believe we have a woman prime minister.'

'Do you go to the Lyon's tea house in Piccadilly? Is it still there?' Edith said, more animated than I'd thus seen her and clearly more interested in a world she'd once been part of. She'd spilled some flakes of pastry on her top but made no attempt to brush herself off – I doubted if she'd even noticed. 'We used to go there for tea, Georgina. Do you remember?'

'Of course I do, Edith. And to the Kardomah for coffee,' Georgina said with a gentle smile. 'Do you know of it?' she asked, turning back to me.

I shook my head. 'I think they must have gone.'

I'd come expecting to dislike my aunts, but was finding it increasingly difficult to do so. Once again, I wondered what had made them shut Mum out. Yet what really could I glean from their manner so far? It was easy to be charming for a day or two – keeping a sustained relationship with a niece required so much more.

Pudding was rhubarb and custard and once it was served, they asked where in London I lived, and what I did in my spare time.

I told them about my flat in Bloomsbury but admitted I did very little outside of work.

'But you are young! You should be having fun and making the most of what London has to offer!' Georgina cried.

'If by fun you mean going out to clubs and bars, I never was much interested in them to tell the truth.'

Edith gave me an approving glance. 'Wouldn't you like to have a beau and get married one day?' she asked.

'My work keeps me so busy, I doubt I'll ever meet a man prepared to put up with my lifestyle.'

A tiny frown plucked at Edith's brow as if my answer hadn't pleased her. 'Don't you want children?' she asked. 'Most women do.'

It was a very personal question to be asking so soon. 'It isn't something I've given much thought to. Perhaps when – if – I meet the right person.' Not that that was very likely. Men didn't tend to ask me out. My friend, Rachel, said they were intimidated by me. I wasn't so sure.

Edith shot a look at Georgina, her frown deepening.

What did my desire or otherwise to have children have to do with them? They weren't obligatory. The flash of irritation disappeared almost as quickly as it had come. Perhaps they regretted not having had children.

Georgina glanced at the clock on the mantelpiece and then at Edith. As if obeying some unspoken command, Edith rose to her feet. 'Would you excuse me?' The earlier animation had left her face, leaving her looking every day of her age.

Georgina and I did the dishes together and while I finished drying them she made a pot of tea and set out a tray. I took it from her and we went into the sitting room. Georgina lit the fire as I poured the tea. The room was bone-achingly cold. I had no idea why we hadn't gone back into the library. I was about to ask when Georgina leant forward.

'My – our – story will take some time to tell. I'm going to have to ask for your patience. I have never spoken about it before, not even with Edith, and parts of it are still very painful to recall. All I ask is that you listen and try not to judge me too harshly. When I come to the end you will have to decide what to do. It will be in your hands. However I must ask you

to promise me you won't make up your mind about anything
I tell you until I have finished my story.'

She certainly had my attention.

'How will I know when that is?'

She smiled slightly. 'You will know.'

Chapter Twenty-Five

Georgina

1941

Georgina settled herself against the mountain of pillows and speared a slice of papaya. As the delicious juice flooded her mouth she gave a sigh of pleasure.

From the moment she'd stepped off the ship and into the hot, humid air of Singapore and taken her first breath of its indefinable scent, a distinct aroma of dried fish and spices, swamps and drains, and as far away from the soft, sweet-smelling rain of Scotland or the smog of London as it was possible to get, her heart had lifted. She'd made the right decision to come.

As she'd adjusted her hat, she drank in the riot of colour and sounds of Keppel Harbour.

The man who was to meet her was waiting to greet her at the quayside. He was wearing white ducks and a panama hat. He had an unremarkable face and a well-cared for moustache.

'Miss Guthrie? I'm Lawrence Murray. Welcome to Singapore.'

'How did you know it was me?'

'You're the only single lady. Besides, I was told by your brother-in-law's friend to watch out for the most beautiful woman disembarking.'

Georgina lifted an eyebrow. 'And the fact that I'm the only woman with red hair didn't come in to it?' When he flushed, Georgina took pity on him. She held out a white-gloved hand. 'How do you do? I'm delighted to be here.'

'Not as much as we are to see you.' If possible he turned an even darker shade of crimson.

One of the porters took her bags and placed them in the waiting car.

'I took the liberty of arranging a room for you in a house just off Beach Road. You'll be sharing it with two others – Miss Amanda Coe and Miss Jessica Hobbs. I hope that's acceptable?'

It had been. Amanda and Jessica were rarely at home and when they were, fun to live with. Something made easier by the number of servants employed to take care of them; servants they seldom saw, but who, as if by magic, took away their laundry, leaving it washed and ironed on their beds, who polished and swept the house, shopped and cooked. Although Georgina was used to being waited on this was at another level. The three women even had an amah each to look after their wardrobe, mend their clothes and help them dress. The garden was tended by even more servants, the rose bushes and other exotic flowers assiduously cared for, so the garden was a constant riot of colour and scent, the lawn kept watered and manicured. Apart from the wide verandas surrounding the house, each bedroom had a small balcony, from where they could see the sea, and if they wished they could walk into the centre of Singapore. Usually, however, it was too hot and much easier to call a taxi or hail a rickshaw.

In the months since her arrival she'd thrown herself into her new life. Singapore was a hotchpotch of people; Indians, Malays and Chinese by far in the majority, the Europeans – plantation owners from up country, district commissioners, bankers and merchants and their wives – forming a small but distinct and privileged enclave. And it had no end of delights on offer: parties, dinners, dances, picnics to name but a few. Georgina accepted every invitation she was offered and there was no shortage of them. Single women were in demand. Most nights she fell into bed, went straight to sleep and the next day

211

it would start all over again. There was no time to brood, no time to dwell on the past. Georgina was always surrounded by men, a smile, even the merest inclination of her head would have them rushing to be the one to buy her a drink, but lately Lawrence was a constant presence at her side and kept the attention of the other men from her. Yet, despite the constant round of socialising, all the attention, the hollow feeling inside had never truly gone away.

And now, after almost two years, life in Singapore was beginning to pall. She was tired of the petty rules the British clung to as if they still lived at home. The ritual attached to social occasions completely inflexible; new arrivals left their cards, one left one's card in return, following up with an invitation to dinner, cocktails, or whatever. It didn't matter that there were all these places to go, one always found oneself in the same company, having the same boring conversations with the same people over and over again. If it weren't for the hours she spent at work, then Georgina thought it likely she would go stark staring mad with boredom. Even then, she was little more than a glorified secretary. She typed letters and communiqués, translating them if necessary from French into English, and delivered them, and helped the governor's aides entertain. She suspected she was there primarily as a pretty face, an amusement, a diversion. She was pretty decent at that.

Sometimes she wondered if she should go back to Britain. For months London had been bombed relentlessly and part of her felt guilty she hadn't been there alongside her fellow countrymen and -women, facing up to the Germans, standing shoulder to shoulder, defiant.

The war might be nearly two years old but in Singapore one would never know there was a war. Nothing, not even the dreadful news of mounting casualties, interrupted the countless rounds of parties, lunches, dinners and other social occasions. Neither was it chic to discuss the war during the course of an evening at Raffles – not over early-evening drinks, or over dinner, certainly not while dancing.

She sipped her lime juice and speared another slice of papaya. Britain might be suffering under rationing, but here there was a boom. If the exotic vegetables, fish and fruit Malaya had to offer wasn't enough, one could dine on Sydney rock oysters and smoked salmon that had been flown in from Australia, or strawberries packed in ice from the up-country station of Cameron Highlands.

As she ate, she flicked through the pages of the *Tatler* which she had delivered from America, ripping out the pages showing models in the latest fashions. All one had to do was take the pages to a tailor and within hours one would have a perfect copy. It was the same with shoes. One described the colour and the design one wanted, placed a foot on a sheet of paper, the cobbler drew an outline, and hey presto, a few days later one would be wearing them. She had so many dresses and shoes her cupboard was quite crammed.

She set aside the magazine and picked up a copy of the *Straits Times*. The headline was about some silly issue with Keppel docks and the supply of rubber, the news of the war relegated to an inside page.

The only relevant thing about the war as far as Singapore was concerned was that in the aftermath of the battles in North Africa, soldiers had flooded into Singapore and Malaya to get a break from the front line and there was an increasing number of uniforms amongst the evening gowns – the soldiers, sailors, and airmen bringing with them a holiday atmosphere. A large number were Australians. Most of the British wives disapproved of them – they were too loud, too brash, hadn't quite the manners expected – but Georgina rather liked them. With their slouch hats, relentless good humour and breezy egalitarianism there was something more elemental about them – more masculine than the British officers with their rigid codes of conduct and stiff upper

213

lip. The Australians reminded her of Findlay. Her stomach lurched. Where was he? Was he even still alive? She clung to the belief he was. For him not to be was unthinkable.

In addition to the flood of soldiers, more British Army Sisters, part of the Queen Alexandria's Imperial Military Nursing Service – QAs – had arrived too.

Thinking of the army nurses and Findlay reminded her of her continued estrangement with Edith. In all the time she'd been in Singapore, Georgina hadn't heard from her sister, despite writing countless letters. Harriet had written, of course, and she'd told her that Edith had joined the QAs and, following a stint in Peebles undergoing military training, had been sent abroad. Being abroad wasn't an excuse not to write. Naturally there had been no mention of Findlay.

Her appetite gone, she pushed her breakfast tray aside and threw back the mosquito net. Although she was reasonably acclimatised to the heat – she no longer went an embarrassing shade of puce – it was still almost unbearable, the fan chugging away on the ceiling more prone to push the humid air around the room rather than disperse it. The heat, along with the mosquitoes and other crawling insects, was one of the things she loathed about Singapore. Often, as she had last night, she slept naked finding even the sheer silk of her nightdress added unnecessary heat. Shrugging into her silk kimono, another purchase from Chinatown, she flung open the window and stepped out onto the balcony. Almost immediately the heavenly scent of jasmine and spices flooded her nostrils.

On a clear day, from here, if she stood on tiptoe, she could just about make out the ships steaming towards the port. Always busy, today it was jam-packed with ships and boats, every size and variety, until it was impossible to imagine how they were able to move, let alone enter or leave the harbour. A shiver of unease ran up her spine. That's where it would come from – the attack. If it came. *When* it came.

214

One of the advantages (or disadvantages depending on one's point of view – sometimes ignorance was bliss) of her job at Government House was that she knew things no one else did. Of course she was forbidden to say anything and not everyone at the office agreed the Japanese would attack, but she'd read enough memos as she'd carried them from one office to another to have formed her own opinion.

She glanced at her wristwatch. She was expected at the Tanglin club for a tennis four, followed by lunch, which as usual would go on well into the afternoon. Then home for a nap before dinner at Raffles with Lawrence. Dear, boring Lawrence. He was pestering her to give him an answer. She was approaching twenty-five, quite incredible when she thought of it, and people expected her to choose someone to marry. Whenever they made pointed remarks to that effect, she'd laugh and quip that Singapore was so full of attractive, eligible men, how on earth was she supposed to choose one?

Not everyone found her response amusing. The tedious matrons and planters' wives certainly didn't. They disapproved of her. As a single woman, disinclined to follow the rules and without a mother to try and matchmake for her, she knew she cut a slightly scandalous figure. Both Amanda and Jessica, the women she'd shared the house with when she'd first arrived, had left. Amanda to Australia and Jessica back to England to marry her sweetheart there. It wasn't really the done thing that she had stayed on by herself. But when had she ever done the right thing?

However, her standing ensured that no one dared slight her, preferring instead to murmur about her behind their gloved hands or to put her down as eccentric. She couldn't give a fig what they thought of her.

Furthermore, a small voice niggled, she hadn't met anyone who had come close to making her feel the way Findlay had. The hollow feeling in her stomach spread to her chest.

'Missy Gutrie, your bath is ready.'

215

She'd been so absorbed in her thoughts she hadn't heard her amah come up behind her. Then again she rarely did. Tsing Tsing never wore shoes and was quiet as a cat.

'What dress will you wear for lunch?'

Georgina smiled. Tsing Tsing was Chinese or Malay – she wasn't sure – tiny with thick dark hair and solemn dark eyes. Georgina stretched her arms above her head. 'I don't know. You choose. Perhaps the white shift?'

Georgina went back inside to the relative cool of her room and into the bathroom. The bath was run, Tsing Tsing had thrown in a few petals to scent it and had already laid out her tennis things. Now she was considering each dress in Georgina's wardrobe for a few seconds, before flicking it across with a decisive click.

Tsing Tsing pulled out a frock and held it up for Georgina's inspection. 'This one?' It was mainly white but with a blue collar and matching belt. 'Mr Lawrence like it. And it makes your eyes bluer.'

Georgina took it from her. It wasn't her favourite but it would do. She wrapped her hair in a bandana to stop it getting wet in the bath. She really had to decide what to do about Lawrence. It wasn't fair to continue to use him to deflect other men's attentions. She smiled grimly to herself, irritated. How she hated having to make decisions.

It was really too hot for tennis but they made an attempt at it; Georgina partnered by Lawrence and Grace by her husband, Bill. As the men quibbled whether Grace's serve had been in or out, Georgina shared an exasperated smile with Grace. The men took the game far too seriously.

'Who cares?' Georgina said. 'Why don't we call it a draw and have a drink instead? It's past twelve, isn't it?' Midday was the acceptable hour to have the first drink of the day.

'I'm up for that,' Grace said, tugging Bill away from Lawrence. 'I can barely hold my racquet my hands are so damp.'

Bill and Lawrence knew each other from the Foreign Office. Lawrence was now a major with the army and responsible for intelligence but neither Georgina nor Grace were exactly sure what Bill did.

'Fair enough,' Bill said. 'Although we were just getting into our stride, weren't we, darling?'

As the two men walked off, towels wrapped around their necks, Grace put her hand on Georgina's arm. 'I'm leaving for Australia next week,' she said. 'Bill says I must. Why don't you come too? We'd be happy to put you up.'

'Why now?' Georgina asked. 'Only last week you were saying you'd never leave. What's changed? What has Bill told you?'

'He just thinks it's safer. There's the children to think of. It's not as if I'm needed here. And you aren't either. Not really. '

Georgina suppressed a flash of annoyance. Despite what she'd been telling herself only a short while earlier, it was one thing to recognise one's own limitations, quite another to have them pointed out. 'I doubt we'll be any safer on a ship.' She dabbed the back of her neck with a towel before passing it to one of the waiters who had rushed over as soon as they'd noticed they'd finished their game. She took a glass of iced water from his tray and drank thirstily, her irritation melting as the cold drink worked its magic. 'I can see why you feel you should go, Grace, but I think I'll stay here for the time being.' Georgina had no wish to go to Australia. If she was bored here, she'd be even more bored there. At least here she had her job – such that it was.

'I'll miss you, of course,' she continued, 'but your children will be delighted to have you back. They must miss you terribly.' Grace and Bill's boys, seven and nine, were in boarding school in Brisbane.

'They probably won't recognise me,' Grace sighed. 'I'm not even sure I'll recognise *them*. Children change so much at that age.'

'So it's all settled then? You're definitely leaving?'

It would be the third friend Georgina had lost in as many months. She tried to cheer herself with the knowledge that there were still enough people left on the island to keep the social life alive. But Grace! She would miss her the most. Of all her friends, she was the one who could be most depended on to have fun. Her and Bill's parties were the best on the island, with everyone who was anyone invited. They always went on until the small hours and, fuelled with copious amounts of alcohol and good food, usually ended up with at least one person in the pool.

She felt a flash of shame. Why on earth was she thinking of parties when the rest of the world was being torn asunder? What sort of shallow bitch did that make her?

The sort of shallow bitch who'd ruined her sister's life.

The men joined them a few moments later and ordered another round of drinks.

'Grace tells me she's leaving, Bill,' Georgina said. 'Do you really think Singapore is in danger?'

'I don't think it's the fortress people think it is,' he said, pausing as they watched a monkey swing from the trees and grab a sandwich from a plate before loping away with a pleased chatter.

'There's no way the Japs will ever be able to land on Singapore Island,' Lawrence scoffed. 'Not with the guns we have. First sight of their ships and we'd blow them to kingdom come. And if they do ever land on Malaya, there's only jungle between them and us. It would be madness and quite impossible for them to even attempt it. But just in case, several regiments of British and Commonwealth soldiers have been sent up north. They'll see those short-sighted, bandy-legged blighters off in hours.'

'I'm not so certain,' Bill said quietly. 'I'd be happier if there was more of an RAF presence – just in case. Belts and buckles! Always better.'

'Singapore Island is as safe as it's possible to be. Trust me,' Lawrence continued, with an annoyed glance at Bill. 'No point in getting people all alarmed without good reason.'

That's what everyone said. But Georgina couldn't quite shake the niggling feeling that they said it too loudly and too often for it to be entirely convincing. If it were so safe, why was Bill insisting Grace left? Did he know something no one else did?

The waiters brought their drinks and Georgina took a long swallow, glancing around at the garden boys snipping away at the lawn with pairs of scissors, the waiters in their white jackets and impenetrable expressions, the other couples sipping their drinks, laughing and chatting.

No, Lawrence had to be right. Bill was just an overly cautious older man. Nothing bad could ever happen in Singapore. Nevertheless, she shivered. It was as if someone had walked across her grave.

A few hours later, feeling slightly worse for wear after two, or was it three, gin slings, Georgina left the club for home.

By the time the rickshaw pulled up in front of her house her head had begun to throb and the heat made her tongue cling to the roof of her mouth. A nap before dinner would sort her out.

On her way in, she noticed an envelope on top of the table in the hall. She recognised the writing straight away. It was from Agatha – Harriet's friend. She took it into the sitting room, calling for the houseboy to bring her some coffee. The blinds had been drawn against the sun and the room was dark and cool, a welcome relief to the scorching heat outside.

She waited until the servant poured her coffee and had retreated before taking a letter opener from her writing desk and slitting the envelope open. It was dated the twelfth of May – almost two months ago.

Dear Georgina,

It is with heavy heart that I write to tell you that your sister Harriet and her husband Peter died in an air attack on London yesterday. Their home suffered a direct hit and was completely destroyed. We should find some comfort in the fact that they both died together and probably instantly.

As you know, your niece Olivia is at boarding school in Perthshire. The poor child is understandably distraught. Given you and Edith are both overseas and there are no other family members alive, I suggest Olivia stays at St Michael's (I will, of course, continue to have her on weekends out) until such time you, or Edith, are in a position to care for her.

I am so very sorry to be the bearer of such terrible news. We all loved Harriet and Peter dearly - as we do Olivia.

Scotland, largely, has been spared the horror of what is happening in London, and you can be assured that in the meantime Olivia is safe and well cared for.

With deepest sympathy and fondest love,
Agatha

The letter fell from Georgina's fingers and onto her lap. Harriet dead! And Peter too! She stumbled to her feet, waving away a concerned-looking houseboy and, on legs that felt boneless, climbed the stairs to her bedroom. She mustn't cry, was all she could think. Not in front of the servants.

Tsing Tsing was in her bedroom putting away laundry.

'Could you send a message to Major Lawrence and let him know I won't be able to meet him for dinner tonight?' Georgina said. Her lips felt frozen – her words sounding as if they came from a great distance.

'What is it, Missy Gutrie? What has happened?' As ever Tsing Tsing was attuned to her moods.

'Not now, Tsing Tsing. Please, just do as I ask.'

Tsing Tsing hesitated.

'Go! Now!' It was the first time Georgina had ever snapped at her and Tsing Tsing's face creased with distress before her usual impenetrable mask came down.

'Of course. Straight away, Missy Gutrie. You rest.'

Georgina closed the shutters and lay down on her bed. As an image of the last time she'd seen Harriet flooded her mind – the horrible censure in her sister's eyes – she covered her face with her hands and wept.

*

Night had fallen by the time she woke up. At first she couldn't think where she was, but almost immediately the memory of the letter and its contents hit her like a mule kicking her chest.

She lay in the darkness for a while, crying some more, biting her pillow to muffle her sobs. Did Edith know? Had Agatha been able to contact her? Where had Harriet and Peter been buried? Agatha hadn't said. She had to write back and ask. And poor little Olivia! To lose both her parents at the one time!

She forced herself out of bed. There were arrangements to be made, matters that needed taken care of. She had to pull herself together. She studied her reflection in her dressing-table mirror. Her cheeks were creased and her eyes puffy from crying. She washed her face in the basin of tepid water on her nightstand and opened the shutters, letting what little breeze there was into the room. She stepped out onto the balcony where – was it only this morning? – she had stood, looking forward to her day with anticipation.

There was a gentle tap on the door and Tsing Tsing entered, bringing a tray of tea. 'I know you said not to disturb – I will go – but you must have something to drink.'

'Thank you, Tsing Tsing. You are very sweet.'

Tsing Tsing laid the tray on the table beside an armchair. 'You have had bad news, I think?'

'Yes. Very bad news. My sister and her husband.' Georgina took a deep, shuddering breath. 'They were killed in a bomb raid. Both of them. Together.'

'I am sorry. Very sorry.' Tsing Tsing paused, her hands folded in front of her. 'Missy, Mr Lawrence downstairs. I told him you not to be disturbed, but he not listen. He say he wait.'

Dash Lawrence. She didn't want to speak to anyone, not right now. However, she knew he wouldn't go until she'd told him to leave herself.

She slipped out of her creased frock and into a clean one, automatically slicked some lipstick over her lips, adding a little to her cheeks and rubbing it in. Taking a deep breath she went downstairs.

He was waiting for her in the sitting room, pacing up and down, a tumbler of whisky in his hand.

'Lawrence,' she said. 'I'm terribly sorry about this evening.'

'What's up, old thing? You were all right earlier. It's not like you to cancel. I thought I should check up on you.'

She suppressed a flash of irritation. Couldn't he have left her alone just this one evening?

'I had some news from home,' she said, trying to stop her voice from shaking. 'My sister and her husband have been killed.'

'Oh, my poor darling, I'm so terribly sorry. Here sit down.' He took her hands in his. 'You're frozen.'

'It was a dreadful shock.'

He poured her a G&T, lit a cigarette and handed both to her.

'Darling, is there anything I can do? You just have to say the word.'

He really was very sweet. Why couldn't she have fallen for him? But she didn't want sweet. She wanted someone who would shout and swear at the stupid senseless waste of life – who wouldn't be horrified if she did . . . Of course she couldn't marry Lawrence. What on earth had made her ever imagine she could?

'They had – have – a daughter.'

'Poor child. Where is she?'

'In Scotland. She's boarding at a school in Scotland, near to friends of Harriet. She's been there since war was declared.'

'Will you go to her?'

'I haven't really thought that far. I should really speak to my sister Edith first, if I can contact her. In the meantime Olivia's being well cared for. I can't imagine that she'd wish an aunt she barely knows to swan in and take her—' Take her where exactly? Back to Singapore? Make her risk a sea-journey when the ship she was travelling on might be bombed? Moreover, Georgina was hardly an appropriate person to care for a young girl. Besides, Olivia was at boarding school. Even if Georgina did go back to Britain, she would almost never see Olivia and what would Georgina do there anyway? She really had no idea. 'No, I think she's best left where she is for the moment.'

'We could get married,' Lawrence blurted. 'Then she could live with us when we return to Britain.' When Georgina stared at him aghast, he flushed. 'Sorry, old thing. Wasn't quite the way I intended to ask. Meant to go down on one knee – the whole bally shooting match.' He looked at her with hopeful eyes. 'You know I'm fond of you.' He cleared his throat. 'For God's sake not just fond – I adore you. You must have guessed how I feel.'

Georgina put out her cigarette and walked over to him. She brushed her fingertips across his face. 'And I am fond of you. But it's not enough, is it? You are so sweet to ask me, so very generous to offer to take on a child you don't even know, but I can't accept your proposal.'

'Is there any chance you'll change your mind? You've just had the most frightful shock. I'm such an idiot.'

'You're not an idiot. You are a kind and generous man and if anyone's a fool, it's me. But no, Lawrence, I'm so sorry, but there is no hope at all.'

Chapter Twenty-Six

Charlotte

1984

While Georgina had been speaking, the generator had given up, plunging the room into darkness. My great-aunt's face was a ghostly disc in the dim light. She lit the oil lamp with trembling fingers.

'Would you mind if I continued tomorrow? I'm feeling a little drained. All these memories ...'

'Of course. You go on up. I'll just let Tiger out before I go to bed.'

Recognising her name being spoken, Tiger sprang to her feet and wagged her tail.

'I'll wait for you and take you up.'

'There's no need. I'm sure I'll find my way.'

'Please. I'd rather. Some of the floorboards are a little dodgy.'

We'd managed perfectly well earlier. 'In that case, I won't be long.'

Outside, the clouds and rain had vanished. It was almost pitch dark and silent except for the gentle grinding of waves against the shore. But the darkness made the light from the moon and the stars bright. I had never seen the Milky Way so clearly.

An owl hooted, flying so low it almost brushed my face, startling me.

At this time of night in London the streets would be brightly lit and thronged with people going to the theatre, tourists and cars, the pubs and wine bars packed. I would still be at chambers preparing for upcoming cases before walking back through the streets to my flat for more work, supper then bed. Some might say, Mum included, that it was a lonely, sterile existence. But my own company had never bothered me. I liked being on my own – doing what I wanted, when I wanted.

My thoughts turned to my conversation with Georgina. So it hadn't been just a tipsy kiss as she wanted everyone to believe. She'd been in love with Findlay. I wonder if she realised she'd let her feelings for him slip when she'd been recounting her time in Singapore? How awful to fall for the man your sister hoped to marry. Despite the brief glimpses I'd seen, I couldn't reconcile the woman she was now with the young, vivacious one my mother had so admired and that she'd been in Singapore. However, what did I know? As a person approached their seventies they were bound to slow down, to prefer the more sedentary pleasures of life. Yet, there were seventy-year-olds around who had better social lives than I did (admittedly not difficult) and who were as fit and active as many a thirty-year-old. And it was into this category I would have placed Georgina. Edith was a different matter.

Feeling an uneasy prickle on the back of my neck, I turned and looked up just in time to see flash of light at an upstairs window as if a curtain had been opened then quickly closed again. So Edith had been watching me.

If I had difficulty reconciling the older Georgina with the woman she'd once been, then it was so much more difficult to imagine the nervous, blank-eyed Edith with the aunt of my mother's childhood. She was so slight, almost wraith-like. How did she fit in to whatever story Georgina had to tell? If she played a part at all? No doubt, I would find out soon enough.

I whistled for Tiger and turned and went back inside.

Georgina accompanied me all the way to my door, came in, lit my lamp for me and wished me goodnight.

I paid a visit to the chilly bathroom and had a stand-up wash, leaving my clothes on as I soaped under my armpits.

Back in my room, I undressed quickly, hurried into my pyjamas and slipped into bed. The sheets were freezing and damp, the bottle Georgina had placed there earlier now stone cold. She had forgotten her promise of a fresh one (and I had forgotten to remind her). I tossed it out of the bed and on to the floor, put out the lamp and wriggled around trying to find some warmth.

With the light out the darkness was dense – almost suffocating. I was unable to see my hand even when I brought it to within an inch of my face.

Knowing I wouldn't sleep as long as I was so cold, I gave up trying. I needed to put something on over my pyjamas. Not wanting to go through the palaver of lighting the lamp again to find what I wanted in my suitcase, I opened the curtains.

The clouds had vanished and the moon was a bright, white disc against an inky black sky studded with a thousand stars, their glow illuminating the room. *I am the soft stars at night.* I could hear Mum's voice as clearly as if she were in the room with me. My heart gave a painful kick. 'Maybe you are, Mum,' I whispered aloud.

I stood there for a while gazing up at the Milky Way and thinking about Mum but as I was about to turn away, I noticed a figure standing in the shadows of the copse close to the front of the house. Despite the starlight, it was too dark for me to make out their features. However, I had the distinct impression that whoever it was was looking up at my window. As I watched, the figure backed into the shadows.

Was it Edith and was she sleepwalking? In which case I should fetch Georgina, but I had no idea which room was hers. It was easier to go after Edith myself. Staying by the window,

I yanked my sweater over my head and was about to pull my jeans over my pyjama bottoms when another figure emerged from the house and scurried towards the trees. I sighed with relief. It had to be Georgina. She must have seen Edith and was going to bring her inside.

Keeping my sweater on and adding socks, I retreated back to bed. I was still cold.

If I were to stay here, even another night, I'd have to buy warmer clothes.

Chapter Twenty-Seven

I was woken by the singing of the birds and therefore up a good hour before breakfast. I took Tiger outside. It was a crisp, beautiful day, the sky an endless blue dome with only the arrow plume of an aeroplane high in the sky to remind me that the modern world existed. I slipped through the gap in the rhododendrons, following the route to the shore Georgina and I had taken the day before. I walked up the hill at the centre of the island, following the steep path, Tiger at my heels. It wasn't high, but one side dropped away sharply, eroded by the wind or time. It was probably why Georgina had advised me against climbing the hill.

From here I could see all around the island and as far as the village of Balcreen. Down by the water's edge an otter waddled across the rocks and into the sea. It was so peaceful and I was beginning to understand why Mum had loved it here so much. It wasn't, however, a place I could imagine myself staying for any length of time. It wasn't London and even if it weren't for the fact London was where my work was, I thrived on the buzz of the city, liked having easy access to shops and restaurants, the coffee shops, museums and galleries. Not that I had been to many in the last few years. I intended to change that.

But I didn't want to think about London. To do so was to think about Lucy and make a decision about what I was going to do about her and Annette, and I was in no state of mind to decide something so important.

At breakfast – tea, toast and deep-yellow-yolked boiled eggs – I told Georgina what I'd seen last night. There was no sign of Edith who was probably still in bed – 'I'm assuming it was Edith? I was about to go down and lead her inside when I saw you.'

Georgina gave me a startled look. 'Oh,' she said faintly.

'I was taking a walk, that was all!' Edith cried from the doorway. Once again, I hadn't heard her approach. She trod so lightly. 'Can't I do that without being watched?'

Georgina crossed over to her and patted her sister's hand. 'You're bound to be unsettled,' she said, before turning back to me. 'Edith was never a good sleeper.'

Edith took her place at the table, lifted her napkin and twisted it between her hands. 'I don't care to have guests and I like it even less when they spy on me! Tell her she mustn't, Georgina!'

'Of course Charlotte isn't spying on anyone! The very thought, Edith!'

'I'm just relieved it wasn't Lady Elizabeth searching for her lost child.'

Instead of laughing at my – albeit rather pathetic – attempt at lightening the atmosphere, Georgina frowned. 'What on earth do you mean?'

'Mum told me when she was last here she thought she heard a child's footsteps and the sound of giggling. Sometimes she thought it must be the ghost of the drowned child. Mum always had a rich imagination.'

It was said light-heartedly but I was unprepared for their reactions. Georgina paled and Edith flung her twisted napkin on the table.

'All this chatter about old stories! And ghosts! You shouldn't be snooping! This is not your house. Not yet. It's us who should be watching you!'

229

'Edith! Dear!' Georgina exclaimed.

Edith scraped back her chair although she hadn't touched her breakfast. 'I should get on. I have things to do.' She hurried out without another word.

I couldn't remember the last time I'd felt this uncomfortable.

'I'm so sorry. I didn't mean to upset her. I wouldn't have said anything about seeing her if I'd known she was listening.'

'Edith likes to believe her sleepwalking days are over.'

'I don't think she's at all happy that I'm here. I could stay in the inn in Balcreen, if you think that would be better?'

'No! Please don't think of it! Edith just needs time to get to know you. It's been so long since we had company and she finds it unsettling. You'll understand better why she is the way she is when I've told you everything. However, I should spend some time with her this morning. You and I can talk more later.' She reached for my hand and covered it with her own. 'Please stay a little longer.'

Why not? It wasn't as if I could go back to work just yet. And it was becoming increasingly clear to me that whatever was going on with the sisters was going to take longer to winkle out than I'd anticipated.

'If you are sure my staying won't upset Edith more?'

'She knows it's important that you're here. She's well aware Greyfriars is partly your house too.'

But not home. I was trained to notice what wasn't said as much as what was.

'In that case, thank you. But if I'm going to stay longer I need to do some shopping. Get some more clothes.'

Her expression relaxed. 'You should find what you need in Oban. You could spend the morning there. Apart from the shops there's a lot to see – the harbour, the folly on the hill.'

I had the distinct feeling Georgina wanted me gone for a few hours at least. No doubt, she also found it difficult to have guests after all this time. My two great-aunts were clearly used to spending all day on their own.

'If you plan to go to Oban,' Georgina continued, 'we should arrange for Ian to come and fetch you, although I took the little boat out of the boathouse and left it down at the jetty in case you wanted to use it.'

'Then I'll row myself. It's not as if it's any distance. If I had longer legs I might even be able to leap across.'

Georgina gave a little choke of laughter.

'Why don't you and Edith come with me?' I said impulsively. 'We could have lunch, then do a little shopping. Afterwards you could show me the sights.'

'It is most kind of you to ask but, really, it is impossible.' She gathered the dishes from the table. 'Edith would never agree to go and I can't leave her here on her own.'

Why not? I couldn't imagine there was anything that could happen to Edith on the island. However it wasn't a question I felt able to ask.

'In that case, I'll get going. I'll take Tiger with me, of course.'

Rowing across used muscles I'd forgotten I had but it was as easy as I'd hoped and I enjoyed the unaccustomed exercise. I tied the small boat up next to the pier on the Balcreen side. Tiger jumped into the front seat of my car, happy as Larry.

Oban was around ten miles from Balcreen village, and the nearest large town. I drove into the town centre and parked my car down at the harbour. I put Tiger on the lead and strolled along the quayside, feeling myself relax. Until now I hadn't realised how tense I'd been at Greyfriars. I found a shop selling jumpers – thick and warm although not to my taste – and bought three, as well as a pair of walking boots and passing McColl's the newsagent, on impulse went in and bought a guide book to the West of Scotland. Finally I stopped off at a fishmonger and bought some fresh, filleted trout. I wandered around some more before having taken in all Oban could offer, then returned to the car and drove back to Balcreen.

*

Despite my attempts to drag out my trip to Oban, I'd only been away for just over an hour and deciding it was too early to return to the claustrophobic atmosphere at Greyfriars, I stopped in Balcreen and took Tiger for a walk by the shore. Freed from the constraints of the car and her leash, she ran in front of me, sniffing all the new smells, poking her nose down rabbit holes to investigate, bounding back to me, her bottom wagging furiously, her nose smudged brown with dirt.

Down at the shore and set back from it by a hundred yards or so was a row of cottages that looked abandoned and beginning their descent into ruin. Except for the one at the end. Next to its bedraggled neighbours it was almost jaunty. It had been whitewashed, the wooden surrounds of the windows painted a glossy blue, and a number of fishing rods were propped up neatly next to the door in front of which stood a very expensive-looking motorbike. It seemed as if a stray Yuppie had extended his reach to the Scottish Highlands.

Tiger plunged into the sea while I watched from a bench looking over the shore. Why had I ever thought she would be frightened of water? I opened my new guidebook. There was nothing about Kerista and only a brief paragraph about the ruins of Stryker Castle which added nothing to what Georgina had already told me. I turned to the section on Oban. I was reading about its history when a yip and whine came from the sea. I looked up and immediately saw that Tiger was in trouble. She was trying to swim towards me, but despite her frantic paddling was making no progress. In fact, I saw with alarm, it seemed she was being pulled further out to sea.

I dropped my book and ran to the shore. 'Come on, Tiger!' I shouted. 'Come to me, sweetie!'

But it was becoming clear she couldn't. There had to be a current just beyond the shore that was preventing her from making her way back.

I looked around searching for help, or even a life buoy. There was nothing and no one.

By this time, Tiger was barely keeping her head above water. I had no choice but to go in after her.

I took off my shoes and my jumper and waded towards her, the pebbles digging painfully into the soles of my feet. The sea was icy cold, my jeans sucking up water as if they were a sponge, making it difficult to move. Fortunately, the sea bed sloped only gradually, although I was aware that that could change at any moment. I plunged on, desperate to reach Tiger before she was carried beyond my reach.

'Come on, Tiger!' I shouted. 'You can do it!'

She was only a few yards away from me but the same current that was preventing her from swimming back to shore was tugging at my legs. I was waist deep in water by now and struggling to keep my footing on the slippery stones underneath. Any deeper and I'd have to swim out to Tiger and attempt to pull her in and I wasn't a great swimmer.

'Hey!' The shout came from behind me and I swivelled around to find a man standing on the beach. 'What the hell are you doing?'

'It's my dog!' I pointed to where only the tip of Tiger's nose was now visible. 'She can't get back. I need to reach her.' I kept my eyes on Tiger, petrified that if I looked away again I'd lose sight of her completely.

'Wait there.'

There was no time for me to wait. In a few minutes Tiger would go under and I might never find her. By the time the man had called the coastguard or went for help it could well be too late.

A sob caught in my throat. I couldn't lose Tiger. Not after Mum. And not when Mum had relied on me to take care of her. I sucked in a deep breath and clenched my jaw. Getting upset and panicking wasn't going to help. She was only a few feet away from me. I lunged for her, catching her by the collar. In the process of reaching for her I'd lost my footing and the beach beneath my feet had disappeared. I had to tread water to keep us

233

both afloat. Tiger was panicking in my arms, her claws scratching at my arms and face. I tightened my grip on her collar, terrified she would wriggle free before I could get us both ashore.

At that moment, I felt myself being grabbed from behind.

'Stay calm,' a man's voice said behind me. 'Just relax, but keep a hold of your dog.'

I did as he asked, and felt myself being dragged back to shore. I held on to Tiger's collar. She'd stopped panicking and had gone back to swimming, helping herself along.

Suddenly it was all over and I was sitting on the beach, a shivering Tiger shaking out her wet coat in between licking my face. My teeth were chattering not just from the cold but from shock. My eyes tracked shoes polished to within an inch of their life, upwards past a pair of trousers that had been worn so often they were a tad shiny, further still past a collarless grandpa shirt until I was gazing up at a stubbled face of a man in his late sixties or early seventies. He was looking down at me as if I were a bad smell, fury blazing in his green eyes. A collie sat obediently next to him.

'That was a bloody stupid thing to do. You could have drowned.' A faint waft of alcohol floated towards me.

'I couldn't leave her.'

'She would have managed to get ashore eventually.'

'You can't know that.'

He murmured something about bloody tourists under his breath and before I had the chance to thank him, stalked off in the direction of the village, his collie at his heels.

The wind had sprung up, my jeans were soaking wet, my blouse clinging to my back, water streaming from my hair.

'Don't ever do that again,' I berated Tiger. 'From now on you're a land dog, do you understand?' When she whimpered I knelt on the ground and pulled her towards me.

Mum would have never forgiven me if anything had happened to Tiger. When the realisation struck that Mum would never know, I pulled my knees up to my chest and gave in to the horrible, desolate emptiness I'd been feeling since Mum died. I allowed myself the luxury of tears for a few minutes then I wiped my hand across my nose and sniffed. I couldn't stay here. I had to get warm. Tiger was fine and that was all that mattered.

'Can I help?'

I looked up into a pair of deep brown eyes, framed by horn-rimmed glasses.

'I'm fine.' Appalled at the picture I must be presenting, at how deranged I must appear – my eyes swollen and red-rimmed, hair in rat's tails, face smeared with dirt and probably snot, my clothes dripping onto the shingle – I scrambled to my feet. The owner of the eyes wasn't much taller than me and slim but with a wiry frame. He was wearing jeans and a white T-shirt. His face was too long to be handsome, but there was something undeniably attractive about him.

'You just happen to like sitting on the beach fully dressed but soaking wet?' He cocked an eyebrow and smiled at me. His was a face that was meant to smile.

'No. Naturally not. Come on, Tiger, let's get on our way.'

'You can't go anywhere like that.'

'I don't have far to go.'

His lovely eyes creased with concern or laughter, I couldn't be sure. He reached towards me. When I backed away he dropped his hand.

'It's okay. I'm not going to hurt you. It's just you have some-thing in your hair. May I remove it for you?'

Before I had a chance to reply he'd plucked something from my head and held out a string of brown bulbous seaweed for my inspection.

'Not really the weather for swimming,' he said with a grin and I found myself smiling back.

'Tiger got into trouble in the water. I went after her. I got into difficulty too.' I wrapped my arms around my body, trying to contain my shivers. 'Thankfully someone came after us and helped us out.'

'And he just left you to fend for yourself?'

'I think he was annoyed he had to come in after us.' Bloody man.

'Are you all right?'

'Freezing, but otherwise fine.'

He pushed his glasses up on his nose and bent and rubbed Tiger under the chin. The little traitor wagged her tail as if she were in seventh heaven. 'Tiger, eh? Should I be frightened?' Tiger wagged her tail even more furiously. 'You seem none the worse for your adventure, but don't go swimming again.'

'I've told her no swimming from now on, haven't I, Tiger? I thought it was shallow. I had no idea she'd get into trouble. She was my mother's dog, you see, and I don't know her that well.'

I knew I was babbling but I couldn't seem to stop myself. I shivered again.

'You need to dry off. My cottage is just back there.' He pointed to the row of cottages behind him. 'Come in and get warm. I'll put a fire on.'

When I hesitated his mouth lifted at the corner, into a lopsided grin. 'I promise you'll be safe.' He reached inside his pocket and pulled out an ID card and held it out for my inspection. 'Inspector James Taylor, Strathclyde Police at your service.'

His photo didn't do him justice. In the flesh he was way cuter. He had an interesting face, a nice smile and I *was* bloody freezing. Even a couple of steps in my sodden jeans was enough to convince me going back to Greyfriars like this would be extremely uncomfortable. A police inspector was hardly going to attack me.

'Fair enough, Inspector,' I murmured. 'Thank you.'

'James will do.' He held out a hand. 'Family and friends call me Jamie.'

'Charlotte Friel,' I replied, taking it. His hand was warm and dry, his grip not too firm and not like a wet fish either. The touch of his fingers made my whole body tingle and we both held on for a moment longer than necessary. I came to my senses and withdrew mine, flustered by my reaction. I told myself not to be silly. Near-death experiences probably did that to a person.

His cottage was the end one of three, the painted one with the fishing gear and motor bike. Having only two small windows the inside of the cottage was gloomy and it took a few moments for my eyes to adjust. We were standing in a kitchen-cum-sitting room. On one side was a sink and an array of cupboards, on the other, a small sofa faced the window overlooking the beach. On it was a hard-back edition of Gavin Maxwell's *Ring of Bright Water*. A kitchen table took up most of the remainder of the room. There was an old-fashioned Aga above which hung several pairs of thick socks with an armchair next to it. Apart from a mug, turned upside down on the worktop beside the sink, the room was immaculately tidy. He went up another notch in my estimation.

'Right, you need to get out of these clothes and into a hot shower. I'll get you a clean towel – and one for Tiger.' He indicated a door with a tip of his head. 'The bathroom's through there, with a dressing gown on a hook. I'll chuck your clothes in the tumble dryer and get a fire going.'

Before I could say anything he'd disappeared, returning moments later with a couple of towels. He passed me one before bending down and enveloping Tiger in the other and beginning to rub her dry. 'Go on,' Jamie said, turning to me. 'The shower's electric. There's a switch for it just outside the door. Tiger will be fine with me.'

My teeth were chattering too much for me to reply. He was right; the sooner I warmed up, the better.

The small bathroom was as clean and tidy as the rest of the house. As I removed my sodden clothes, I glanced around. It was bare, apart from a toothbrush and a tube of toothpaste in a mug along with an electric shaver on the window sill. There was no sign of anything feminine.

The shower was above a spotlessly clean avocado-coloured bath. I shoved aside the plastic curtain, stepped in and turned the dial. The water was hot and I luxuriated in its heat, staying under the spray until I was sure that the blood had returned to every cell.

I dried myself briskly and, finding the dressing gown he mentioned which smelled of wood-smoke and soap, put it on. I picked up my sodden clothes and went in search of my host. An ecstatic and apparently fully recovered Tiger greeted me as if she hadn't seen me for years.

'Feeling better?' Jamie asked, taking my wet clothes from me with one hand and removing the book from the sofa so I could sit with the other. Heat radiated from the Aga and the room was already warmer than it had been.

'Much, much better. Thank you, Jamie. I don't usually do the damsel in distress thing.' Tiger sat by my feet and I tickled her behind her ears.

'I'm sure you don't.' He bent down and thrust my clothes into the tumble dryer and switched it on before turning back to me.

'So what brings you to Balcreen? Holiday?' He poured a finger of whisky into a glass and handed it to me.

'Not exactly. I've come to visit family.'

He sat facing me in the armchair. Tiger had abandoned me and placed her head on his feet gazing up at him with adoring eyes. She wasn't usually so friendly. Jamie must have fed her a treat or two while I'd been in the shower.

'You have family here?' he asked, bending down to stroke Tiger.

'Yes. Great-aunts. I'm staying with them on Kerista Island.'

'The Misses Guthrie are your aunts?' He couldn't have sounded more astonished had I told him I was a mermaid. He let out a low whistle. 'You must be the first guest they've had in years.'

'So I gather. You know them?'

238

'Know of them. I was beginning to wonder whether they existed – if it wasn't for the fact people see a light at night and that Ian delivers their groceries on a weekly basis I'd doubt whether they even existed.' Whenever he smiled, one side of his mouth turned up more than the other. 'What are they like?'

'I don't know them very well – at all really.' I had no idea how to describe them. Sweet old ladies wasn't the first description that came to mind.

His smile grew wider. 'Are you sure they aren't growing cannabis or something out there? They could easily arrange for it to be picked up by boat to sell in Europe. It would be the perfect spot and the perfect cover.'

'You don't really believe that! I can't imagine two women less likely to be drug smugglers!'

'As a policeman I've come to realise nothing is impossible.'

I was about to protest again, when, catching the glint in his eyes I realised he'd been teasing me. I smiled back at him. 'If you met them you'd know the most they grow are carrots and potatoes.'

'So why now?'

'Why now what?'

'What brought you to visit your great-aunts now? You said you barely know them.'

It wasn't a question I particularly wanted to answer.

He stayed quiet. I knew the tactic well. It was the same one I used when I suspected a client or a witness had more to reveal.

'I had no idea they existed until recently. They wrote to my mother a few weeks ago asking her to come and see them. I'm here in her stead.'

'Your mother didn't want to come herself?'

Suddenly and humiliatingly I was on the verge of tears again. 'She couldn't. She died. Just over a week ago.'

'That recently!'

I could see the questions in his eyes but I ducked my head so

239

I wouldn't have to meet his enquiring gaze. 'She was sick for a while,' I added as if that explained everything. I took a gulp of whisky, grimacing as it burned my throat. I never drank spirits – rarely drank anything at all apart from the odd glass of wine if I were out for dinner. I'd drunk too much vodka once at university and ended up throwing up over the person next to me. I'd sworn I'd never touch spirits again and I'd never had but today I welcomed the way the whisky's warmth was spreading through my limbs.

'I would have liked to have thanked the man who rescued Tiger and me, but he stomped off before I could,' I told Jamie, wanting to turn the conversation away from me and Mum.

'Was he elderly? Tall? Did he have a collie with him? One with a chunk out of his ear?'

'As a matter of fact, he did. How do you know?'

'Didn't take too much detective work. Findlay goes down there every day around the same time. You can set your watch by him. Luckily for you.'

I latched on to the name. It couldn't be the same Findlay, surely? Yet he was around the right age and Findlay wasn't a common name.

'Findlay who?'

'Armstrong. Why do you ask?'

It had to be the same Findlay. In which case, did my aunts know he was here? I realised Jamie was waiting for my reply, so I thought quickly. Not only did I feel a perverse need to protect my great-aunt's privacy, as a lawyer I was used to keeping information to myself.

'I just want to know who I have to thank.'

His mouth tilted up at the corner. 'I doubt Findlay will expect, or want, your thanks.'

'I gather he's not the friendliest of men.'

His smile grew broader and something strange happened inside my chest. It was as if my heart had done a little dance.

'I would say that's a fair assessment.'

'How do you know him?'

'Know is a relative word with Findlay. Despite the common view, he's a good man at heart.'

I raised an eyebrow inviting him to continue.

'I've known of him – about him – most of my life, although I only met him a couple of years ago.' He swirled his whisky around his glass. 'I was visiting and just happened to be at the station in Oban looking up an old pal when Findlay was brought in. He'd got into a fight with a fisherman – can't remember what about – if anyone ever knew. Findlay had been drinking in the Balcreen Inn all day and could hardly stand, but it had taken four people to restrain him – men known to be tough – and not before he'd managed to crack a jaw and break a nose.'

'Good God!'

'I hung about. I don't think the sergeant fancied dealing with him with just a constable for help – even though Findlay was handcuffed.' Jamie grinned again. 'I could tell immediately he was ex-army and almost certainly an officer.'

'How?'

'There are signs – the way men carry themselves – a certain look in their eye. There was still enough of the soldier in me to want to protect him from himself. Not that I wanted him going around putting men in hospital either. I saluted him and instinctively he saluted me back – then glared at me. I worked out pretty quickly that if he'd been in the forces he must have served in the war – like my godfather, Michael. My godfather was one of the few men who was prepared to share their war stories.' His eyes took on a faraway look. 'The things those poor buggers had to go through – no wonder half of them are a little mad. And then we have to go and do it all again in the Falklands.'

'You were in the army?' Not wanting to interrupt, I had filed away his earlier comment. 'Did you serve in the Falklands?'

'Yes to being in the army – no to serving in the Falklands

but I had friends who did.' There was no longer any trace of the earlier amusement in his eyes.

'And did you talk to Findlay?'

'Not then. He was still drunk. But the next morning I went back and persuaded the sergeant to release him into my care.'

'Weren't there charges?'

'There should have been. But things are done differently here. The men he'd been fighting with decided not to go ahead and make a complaint.'

'Why ever not?'

'I had a word with them. The police in these parts tend to turn a blind eye to lock-ins, the odd spot of poaching, driving without road tax, and no one wants to get on their wrong side. They know I'm a cop.'

It all sounded very irregular.

'I drove him back to his house,' Jamie continued. 'He was sober by then. But if I expected him to be grateful I was to be disappointed. He got out of the car without a word of thanks. I went back to see him a couple of nights later. I had given my word to the sergeant that I would keep an eye on him. Findlay had been barred from the pub for a month and I wanted to make sure he wouldn't attempt to ignore the ban. Since then I drop in on him every time I come home.'

So much of what he'd said intrigued me. Perhaps it was the relaxing effect of the whisky or because Tiger was fast asleep in front of the fire and it would be a while yet before my clothes were dry, but I was reluctant to move. Or perhaps it was my insatiable curiosity to know a person's story. I stretched my feet out in front of me and smiled at Jamie. I'd only spent a short while in his company but already I had the strong impression that Jamie was a what-you-see-is-what-you-get kind of man. So different to the men in London I had dated. As it struck home what I was thinking, I felt myself flush and quickly bent down, ostensibly to pat Tiger, but in reality to hide my face.

When I glanced back up it was to find him looking at me, amusement in his warm brown eyes. Almost as if he knew what I'd been thinking moments before.

'You're from Balcreen, then?' I said, hoping he'd think my flushed face was from the whisky.

'Not exactly. Oban.'

'And you're here on holiday?'

He linked his hands behind his neck. 'Two whole weeks – or to be more precise two weeks minus four days. I come every year.'

'Why did you become a policeman?'

'When I was at university I joined the cadets. My parents weren't very well off and the cadets paid you while you were with them. It helped. Besides, I liked it that they always had plenty going on at weekends – sailing, climbing, pot holing – all stuff I liked to do. Part of the deal was that when cadets finished university they joined the army for five years – to pay back the training and money the army had invested. I served my time but when it was up, I realised the army wasn't for me. But,' it was his turn to look sheepish, 'I still wanted to serve, so I joined the force. I liked the thought of catching bad guys.'

'And do you? Catch many?'

He smiled and my heart skipped a beat. If my direct questioning made him uncomfortable, he gave no inkling of it.

'Not as many as I'd like. Dealing with criminals is like watching a revolving door. Doesn't matter how many you put away there's always more to take their place. The part I find most frustrating is that we catch them and then some smart-arse lawyer gets them off on a technicality.'

It was as if a cool wind had swept over my skin. Police and defence lawyers were natural enemies. They hated us for getting people they thought of as scum off, we disliked and mistrusted them for their bullying tactics and the way they sometimes twisted the truth to get a result. If they did their jobs better I wouldn't be able to get so many criminals off.

'Don't you think everyone deserves a fair trial? Even the guilty?'

'Not if it means that they are back on the streets to rape and murder – no.'

I winced inside. If only he knew how close to the mark his words were. I hesitated, reluctant to tell him I was one of the smart-arsed lawyers he'd so bitterly referred to. But what the hell! I was proud of what I did – I winced again – or had been until recently.

'I should tell you that I'm a barrister.' Despite what I'd just been telling myself, I was aware I sounded defensive.

He tipped his head to the side and I could tell he was reassessing me.

'I hope you are going to tell me you are on the side of the angels,' he said finally, referring to the way policemen describe lawyers who work for the prosecution.

I shook my head. 'Not unless you call defending the innocent the side of the angels.'

His eyes darkened with disapproval.

'Not all policemen are on the side of the angels,' I went on. 'Some are no better, worse even, than the criminals they purport to despise.'

I saw the dawning recognition. He leaned forward and regarded me intently. 'I thought I'd seen you before – in the newspaper. You were one of the barristers who defended the woman who murdered her policeman husband.'

I'd forgotten my picture had been in the press. That time seemed so long ago.

'I didn't recognise you at first,' Jamie continued.

It was hardly surprising, the crumpled heap he'd come across earlier couldn't have looked less like the woman in the photo.

'She didn't murder her husband – it was self-defence.'

'She stabbed him six times, if I remember correctly!'

'And he had spent the previous ten years beating the crap out of her. She was terrified of him.'

'Yet she stayed.'

I clicked my tongue. 'She had nowhere else to go, no money of her own. She tried to get help from the police – I found records of thirty-four phone calls. Not one of them ended in an arrest; on the contrary all of them resulted in a beating that was even worse than the one that instigated the 999 call in the first place. Unsurprisingly she gave up looking to the police for protection. It was only when her husband – her *police* husband – turned on their son – who'd tried to come to her aid, that something snapped. I'm only surprised she didn't do it sooner.'

'Touché,' he said. 'Okay then, let's agree, not every policeman is on the side of the angels.' He continued to study me with his lovely brown eyes. Something passed between us at that moment. A shock of mutual recognition. 'You really care, don't you?'

I held his gaze. 'I do.' Even if I didn't always get it right.

'What made you choose law?' he continued after a long pause.

'Dickens,' I said without hesitation. 'Or more exactly *Bleak House*. You read it?'

'S'matter of fact I have. Jarndyce and Jarndyce?'

He might be a policeman but there was definitely a connection between us.

'I felt so bad for them and so angry with the lawyers. I thought, all they need is one good lawyer, someone like me. I would sort it out. I was never one for doubting my capabilities.' I smiled, remembering. 'Then when I was sixteen, Mum took me on a trip to London. We visited all the places in London where Dickens lived and worked, including the Inns of Court. She also took me to the Old Bailey and we sat in on a trial and I fell even more in love with the idea of being a lawyer. Not just an ordinary lawyer, but a barrister. I wanted to be the person in the gown and wig, defending the helpless, the desperate, the weak. I wanted to be the one addressing the court

245

who had everyone hanging on her every word.' I trailed off. I couldn't remember ever telling anyone that before.

'Have you thought about changing sides?'

'I do my share of cases for the prosecution,' I flared. 'Everyone in my set takes on a couple every year.'

He stared at me intently. 'Only a couple?'

'If prosecution was all I did, I could barely make enough to survive.'

'But many barristers do, don't they?' He pushed up the frame of his glasses with a finger. 'I'm not getting at you, although to be honest we policemen don't exactly love defence barristers. We spend hours making a case as strong and as tight as possible, only to have it torn to shreds by some hot-shot lawyer who appears to be only interested in making a name for him '– he slanted me a look '– or herself.'

'I should be going,' I said, setting my whisky glass down. I'd had enough of being made to feel guilty. I was perfectly able to do that to myself. 'My great-aunts are expecting me back.'

'Your clothes won't be dry yet.'

I told him they would be fine, retrieved them from the dryer and returned to the bathroom. My pants and bra were fine, but my jeans required a great deal of manipulation before I could drag them on. My blouse was uncomfortably damp but I would exchange it for one of my new jumpers as soon as I was back in the car. There was little I could do about my hair. As always when it dried and I had no access to a hairdryer, it curled. My cheeks were flushed, whether from the heat of the room, the whisky or the attention of a man I had to admit I found intriguing and attractive, I couldn't be sure. Whatever the reason, my eyes were brighter than they had been for weeks and my skin had lost some of its pallor.

He was rinsing our glasses when I returned to the kitchen. Hearing me, he turned and smiled. 'How long are you here for?'

'I'm not sure. Another few days.'

'Are you free tomorrow?'

Give him his due, he wasted no time.

'We could walk up the Black Hills,' he continued when I didn't reply. 'You said you wanted to thank Findlay. He lives up there. I could take you to see him, if you like, although I can't guarantee what reception we'll get.'

I hesitated. Didn't I have enough on my plate without getting involved with someone – a policeman no less? The sensible thing to do would be to say goodbye and leave it at that.

Mum's words about being more impulsive rushed back. I had days yet to spend with the aunts and for the first time I had nowhere I had to be, no strict timetable in my head. Besides, I liked him – despite the way he'd needled me – and he'd be a diversion – something to take my mind off myself and my grief and worry.

'What time tomorrow?'

'Ten? Would you like me to come for you?'

'Let's meet at the pier on the Balcreen side.' I patted my leg. 'Come on, Tiger, let's go.' At the door I turned. 'Thanks for the drink and the use of the dryer.'

He grinned. 'Anytime. Anytime at all.'

Chapter Twenty-Eight

I rowed back to the island, Tiger at the prow, nose to the wind. Her scare in the water hadn't affected her at all.

I tied the boat up to the pier and, feeling lighter than I'd felt in a long time, walked towards the house. It'd been good to spend time away from Greyfriars with someone so completely normal and I was glad I'd agreed to see him again. And curious to meet Findlay.

Could it really be the same Findlay Edith had been almost engaged to? If he was, did the aunts know he lived close by? If I hadn't seen for myself how isolated they were I would have assumed it was impossible for them not to.

The wind was picking up again and it rustled through the rhododendron leaves. As I emerged from the short tunnel, once again I had the impression of a face at one of the upstairs windows. I was uneasy at the thought my aunts might be watching me. But was it really surprising when they lived as they did? Even small events must assume an importance in an otherwise uneventful day.

As the front of the house came into view I saw a figure balanced on the roof of the side porch. At first I thought my aunts had hired someone from Balcreen to replace the missing tiles but as I drew closer, to my shock, I realised it was Georgina.

My great-aunt was wearing trousers and was straddled across the eaves, a hammer in one hand, nails between her lips.

Frightened to call out in case I startled her and caused her to lose her balance, I stood stock-still and watched, heart in my mouth, as my great-aunt expertly removed a tile and replaced it with another.

Tiger barked and Georgina turned around, looked down and waved. 'So you're back! Did you get what you wanted?'

'I did.'

'Go inside, I'll be finished here in a mo.'

'Shouldn't you let someone else do that?' I called back.

My great-aunt's laughter floated on the wind. 'Perfectly able to do it myself.'

'Can I help?'

'You can pass me some more nails. Save me coming down for them. They're on the ground. In a box.'

'How many do you need?'

'Half a dozen should do it.'

I located the box and counted out the number she asked. I clambered up the ladder, my damp jeans still clinging to my legs, and handed them to her. 'Do you need me to stand by in case you need any more?'

'No. This will be enough. You go on in.'

Inside, the house seemed empty. I went through to the kitchen to put away the fish in the larder. Just as it had been in Mum's day it was stacked from floor to ceiling with tins of every sort. Baked beans, tuna, Fray Bentos steak and kidney pies, tins of peas, tins of fruit, tins of evaporated milk, canned soup of all varieties. Apart from those there were bags of rice and flour, so old they didn't even have sell-by dates on them. If ever there was a nuclear war or some other kind of apocalypse I knew where I would want to be.

Trout put away, I popped back outside. Georgina was still on the roof and not wanting to distract her, I ran up to my room and put my new jumpers in the chest of drawers. I changed out of my damp clothes and hurried back downstairs, expecting at any moment to hear a cry and a thump as my great-aunt fell from the roof. Instead, to my relief, I found Georgina at the bottom of the stairs, looking decidedly pleased with herself.

'There. That should hold that particular leak for a month or two.'

'Couldn't someone from the village do it for you?' I asked.

'No need. I can manage perfectly well. It's not the first time I've fixed a roof.' A shadow crossed her face, then she smiled. 'How did you like Oban?'

'I thought it was very pretty. I bought us some fresh trout for dinner. I put it in the larder. I'm happy to cook. I assume you and Edith eat fish.' There was no point telling her about the escapade in the water, or that I'd thought the man who rescued Tiger and me was the same Findlay Edith had been engaged to. I wanted to know for certain that it was him before I mentioned meeting him. What would I have said anyway? I think I was pulled out of the water by the man you loved – the man your sister was hoping to marry.

'You'll discover there is very little Edith and I won't eat.' Her face clouded again. 'There was a time that we considered insects a gastronomic delight.'

'Was this during the war? I gather you and Edith were prisoners of the Japanese.'

She gave a small shake of her head. 'That's part of my story. And for later. But we couldn't live surrounded by the sea and not eat fish. It's a shame we don't have a stocked loch here otherwise we would catch our own. Most of what the local fishermen catch gets sent off to Spain. Ian sends us whatever they don't want.'

'So that's settled,' I said. 'I'm making dinner. You and Edith can relax – keep me company in the kitchen if you prefer – you can continue your story then.'

She frowned. 'No, as I said, not while Edith is present. She doesn't like to be reminded of the past.'

In which case it was just as well I hadn't mentioned Findlay. 'How is she?'

Georgina frowned.

'Edith. Is she feeling better?'

'Oh Edith!' She gave an odd little laugh. 'Yes. I think so.'

'Then why don't we chat now? There's an hour or so before I have to start preparing supper. If Edith comes in you can stop.'

'Very well then. Shall we go into the library? The fire's lit.'

I had a sense that the room had only been recently vacated. There was a book open on one side table and some simple needlework on the other and when I sat down, the sofa cushion was still warm as if someone had been sitting there only moments before. If it had been Edith she'd clearly just scuttled away. In an attempt to avoid me, or so that she wouldn't have to listen to what Georgina wanted to tell me?

Georgina settled back in her chair. 'Where had I got to?'

'You'd just heard about my grandparents – Harriet and Peter?'

'Oh, yes. Dear Harriet. She was so young. I still miss her. It was a terrible shock.' She looked at me through her thick lashes. 'An even worse shock for Olivia, no doubt. As it turned out it was a good decision not to send for her.'

'Mum was only eleven,' I reminded her, not quite ready to let her off the hook. 'And you and Edith the only family she had left.'

'She was settled at boarding school. Even if I'd gone to her, I would have hardly seen her. I'd written to Agatha asking her if she could have Olivia on weekends out and holidays until alternative arrangements could be made. And she wrote back saying she was happy to act as guardian until Edith or I could take over. In those days it was different. Many of our sort spent years at boarding school, and if their parents were abroad, didn't see them for years. You can't judge the past by the standards of today.'

'But later – after the war was over?'

251

She gave an exasperated click of her tongue. 'I did say I would explain and you promised you would hear me out.'

I had. Hiding my impatience, I sat back in my chair. 'I'm sorry. Please, carry on.'

Georgina took a cigarette from a lacquered box on the side table next to her and lit it. 'I rarely smoke, these days. You don't mind, do you?

'Not at all.'

She took a couple of quick puffs before stubbing it out. 'With Harriet gone, I missed Edith even more. She hadn't written to me, not even after Harriet's death and without an address I couldn't write to her. The best I could do was send the letters I wrote to Agatha, asking her to forward them. But I never received a reply from Edith. Then, out of the blue, I bumped into her.'

Chapter Twenty-Nine

Georgina

November 1941

Georgina leaned back in her chair making the most of the cool, air-conditioned interior of the tea room in Robinson's department store. As always the place was packed. She was due to join Lawrence and a group of friends at Raffles later for dinner, but before that she had a few hours to kill and she planned to go to the Chinese market and then to the Indian tailor to get a new evening dress made up. She said as much to Eleanor who had joined her for tea. Grace had left and Georgina still missed her. Eleanor wasn't nearly as much fun.

'It's far too hot for Chinatown, don't you think?' Eleanor said, when Georgina asked whether she wanted to come too. 'And don't you have enough evening dresses to last you a lifetime? Besides, I'd much prefer to have a lie-down before the dance tonight. Are you going?'

'Naturally,' Georgina said. 'I don't think there's much else on.'

A group of army nurses in their crisp white tropical uniforms arrived at that moment causing a flurry of activity as the waiting staff rushed to find enough empty seats to allow them to sit together. As always, whenever she saw army nurses she thought of Edith, wishing she knew for certain that she was safe.

And then it was as if she'd conjured her up. Taking a seat

at one of the tables and smiling at the Chinese waiter was her sister. Georgina's heart lurched.

'What is it?' Eleanor asked. 'You've gone as white as a sheet.' She followed Georgina's gaze to the laughing and chatting nurses. 'Do you know them?'

But Georgina had already got to her feet and was pushing through the throng of customers.

'Edith!' she cried, placing a hand on her sister's shoulder. 'Is it really you?'

Edith's shoulders stiffened under Georgina's fingertips. She turned around and regarded Georgina with her cool, light-blue eyes. 'Georgina, I wondered if we would meet.'

'I can't believe it! You're in Singapore! When did you arrive?'

'Wednesday.'

'You've been here two days already! Why didn't you let me know?' It was one thing Edith not replying to Georgina's letters, quite another being in the same city and not getting in touch.

'I was planning to.' Edith shrugged. 'But we've been rather busy since we got here. People have insisted on showing us the sights.'

Georgina had no doubt. The army sisters held officer rank and the moment their ships docked in Singapore they were whisked away in their white dresses and red capes to join the throng in Raffles.

'Too busy to send a note?'

The nurses with Edith had fallen silent and were regarding the two women with a mixture of puzzlement and curiosity, bewildered smiles frozen on their faces.

Edith appeared to recover. 'Everyone, this is my sister Georgina.' She gave a brittle smile. 'We haven't seen each other for a while. Would you excuse us for a moment?'

She stood and she and Georgina moved out of earshot.

'So you haven't forgiven me yet?' Georgina said. 'It's been over two years.'

'Really? That long?'

'You never wrote — not even after Harriet died.'

Edith's expression softened. 'Poor, darling Harry. I couldn't believe it when I heard. Still can't.'

'Look, we can't talk here. Why don't you come home with me?'

Edith glanced at her watch. 'I have plans.'

'Later then? We could have dinner.'

'I'm having dinner with friends. At Chez Wein. I understand they make the most divine cocktails. Then I have to pack. Our unit is being sent to a hospital up north tomorrow.'

Georgina's heart dropped. She'd found her sister only to lose her again.

'After dinner then? You can spare half an hour surely?'

'Georgina, I'm already dead on my feet. I'll be no use to man nor beast unless I get a good night's sleep.'

'What about tomorrow? Before you leave? We could meet anywhere and anytime you like.' She glanced behind her to find Eleanor making her way towards them. 'We *have* to talk ...'

Edith looked as if she were about to find another excuse but then she sighed. 'Come to the hospital. About ten. I should have some time then. I'll find somewhere we won't be disturbed. Now if you'll excuse me, I should return to my friends.' Georgina winced. There was a time Edith would have considered *her* a friend as well as her sister and would have been only too delighted to have her join them. Edith kissed Georgina on the cheek, the merest brush of her lips, and then, in the seconds before Eleanor was upon them, she turned away and rejoined her fellow nurses at the table.

'Someone you know?' Eleanor said, nodding in Edith's direction.

'My sister, Edith.'

Eleanor's eyes widened before swivelling to Edith and the other nurses. 'She didn't seem very pleased to see you.'

'Edith has always hated public shows of affection.'

'There's public shows and downright coldness,' Eleanor said.

'For Heaven's sake, Eleanor, just shut up! You know nothing about it.' The look of hurt dismay on Eleanor's face brought Georgina to her senses.

'Forgive me. I didn't mean to snap at you. It was a shock seeing her, that's all. To be honest the last time we parted it wasn't on the best of terms.'

A look of malicious, greedy curiosity passed over Eleanor's face. 'Why don't we have a drink at the Swimming Club and you can tell me all?'

The biggest drawback to living in Singapore was that essentially it was a small community. Everyone knew each other's business and gossip, amongst the men almost as much as amongst the woman, was one of the main sources of amusement. Georgina had no doubt she had been the main topic on more than one occasion and that bothered her less than perhaps it should have. But she was damned if she were going to have her difficulties with Edith dissected over that evening's gin slings. Edith, she was certain, wouldn't breathe a word at her end.

'I have plans for this afternoon, remember?' Georgina said. 'It's good of you to take such an interest but really there is nothing to tell. I'm seeing Edith tomorrow and we'll iron out any differences then.'

'You're still coming to the dance tonight?'

Georgina sighed inwardly. It was the last thing she felt like doing, but if she didn't, Eleanor was bound to make more of the meeting with Edith than she'd done already. 'Of course. I wouldn't miss it for the world.'

Normally Georgina loved strolling through Chinatown's labyrinth of narrow streets, with its gaudily painted shop houses selling porcelain and jade, silk and ivory, the locals' washing draped on poles sticking out like flags from upstairs windows, the glittering temples, the junks and sampans packed tightly together along the muddy river, the satay stalls offering delicious snacks, the hawkers with their wares swinging from bamboo sticks bent across bony shoulders. But today, even its delights couldn't distract her.

Although she did order a new dress her heart wasn't in it. It had been easy to excuse Edith's long silence, at least in part, to her working abroad and being unable to write, but it was clear her sister still hadn't forgiven her.

She hailed a passing rickshaw, and sat deep in thought, hardly noticing as the narrow streets of Chinatown were replaced by wide avenues with cropped grass verges, flame-of-the forest and frangipani trees.

Edith had always been stubborn. Once she picked a course it was difficult, if not impossible, to get her to deviate from it. But with that stubbornness came a fierce loyalty. To Edith, loyalty, whether it was to King and country, to friends, or to family, was paramount. And Georgina had been as disloyal as it was possible to get.

But it had been over two years unless – alarm spiralled through her – did Edith know the whole truth? No, there was no way she could. The continuing rift was far more likely due to Edith's stubbornness. And that couldn't be allowed to continue. When she saw her tomorrow, she would make Edith see that.

Her journey back to Beach Road took her past St Andrew's Cathedral with its slim spire on its island of carefully tended green lawn, the Supreme Court and the gentlemanly government offices, separated from the waterfront by the green rectangle Padang and the cricket club. If they could make up, Edith might spend some time with Georgina in Singapore and she could show her all the sights. She smiled. It would be just like old times and Singapore would be a different place with Edith in it.

She forced herself to go to the dance at Raffles that night.

She and Lawrence swept up to the front door, passing the door that was guarded day and night lest those not permitted inside the hotel tried to sneak in, and into the familiar wide bar with its potted palms and white-coated waiters. It was difficult to be despondent at Raffles – there was always such a cheerful atmosphere. Tonight it was even more crowded than usual, mostly because of the troops – all officers naturally. The other ranks had their own places. Although Lawrence appeared to have accepted she would never marry him, he'd insisted they stay friends and she was only too happy to agree. She might not love him but she liked him enormously.

She'd returned to her seat after dancing a particularly energetic quickstep with Lawrence, tapping her foot to the rhythm as the band immediately swung into a foxtrot.

'You look unusually pensive tonight, darling,' Lawrence said, clicking his fingers for another round of drinks. 'Is anything the matter?'

For a second she was tempted to tell him about Edith and their estrangement – but only for a second. If she told him she'd also have to reveal her part in the row and she shrank from doing that. Lawrence's good opinion of her was one of the few that mattered.

'I've been thinking about the war. I'm worried. Do you really think we're safe here?'

Instead of laughing off her worries, he frowned. 'Why do you ask?'

'You truly believe the Japs could never capture Singapore?'

'My dear, man has as much chance of landing on the moon.' As the foxtrot segued into a waltz he reached for her hand. 'Come on, let's dance those blues away.'

The next morning, feeling unaccountably nervous, she studied her wardrobe. What to wear for her meeting with Edith? She picked out a dress, then tossed it on the bed. It was too low cut. A skirt and blouse ensemble landed on top of the dress. Skirts and blouses were all very well for workwear, but simply wouldn't do otherwise. She wanted to appear repentant, not frumpy.

The best part of an hour had passed and clothes were heaped on her bed and floor before she settled on a simple cotton frock with pearl buttons that reached almost, but not quite up to the neck, and which was inoffensively bland, without being too matronly. There was, however, no way she was going out without the full make-up; foundation, deep red lipstick and blusher. When her face was made up to her satisfaction, she wound her long hair into a victory roll. She picked up her white cotton gloves, pinned her wide-brimmed straw hat into place and slipped on a pair of heels. Pleased that she struck the exact note she intended, she told the houseboy to call for a rickshaw.

Outside, the combination of heat, noise and smells was intense; rickshaws jamming the narrow streets, locals crouching over fires cooking meals to sell to passers-by, little yellow Ford taxis scooting about, tooting their horns at ponderously slow-moving bullock carts getting in their way, the smell of dung merging with spices, the dazzling shimmer of the sun on the sea,

The British military hospital was a modern, large, three-storey white building with red-tiled roofs and verandas, surrounded by lush, tropical gardens.

Georgina stopped a nurse who was heading back to the hospital having wheeled a patient towards a waiting ambulance.

'I'm looking for Sister Guthrie. Might you be able to tell me where I can find her?'

The nurse looked at her blankly. 'Sorry. Don't know the name. There's so many nurses coming and going these days, it's difficult to keep track.'

She was about to turn away when Georgina grabbed her arm. 'Is there anyone who might know?'

'Home Sister, probably. You'll find her in the sisters' mess. Those buildings over there.' She pointed to a group of bungalows on the edge of the hospital grounds.

Georgina made her way through the benches and chairs

occupied by patients, following a path that led to the bungalows. There were three in a row. She chose the middle one
and found Home Sister in the hall.

'Excuse me, Sister, but I'm looking for Sister Guthrie.'

'Sister Guthrie? I'm not sure I know that name.'

'She's with the 21st Combined Unit.'

'Oh, them! They were sent up north. They left last night.'

'They can't have done! My sister said she wasn't leaving until
this morning.'

'Orders can change at any moment. Let me check and see
if she left a message for you.'

She left Georgina kicking her heels in the corridor. It
seemed an age before she returned.

'Found this.' She handed Georgina an envelope with her
name written on it in Edith's elegant writing and waited while
Georgina read it. It didn't take long.

> Georgina,
>   I'm afraid my unit has been sent up
> north sooner than we expected. I would
> have sent you a note but I really
> don't think us meeting up would serve
> any purpose, except to embarrass us
> both. Everything we have to say to one
> another has already been said.
>   Despite everything, I wish you well.
>   Edith.

So there was to be no reconciliation. It had been so long and
with Harriet's death there was only the two of them. Surely
with the war raging, no one knowing how long they might
survive, Edith might have let bygones be bygones?

'Is there anything else?' Home Sister asked. 'Because I have
a sick nurse to see to.'

'No, thank you.'

Home Sister opened the door and Georgina stepped out and back into the oppressive heat.

Damn Edith and her stubbornness. She would write to her one more time, but really she'd done enough grovelling. It was up to Edith now.

Chapter Thirty

Charlotte

1984

The grandfather clock in the hall struck seven and Georgina looked at me, a startled expression on her face, as if she'd forgotten I was there. 'Goodness me, is that really the time? I need to freshen up before dinner.'

There had been no sign of Edith while we'd been talking. I'd hardly seen her. The house seemed to swallow her up only to spit her out at indeterminate intervals.

'I'll go and start preparing it, shall I? Perhaps you can continue with your story afterwards?' I was seething with impatience for her to get to the crux of why they'd invited me here, although I still couldn't see what the continuing breakdown of the sisters' relationship had to do with what Georgina wanted to explain. They had clearly repaired their relationship since then.

I left Georgina at the foot of the stairs and went to the kitchen. I removed the trout from the pantry and a large frying pan from the shelf, almost dropping it as I did. My upper arms were aching slightly from rowing and the thing had to weigh a ton.

I set the pan on top of the stove to heat. The trout had been boned and filleted so it was ready to fry. All I needed to do was boil some potatoes – even I could manage that – and make a salad. It was no restaurant meal but it would be tasty enough.

As I cooked, my thoughts strayed back to Jamie. I had rarely, if ever, felt such an instant attraction to someone. However, I was down and anxious and bound to feel drawn to anyone who showed me a smidgen of kindness, but I knew that wasn't the whole truth. There was something about him that drew me. It was almost as if I knew him – as if I'd always known him. I shook my head. I wasn't usually prone to such flights of fancy. Greyfriars and its atmosphere was clearly getting to me. Moreover, losing Mum had left a chasm inside me as big as a canyon waiting for something to fill it. I couldn't remember feeling this vulnerable and I hated it.

The aunts joined me a few minutes before everything was ready. As they had the previous night, they'd changed into fresh clothes and had done their hair.

When the fish was ready I removed the plates I had placed in the warming part of the oven earlier and set them on the worktop. Georgina rose from her chair and took a large tureen from the shelf of the Welsh dresser and set it down on the table. 'For the potatoes. I'll get you another one for the carrots.'

'And what has Georgina been telling you this afternoon?' Edith seemed to have recovered from this morning's distress.

Georgina was watching her closely, almost as if she were ready to leap in to stop Edith in mid-sentence if necessary.

'Why don't we talk about Charlotte while we eat?' Georgina said firmly. 'Tell us more, Charlotte. Why did you become a lawyer?'

I gave them the potted version of the one I'd given Jamie.

'Do you think right and wrong is always black and white?' Georgina asked.

'No, I believe that justice and the law aren't always the same.' More than believed, I knew they weren't the same. Lucy had been the one really on trial, not Simon. Not wishing to mention Lucy, I told them about the Curtis case. 'She had committed a crime – a very serious one – but it seemed to me, and thankfully the jury, that she had no choice.'

263

'But shouldn't she have to pay for her actions?' Georgina asked, delicately disecting her trout.

'I believe she has. I doubt the events of that night will ever leave her, or her son. I suspect she'll be paying for what she did, one way or another, for the rest of her life.'

'What about restitution?' Edith asked, giving her sister a sideways glance.

'Restitution?'

'Is making restitution the same thing as paying for one's sins?'

'I'm not certain I believe in the concept of sin.'

'What about evil?' This time the question came from Georgina.

'Are you asking whether I believe in evil?'

'Yes.'

I thought for a moment. 'I'm not sure. Certainly people can commit evil acts. But I also think what some people think of as an evil act might, in some cases, be attributed to mental illness – the mother who kills her child, for example.'

'What about Hitler?'

'Yes. There's no doubt he was evil. I believe evil people are rarer than we think, however. And I don't necessarily go along with the belief that the ordinary German was evil too – I'm talking about those who knew what was going on yet did nothing. I'm not sure any of us know what we would do when in fear of our lives.'

Georgina seemed pleased with my response. 'Who was it who said "All that is necessary for the triumph of evil is that good men do nothing"?' she asked.

If she'd wanted to pick a quote to pierce my soul she couldn't have chosen a better one. Of course she couldn't possibly know how meaningful it was for me.

'It was Edmund Burke. And yes, I can see why he would say that.' I'd finished my supper and laid my knife and fork down. 'What did you two ladies do with your day?'

'More questions!' Edith muttered.

Georgina placed a hand over her sister's. 'Charlotte is only

264

being polite, darling.' She turned back to me. 'Our days are rather uneventful. We'd much rather hear about you.'

'I've agreed to meet someone tomorrow.'

Georgina frowned. 'I didn't realise you knew anyone in this part of the world.'

'I only met him today.'

'You're meeting someone you don't know?'

I was amused and touched by the concern in her eyes. If only she knew the low-lives I dealt with on a daily basis. 'Don't worry, I'll be safe enough. He's a policeman.'

Her head snapped up. 'A policeman! How did you meet him?' She seemed annoyed and I bristled. Concern was one thing, this quite another. She had no right to question me as if she were responsible for me.

'There was an incident with Tiger. She went in to the sea and got caught in a current. We had to be helped ashore.' I held back from saying rescued and who had done the rescuing. 'Jamie took me into his house to dry off. He's visiting for a couple of weeks, apparently. He said he'd collect me from the pier on the other side.'

While I'd been talking, Edith had leapt to her feet, collected our supper dishes and taken them away. I heard a clatter coming from the scullery as if she'd just dumped them in the sink.

'I really wish you wouldn't invite anyone to Greyfriars,' Georgina said.

'Oh, he's not coming here. I said I'd meet him at the pier on the other side.'

She appeared to relax.

'I'll row myself across and back,' I added.

Edith returned to the kitchen. 'When are you going? When will you be back?'

'I don't know. I'll leave after breakfast and return sometime in the afternoon, I imagine.'

'Can't you be more precise? We have our routines, you know, and they mustn't be upset.'

265

I shook off my irritation. 'If it helps, I'll make sure I'm back in time for supper.'

Edith looked at Georgina as if seeking her support. Georgina gave her a slight shake of her head, before turning back to me. 'You must feel free to come and go as you please. Have a lovely time and we'll expect you when we see you.'

After dinner, when Georgina and I had washed and put away the dishes, that had, as I'd suspected, been abandoned in an untidy heap in the kitchen sink, we retreated to the library. Georgina offered me a sherry. 'I don't know about you but I think I'll need one.'

When I nodded she filled two crystal sherry glasses from a decanter on a silver tray. She poked the fire and added some more coal. When it was blazing to her satisfaction she sat down and sighed. 'I'm getting to the difficult part.' She took another sip of sherry and raised an eyebrow. 'Do you know what the Japanese did in 1936?'

I shook my head.

'They invaded China and murdered hundreds of thousands of the local population in a place called Nanking. They raped women and children in front of their relatives – daughters in front of mothers, wives in front of husbands, often out on the street – sometimes several times over and then when they were done, when their victims were half-dead anyway, they bayoneted them where they lay – laughing as they did so.'

Nausea curdled in my stomach.

'I'm ashamed to say that at that time what was happening on the other side of the world didn't seem to have very much to do with us,' Georgina continued, a faraway look in her eyes. 'But we should have paid more attention. We should have done something to punish them, at the very least we should have realised that the Japanese had to be taken seriously. That they were not an honourable army. But we didn't. Not until it was far too late.'

Chapter Thirty-One

Georgina

Singapore, December 1941

In the early hours of the morning, just over a week since she'd seen Edith, Georgina was jerked from sleep by bangs that shook the house and rattled the window panes. Her heart in her throat, she ran to the window and looked out, almost unable to believe her eyes. Parts of the city were in flames and, even as she watched, planes appeared from out of the thick cloud. Singapore was being attacked! Where were the guns? Where was the RAF? For crying out loud, Singapore was lit up like a Christmas tree! Only yesterday the radio had spoken, very casually, as if it were of no concern, of Japanese landings on Kota Bahru and of their warships lying off the east coast. Yet, even then, Singapore hadn't bothered to enforce the blackout. Damn the Singapore government and their insistence in not taking the threats from the Japs seriously. Thank God the British government seemed to. A few days earlier two British battleships, the *Repulse* and the *Prince of Wales* had sailed in to reinforce the Far Eastern fleet.

The sound of stuttering returning fire came at last, either from the heavy guns facing out to sea or from the battleships. At least Singapore was being defended. Half an hour later it was all over.

The next morning, she heard on the radio that Pearl Harbor had been bombed by the Japanese and almost the entire

American navy wiped out. In response, America had declared war. In Singapore, although Raffles Place had suffered a direct hit, Chinatown had endured the worst of it. Dozens of people had been killed and hundreds more injured. The day after the attacks, news reached them of the sinking of the *Repulse* and the *Prince of Wales* battleships. They had only been in Singapore a week! And the very next day news broke of the destruction of the airfield at Butterworth, and Georgina thought it inevitable that people would now sit up and pay attention. Who could doubt the Japanese army's intent now? But no. Singapore picked itself up and shrugged the news off as if it was only a minor inconvenience and really nothing to do with them.

On Sunday, a week after the bombing of Singapore and Pearl Harbor, Georgina and Lawrence drove out to the Sea View Hotel on the east coast road leading to Changi. Sunday morning was a Sea View morning for most of the Europeans in Singapore and it was Lawrence's and her habit to go there every Sunday for lunch. Not even the Japanese attacks would be allowed to change that. They were all nothing if not creatures of habit.

Everything was just the same as every other day, adding to the sense of unreality. The large rectangular ballroom was open to the sea along one side, its floor crowded with small tables, each able to seat four people, leaving a square in the middle for dancing once the tables had been pushed back after the meal was over.

At the far end of the hotel's pillared terrace, with its dome in the centre, flowers in tubs lined a platform on which an orchestra, violins predominating, played light classical music. Most of the men not in uniform were in the more casual dress permitted on a Sunday – open-necked shirts and shorts. Many of the women also wore shorts, their hair and skin protected by wide-brimmed hats or bandanas, with sunglasses to shield their eyes from the glare of the sun.

Lawrence held out a chair for Georgina at one of the tables on the terrace facing the hotel beach, signalling for a Tiger beer for himself and an ice-cold gimlet served in a frosty glass for her.

They sat in silence as they waited for their drinks to arrive, taking in the spidery lines of Malay fishing traps between the green islands and the sea.

'Surely the government is going to do something now?' Georgina said, when they'd been served, taking a sip of her drink. 'They've refused to take the war seriously so far.' And were still not taking it seriously. If the *Straits Times* were to be believed, nothing at all was happening. At least Singapore had finally implemented the blackout they should have implemented months ago.

'Darling, you have to leave these matters to people who know best. I promise there is nothing to worry about, but if you are at all concerned why don't you go back to Britain? I can easily get you a ticket.'

'I have no intention of leaving!' Certainly not as long as Edith was in Singapore. 'I'm going to make myself useful. I'm taking a course in first aid with a view to volunteering at one of the hospitals. People have been wounded and killed, Lawrence, and the hospitals are feeling the strain. As you keep pointing out, my job here is practically redundant these days and I refuse to be a useless mouth.'

To her fury he laughed. 'You! Take care of the sick? Empty bedpans and fetch and carry for the nurses? You can't be serious.'

'Just bloody well watch me, Lawrence.' She picked up her handbag and glared at him. 'That is one of the many reasons I could never marry you. You think you know everything there is to know about me, but you don't. You don't know me at all.'

Over the days that followed it became increasingly clear that the Singapore government was determined to persist with their bury-your-head-in-the-sand attitude and that the rest of Singapore was going along with it. As December wore on the first festive decorations started sprouting in shop windows and adverts for hotel rooms in the up-country stations of Fraser's Hill and Cameron Highlands appeared in the newspapers with the headline: *Don't let rumour spoil your Christmas!*

Georgina had thrown the newspaper down in disgust. No wonder most people still refused to believe, even for a moment, that the Japanese would ever be able to occupy Malaya, never mind Singapore.

If anything the atmosphere grew more heady and frenetic. More troops poured in as did army nurses yet Singapore carried on partying. But people from up country were fleeing to Singapore; trekking across ravines and through the jungle, stumbling into buffalo wallows filled with mud and excrement, some arriving in Singapore with only the clothes they stood up in. Undaunted, many of the up-country women would find their way to the Swimming Club, where they'd shower, wash their clothes and lay them on the lawn to dry before taking a seat under a beach umbrella by the side of the large, tiled pool and ordering a drink from one of the impeccably dressed Chinese waiters. Georgina had to admire their sangfroid.

Christmas Day arrived without a word, or even a card, from Edith. Georgina had completed her first aid course – but to her chagrin Lawrence had been correct – she was a hopeless nurse. The sight of blood sickened her. So she'd offered her services to one of the many refugee centres that were springing up throughout Singapore as more and more people arrived from the north. She might be no use as a nurse's aide but she could ensure that refreshments and clothes were in plentiful supply for those who needed it.

By now even the army was retreating. The Japs had landed in Hong Kong the same day they attacked Pearl Harbor. The commonwealth forces held out as long as they could, but it was hopeless and eighteen days later, on Christmas Day, Hong Kong surrendered.

Georgina was in Lawrence's office waiting for him to finish so they could have supper. She was perched on the edge of his desk, examining her nails and wondering whether to schedule a manicure for the following day when a corporal rushed in, barely remembering to salute his superior officer who was seated at the other desk.

'Sir, you need to read this.' The corporal's face was pale, the hand that held the telegram shaking.

The captain snatched it from him, read it, and blanched.

'Jesus,' he breathed.

'What is it?' Georgina asked, her nails forgotten, a cold feeling growing in the pit of her stomach.

Ever after she would recall the swishing of the overhead fan, the distant sound of explosions, the beads of moisture on lips and foreheads.

Instead of replying, the captain turned on his heel and hurried out of the room, the telegram still clutched in his hand. The corporal just stood there as if he had no idea where he was.

'What did it say?' Georgina demanded.

The soldier collapsed into the chair recently vacated by the captain. 'My girl was there. Dear God, my girl was there.'

'Where? What has happened?' Georgina felt icy cold despite the heat.

The corporal seemed to collect himself. He gave a small shake of his head. 'Better you don't know, miss.'

She strode over to him and stood directly in front of him. 'Better I don't know what?'

He looked up at her, his eyes swimming with tears.

She crouched down in front of him and pressed his shoulder. 'Tell me,' she whispered. 'You'll know I'll find out later anyway.'

He was silent for a long time. 'They've murdered them.'

'Murdered who?' She could barely speak.

'The nurses. And the doctors. In Hong Kong. And the men. Dear God, even those who were sick or wounded, the bastards killed the lot of them.'

Acid bile rushed to Georgina's throat. 'Tell me about the nurses!'

'Raped. And murdered too.'

'All of them!' It couldn't be true.

'No, some they took prisoner, some escaped. That's how we know.' He turned his head away from her and vomited into the wastepaper basket that Georgina had hurriedly placed next to him, having just about enough wits left to anticipate what he was about to do.

'But they can't have. It's a hospital! Why would the Japs kill women and doctors and sick men? The communiqué must be wrong.'

He lifted his head, wiping his mouth with the back of his hand. 'It's true, miss. The doctors held up white flags – they came out with them – but the bastards killed them anyway. Then the Japs went inside the hospital. Some of the doctors were in the middle of operating. Didn't make a difference. They shot them, or bayoneted them, then all the poor buggers who were lying helpless. It was a massacre.' He started crying again. 'My Laura was one of the nurses. No one knows for certain who's alive or dead.'

Georgina took a breath in an attempt to slow her racing heart.

'It might not be as bad as it sounds. You know how things can get confused – exaggerated.' But, dear God, even if only a small part of it was . . .

'They've landed on Malaya too,' the corporal said. 'Everyone said they couldn't.'

She went to the adjoining bathroom and poured some water into a small basin and handed it to the corporal. 'Wash your face,' she said, making herself sound stern, although she wanted nothing more than to weep with him, 'and for God's sake pull yourself together. It'll do no one any good if we cause a panic.'

She waited in Lawrence's office for hours pacing up and down, fretting and refusing to leave until she'd seen him. She had to know if what had happened at the hospital in Hong Kong was true. And had the Japanese really landed on Malaya too? Everyone believed that the Japanese couldn't get to Singapore – not through the jungle – and definitely not through the port. But what if it was their intention to try? What would they do to the hospitals in their way? There were several – one of which was where Edith was – lying between the north of Malaya and Singapore.

The troops would stop them. Of course they would. Hong Kong was much more difficult to defend than Malaya. Nevertheless, it would be far safer for Edith and her fellow nurses to return to Singapore. God knew nurses were needed here as much as anywhere.

But, she forced herself to calm down, as soon as the Governor's office knew what had happened in Hong Kong, if it were true, surely they would abandon their stupid pretence that everything was still going to be all right and demand that the nurses be brought to safety?

More information trickled in over the next hours, each new detail almost worse than what they'd learned before. The hospital in Hong Kong where the massacre had happened, had been set up in St Stephen's college to help deal with the wounded. Staffed by QAs as well as civilian nurses and VADs, it had been packed with injured men, the nurses run off their feet and the doctors operating almost non-stop. A Red Cross flag had been prominently draped over the front door and no one doubted for a minute this would give them protection should the worst happen and Hong Kong was taken.

273

The worst did happen. After fighting bravely and fiercely, on Christmas morning the colony had accepted the inevitable and surrendered. Despite this, the Japanese army had bayoneted the disarmed soldiers before, fuelled by vast amounts of looted alcohol, going on the rampage. When they arrived at St Stephen's, two army doctors went out to meet them but, to the horror of those watching, were immediately shot and bayoneted. It didn't stop there. The soldiers swarmed through the hospital, ripping bandages from injured soldiers' wounds before bayoneting the helpless men too. Anyone who tried to stop them was instantly killed.

The nurses were gathered together and taken to a room. Throughout the night, Japanese soldiers came and selecting several took them away where they were raped repeatedly. Three women were raped and then murdered, their bodies left casually in a heap.

It was very late before Georgina was able to speak to Lawrence. When he eventually appeared, he looked haggard and drawn.

'Georgina! Why on earth are you still here?'

'Oh, Lawrence, I heard what happened in Hong Kong. It's too dreadful to believe.'

'Bloody savages,' Lawrence muttered, closing the door behind him. Georgina thought it was so Lawrence could take her in his arms to comfort her. But she was mistaken. Instead, he went to his desk, opened the drawer, removed a bottle of whisky and two glasses and poured them each a large measure.

'Darling, you are not to tell anyone what you've heard.'

'You can't be serious! Of course people must know – it must be reported!'

Lawrence's mouth flattened into a straight line. 'You signed the official secrets act, did you not?'

'But . . .'

'If you tell anyone, even a single person, what you have discovered here, you will be committing an act of treason. Do you understand?'

This was a side of Lawrence she'd never seen before.

'But that's outrageous,' she said furiously.

'Those orders come from the highest authority. To tell people will only cause panic.'

'What about the nurses in Malaya? What's being done about them? Are they to be evacuated? They have the right to know what happened – what could well happen to them. They should be given the opportunity to come back to Singapore for their own safety.'

'For God's sake, Georgina. Can you imagine what would happen to our injured men if the nurses take it into their heads to jump ship?'

'How can you not tell them! We are talking about defenceless women.' She gripped his arm. He must be made to see reason. 'What if the same thing happens at the hospital where Edith works? At any of the Malaya hospitals?'

'We won't let them be raped.'

'And how exactly are you going to prevent it? These women don't have any means of protecting themselves.'

He looked down at his feet and flushed.

'How, Lawrence?' she demanded. 'Tell me how you or anyone can guarantee they won't be raped and murdered.'

'Their commanding officers – well, some of them think it would be better – for Heaven's sake, Georgina, this is not something you need to know.'

'If you don't tell me, I'll go to the press and tell them everything I've heard.'

'They won't print it. They've been told not to.'

'Then I'll go to your commanding officer and tell him you've been sharing information with me that has been classified above my level. I can't imagine he'll be pleased to hear that. You might even be court-martialled.'

He stared at her, appalled. 'You wouldn't. I allowed you into the office and you had no right to any of the information you garnered here. I trusted you.'

'Then perhaps you shouldn't have. Just tell me.'

He took a long swallow of whisky. 'Some suggest the women should be shot if it looks like they are in imminent danger of being –' he flushed and looked into the middle distance '– you know.'

'Shot by whom? You can't mean ... Dear God. You can't mean that our officers intend to shoot them! As if they were animals that needed to be put down. Tell me that's not true.'

'I doubt it will get approval. Can you imagine the stink if it ever came out? In any case I can't imagine they could bring themselves to do it even if it were an order from high up.'

'Doubt isn't good enough. If you can't promise me that won't happen, I'll go to the press myself and tell them. I'll make sure everyone in Singapore and beyond knows. I'll—'

'Oh, get off your high horse, Georgina. We'll see those bandy-legged blighters off by sundown. There's not a hope in hell of them making it beyond their landing site. It's all just a ruse to get us to send more troops up north.'

'But what if ... What if the Japs do make it through the jungle?'

'I promise you, Georgina. It will never happen.'

She still wasn't convinced. 'If people were so sure of that then why even discuss what they'd do if the Japs did make it through the jungle?'

'Because some of our officers panic more easily than others.'

'I don't find that reassuring, Lawrence. Can't you persuade someone to order the nurses back to Singapore?'

He rubbed his forehead as if to dispel an encroaching headache. 'The nurses are part of the army. They knew the risks.'

'They are women. And not all of them are army nurses. You know there are hundreds of civilians amongst them, as well as volunteers. Do you think they truly knew what they were letting themselves in for? Their officer status was supposed to protect them – much damn use it did.'

He sat down behind his desk and opened the drawer, lifting

out a sheaf of papers. 'You are going to have to excuse me. I have work to be getting on with.' The sun had risen while she'd been waiting for him. 'But I will promise you, if it looks like the nurses are in danger, I will personally insist that they are evacuated.' He picked up his fountain pen. 'That is the best I can do.'

Chapter Thirty-Two

Charlotte

1984

Georgina took a deep, shuddering breath. 'How could one human do that to another? How could they murder doctors and nurses? It wasn't as if they could do them any harm. It was impossible to believe. At first. We came to know differently later. And the fear that my sister could be caught up in that . . . ' she squeezed her eyes shut '. . . didn't bear thinking about.'

I shook my head. I'd known none of this. When we learned about the war, it was always about what had happened during the holocaust. Millions of innocent men, women and children had been murdered then too – on a scale that was difficult to imagine. My generation couldn't really conceive it – the Germans were our friends now – but those that had carried out those crimes or at least were aware of them, still lived. And those who had been their victims lived too. How does a person ever come to terms with man's inhumanity when they have been forced to face it? I didn't know. This had to be why Georgina had asked me whether I believed in evil.

'I think that's enough for one night, don't you?' Georgina said. She glanced at her wristwatch. 'There is an hour or so before the generator cuts out. Why don't you tell me a little more about you?'

Before I could say anything I heard a smothered cry coming

from behind us. Edith stood in the doorway, her hand over her mouth, her eyes glassy.

Georgina jumped up, strode towards her sister and took her hands in hers. 'Darling, how much did you hear?'

Edith shook her head from side to side. Tears flowed, unchecked, down her cheeks.

'I need you,' she whispered.

A look passed between the two women. Then Edith spun away, her quick, light steps fading into the distance.

Georgina turned back to me. 'Please excuse me. I must go with her.'

'Of course. I'm ready for bed myself. I'll just take Tiger outside first.'

But I was already talking to an empty room.

My dreams that night were of blood-streaked women holding out their hands to me, their eyes begging me to do something.

I jerked awake, my heart hammering against my ribs. It was dark – that dense, almost tangible darkness through which I could see nothing. My bedclothes were tangled, as if I'd been fighting them in my sleep, my pyjamas damp with perspiration, around me only silence.

Something had woken me. I was certain someone was in the room with me. I lay rigid, straining my ears for the sound of someone moving about. But if someone had been in my room, or still was, Tiger would have alerted me. Surely. Although by now she was used to Edith and Georgina.

'Who's there?' I said, my voice a strangled croak. 'Is that you, Georgina? Edith?'

Although why either of the women would be in my room in the middle of the night I couldn't imagine.

There was no reply. Fumbling in the darkness, I located the paraffin lamp next to my bed and the box of vesta matches alongside it and with shaking fingers managed to strike a match and hold it to the wick of the lamp, breathing easier when it eventually lit. It only gave off a small pool of light, the rest of the room remained in shadow. But it was enough for me to see Tiger fully alert, her ears pricked up. Knowing I wouldn't get back to sleep until I checked that I was alone – even though common sense told me I had to be – I pushed the blankets aside, shivering as the cold, damp air wrapped around me.

Holding my lamp in front of me, my heart still pounding, I peered into the darker recesses of the room where the light didn't reach. I investigated all the corners, even going as far as searching under the bed and opening the wardrobe door to look inside, berating myself as I did so. There was, of course, no one anywhere in my room but I couldn't shake the feeling that there had been. It must have been the remnants of my nightmare that had frightened me.

I was about to return to bed when I noticed a sliver of light coming from the other side of my door. It was only there for the briefest of moments as if someone had passed by with a candle or a lamp, and paused outside my room before moving on.

I hurried over to the door and flung it open, but there was no one there. I glanced down either side of the corridor and considered investigating further but I was cold and what would I do anyway if I came across Edith or Georgina? It wasn't as if they didn't have the right to wander the corridors of Greyfriars any time they chose. But they slept on the other side of the house. Why come to this wing? To check up on me?

Just then a movement from the far end of the corridor caught my attention and my breath caught in my throat as I saw a figure glide away from me. It had to be Edith, sleep-walking. Had she wandered into my room while asleep? The thought of Edith standing over me while I slept chilled me. Nevertheless, I should check she was okay.

Whispering to Tiger to stay where she was, I gently closed

my bedroom door behind me and hurried down the corridor. If it were Edith I couldn't risk calling out to her; Georgina had said Edith wasn't to be woken when sleepwalking. She was moving quickly despite having no lamp to guide her and had disappeared from view. The light from my own was too feeble to allow me to see more than a few feet ahead.

I paused at the top of the back stairs that led to the kitchen. There was no sign of movement from there. Neither was she in the corridor leading to Edith and Georgina's wing although the door to it was open. I had only ever seen it closed. Perhaps Edith had returned to her room and was, even now, sliding under her bedcovers? The house was freezing and despite the thick pullover I wore over my pyjamas, I was shivering and wanted nothing more than to creep back to my room and bury myself under my blankets. What harm could possibly come to Edith? Just then, I thought I heard the faintest click of a door closing from the servants' staircase halfway down the corridor that led to the west wing. Georgina had said that the west wing was almost an exact replica of the one I slept in, so in all probability there was a similar servants' staircase bisecting the corridor although I couldn't visualise where it might lead. I had a vague recollection of my mother telling me about the nursery and the secret staircase that led from it and to the ramparts. What if Edith had taken it into her head to go up there? In which case I'd have to go after her. She'd been upset earlier and was clearly vulnerable.

I swore under my breath and followed the west wing corridor until I came to a stair. I'd been right then. Unlike the one in my wing this one only led upwards. I hurried up the stone steps to another corridor, narrower than the one below and uncarpeted. Halfway along, on my left, a door was slightly open. I pushed it gently, hardly daring to breathe, and stepped inside. It was even darker, almost pitch-black, no doubt because the shutters were closed. I held my lamp high and, as my eyes adjusted, I made out a single bed, a rocking horse and a bookcase – and right in the corner, the shape of someone watching me.

'Edith?' I whispered, my heart in my mouth.

When there was no reply, and fighting an increasing desire to turn tail and run back to my room, I forced myself to go forward. The light of my lamp cast flickering, magnified shadows on the wall.

The figure was wearing some sort of dress but, I clasped my hand over my mouth, it was headless. Was I still in the throes of my nightmare? Had I not woken up at all?

I stepped closer. And then, when I saw what it was, I almost laughed out loud.

The figure was nothing more than an old-fashioned wooden tailor's dummy such that I'd only ever seen in old photographs. Georgina had said that they made their own clothes and I'd seen a number of Simplicity patterns lying around. When I was younger Mum had made her own clothes too, laying cloth on the table before pinning on the tissue patterns and cutting around the silhouette.

But I was almost sure I hadn't imagined the figure in the corridor and if I hadn't, then she had to be still here or have taken the secret staircase. If this had once been the nursery and it seemed it was, then the door to the secret staircase was at the back of the cupboard.

I found the cupboard easily enough at the side of the room. Placing my lamp on the floor, I pushed the clothes to the side and, lifting my lamp again, peered at the back of the cupboard. There was no handle, no keyhole, nothing to indicate that there was a door. Was the story about the secret staircase a fabrication, a story made up by Georgina to intrigue a little girl?

I hadn't realised I was holding my breath until it came out in a rush.

I'd definitely seen Edith in the corridor earlier, somehow she must have slipped by me and gone back to bed. Everything else was my imagination, the result of the terror of the nightmare I'd been having when I'd woken. Shaking my head at my idiocy, I retreated back to my bedroom.

Tiger was waiting by the door for me and I patted her and for once invited her onto the bed to sleep. She bounded up as if she couldn't believe her luck. I told myself it was her warmth I craved, but I knew it was a friendly presence.

Still shivering I ran over the events in my head. I'd been having a nightmare. That had made my heart race – no wonder I had imagined someone in my room.

But I hadn't imagined Tiger, the hairs on her neck standing on end, and I hadn't imagined the figure fleeing in front of me. And if I hadn't imagined it where had she gone? There was only one door at the end of that corridor and it was too narrow for two people to pass without brushing against each other. So she couldn't have slipped past me without my noticing. Neither could she have disappeared like a puff of smoke. Unless – and the thought chilled me to the marrow – unless it hadn't been Edith I'd seen. Perhaps it had been something far less corporeal? I couldn't help but remember what my mother had told me – that Greyfriars was haunted by the Jacobite woman who had been torn from her child. I almost laughed. I'd been here less than forty-eight hours and already I was thinking of ghostly reasons for something that was bound to have a perfectly reasonable explanation.

I was beginning to feel as if I'd stepped into a different world, as if the person I was, had been, was being swallowed up by Greyfriars and might disappear without a trace. Of course, I didn't believe in ghosts. They did not exist. There had to be another explanation although I was damned if I could think of what it was.

I contemplated wedging a chair under the handle of the door in case my visitor chose to return but decided against it. I absolutely refused to give in to these ridiculous notions.

*

283

By morning, last night's fears and flights of fancy seemed even more absurd. Nevertheless, I felt tired and on edge. The atmosphere at Greyfriars and Georgina's recounting of events in Singapore, coupled with my grief over Mum and my anxiety about work, was clearly affecting me.

It wasn't just that; the great-aunts unsettled me too, Edith in particular. I was certain I wasn't imagining it when I felt she was watching me, or how easily she started at the slightest noise. She reminded me of the starlings that roosted on the rowan tree outside my room at Greyfriars – the way they'd take flight as I approached and fly away in a thick black cloud only to re-alight moments later. At that moment if it hadn't been for the promise I'd made to Mum I might well have packed my leather suitcase and left. As it was, I was glad to be leaving the island behind me for the day. Some time away from the claustrophobic atmosphere of Greyfriars could only do me good.

It was fully light by the time I had used the plastic shower hose to have a lukewarm shower, and dressed in a clean pair of jeans and a silk blouse that picked out the colour of my eyes. Outside it was drizzling again, the sky drained of all colour although it wasn't windy and there was clear sky in the distance and even a hint of sun. I'd already made up my mind, whatever the weather I was going on that walk with Jamie.

I left after breakfast, having said nothing about last night to my aunts – Edith was clearly none the worse for her night-time wanderings and it seemed insensitive to mention it, particularly after her previous reaction. Stopping only to don my new pair of walking boots and shrug into the jacket Georgina had given me the day I'd arrived, I hurried off down to the pier feeling a sense of nervous anticipation. It wasn't a date, I reminded myself, but deep down I didn't really believe it wasn't. Then again, my experience of men was limited. Very limited.

I'd never really got the whole dating thing – especially when to advance and when to retreat – what people called flirting. It wasn't as if I wasn't good at reading body language, I was, I had a reasonable idea when someone fancied me, they simply rarely asked me out. The two men I'd had relationships with I'd met through work. Cyril the Weasel (as Rachel referred to him) was a barrister in another set. He'd asked me out, I'd agreed, dated him for a few weeks – and broken up with him as soon as I'd realised he talked about nothing but himself. I'd also met Christopher through work. I'd needed a medical opinion and Rachel had put me in touch with him. He had lasted longer although, or perhaps because, we'd rarely seen each other and while I'd liked him a great deal, I realised eventually I wasn't in love with him.

The Guthrie women were not great at picking men, that much was evident. Perhaps, like my great-aunts and my mother, I was destined to live on my own. The thought had never and, I told myself firmly, still didn't worry me.

Jamie was waiting for me on the opposite side. He was wearing jeans and a thin sweater and looked good. More importantly he looked safe, solid and normal. He grinned when I stepped ashore and my heart fluttered behind my ribs.

'Ready to go?'

'Whenever you are.'

He pointed to the hills behind him. 'It'll take a couple of hours to reach the top. You okay with that?'

'Of course.' I hoped my thighs were up to it. The weather was clearing, the sun out, the earlier rain on the grass evaporating in ankle-high mist.

As we walked along the road and towards the hills, Tiger trotting happily beside us, we chatted. He liked country music, I hated it, I loved Dylan, he didn't, but we agreed on a dislike of punk, a fondness for Sade and a loyalty to the Rolling Stones. He liked going to the opera, I'd never been. I enjoyed

285

ballet, but he didn't get it. He liked having a pint in the pub, hiking, sailing and mountain climbing. I did none of these. We spoke about the recent gang murders in Moss Side in Manchester and the IRA, both agreeing that there seemed to be no simple solution to either problem. Every now and again he would pause to point out a bird or a deer almost completely disguised by its surroundings.

He was so easy to be with, I found it hard to believe this was only the second time I'd met him. Being with him I forgot for long stretches of time my own misery and anxiety.

Soon we were climbing the steep path and it became almost impossible for me to breathe and talk at the same time and we completed the rest of the way in companionable silence. When we reached the summit, I sank to the ground, Tiger flopping beside me, and rested my back against a rock, glad of a chance to get my breath. The views were amazing. I could see as far as Oban, and Jamie pointed out Mull and Colonsay, as well as many of the other, smaller islands. I could even see the top of Greyfriars' turret.

Out here under the massive blue sky, last night's fears seemed even more ridiculous; the person stumbling around last night not me, but some other deranged woman.

'I brought coffee and sandwiches,' Jamie said, plonking himself beside me and reaching into the small rucksack he'd carried on his back. He brought out a brown paper bag and held it up for my inspection. 'Egg mayonnaise, cheese and tomato and tuna.'

My stomach grumbled in response. I'd had no appetite for breakfast earlier.

'And,' he glanced at Tiger who was looking at him wagging her tail hopefully, 'some treats for you, Tiger.'

The man was practically perfect.

'You must miss all this empty space in Glasgow,' I said as I nibbled on my egg sandwich. Tiger had wolfed down her treats and headed off to explore a tussock of grass.

He grinned. 'That's why I need my annual fix here. More often if I can manage. It lets me forget about the creeps for a while. As a police officer your view gets skewed. You tend to think the world is full of bad people. Every now and again I need to be reminded that the world is a great place, with more good people than bad in it.'

'That's what Mum used to tell me.' Would Mum have recognised the terror-filled woman from last night? Or the one sitting here, her heart tripping? I doubted it.

'Were you close?'

'When I was a child, and in the end, yes.' My voice caught. 'In the middle not so much. I wish I'd spent more time with her before she got sick.'

He stayed silent, waiting for me to go on.

'I wasted so many years. I kept telling myself when I accepted a case that I would see it thorough to its conclusion, then I would take a break, go on holiday, spend more time with Mum. But it never happened. It never seemed to be the right time. Before she died, she made me promise to spend less time at work and more time enjoying life. I think she would like to know I'm on this hill. That I kept my promise to come and see my aunts.'

He studied me with his big brown eyes. 'How are you getting on with them? What are they like?'

Tiger had returned from her explorations and was resting, her head in Jamie's lap.

'Neither of them are the way I imagined. It's difficult not to like Georgina. There's something warm and charming about her. She must have been very beautiful at one time – still is really. I don't see much of Edith. She's quieter. I get the impression if anyone raised their voice, she'd burst into tears.' I accepted the plastic cup of coffee he'd poured for me. 'I'm still not sure why they wanted me to come.'

I told him about them not being in touch with Mum despite the death of her parents and how mystified and hurt

Mum had been, and how Georgina had started to tell me about the past.

'I don't know if they are trying to make amends – via me now Mum is dead – or hoping to excuse, at the very least explain, their behaviour towards her. I sometimes wonder if they're scared I will sell my share of Greyfriars – I don't think they could afford to buy me out – but I don't really think that's the reason. All I do know is that the house feels . . . ' I tried to find the words to explain but couldn't. Sort of sad and haunted, as if it holds secrets? 'Not quite right,' I finished lamely.

'What do you mean?'

I tried to laugh it off. 'Oh, nothing. The house is so big, so dark, it's difficult not to feel spooked. I'm far more used to bright lights and traffic.'

'Have you always lived in London?'

'No. I was brought up in Edinburgh. That's where I went to school.'

'Did you go to university there?'

'No. Cambridge, actually.'

He whistled. 'Lucky you. It's a beautiful city.'

'I know I was lucky, but I wasn't always happy.' The words were out before I could stop them. I could just imagine him with a suspect – he'd have them confessing all sorts of stuff before they knew what they were doing.

'So why weren't you happy?' I'd hoped my confession had slipped past him – although I already knew enough about him to suspect that little did.

I was quiet for a while, wondering what to tell him. He stayed silent, allowing me time to gather my thoughts. I wasn't used to talking about myself. Most men I knew tended to talk over women and, particularly in the company of other men, only wanted to talk about themselves, jostling each other with their words and their need to impress. Jamie didn't appear to feel the need and subsequently struck me as more confident, more self-assured.

288

'When I first went to Cambridge I was a bit of an oddball. I didn't have many friends at school. I rarely, if ever, went to the other girls' homes or even into town with them. I spent most of my time with Mum in the library out of school hours. I was shy and awkward in company, and even more so by the time I went to university. Up until then I'd had little interest in clothes or hair styles – or boys for that matter – any of the stuff most girls my age were interested in.' I glanced over at him. He was still listening intently. 'Everyone at university appeared so confident, as if they knew everything there was to know. To be honest, to begin with, I was intimidated. There was such a competitive atmosphere. Even from first year, people spoke of changing the world, getting in to the best chambers. But although they talked about it, I knew I could make it happen. If I wanted it badly enough. And I did. I spent every waking moment in the law library. Looking back, it was easier to closet myself away there. Libraries were always the places where I felt most at home and it meant I had an excuse, even if only to myself, not to go to all the parties everyone else went to. In fact I rarely went anywhere – never drank – apart from once when I made a bit of an idiot of myself – didn't join any societies or clubs. God, I was so boring! The archetypal, introverted swot!'

I slid him another look. He was still looking at me, a small smile playing around his mouth. 'I find it difficult to imagine you as that girl.'

I didn't. In many ways, hidden, deep down inside I was still her. 'I made it my goal to come first in all of the exams. Law isn't so much about brains, you know, it's about the ability to memorise.'

'It must require some brains,' he teased.

'Yes, of course. But a good memory is even more important. First you memorise – then you apply your brain to see how one case might be relevant to another. Luckily that seemed to be a particular skill I had. Because I loved reading I was very fast at it and read as many of the old law books I could fit in around my lectures. I also read books on psychology. The more I read, the more I was fascinated by the detail of crimes, in particular why a person did what they did. I realised quite early on that if I understood what sort of person the victim was and the background of the accused, I could make a case to myself and once I made the case, it was a simple next step to finding the evidence to support it.'

I smiled ruefully. 'All that swotting and not going out eventually paid off. I got a first and a pupillage in Lambert and Lambert, the chambers I'd set my sights on before I even started the post-graduate course. Even then I had to prove myself. I had to be better than the men, more determined – and way more ruthless. We might have a woman prime minister but the glass ceiling is still very much there. My pupil mistress was one of the first women who'd been called to the bar and she drilled me constantly. After my pupillage I applied for a tenancy at Lambert and Lambert and was accepted. If I'd worked hard before, it was nothing compared to the hours I put in then. I worked all the time, and still rarely went any-where. The first two years were tough in every way – I barely made enough to cover the cost of my tenancy at chambers. Most of the cases I was offered were rapes, domestic abuse, child neglect and not what I had in mind. But every barrister needs to start somewhere. I kept on telling myself that in time I would get the kind of cases I really wanted – the chance to defend innocent people of crimes they hadn't committed – and in the meantime I could put up with anything. So I continued to accept all the rubbish cases, the ones no one else wanted. But here's the thing – I won. And kept on winning. The trouble was that the more successful I was at winning those cases, the more of them I was asked to take on.

'If that sounds self-pitying, it's not meant to be,' I added quickly. It was important he understood. 'I knew how lucky I was. There were women, and many men, who would give an arm and a leg to be in my position. In the last few years, I've been able to pick and choose my cases.' With one regrettable exception. Lucy and her trial wasn't something I was ready to share with him. 'I make good money now – enough to have bought a flat in central London and a decent car.'

He shot me that quirky smile of his and I felt my cheeks flame. 'Now I sound big-headed, but I'm not. It's the simple truth. I've never had any time for coy women.'

'I've never cared for coy women either.'

The look in his eyes made my heart give a little run of beats. 'But the financial rewards are the least of it. I love what I do.' I crumbled the remains of my sandwich between my fingers, feeling as if I'd done a bad job explaining myself. Me, who was usually so articulate. But I wanted to try and make Jamie understand how important my job was to me, how it defined me. It felt important that he did. I flung some crumbs to a seagull who'd been watching us for the last few minutes. It gave a pleased squawk and gobbled it up.

'What's the most excited you've ever felt? The most alive?' I asked.

'Apart from catching a bad guy and seeing him go down?'

'I'll take that as a given.'

He took his time thinking about what I'd asked.

'When I reach the top of a mountain – when I'm sailing and the weather turns. Anything where I'm pitching myself against the elements, pushing myself harder, further than before.'

'That's how I feel in a court room. It's an adrenalin rush – my very own rollercoaster ride. It makes me feel alive – and powerful. Too powerful, I've begun to realise . . . ' I trailed off, dismayed at how much I'd revealed about myself.

But if I'd thought he wouldn't pick up on my words, once more I was mistaken.

His gaze sharpened. 'What do you mean "too powerful"?'

No wonder he'd made Inspector.

'Justice being served isn't the same thing as winning,' I said, recalling the conversation I'd had with Georgina and Edith. I'd started off wanting to defend the powerless but somewhere along the line, I'd lost my way.

'What about Susan Curtis? You saved her from prison, didn't you? Don't you think you achieved justice for her?'

'I thought you didn't approve . . . '

'I don't approve of bullies. In particular those who abuse women. You must have felt good when you won that case?'

'More than good. I felt fantastic. At that moment, life was perfect . . . ' Until I'd learned about Lucy and hard on the heels of that had come the news about Mum. In less than a day I'd gone from feeling on top of the world, to doubting everything about myself.

A sudden breeze whipped my hair around my face. I'd rarely spoken as much about myself, said some things I hadn't even admitted to myself. I wasn't, however, ready to tell him everything.

Anxiety rippled through me, making my stomach clench. What if Giles stopped me coming back to Lambert and Lambert? And though I'd tried not to worry about it, I still wondered if someone would report me to the Law Society. In which case, I might be barred from working as a lawyer at all.

He eyed me speculatively as if well aware I was keeping something back from him. I averted my eyes. A large bird swooped overhead, scattering the flock of seagulls that had joined their pal in hopeful anticipation of more crumbs.

'It's a golden eagle,' Jamie said, following my gaze.

'"I am the swift uplifting rush/ Of quiet birds in circled flight,"' I murmured.

Jamie cocked a questioning eyebrow.

'Lines from a poem Mum and I both loved. Enough about me,' I said, before he could probe further. 'Tell me more about you.'

He leaned back against the rock and tucked his hands behind his head. 'What else would you like to know?'

'Everything' was the simple answer although I didn't say that. What he'd been like as a child? Was he married? Dating? Had he ever been in love?

'Let's start with your connection with Balcreen. You say you come every year?'

'My family comes from Oban. It's where I went to school.'

'Oh. Have they moved on?'

'No. Mum still lives in the house where I was born. Dad died from a heart attack when I was fifteen.'

'I'm sorry. That must have been tough.'

'It was. He was a good man.'

'Don't you get on with your mother?' I asked, sitting up and wrapping my hands around my knees.

'We get on great. She's amazing. You should meet her.'

'Then why don't you stay with her instead of renting a cottage?'

'Partly because I'm used to living on my own–' in which case he couldn't be married I thought with a lift of my heart '–and partly because one or more of my sisters is always at Mum's with their kids.'

'You don't like children?'

'It's not them. They're cute – in reasonable doses. If you met my sisters you would know what I mean. I love them, a lot, but they don't know the meaning of the word privacy.'

'How many sisters do you have?'

'Four. All older.'

'What do they do?'

'Two are married – Becky and Catriona – and live in Oban – Becky is a teacher, and Catriona is a nurse. She has three children. Bethany, the eldest, breeds horses in Kent, and has two under five. Marcia – she's the youngest, has a deli near Oxford. They are all at home at the moment. I'm expected there for lunch tomorrow.' He removed his glasses, and polished them on his T-shirt before replacing them. 'Why don't you come too? We could sail there and back.'

I hesitated. It was another step in a direction I wasn't sure I wanted to take.

'I'll tell them we're friends.' He smiled ruefully. 'Though I suspect my sisters won't believe me for a second.'

Everything was there in the space between his words. We both knew that we were already more than friends – or could be.

He sat up. 'Please come. So what if they jump to conclusions? I'd like them to meet you. My family rarely gets together.' He lifted an eyebrow. 'Although I'm warning you they can be a bit overwhelming.'

There was a challenge in his eyes as well as his mouth.

'I wouldn't like to impose.'

'You wouldn't be. You'd be doing me a favour.' He lowered his voice. 'I want to spend more time with you while I can.' He reached across and brushed my fringe away from my eyes. 'Much more time.'

My skin tingled under his fingertips. Wasn't this all too soon? Where was the in-between bit, where we pretended to be less interested in one another than we were?

He leaned towards me, drawing his finger along the contour of my cheek and under my chin. He lifted my face and kissed me. His lips were warm and firm and I relaxed into him, placing my palm against his stubbled cheek and returning his kiss, feeling every nerve in my body come alive. Tiger whimpered and thrust her body between us, forcing us apart.

'Can I take that as a yes?' His lovely eyes were dancing. 'You will come tomorrow?'

I nodded.

'I don't know what it is about you,' he said, kissing me on the lobe of my ear and sending a shockwave of desire from the tips of my toes to the roots of my hair. 'But I can't remember the last time I wanted to get to know someone as much as I want to get to know you.'

We were definitely missing out the in-between bit. 'You know pretty much everything there is to know.' I pulled away, uncertain whether I wanted to start something, particularly when I had no idea where it would end.

'Tell me more about Findlay,' I said, moving the conversation to safer ground.

'What's your interest? Apart from the fact he rescued you and Tiger?' If Jamie was disappointed in my reaction he didn't show it.

'I think he might once have been engaged to my Aunt Edith – if he's the same Findlay.'

Jamie gave a low whistle. 'The old dog. I hadn't a clue.' He looked thoughtful. 'He did tell me once, when he was drunk, that he'd been in love but she broke it off. Apart from that one time, we never speak about our personal lives. All we talk about is our time in the army. Particularly his. It's far more interesting than mine ever was.'

The sun had come out and was making me feel pleasantly drowsy. I leaned back on my elbows and turned my face to the sun. 'Go on,' I prompted.

Jamie leaned back against his rock. 'That first time, when I took him home, I noticed the beret in his house, and recognised the emblem of the SAS. Michael, my godfather, was one of the Originals so I knew a bit about them. I asked Findlay about it and eventually, grudgingly, the story of his time with the SAS came out. I doubt he would have spoken to me about it if I hadn't been an army man myself once. You've heard of the SAS?'

'Of course. I hadn't known they still existed until the Iranian siege.'

Four years ago the Iranian Embassy in London had been taken over by dissidents and the occupants held hostage for six days. The BBC and ITV news had covered events as they unfolded and people had watched fascinated as the SAS, their faces concealed by masks, had stormed the embassy and overcome the hostage takers. The siege had brought the SAS to the public's attention and the hitherto little-known army regiment had received almost universal approval. Some, however, had questioned whether their killing of four out of the five hostage takers had been necessary.

'They've always worked under the radar. That was their *raison d'être*. Not many people know that they were formed during World War Two by a friend of my godfather – David Stirling. A Scot as it happens. And quite a legend in these parts. When I returned to Glasgow I asked Michael whether he'd known Findlay. Turns out he did. Pretty well, as it happened. It was Michael who recruited him to the SAS.'

A cloud passed across the sun, the breeze picking up a little.

'To understand Findlay you have to know a little about the SAS. Near the beginning of the war, David Stirling ended up having to have a spell in hospital. While he was flat on his back he got to thinking. He concluded that what was needed was a regiment that could be broken into small groups of men. This, he believed, would allow them to move with a lot more stealth and speed behind enemy lines. It took him a while to get agreement from Churchill but he did eventually. Then he started looking for men to join this company. He knew the kind of men he wanted – men who were used to acting on their own initiative as well as being fearless – and he set out to find them. Michael was one of Stirling's first recruits. Michael had known Findlay for years, they were at Oxford together and he knew that he was exactly the kind of man Stirling wanted for his company.

'Findlay was a rugby blue – Michael played on his team. Even then Findlay had a ruthless streak – nothing would do but a win. When he wasn't playing rugby he was partying hard and lucky not to have been sent down. He gave his studies minimum attention. Not that Findlay wasn't bright – he was – he simply preferred playing rugby and having a good time to getting a decent degree.

'Findlay was popular. With men and women. There was a roughness about him – he didn't particularly care about how he dressed or who he offended – but he could be charming too. He was a man who enjoyed life but no one really knew how he'd end up. People did think he had a good chance of playing rugby professionally – it would have suited his character, Michael thought.'

I sat up. Jamie had the natural instinct of a story teller. 'But he didn't? '

'No. I don't think he had the discipline, or the desire. And then the war came and David Stirling's unit. The trouble was that Findlay was in a military prison for striking a fellow officer after a prolonged drinking session in a pub, for some slight – real or imagined. But Stirling agreed with Michael that Armstrong was perfect for his new regiment. To cut a long story short, Stirling got Armstrong. It also turned out my godfather's instincts were right. Findlay was one of the Originals as they came to be known and one of their most successful recruits.

'Stirling had picked the right men. They were audacious and brave, to the point of recklessness. They taught themselves how to parachute, practised landing by throwing themselves from moving jeeps and trained by sneaking up on other units and stealing their tents and equipment,' Jamie grinned, 'even a piano.

'Things didn't go well to begin with. Their first mission was a disaster and they lost about two thirds of their already small detachment. For most people, not Stirling or Findlay however, that would have meant the end of the SAS. So they didn't report back to base. If they had, they would almost certainly have been disbanded. As it was they weren't and they went on to do great things.'

Jamie scrambled to his feet. 'Those clouds look nasty. Let's get going.'

I'd been so absorbed in what he'd been saying I hadn't noticed that black clouds had come in from the west.

He picked up his rucksack, took my hand and we ran helter-skelter down a different path, leaping over patches of scree, before skidding to a halt in front of a house. I was panting and out of breath, but exhilarated; all my earlier anxiety having sloughed off from being in Jamie's company.

'Do you still want to meet Findlay?' Jamie asked.

I nodded. 'More than ever.'

Jamie only let go of my hand when he knocked on the door of the detached house. I tried not to look at him, the nape of his neck, the way his dark hair curled just over his ears, and instead made a show of studying the house and surroundings, which were well maintained. There was a bench by the front door, alongside which were a pile of creels.

When Findlay opened the door he looked far from pleased to see us.

'I suppose you'd better come in,' he muttered, turning on his heel.

Jamie gave me a quick smile and a shrug of his shoulders, stepping aside to let me go in front of him.

We followed Findlay through the hall and into the kitchen. It was bigger than Jamie's but just as neat. There were no dishes on counters or in the sink, newspapers were stacked in a basket next to another basket of logs, and the kitchen table was covered in a plastic table cloth that had been wiped since anyone last ate there.

'You know I don't particularly care for visitors,' Findlay said rudely. In contrast to the spartan tidiness of his living accommodation, his hair was mussed, his face unshaven, his eyes blood-shot. There was also the unmistakable smell of alcohol on his breath.

'Charlotte, this is Findlay Armstrong, Findlay, this is Charlotte Friel. She wanted to thank you for rescuing her and her dog.'

'Bloody stupid to go after a dog.' He nodded in my direction. 'She could have drowned.'

Not exactly the reception I had been anticipating.

But my attention had been drawn to a couple of photographs on the mantelpiece above the fireplace. I crossed over to get a better look. The first was an enlarged and framed version of the one Mum had shown me – the one taken outside Greyfriars with Mum and the sisters gathered on the lawn. He must have kept a copy for himself.

There was no longer any doubt that he was the Findlay Armstrong Edith had loved. Was it possible he still held a torch for her, after all these years?

The other photograph was of a group of men in an army jeep, all but one grinning at the camera. Although they were all in uniform, instead of hats they were wearing Arab head dress and were all unshaven. I recognised the unsmiling driver immediately: Findlay. Despite the stubble covering his face he was very good-looking. Except good-looking wasn't the exact word – hunky, gorgeous, even compelling suited better.

'Seen enough?' I turned around to find Findlay, arms folded across his chest, glaring at me.

It was difficult to see the man he once was – a war hero and the man Edith had hoped to spend the rest of her life with and the one Georgina tried to seduce. Yet, despite his dishevelled appearance, he was upright and tall, and still radiated the kind of masculine assurance most men appeared to long for, but few achieved. With the possible exception of Jamie.

'So you are the Findlay Armstrong my aunts knew!' I said.

'Your aunts?' Findlay frowned.

'Charlotte is staying at Greyfriars for a few days,' Jamie said. 'With the Misses Guthrie.'

Findlay started. 'With Edith and Georgina?'

Several emotions crossed his face in quick succession, too quick for me to pinpoint. Longing? Hope? Shame? Anger?

I nodded towards the photo. 'I gather you knew them once.'

'They told you? What did they say?' He sounded almost eager.

'Only that you were the cause of a falling-out between them. I know you and Aunt Edith intended once to marry. My mother remembered meeting you in 1939 at Greyfriars. She was only a child then but you obviously made an impression on her.'

'Did she send you?' His expression was still unreadable, but he was staring at me with glittering eyes.

'My great-aunt? No, she didn't.'

The light in his eyes faded. 'Then why are you here?'

'Findlay,' Jamie said warningly. 'I explained. Charlotte wanted to thank you.'

'I don't need or want her thanks.'

'You could at least be a little more civil.' Jamie didn't seem the least bit put out by Findlay's rudeness.

Findlay ignored him and spoke directly to me. 'How is she?'

'Edith? She's frail.'

'And Georgina?'

'She seems the stronger of the two. No one who met her would take her for someone who's almost seventy years old.'

He set furious eyes on me. 'God, the young can be so damn condescending. You think that just because a body gets old, that the person inside changes?'

I flinched from the fury in his eyes and had to force myself not to take a step back.

'Do my great-aunts know you live here?' It was the first thing I thought to ask. I had so many questions I didn't know where to start. Why was he here? Had he seen my aunts? Kept in touch? Had he fallen in love with someone else? In which case what had happened to her?

If possible his expression darkened even further. 'I think it's none of your business. I'm sorry, Jamie, but you and your friend will have to excuse me. I have somewhere I need to be.'

'That didn't go too well,' I said, when we were outside again.

'I did try to warn you,' Jamie replied as we headed downhill. 'Some days he's better than others.'

'What happened to him?' It was difficult to reconcile the bitter man I'd met with the charming one my mother had described.

'During the war? He was decorated. Stirling's unit practically destroyed the Luftwaffe in Africa single-handedly.'

'And after?'

'Findlay was one of those men who relished the excitement of combat. I think he became addicted to it. After the war was over he stayed with the SAS for a while, but I understand his behaviour became increasingly unpredictable. From what I can gather he became a professional gambler before ending up here.' He gave me a sideways look. 'When he's not in the pub, or down at the shore, he fishes.'

'Did he marry?'

'Not as far as I know.'

Just then there was a low rumble followed by a flash of lightning. Jamie grabbed my hand again as the sky opened and we ran the rest of the way, stopping only when we reached the shelter of some trees at the start of the road to Greyfriars.

We stood facing each other, both panting from our exertions – me more than him. My heart was beating painfully fast and it wasn't just from running.

He smiled down at me, before cupping my face in his hands and pulling me towards him. Then his mouth was on mine, his lips tasting of the sun. I returned his kiss with a need that shocked me, savouring the long, lean, length of him against my body. When we pulled away I was even more breathless than before.

'I should get back.' My voice was little more than a croak.

'Now? Can't you stay? Come home with me. I'll make dinner. I can't promise it will be edible, though.'

I was tempted. Very tempted. It wasn't dinner I was thinking of and I was certain, neither was he. But I hardly knew him. I remembered what Mum had said to me, about how I needed to let myself go. Grab at life. I was not sure this was what she had in mind.

He was kissing my neck, making it difficult for me to think.

I pressed my hands against his chest, leaning away from him until I could see his eyes. 'I'm not on the pill.' I swallowed, glad of the semi-darkness.

He looked at me, his gaze full of hunger. 'Nothing to worry about. Back at the cottage. In my wallet.'

I pulled him back towards me. 'Then what are we waiting for?'

At his place he kissed me again, more thoroughly this time until my head was spinning, my body on fire. Sensing this he picked me up and set me down on the work top.

'You sure?' he asked, his fingers working on the buttons of my blouse.

I nodded. I was never more sure of anything.

He slipped my blouse off my shoulders where it fell to the ground. The old me would have stopped to pick it up, but this me didn't give it a second thought. My bra straps were off my shoulders, his lips on the swell of my breasts, my hands tugging at his T-shirt. He stopped kissing me long enough for me to get it over his head, then my bra was off and my naked skin was next to his.

'You are so beautiful,' he groaned.

My jeans followed my blouse in a flurry of hands, mine or his I couldn't tell, and he stepped out of his, his underpants following in quick succession. He removed my panties and spread my legs. And then, I stopped thinking at all.

Later, lying in his bed, his long fingers on my scalp, my head on his chest, the rain beating a tattoo on the roof, I felt more peaceful than I had for a very long time – as if the little splinters of me that had been flying in all directions were slowly coming together.

'What are you thinking about? You have a little frown just here.' He ran a fingertip between my brows. 'Not regretting sleeping with the enemy?'

I turned on my side to face him and propped my head on my hand. 'No. You?'

He laughed. 'You kidding? Besides, I have a feeling that you'll defect to the side of the angels.'

'Don't hold your breath.' I mulled over his words. What was the side of the angels? As a prosecutor I could win a guilty verdict on behalf of a victim as easily as I could defend someone who was innocent! The financial side of it wasn't the issue. What had I done with the money I had accumulated in the years I had worked at Lambert and Lambert? Apart from buying a car and a flat, very little. I hadn't even gone on holiday. I owned my flat outright, the car could go without too much pain and I could survive on very little. I could pick and choose the cases I wanted to – the cases where I believed in the innocence of my client. Supposing I was allowed to continue to practice. A knot formed in my stomach.

'What time is it?' I asked Jamie.

'After seven. You're not hungry, are you?'

I kissed him quickly on the lips and before he could respond, threw the blankets back. 'I need to get back to Greyfriars.' I glanced around for my clothes, before I remembered they were in the kitchen.

'I'll take you. Later.' He held out a hand to me and I stepped back. If I let him touch me, I would never make it out of here.

'No. Better not. My aunts will be worried if I don't return soon.'

'We still on for tomorrow?' He hitched himself up on his elbows.

I nodded.

'We'll leave from the bay and call in at my mum's on the way back. We don't have to stay long.' He reached for his glasses. 'I promise it's no big deal.' I must have looked as anxious as I

303

felt. He grinned. 'If you do come it'll stop the endless questions about why I don't have a woman in my life.'

'What time?'

'Eight too early? I like to get out at first light.'

I smiled back at him. 'Do you want me to come here?'

'I could pick you up at Kerista. There's a jetty there, isn't there?' He flung back the bedcovers and followed me, naked, into the kitchen. Tiger greeted us with ecstatic wags of her tail. I reached for my clothes, hopping from one foot to the other as I put on my jeans.

'Great.' I kissed him, twisting away from his arms before he could pull me against him, otherwise I'd never be able to resist dragging him back to bed. 'I'll see you then.'

I couldn't help it; I smiled all the way as I rowed across to Greyfriars.

Edith was waiting for me on the doorstep. 'Supper's been ready for a while. Where have you been?'

There was something child-like about the plaintive note in her voice.

'I'm sorry, I hadn't intended to be out so long.'

'We need to know where you are and when you are coming back. We are used to order in this house – schedules. You can't just come and go as you please.'

'Edith, it's all right.' Georgina appeared in the doorway. The two women exchanged a look and Georgina gave a small nod. *'Everything's* all right. Why don't you take a tray upstairs and leave Charlotte and me to talk?'

Edith narrowed her eyes at her sister but, as always, did as Georgina asked.

'I know supper's waiting but would you mind if I changed first?' I was conscious that the scent of sex might still cling to me.

'Of course.'

'How was your day?' Georgina asked when I came back

downstairs. I'd found her in the kitchen. She gave me one of her mischievous smiles. 'I have to say you have a bit of a glow about you.'

Annoyingly, I reddened. 'Lovely. Thank you.' While I'd been freshening up, I'd thought about mentioning I'd met Findlay, but once more, had decided against it. Better to wait until either sister mentioned him. 'Is Edith all right?'

'She's a little out of sorts. She likes her routines – we both do.' She gave her head a little shake as if bemused by her own foibles. 'Supper is keeping warm in the oven. Let me get it out.'

'Thank you. I'll try not to be late again.'

Georgina set it on the table – some sort of fried spam with more potatoes and carrots – and I thought longingly of the missed dinner in Jamie's cottage.

'It's not very appetising, is it?' Georgina said with a grimace, pushing her plate away. 'But Edith and I never learned to cook. No real interest, I'm afraid.'

'I feel the same,' I admitted. 'That's why I eat out most days.' I hesitated. 'I'm going sailing with Jamie tomorrow.'

She widened her eyes at me theatrically and I blushed again. 'What is he like?'

'He's kind. And honest.' And so much more. 'I think you'd like him.'

'Perhaps I'll meet him some time?'

'It's early days yet and I probably won't be here very much longer. A day or two?'

A look of genuine regret crossed Georgina's face. 'So soon? In that case, I need to carry on with my story. You go through to the library. I'll bring coffee.' She looked at our barely touched plates. 'And a plate of biscuits?'

Chapter Thirty-Three

Georgina

Singapore, 1942

With the arrival of January the news only got worse. Not only were the Japanese making progress south and through the jungle but they were outwitting and defeating the Allied troops at every turn. In recent days they'd started bombing Singapore during the day as well as the night and untold numbers were being killed or hideously maimed.

Edith was never far from Georgina's thoughts and she worried all the time about her sister's safety. Georgina tried to persuade Lawrence to arrange a lift for her to Edith's hospital up north but he told her in no uncertain terms that it was impossible. Since the night they'd argued about the nurses' safety they'd hardly seen each other. Lawrence was kept occupied with his army duties and Georgina spent most of her free time volunteering at the refugee centres.

Civilians from up north continued to pour in, most in only the clothes they stood up in. Trains were sporadic if at all and many had walked, arriving in Singapore worn out, dishevelled and shocked, suitcases in one hand, a child holding on to the other. It wasn't only civilians that flooded into Singapore, there were retreating soldiers too. If possible they looked even more stunned than the civilians.

By mid January the Japanese were only fifty miles from

Singapore, having made their way on bicycles, hacking through the forests and towards Singapore.

It was as if Singapore were divided in two: one side filled destruction and death, the other as if nothing untoward was happening. There was still dancing every night, even at tea time, and people still lunched at the cricket club, swam at the Tanglin or went to the cinema despite having to strain to hear the movie above the racket of bombs and crump of guns. The shops remained full of goods and one could still buy anything one wanted – the *Straits Times* carrying advertisements for silk stockings and several different types of refrigerators, as well as advertising accommodation to let.

But if one perused the personal message columns in the *Straits Times*, the evidence of a country in trouble was clearly there; people looking for missing relatives, abandoned suitcases waiting to be claimed. And when in mid-January the Chinese stopped the chit system that allowed the British to run accounts, insisting on being paid in cash instead, it was clear they, at least, knew the end was in sight.

To deal with the injured and dying, all sorts of buildings had been requisitioned for extra hospitals, including some of the grander homes.

To Georgina's relief, as the situation in the north worsened, the nurses began retreating too, coming to staff the new hospitals that had sprung up in Singapore in an attempt to deal with the increasing number of casualties. At last came the news Georgina had been longing for: Edith's unit had been sent to a makeshift hospital on the Changi road.

Immediately she hailed a taxi, paying twice the normal fare in Straits dollars and headed out there.

The hospital was little more than a collection of bungalows with stretchers holding injured men and women laid all across the grass. But the nurses appeared cool and collected in their pristine white uniforms and veils. They might have been nursing at home before the war for all the concern or fear they showed.

307

When Georgina asked if she might speak to Sister Guthrie, she was shown into a tiny, windowless room and told to wait.

It seemed a very long time before Edith appeared. She looked awful. Her apron was splashed with blood and there were dark shadows under her eyes like bruises, lines around her mouth that hadn't been there before. She was also thinner than when Georgina had last seen her. Georgina's chest constricted. This was her baby sister.

Georgina jumped to her feet, her hands outstretched, doing her best to hide her dismay at her sister's appearance. 'Edith! It's so good to see you.'

If she'd hoped Edith would let her take her in her arms she'd been mistaken. Edith stepped back out of Georgina's reach.

'What on earth are you doing here?'

'I was worried . . . I wanted to see you. To make sure you were all right.'

An irritated frown creased her brow. 'As you can see, I'm perfectly fine.'

Georgina's heart sank. In every other respect she still was the same Edith. Tight-lipped and disapproving.

'Look, can we go outside? I find this room a little claustrophobic.'

'Very well. I have fifteen minutes and could do with a breath of fresh air.'

They stepped back outside and into the humid, earthy air. They found a bench on the lawn in front of the hospital and Edith lit a cigarette. She inhaled deeply and released the smoke thorough her nostrils.

'I didn't know you smoked,' Georgina said.

'There's a great deal we don't know about one another.' When she gave Georgina a hard stare Georgina knew she was referring obliquely to what had happened with Findlay.

'How did you get here? Don't tell me you're driving ambulances now?' Edith continued.

'I would if they let me. I've being volunteering – making myself useful. Or at least trying to.'

308

Edith raised her brows in astonishment. 'You never struck me as the Nightingale sort.'

'I'd never struck myself as the Nightingale sort.' She didn't tell Edith that she wasn't volunteering at the hospital, but at one of the refugee centres – that she didn't have the stomach for blood and gore. She had some pride left.

They shared a smile – the first they had in years – before Edith clearly remembered she hadn't forgiven Georgina, frowned again and glanced pointedly at the fob watch she wore pinned to her uniform.

'I've come to tell you that you need to leave Singapore,' Georgina said quickly, realising Edith was about to get up and return to work. At one time they could practically read each other's thoughts.

'Leave?'

'Yes, leave! It's too dangerous for you to stay. You must go back to Britain. You can nurse in one of the hospitals there just as easily.'

Edith laughed shortly. 'I can't simply leave just because you've taken it into your head that I should! You forget I am part of the British Army and an officer. We go where we're told to. And that's how it should be.' She gestured towards the hospital. 'Every inch of space is taken up with patients – we couldn't possibly abandon them.'

'Perhaps the Japanese will take care of them.'

Edith's lips twisted. 'The way they did in Hong Kong?'

'You heard what happened?'

Edith's expression softened and her eyes filled. She took a shaky draw of her cigarette. 'I wanted to get off with the nurses in Hong Kong. Not just because I didn't want to come to Singapore—'

Georgina winced.

'But because my friend Anne was one of the QAs who was allocated to work there. We'd gone through all our training together, worked side by side in the military hospital in

309

Edinburgh before we were sent overseas.' She gripped Georgina by the arm. 'She was in Hong Kong, Georgie, when the Japs invaded. You know people. Can you find out what happened to her? I'm going mad thinking about it.'

It felt good to have Edith talking to her again, even better that she was asking for Georgina's help.

'I'll do my best,' Georgina said. 'I promise. But, Edith, what the Japanese soldiers did in Hong Kong is why you need to leave here. What if they do the same thing here? Oh, Eadie, I couldn't bear it if something happened to you.'

But the small fissure in Edith's coolness had closed again. 'A bit late to be acting the concerned big sister, don't you think?'

'Don't – please don't – make what I did to you the reason you won't leave. They need nurses in Britain. What use will you be to anyone if the Japs overrun the hospital?'

'I can't go. I'm needed. Besides, as I said, we're as much a part of the army as anyone else. We don't retreat just because we're frightened. Imagine if we all did that! We might as well all go home.' She glanced at her fob watch again. 'But there is nothing stopping you from leaving Singapore. Go home, Georgina,' she said. 'I don't understand why you stay.'

'Because you think I don't do anything useful? Because I'm a useless mouth as they like to call us?' Georgina couldn't help but smile. 'I've been called many things in my life, but that is one of the worst.'

'There is no point in us both risking our necks!' Edith's expression softened again. 'Go home, Georgina. As soon as you can book a berth. Think of Olivia. She needs one of us. It's what Harriet would have wanted and expected.'

'I'm not leaving without you. We're in this together. You're my sister.'

'You should have remembered that before now.'

'And you shouldn't keep bringing that up,' Georgina retorted, exasperated. 'It's been years, Edith. I've begged you

310

to forgive me. I've said I'm sorry. Tell me what else you want me to do and I'll do it.'

Edith took a draw of her cigarette. 'I saw him, you know.'

'Findlay?' Georgina's heart banged against her ribs.

'He came to see me when I was in Peebles. He was going to join his regiment abroad.'

Georgina stayed silent, her whole body stiff with the effort not to show a reaction.

'We talked. He told me what happened.'

Georgina's heart stood still. 'What did he say?'

'More or less what you did. He wants us to get back together.'

Georgina wasn't sure if she felt relieved or dismayed. 'And will you?'

Edith removed a strand of tobacco from her tongue. 'I think so. After this is all over. Supposing we survive.' She narrowed her eyes against the cigarette smoke. 'I still love him. And I believe he still loves me. One thing this God-awful war has taught me is that life is too short not to forgive. Or to have regrets.'

'Does that mean you forgive me?' Her throat was tight and she had a crushing pain in her chest.

'It's harder with you. You were the one who was supposed to watch out for me. Sisters are supposed to stick together. Why did you have to go after him?'

There was no answer to that – at least not one Georgina could share with her.

The sound of grinding gears caught their attention as several trucks with red crosses pulled up outside the hospital.

Edith ground out the cigarette beneath her heel. 'Looks like it's starting again. I need to go.'

'I'll come back,' Georgina shouted. 'I'll keep coming until you agree to leave.'

But her sister was already gone.

Over the next weeks, Singapore descended into chaos. Drunk, shocked, dazed soldiers wandered the streets and the dead, too many for the ambulances to collect when the wounded had to take priority, lay unburied on the streets. Even the additional hospitals couldn't cope with the number of casualties. When beds ran out they lay everywhere; on the floors, in the corridors, on verandas, even in garages of requisitioned houses or in the ditches the troops had dug.

Yet, astonishingly, people more or less carried on as normal. Houses for sale or rent were still advertised in the press.

It was as if everyone had gone completely mad.

At end of January Winston Churchill sent a message, broadcasted from the House of Commons. 'Bad news from the Far East . . . and highly probable we shall have more.'

The army had been told to hold on as long as possible – to fight to the last man. It was finally an admission that Singapore was lost and, worse, on its own. No more help would be coming from Britain.

Within days the authorities had made four troopships available for 'useless mouths' and finally people were making for the docks in earnest.

But the government's final admission that Singapore was in deep trouble came far too late, and was made even worse by the ineptness of the way in which they went about organising the evacuation. The P&O line were put in charge. It turned out to be a terrible decision that ended up costing lives. Instead of piling as many as they could reasonably fit on to the ships, people had to buy tickets and book berths. To Georgina it was the equivalent of taking bookings for lifeboats – not that many appeared to agree with her. Her voice was a lone one. And as if to make securing a berth even more difficult, despite the constant bombardment that made it almost impossible to travel any distance along Singapore's roads, the P&O moved their booking office out of the city to a bungalow several miles away from the docks. It was as if no one in Singapore could let themselves believe what was actually happening. The British sang froid was one thing, burying one's head in the sand, another.

312

Everyone lined up outside the bungalow and the queues stretched for miles, countless feet tramping the lawn into mud. People would take shelter as Japanese planes flew over dropping bombs, flinging themselves to the ground before calmly retaking their place in the queue.

There were two queues: one for those wanting to go to Britain and another for those wishing to go to Colombia. But even the constant bombardment, and the fact that Singapore was holding on by a thread, didn't stop those manning the desks from demanding passports and money for fares from people who had lost everything they owned. Women were even asked to produce their marriage certificates – as if that had the slightest bearing on anything. And if that wasn't bad enough, even after the passengers had their tickets, after everything they'd gone through to get them, when they made it back to the docks, they were forced to queue again at a small gate where a single clerk made out their tickets, taking his time to write each person's name in copperplate. If Georgina hadn't seen it for herself, she wouldn't have believed it. She had held off buying a ticket for one of the ships, but knew time was fast running out.

Tsing Tsing had long since gone into the jungle with Georgina's blessing. There were no berths to be had for non-Europeans and nowhere for them to go even if there had been. Georgina was ashamed of the way they'd let the locals down. They'd abandoned the servants and employees who had served them well in north Malaya and were essentially doing the same all over again. As it turned out, Tsing Tsing had made the right decision.

On the tenth of February the Japanese reached Bukit Timah only five miles from the city and no one could doubt any longer that Singapore would fall. Robinson's store began to give their stock away. Mothers and children with only what they stood up in were given two complete sets of clothes – one to wear – one immaculately wrapped. Aimless and exhausted soldiers wandered the streets, getting drunk whenever the opportunity presented itself. Even order at Raffles Hotel had collapsed, the ballroom full of drunken servicemen and the floor littered with beer cans. Yet in a city where services, gas, water, electricity, drainage were collapsing under the constant bombardment, the last issue of the *Straits Times* – reduced to a single sheet – still carried the headline *Singapore Must Stand; It SHALL Stand.*

But at last, the news Georgina had been holding on for; the nurses were being evacuated.

Chapter Thirty-Four

Dodging bombs and shells and the scores of unburied bodies that almost blocked the streets, Georgina ran towards the hospital. She held a handkerchief over her nose in a futile attempt to keep out the stench of putrefying bodies and overflowing sewage, that mingled with the alcohol spilled in an attempt to stop the Japanese getting hold of it and going on another violent rampage. Fires blazed everywhere and a thick black pall of smoke hung over the city, stinging her eyes and blurring her vision.

Brand new cars had been driven over the edge and into the sea, others abandoned amongst the dead and set alight. Everything that could be of use to the Japanese had been set on fire, including the oil tanks on the naval base.

The Japanese planes bombed continuously, Allied soldiers wandered dazed and bewildered without hope or direction. The best anyone could hope for now was to make it onto one of the few remaining ships.

Georgina fought her way through the crowds, pushing aside anyone who got in her way – the need to get to Edith all she could think about.

She almost sobbed with relief when she saw her sister amongst the other nurses waiting by a truck, their suitcases beside them.

'Dear God, Georgina. What are you doing here? I was sure you'd have left by now.'

'I couldn't leave. I said I wouldn't without you.'

'Tell me you have a ticket.'

'I don't think it matters whether one has a ticket any more. It's pandemonium at the docks. They're trying to squeeze people on wherever they can find a space.'

'Sister, you need to get in,' a soldier said, holding his hand out to Edith.

'Push up, girls.' Edith leapt on board, ignoring his hand 'We need to make space for one more. Come on, Georgina.'

The truck was revving, the driver clearly impatient to get going. The racket of artillery fire sounded as if it was almost on them. Georgina grabbed the soldier's hand and followed Edith onto the truck.

If it were possible the dock was even more chaotic than it had been in the days before. Now there was no longer even a pretence of people queuing. Scores of women and children stood right up to the very edge of Clifford Pier, the girls in white dresses, ribbons in their hair, the boys neatly dressed in shorts and shirts.

As each launch approached the quayside people poured in, clutching their suitcases in one hand, their children in another. The boats filled in minutes and set off back to the waiting ships. Just when Georgina was giving up hope they would ever find a space on one of the ships, the helmsman of a launch, already two thirds filled, gestured to the group of nurses. 'Sisters! Over here.'

Georgina hoped that she'd be included in the group, that her civilian status wouldn't mean she would be left behind, but the helmsman looked at her and shook his head.

Edith grabbed her hand and pulled her forward. 'She comes,' she said flatly, giving him a hard look. Georgina couldn't help but smile. If this was how Edith was when she was looking after her patients, God help them.

Georgina tumbled onto the launch with the remaining nurses and within moments they were pulling away. Along with the majority of the women and children on board, Georgina turned to face the city that had been home these last few years. Some sobbed silently, but most sat straight backed, chins held high, fighting back tears. Most would have left husbands, brothers, sons and fathers behind to who knew what fate. Georgina hadn't seen Lawrence for days. Naturally he had to remain with his regiment. Georgina sent a quick prayer heavenwards for them all.

As the sky burned red from the fires, Georgina reached for Edith's hand and for once Edith didn't pull hers away.

Even on board the ship they weren't out of danger. The strait was heavily mined and out at sea, Japanese warships lay in wait. The captain, hoping that the Japanese would miss them in the darkness, waited for night to fall.

Georgina and Edith stayed on deck as did many of the other nurses and passengers. It was so crowded there was no room to lie down. Georgina sat next to Edith, her back against one of the bulkheads.

'You should go down below,' Edith said to Georgina. 'Where it's safer.'

'If we're going to be bombed I'd rather get blown to pieces than get trapped down there,' Georgina said. The cargo hold would be even more crowded. Hot as hell, dark and airless.

'Do you always have to be so dramatic?' Edith hissed. 'For God's sake, there are children. Do you want to frighten them completely out of their wits?'

Although night had fallen, the heat was still intense. Bodies pressed up against each other and the murmurs of mothers soothing their children filtered through the still air. It was a relief when the boat finally moved out to sea.

'What will you do when we get back?' Edith asked after a while.

'I have no idea. Try and make myself useful. You?'

'I'll be sent somewhere else, I imagine. We nurses would have stayed in Singapore given the choice.'

317

'Will they give you leave, do you think?'

'Perhaps a week or two. Do you know, for the first time, I think I'm actually looking forward to a British winter. I've been so hot these last months.'

'What's it been like for you? The war, I mean.'

'Terrible and awful, but exciting too. I'm glad I was part of it. '

They fell silent and Georgina dozed a little, allowing herself to hope that they might make it.

She was jolted awake by an enormous explosion. Debris, and body parts of people who only moments before had been squashed up against her were sent flying into the air. Dazed and with her ears ringing, at first Georgina couldn't take in what had happened. But as the boat began to keel over and screams filled the air, she realised they must have been torpedoed. She couldn't see Edith in the thick smoke. She had to find her!

As the boat began to list even further, Georgina, a sob in her throat, scrambled on her hands and knees searching for Edith. Then as the smoke cleared, she saw her. Her foolish, brave sister was already moving towards the injured, even though it was clear the ship was doomed.

Georgina lurched towards her and grabbed her arm. 'There's no time. We're sinking!'

Edith tried to shrug her away, but Georgina tightened her grip. As the ship tipped to the side, they were unable to prevent themselves from slithering into the crowd of people desperately clutching on to the sides as the lifeboats were lowered.

Then – Georgina didn't know how – whether it was the angle of the ship or the pressure of bodies behind her, but she found herself in the water. She surfaced, gagging on the sea water she'd swallowed. Survivors bobbed in every direction, held up by the buoyancy of their life jackets. Mothers called for children or desperately reached out for them. Not everyone alive in the water had a jacket on – some had decided not to bother as the heat was bad enough without them – and they clung to whoever or whatever they could find.

At first she wasn't any more frightened than she had been on the ship. She was wearing a buoyancy aid, and even if she hadn't been, she was a decent swimmer and she'd kept up by doing several laps a couple of times a week at the swimming club. There were also some lifeboats around. One of them would pick her up, and if they didn't, they couldn't be that far from land.

She scanned the sea, desperate to catch a glimpse of Edith, but it was impossible to see her amongst the bodies and wreckage. She screamed her name, but her voice was drowned out by the shouts and cries of others. The crew, or what remained of them, were still trying to launch the remaining lifeboats. Anyone could see there wouldn't be enough for everyone.

One overloaded boat slipped into the water but sank a few minutes later. It was either holed or there were too many people in it.

The sea was lit by the burning ship. Almost blood red. This, Georgina thought, was what hell would be like.

Away from the flames, it was darker. She'd become separated from the rest of the survivors having put some distance between herself and the sinking vessel, realising that if she stayed too close she might be sucked under alongside it. She prayed Edith had thought to do the same. The moon's reflection on the sea invoked memories of evening dinner dances at the Sea View Hotel. If it hadn't been for the terrible cries around her she might have been back there. Still treading water she conjured up a mental image of the route the ship had taken, how long they'd been at sea and the relative knots of the boat. If she was right, they couldn't be too far from land. All she had to do was stay calm, wait for dawn and try to spot land and swim towards it. No doubt those on the lifeboats would be thinking the same thing.

319

But then, louder than the cries around her, a scream rose into the night air. 'Jack! Where's my Jack? Please! Someone help us. He can't swim.'

She glanced around. Amongst the survivors and, God help them, the floating corpses, was a small child clinging on to a piece of flotsam. His mouth was gaping open and his small hands couldn't continue to hold on for too long. The nearest lifeboat to him was a considerable distance away.

Georgina turned on to her front and began swimming. Now the life jacket was more of a hindrance than a help, but she daren't stop to remove it. Furthermore she would need it for the child.

The ship was sinking fast, pulling the current towards it and she had to strike out hard to prevent herself from being pulled towards it. Her soaking wet dress and her shoes didn't help either. She stopped and slipped off her shoes, keeping her gaze pinned on the struggling child, knowing that at any moment he might let go and disappear under the waves.

His head had slipped under once by the time she reached him, but he was still holding tightly to the piece of flotsam. This, she knew, was the most dangerous bit. If the child panicked he could drag them both under.

Treading water again she untied her life vest, talking to the child all the while in a low, soft voice. 'Everything's going to be all right, Jack. I'm going to take you to your mother and then we're going to get on a boat with her.'

As she reached for him, the thing that she'd worried about happened. He gave an almighty cry and flung himself towards her, wrapping his arms and legs around her head, blinding and disorienting her, his weight pushing her down.

She swallowed water, and had to fight the panic that threatened to overwhelm her, knowing if she let it, she might push the child away. Under any other circumstances she might have laughed at the image the pair of them must have made.

She shouted at him to be still, turned him around, slipped

her life jacket off and over his head. She dragged him over to a lifeboat where willing hands hauled him on board. A hand reached for her too and she was about to grab it, when she looked over her shoulder. There were several others still in the water clinging to any piece of flotsam they could find. Some of them looked as if they might have been injured in the explosion and couldn't hold on much longer. She had no choice. Not really.

She went after them. She only managed two – a young Eurasian girl and an elderly matron – before she realised she was too exhausted to continue. Yet she couldn't stop – not while there were people still in the sea. She hung on to the side of the lifeboat for a few moments, just long enough to regain her breath, and struck out again.

Corpses, some with limbs missing, littered the sea. As she swam past, if there was any suggestion the person might still be alive, she checked, and if they were dead, which most were, she tore off their life jackets and handed it to one of those clutching desperately to anything that floated.

She collected a boy of fifteen and a woman she vaguely remembered meeting at the tennis club. The woman's hand was missing.

Every time Georgina returned to the lifeboat it was at the mercy of the current, drifting further and further out to sea until finally it was out of sight. She trod water, knowing she had no energy left to do more than try to keep herself afloat and wait for daylight.

But her strength was already exhausted – whether from the effort of swimming or from shock, she couldn't be sure. All she did know for certain was that she would never make daylight.

She made her legs keep moving, holding on to the hope that a lifeboat would come past, but none did. So this was how her life would end. She thought of Findlay; that last summer at Greyfriars; she, Edith and Harriet as children, and felt peaceful. She was getting so sleepy. All she had to do was close her eyes and let herself drift away.

Then she heard someone screaming her name. It was Edith! The sound of her sister's voice made her want to cry. She tried to swim towards her but she had no energy left. Minutes later, Edith grabbed Georgina under her armpits.

'I've got you now,' Edith shouted in her ear. 'Just float and I'll pull you.' Georgina did as Edith asked. Her sister had always been the stronger swimmer, but to stay in the water until she'd found her . . .

How could she have ever doubted her love?

It seemed like ages until a lifeboat came alongside and she was being hauled aboard. People were still in the water, crying for help, but Georgina knew she was utterly spent and could do no more. But to her dismay, Edith didn't follow her aboard. Instead she swam back into the darkness and disappeared from sight. Georgina spent the remainder of the night shivering, searching the water for a sign of Edith, praying she was on a life raft.

But the horror wasn't over. Dawn was beginning to light the sky when they heard the familiar, dreadful sound of Japanese planes. Even after everything she'd witnessed, Georgina prayed they would leave them alone. It was obvious the survivors were mainly women and children. Her prayers weren't answered.

The pilots opened fire, strafing the people still in the sea, the lifeboats. They kept coming back. Again and again and again. Many who'd survived the night were killed.

When it was over there were dozens more bodies floating in the sea. The ship had finally gone under and the other lifeboats had disappeared. To her utter despair, there was no sign of Edith.

They spent a whole day and another night in the lifeboat with corpses and occasionally parts of bodies floating past them. Many in the lifeboat didn't make it, either because of the severity of their wounds or because of shock and sunstroke, most likely a combination of all three. There was an Australian nurse on board, who checked everyone, but as soon as she was sure there was no sign of life, they said a quick prayer and pushed the body over the side.

Eventually, they made land. Not from any real effort on their part but because a combination of wind and tide brought them in. If it had been a boat with a sail Georgina might, she supposed, have managed to do something to make it go where they wanted – however, it was good luck they had to thank.

But it wasn't good luck at all, although they were only to find that out later. Then, the island seemed like an oasis; a sanctuary. They were all burnt from the sun, deathly thirsty and, those still alive, on the verge of collapse.

They stumbled ashore. Some of the other lifeboats had washed up there too. To Georgina's enormous joy and relief, she saw a familiar figure, wearing only pants and a brassiere, bustling around with two other QAs and a few nurses from the Australian army. She stumbled over to her sister and enfolded her in her arms. They clung to one another for a while before Edith pushed Georgina gently away. 'I have patients to see to. Are you all right?'

Georgina nodded. Apart from sunburn and a few scrapes. Nothing compared to the injuries others had sustained. And nothing that mattered, now she'd found Edith alive.

There was little the nursing sisters could do for the injured. One nurse had managed to hang on to her handbag in which she'd stuffed some basics; cotton wool, antiseptic, a bottle or two of quinine – but that was all and had to be shared amongst everyone.

All that day they sat on the beach too stunned to move, still clinging desperately to the hope that other survivors would make it ashore and, indeed, a party did come around from another part of the island but in the end, out of six hundred on that ship, only fifty or so made it to the beach.

They waited, hoping against hope that more survivors might make it, but only corpses, body parts and flotsam washed up on the shore. Several suitcases floated in too. Some of the women fell upon them, claiming them as their own. No doubt mostly they were. They were still a civilised bunch then and it wouldn't have done to steal someone else's belongings, even if they were almost certainly dead.

When it became clear they couldn't stay on the beach without anything to eat or, more importantly, drink, they agreed they'd spend one more night there and walk to the nearest village as soon as it was light in hope of finding a villager willing to give them food and water. At worst, they would be captured by the Japanese. Despite what had happened to the ship, the way the Japanese pilots had strafed them when they'd been helpless in the water, they still believed that their captors would treat them decently. It could only be a matter of time before the British or the Americans got the upper hand and they'd be home again.

Chapter Thirty-Five

Charlotte

1984

Georgina sighed. 'Little did we know most of us wouldn't make it and for the rest of us, it would be four long years before we saw home again.'

My great-aunt looked completely drained, as if she'd relived every moment of that horrible experience. At times during her story, Georgina had almost faltered, her words coming in short gasps.

We sat in silence for a while listening to the wind, the ticking of the clock, the creaking of the house.

'The Edith you see now is not the woman she was back then,' Georgina said sadly. 'I wish you could have known her then. She was so brave, almost fearless. She risked her life repeatedly to save countless lives. And mine.' There was a note of wonder in her voice. 'And for years she held on to that courage.'

I did wish I could have met that Edith. I was finally beginning to understand why she always appeared so fearful. I vowed to be less impatient with her.

'You were brave too,' I said. 'You saved that little boy's life. I'm not sure I would have been as brave.'

Her face flushed. 'You must listen to the rest of the story before you make up your mind. I doubt you'll feel much admiration for me by the time I've finished. I'm only telling you how it was so you understand what we both went through and why we made the choices we did.' She gave a wan smile. 'And perhaps, part of me wants you to know I wasn't all bad.'

'I would never think that!' And I meant it. Whatever wrong Georgina thought she had done she, like Edith, had risked her life to save others. She'd been bombed, strafed by the Japanese, endured being shipwrecked. No one could have gone through what she and Edith had and remained unaffected. Any normal person would have been sent over the edge, but Georgina was clearly made of sterner stuff. It was impossible not to admire her for it – and Edith for that matter. I had two exceptional women as great-aunts.

'What about the little boy? Jack, I think you said?'

Georgina's face clouded. 'I hope he made it. I like to think he did. I never saw him or his mother again.'

'Shall I pour us a sherry?' I asked. 'Or make some more tea?'

'No, thank you. I'm all right. I'd rather plough on. Get through the next bit. If you can bear to listen? It doesn't get much better I'm afraid.'

'You can tell me as much, or as little as you want to,' I re-assured her.

Georgina took a deep breath and folded her hands in her lap. 'We soon learned that everything we'd heard and seen of the Japanese army was only the beginning. All of us who made it onto that beach were one thing the evening we fled from Singapore, and by the end of the war, something else completely.'

'You were captured?'

She nodded. 'If we'd known what was to happen to us, we would have taken our chances in the jungle.'

Chapter Thirty-Six

Georgina

1942

Before they left the beach, Georgina opened the suitcases that hadn't been claimed. She'd lost her luggage and shoes and all she had was the dress she was wearing which had dried to a cardboard-like texture from the salt water.

Ignoring the appalled looks some sent her way, she pillaged everything she thought might be useful; dresses, shorts, hats, medicines. Nevertheless, the nurses accepted the medicines she had gathered – that was for the common use after all – and Edith took a pair of shorts and a top, pulling them on over her brassiere and pants. Georgina changed out of the dress she was wearing and into a flower-sprigged frock that was a little too big for her, but all right once she'd found a belt to tie around her waist. She also found a scarf which she wound around her head to protect her scalp from the fierce rays of the sun. Disappointingly, there were no shoes that fitted. She bundled the remaining items into a shawl and slung it over her shoulder.

They headed inland, a scraggly bunch of stunned survivors. Some could barely move from lack of food and water or shock and their wounds. They walked the whole day, the men using whatever they could to hack their way through the jungle, stopping only to rest for short periods. It was dusk before they finally stumbled across a small village. They waited until they were certain there were no Japanese about before they approached.

As Georgina was the only one with more than a few words of Malay, she was elected spokesman. The village elder was frightened and wanted them to go, but eventually, reluctantly, probably because there were women and children in the group in a bad way, he agreed they could stay, but only for the night. They would have to leave in the morning.

The villagers shared what food they had with them. The survivors were all so exhausted they ate in silence. The mothers with children were given a hut to sleep in while everyone else had to make do with a patch of hard ground under the huts. They made themselves as comfortable as they could and went to sleep.

At dawn they were woken by shouts, cries and the firing of guns. They scrambled out from their make-shift beds to find to their horror, that they were surrounded by Japanese. The villagers streamed out of their huts and some tried to run into the jungle. Two were shot before they made it to safety.

Most of the soldiers were on foot or on bicycles, stained with sweat, their faces grimy from battle. In front was a jeep with an officer in a pristine uniform. He was about fifty with greying hair and a small moustache. There was almost something avuncular about him. Little did Georgina know then that he would haunt her dreams for the rest of her life.

The soldiers prodded everyone into line with the tips of their bayonets. They were made to stand to one side, the villagers to another. The mothers shielded their children's faces, wrapping their arms around them and whispering soothing words. The rest stood ramrod straight. Edith was next to Georgina and they shared sad smiles before grasping hands. So once again they faced death. They held tight, trying to give each other courage. The sun was up by this time and Georgina believed she'd just seen her last sunrise.

The Japanese officer exchanged a few words with the elder who had dropped to his knees in front of him, pleading for the lives of the villagers – saying if anyone had to be blamed for sheltering the Europeans it should be him. It made no difference. The officer barked a command and the Japanese soldiers set upon the villagers. They bayoneted them all.

Chapter Thirty-Seven

Charlotte

1984

Georgina's voice cracked and a spasm ran through her. 'I don't think any of us could believe what was happening. One of the crewmen tried to intervene but he was restrained. After all the villagers were slaughtered, the Japanese officer made the sailor take off all his clothes and kneel naked in front of him. He took his sword from his belt and sliced the sailor's head from his neck. Then the soldiers set the village alight. We could smell it burning for a long time.'

She stood. Her face was ashen in the gathering dark, her eyes enormous. She passed a hand over her face. 'I'm sorry. It's all rather taken it out of me. Would you mind if I left off here?'

Appalled and sickened by her story, I was nevertheless desperate to know what happened next and what it had to do with the help they imagined they needed now. But I could see the toll the telling of her story had taken on her. 'Of course,' I said softly. 'I'm a little tired myself. I'll take Tiger out and then I think I'll head for bed.'

The truth was Georgina's account had left me feeling drained and nauseous, as if all oxygen had been sucked from the room and the house was closing in on me.

'In that case, I'll bid you goodnight.'

A lump in my throat, I watched her walk away, stiff backed and proud, apart from the slight stoop to her shoulders, the ever-present pencil jammed in her hair. This woman – these two aunts – had faced death with courage I doubted I possessed. Whatever they'd done in the past, I was proud to be their grand niece.

Outside, I drew in deep lungfuls of air. The rain had cleared as had most of the clouds and the moon was a ragged disc in the sky. With no need for a torch in the moonlight, I headed towards the shore, following the path Georgina had taken me – was it really only three days ago? From there I knew I would be able to see the lights of Balcreen and, in particular, Jamie's cottage. I had a need to connect with him, even though he was on the other side of the water.

Just then a movement caught my eye. A figure was in front of me, too far from me to see who it was, also moving towards the west side of the island.

It had to be Edith again. Not wanting to call out lest I frighten her, I hurried to catch up with her, Tiger at my heels. I slipped through the gap in the rhododendrons but despite moving as fast as I dared without the light of a torch to guide me, she had disappeared by the time I emerged. I peered into the shadowy darkness.

She could be anywhere; amongst the copse of trees, down by the shore, she might even be making her way towards the farm. I had no way of knowing. I hesitated, straining to catch a glimpse of her, wondering what to do. If I went back to the house to find Georgina it might be too late. Although Georgina had told me she and Edith knew Kerista like the back of their hands, the ground underfoot was overgrown and uneven. Edith could stumble and fall, her thin bones snapping like twigs.

'Where is she, Tiger?' I said, my voice sounding unnaturally loud in the silence.

Tiger looked up at me and whined. Then, as if she knew what I wanted her to do, she put her nose to the ground and set off, checking behind her to make sure I was following.

We found Edith at the shore's edge, close to the rocks and staring out over the water towards the distant lights of Balcreen. Suppressing a shiver of apprehension, I moved towards her and came to stand next to her. Although she didn't acknowledge my presence she seemed aware of me.

'Shall we go back in, Aunt Edith?' I murmured, putting my hand very gently on her shoulder.

When she didn't reply, I drew her towards me, tucked her arm into mine and very carefully led her back to the house.

Chapter Thirty-Eight

I slept badly. Every time I closed my eyes my head was filled with images of the dead and dying; of body parts floating in the sea, of mothers desperate to protect their children from exploding bombs and raining bullets or the blade of a bayonet. Could there be anything more terrible than being unable to protect your child? My thoughts kept straying to Alfred Corrigle, Lucy's father, and how he must have sat next to his daughter in hospital, terrified she would die.

I was relieved when the chorus of the birds alerted me that it was almost daylight and I could reasonably get up.

I washed and dressed quickly, wondering whether Edith had remained in bed for the rest of the night or if she'd spent it roaming the house, searching for who knew what but most likely freedom from the nightmares that must surely plague *her*.

I found Georgina in the kitchen, stirring a pot of porridge on the stove.

She turned and smiled at me but I couldn't help but notice that the tender area beneath her eyes was dark as if she too had spent most of the night awake.

'Tea?' she asked.

'I'll make it.' I spooned tea leaves into a china pot and upended two mugs I found on the draining board. 'Is Edith okay this morning?'

Georgina's smile was replaced by a frown. 'As far as I'm aware. Why do you ask?'

'When I went outside, after we'd said goodnight, I saw Edith heading towards the shore. I worried she was sleepwalking again so followed her. I caught up with her at the shore where there's those big rocks. You know which ones I mean? She woke up when we got back to the house. She didn't seem to be surprised, just said goodnight and went off to bed.'

I was unprepared for Georgina's reaction. All the blood drained from her face and she swayed on her feet, grabbing the back of a kitchen chair for support.

'By the shore? By Sarah's rocks?' she whispered. 'Oh, no.' She sank into the chair.

'I thought Edith sleepwalked regularly?'

Surely Georgina was used it by now?

'Yes. But . . .'

'What is it, Georgina?'

She scraped back her chair and returned to the stove where she crouched, fiddling with the dampers. By the time she turned to face me she seemed more composed.

'Edith started sleepwalking when we first came back to Greyfriars.' She ran a tongue over her lips. 'Then . . .' She cleared her throat. 'She stopped. When your mother came . . . it started again. And now! Oh, dear!'

Georgina tugged at the buttons on her cardigan, more agitated than I'd ever seen her.

'Do you think it's my being here that's unsettling her?'

She was quiet for a while as if holding a silent conversation with herself and I had the impression that she was turning something over in her mind, debating whether to share it with me.

'We are so unused to people these days,' she said eventually. Her wan smile seemed to cost her a great deal of effort. 'We haven't had guests since your mother. People frighten Edith. It's understandable, after everything she went through.'

After what they'd both been through, surely? Georgina could have hardly been unaffected. 'If you feel it would help I could take a room at the inn at Balcreen.'

'No. Please don't. I'd like you to stay,' I offered.

'In that case, is there anything I can do for you or Edith? I'm supposed to be meeting Jamie but would you prefer if I didn't go? I could cancel. Stay here for the day?'

'No! Really. Don't let us get in the way of your plans. Leave Tiger here if you like. But now I should . . . ' she looked up at the ceiling '. . . see to things. Please excuse me. I need to go . . . ' And before I could say another word, she hurried from the kitchen with Tiger at her heels.

I left a short while later and found Jamie waiting for me down at the pier with his boat, a small yacht, tied up alongside.

When he smiled at me, my heart thumped crazily.

'The weather didn't put you off?' he said, offering me his hand for support as I stepped on board. It was drizzling again.

'Not at all.' If there had been a force twelve storm I would have come anyway.

He handed me a life vest, insisting I put it on. As he helped me with the ties his knuckles brushed against my stomach, making my insides swoop.

'I'll take her out. Are you up to handling the jib?'

'Sure, as long as you show me how to.'

He explained what I needed to do to adjust the sails. 'I'll let you know when.' The air smelled of the sea, rotting seaweed and freedom.

Soon the island was barely visible, the houses in Balcreen matchstick size on the horizon. We talked of little of consequence but each glance between us was charged and every time our hands met, my whole body tingled.

It was almost noon before he sailed the boat into Oban Bay. Once inside he turned its nose into the wind, grabbed the painter and tied it to a rock. A flock of seagulls hovered overhead making a racket. We removed our life vests and stored them.

Jamie pointed to a large house overlooking the bay. 'That's Mum's. It's a bit of a climb.'

We took a shortcut up a steep, rocky path and came out at the bottom of a driveway. Jamie took my hand and squeezed it. 'You okay?'

I had only time to nod before the front door opened and a stout woman hurried towards us with a wide smile that was almost an exact replica of Jamie's.

'Jamie! You're here. At last!'

He picked her up and swung her round. 'Don't act as if it's been years instead of days since you saw me, Mum.'

She laughed down at him. 'It feels like years. You know how much I miss you.'

Four other women – his sisters I assumed, judging by their similarities to Jamie – came out to join us.

'Mum, girls, this is Charlotte Friel. She is staying with her aunts in Greyfriars.'

Their greetings were perfectly warm and friendly but I felt myself warned. Do not hurt him. Their body language couldn't have been clearer had they said the words out loud.

'Charlotte.' Jamie's mother took my hands in hers as if we'd known each other all our lives. 'It is so lovely to meet you. Come inside and have a drink.'

Still with my hand in hers, she led me towards the house as the four sisters enveloped Jamie in hugs and kisses. I glanced over my shoulder to see him laughing as he pushed them away, before flinging an arm around two of them. Behind me I heard a cacophony of chatter and questions.

'You'll never get a word in edgeways with that lot.' Jamie's mother indicated behind her with a nod of her head. 'They still treat him as if he's their baby brother and not an inspector in the police force.'

She was clearly very proud of her only son.

I was taken through a hall and into a sitting room flooded with light from large bay windows overlooking the sea. My next impression was that a small bomb had been detonated. There were sweaters and handbags, discarded shoes, half-empty glasses, even a scarf hanging from a lampshade as if the owner, looking for a suitable place to hang it and finding nowhere, draped it over the first thing that came to hand. I narrowly missed slipping on a Dinky truck among the other toys scattered across the floor. Suddenly, with a shriek like a passing train, five children hurled in, chasing each other. When they saw their uncle they whooped and ran into his arms. He picked up the youngest, a little boy of around four, and popped him onto his shoulders, while tossing another onto the sofa, where he landed with a squeal and a cloud of dust.

Messy and haphazard this home might be, but it was suffused with love and laughter. I hung back as an unexpected and almost unrecognisable feeling washed over me. It took me a minute or so to work out what it was – envy – and a terrible, shameful feeling of loneliness.

But then a glass was shoved in my hand, a chair cleared for me to sit on, and children chased from the room. The four sisters, having found seats, were studying me with unabashed curiosity. Marcia was perched on the arm of Jamie's chair, her arm draped protectively around his shoulder.

'So, Charlotte,' Marcia – or was it Becky said. 'How did you and Jamie meet?'

I explained about Tiger getting into trouble. 'I was sitting on the beach, soaked to the skin and he invited me to his place to dry off.'

'Ah, Jamie never could resist a damsel in distress,' she replied, ruffling his hair.

'Could never resist a good-looking woman,' Bethany said.

'Girls,' Jamie growled with an apologetic smile in my direction. 'Give Charlotte some space to speak.'

The questions flew thick and fast. Where did I live? What did I do? Did I have brothers or sisters? How did I like Oban? Had I visited before?

It was almost unnerving being the centre of Jamie's sisters' attention. Then lunch was served and thankfully, the conversation became more general and the focus shifted to getting children fed.

When lunch was over Jamie took me outside, telling his mother he wanted to show me the garden. I suspected he realised I needed a break from his family.

The sun was a round, bright orb, lighting up the sea so that the water seemed to sparkle. The view was quite spectacular. I asked Jamie whether we could see Kerista from here.

He pointed to the east and to a speck in the distance. 'There.' He gave a wry smile. 'Sorry about that back there. I'd forgotten how intense they can be when they are all together.'

'You have a charming family.'

In the way fluffy terriers can be charming until they show you their teeth.

He laughed. 'You wouldn't say that if you saw them squabbling. But they stick together and they mean well.'

'They seem very protective of you.'

A shadow darkened his eyes and he looked at me for a long moment. 'They are. I was married once. To a friend of Becky's. My wife, Gillian, died from a subarachnoid haemorrhage when she was twenty-five. We'd only been married for a couple of years.'

His reply threw me. Whatever I'd expected him to say it hadn't been this.

'I'm so sorry.' No wonder I'd felt myself warned by the sisters.

'It's been five years. I haven't been with anyone since Gillian. Until you. It's why those Furies in there,' he cocked his head in the direction of the house, where right enough there were four faces pressed close to the kitchen window staring out at us, 'gave you the third degree. They've tried to set me up countless times but I wasn't interested. You're the first woman since Gillian I've brought to meet them.'

A shot of panic ran up my spine. Was I ready for this? Could anyone ever live up to a dead wife? I wished I'd known before I'd slept with him. But would it honestly have made any difference?

As if sensing my confusion, Jamie touched my cheek. 'Why don't we go back inside, say our goodbyes and get the hell out of here.'

It took a while to extract ourselves and take our leave although Jamie promised to return in a day or two. He didn't say whether he'd be bringing me and, apart from a couple of sharp looks, no one asked.

Down at the harbour Jamie turned to me. 'My place?'

'I should get back to Greyfriars. The aunts are expecting me.'

It wasn't exactly the truth, nor was it entirely a lie. Georgina had said only this morning that there was an urgency about finishing her story and I owed it to her to be around to hear it. But that was only part of the reason I said no. His comment about me being the first woman he'd been with since Gillian died had been preying on my mind. What did he expect or want from me? It was all beginning to feel much too fast. Much too soon. I wasn't sure if I was worried about hurting Jamie or having my own heart broken. All I knew was that I felt anxious and vulnerable.

He looked disappointed but said nothing, waiting until I was seated before letting the sails out.

'The wind's picking up,' he said after we'd left the bay. 'Do you want to see how fast this little lady can go? I think you may find it as exciting as being in court.'

'Sure.'

339

He showed me how to tuck my feet under a strap that ran across the midsection of the boat.

'When I let the sail out the boat will heel. That's when we need to lean back to balance her. Just do what I do and you'll be fine.'

Out at sea, he pulled the sails in, bringing the boat close to the wind. I balanced on the edge of the boat and, following his example, tucked my feet under the straps.

Soon we were scooting along and as the boat gathered speed we leaned further and further out until we were inches from the waves. I laughed as the wind tore at my hair and made my eyes water.

It was just us, the wind and the sea. I had to concentrate, remembering what to do when he shouted, releasing my feet and edging forward before, as the boat tacked or jibed, we bounded over to the other side ducking our heads to avoid the boom and repeated the process all over again.

As we neared Greyfriars he reduced the speed of the boat, bringing it back to an even keel. He drew up next to the pier and hooked the painter over the post and came to help me with my life vest. Once it was off, he lifted his hand and tucked a lock of my hair behind my ear. 'What are you so afraid of, Charlotte Friel?'

I shook my head, completely unable to articulate what I was feeling.

'I've pushed things too fast. I'm sorry,' he said. His breath was warm on my face. Although I wanted nothing more than to lean into him, I took a step back and out of his reach.

'It's not that. It's, oh, everything.' But he was right. I was afraid. Afraid to take the next step. Afraid to let someone else into my life who might, probably would, disrupt it. Afraid to be compared to his dead wife and found lacking. I didn't want to risk any of that.

He considered me for a long moment. 'I know what I want – you. I can't pretend otherwise. I also know life is too short not to grab happiness when you can. Whatever the risk.'

His words gave me a jolt. It was the same thing Mum had said to me before she died.

'I believe you want me too,' Jamie continued. 'So whenever you're ready, I'll be waiting. You know where to find me.'

I gave him a grateful smile. I might not be ready for anything serious, but neither was I ready to let him go. I waved him off and walked back to the house.

Once more I found Edith waiting for me at the door.

'We don't like people coming to the island,' she said with a frown.

'He's gone now,' I said gently. 'I won't invite him to meet you until I know you are happy with it.' And until I knew how I felt.

She made no mention of last night so neither did I, but she seemed more agitated than before. She plucked continuously at the necklace around her throat, her thick stockings had a hole above the knee and I couldn't help noticing there were more stains on her blouse.

'Thank you. Won't you go through to the library? Georgina is waiting for you.'

In the library Georgina was staring out of the window. She whirled around to face me.

'Was that your young man?'

'I'm not sure if I'd describe him as my young man exactly. But yes, that was Jamie. Don't worry I've already promised Edith I won't ask him up to the house. Not until you invite him.'

She relaxed and a small smile lifted the corners of her mouth. 'I think that's best for now. When I've told you everything you need to know, perhaps then you could bring him over? Although we'd have to prepare Edith.'

'He leaves soon to go back to work.' I couldn't help the note of despondency in my voice.

'You like him?'

'A great deal.' Unused to talking about my personal life, I hesitated, but perhaps Georgina was exactly the right person to confide in. 'He was married before. His wife died suddenly. Five years ago.'

'I see. And the fact he was married before troubles you?'

'Yes. I mean no. I'm not sure. I just know that being with him feels as natural as breathing, as if we were meant to be with each other. It's like there's been a hole inside me and he fills it.' I grimaced. 'I never thought I'd ever find myself saying something so ridiculously corny.' I didn't need other people to make me whole – the only person who could do that was me.

I pushed my hair from my face. 'I don't think I'm myself. I miss Mum.' And now, to my mortification, I was on the verge of tears.

'You're still grieving, Charlotte. It's hardly surprising you don't know what you feel.'

'So you understand why I can't be sure of anything? Whether I'll still feel the same way about anything tomorrow, or in a month, or a year's time?'

'Loving someone can bring great pain but great joy as well,' Georgina continued, a wistful expression on her face.

It was the same thing Mum had said about my father. But I wondered if it were better not to love. Since Mum had died I'd felt fragile and uncertain and I hated feeling that way.

I leaned forward. 'I'm used to being on my own. I like it that way. I have a good, fulfilling life.' I wasn't sure who I was trying to convince – Georgina, or myself.

Georgina grasped my wrist with sudden urgency. 'We only have one life, my dear, and so few chances of happiness. Your mother lost her love. I lost mine. As did Edith. Don't let the same happen to you.'

'You're talking about Findlay, aren't you?'

Georgina paled and there was a long pause.

'It wasn't just a tipsy kiss, was it?' I persisted. 'At least not on your part.'

342

'No,' she admitted after a long pause. 'I probably would never have followed him down to the shore that night if I hadn't drunk too much champagne, but yes, I did love him. Almost from the moment I set eyes on him.'

She was silent for a long time. When she started to speak again her eyes had taken on a faraway look.

'That summer I was at home at our house in Edinburgh. I had arrived back from Paris a week earlier and spent a few days in London before taking the train north. Harriet and Peter had gone on to Edinburgh a couple of days before and I could have travelled up with them, should have as it turned out, but I had friends I hadn't seen for a while with whom I wanted to catch up in London. I'd left Paris under a bit of a cloud. There were rumours – gossip and speculation – about my having an affair with a married man which made me glad to leave.'

'And were you? Having an affair, I mean?'

'On this occasion, as it happens, no. He was being rather silly. Mistook some light-hearted flirtation for something more serious. Told his wife he wanted a divorce so he could marry me. It was total nonsense, but enough people believed it to make life uncomfortable for me. And as I told you, my work as a model had more or less come to an end. Besides, I suspected war was coming and I wanted to come home, see my sisters, spend time with them. If war did come, I knew it might be a very long time before I saw them again.

'Harriet, Peter, Olivia and Edith had already left for Greyfriars by the time I arrived in Edinburgh. My plan was to spend a couple of nights there before joining them. Edith had told me that her beau would be joining us for a week and that she had some exciting news for me – news that she wished to tell me in person.

'I knew it could really only mean one thing. She and her new beau were planning to get married. I was thrilled for her. She hadn't had a suitor before. Edith could come across as rather straight-laced and that put men off and she, quite

343

justifiably, was fussy. Not only that, she had little opportunity to meet them. As a nurse at the Royal Infirmary she had to live in the nurses' home and if the ridiculous hours nurses were made to work wasn't bad enough, they only had one evening off a week and every second or third weekend. Even then there were strict rules about curfews and that sort of thing.

'It didn't bother her, but it was rather curtailing when it came to romance. Besides, she'd always been dead set against getting married – some nonsense about devoting herself to her nursing career. At that time one had to give it all up if one married.

'There was some mix-up with arrangements. I was getting ready to go to the cinema with friends when Findlay arrived at the house looking for Edith.'

Georgina's sigh seemed to come from deep within her.

'I'd heard people talk about love at first sight but I never believed it, not until that moment. As soon as I saw him, it was as if all my senses went on high alert. I'd never ever felt like that before – my body literally hummed. And to feel it for my sister's soon-to-be fiancé shook me to the core. I should have said I had a prior engagement and sent him on his way, but I didn't. I cancelled my arrangement with my friends and went to dinner with him instead.

'We talked all the way through dinner. I'd never met anyone quite like him. He was the son of a vicar, would you believe? His mother had died when he was three and he'd been brought up by an aunt before he was sent to boarding school when he was five. His father was given a post abroad and took it, leaving Findlay behind. He was in boarding school until he was eighteen and won a scholarship to Oxford on the back of the fact he was brilliant at rugby. I always think that the Scots should be better at rugby than they are because who else is better used to rolling around in wet mud and claiming to enjoy it.' She gave a delicious chuckle, all trace of her earlier distress submerged by her memories.

344

'Of course, there he got in with other rugger sorts and he was invited to their homes at weekends and holidays. You can't imagine how many country house parties there used to be back then. If one wanted, and knew enough of the right sort of people, one could spend a reasonable chunk of one's life without having a home of one's own.

'He wasn't nearly as well off as his friends but no one cared. Least of all Findlay. Luckily for him he was very good with a pack of cards and by spending a couple of nights every week gambling, he managed to buy the right sort of clothes and furnish himself with enough money so that he could at least pay his way.

'He wasn't at all embarrassed to tell me this or that everyone knew. He said most of the chaps' fathers had inherited their wealth without doing a hand's turn, usually by gambling on this investment or that, and he was no different. He made it a point of honour never to win more than his fellow card players could afford to lose, and he never cheated, but anything else was fair game. I believe he even gambled on bare fist fighting – tried it himself I found out later. Naturally, although he never hid it from anyone, he was discreet around his friends' mamas and papas. They might not have been so keen to have him as a house guest if they'd known how he spent his spare time.

'He met Edith at one of those weekend house parties. He was immediately drawn to her. Women flocked around him, you see. But not her. She told me later she immediately disapproved of him; he was so sure of himself, so arrogant. It was because she dismissed him so easily that he pursued her at first. But then he fell in love with her. She was everything he thought he wanted in a wife. She could ride and sail along with the best of them and was a wizard at tennis, but most of all he loved her quiet dignity. She made him feel peaceful inside. She made him believe he could be a good man with her by his side – as if he could achieve great things. She was to be his salvation.

345

'Edith would have made a good vicar's wife. Findlay told me that first evening that she made him think of his mother – or at least the vision of his mother that he had carried around in his head ever since he was a small boy.

'He told me that he and Edith planned to formally announce their engagement at Greyfriars. His eyes were soft when he spoke of her and I felt a stab of jealousy. I wished I had someone who would love me like that.

'As if realising he was going on a bit, he asked about me. I was still smarting a little from the treatment I'd received in Paris but I made light of it and set out to amuse him, to banish the darkness I thought I saw in his eyes. I was, I told myself, doing it for Edith.

'It was late when he left to return to his hotel. We were both getting the same train to Balcreen the next day so it was natural that we would travel up together. He asked if he could arrange for a taxi to collect me and my luggage but I told him I would see him at the station. When he saw the amount of luggage I had brought with me, he laughed and teased me as easily as if we'd known each other all our lives. I was desperately in love with him already.

Georgina tucked a lock of hair behind her ear and gave me a shaky smile. 'I thought that all I had to do was to get through those two weeks at Greyfriars. I was due to leave for Singapore and our paths wouldn't have to cross again until after he and Edith married. I had never envied my little sister more, yet, believe me when I say, I wanted her to be happy.

'At Greyfriars it was difficult to be in the same room as Findlay and not show everyone how besotted I was with him. There was a strange atmosphere at Greyfriars that summer – everyone was keyed up and overexcited at the thought of war. They were used to me making myself the centre of attention and if they noticed I was quieter, that I avoided being alone with him, they put it down to my foreboding about the war. But I dreaded the moment when Edith would announce

346

their engagement and I dreaded even more the day he was to leave. For almost two weeks I managed to keep my feelings to myself. But I didn't think about those sharp eyes of your mother. She was such a quiet little thing and it was easy to forget she was there. And then Findlay told us he was going to join up. He knew war was coming.

'It was only because I had had too much champagne – that and the talk of war – everything was heightened. All I could think about was that I might never see him again. Or perhaps that is just an excuse – maybe I meant to have him all the time. I saw him going down to the loch side carrying his towel. Everyone else was in bed, but I wasn't the least bit tired. He hadn't proposed to Edith yet and I told myself that I would ask him why.' She sighed. 'All the little lies one tells oneself.'

'I grabbed an open bottle of champagne and a couple of glasses and picked my way down to the shore. When I stumbled in my heels I slipped them off and left them on the lawn. The cool feel of the grass beneath my feet was exquisite. It was one of those still perfect evenings you get in a Scottish summer – where the sky hardly gets dark. It was almost midnight yet still light enough for me to find my way without a torch. And, as it turns out, light enough for inquisitive eyes to see me.' She gave me a pained smile. 'But loving him was not an excuse for what I did. And it didn't make me any less responsible for the situation Edith subsequently found herself in. If I'd kept away from him, they would have married. She would never have been in Singapore. Never have had to go through what she did. I promised myself when we faced death together that morning at the village that if we survived, I would do whatever it took to ensure Edith made it home.'

Chapter Thirty-Nine
Georgina and Edith

1942

As the smell of blood, smoke and charred flesh filled the air, the officer drove off in his jeep, his soldiers taking the male prisoners with them, three soldiers remaining behind to take charge of the women and children.

Bellowing commands and jabbing at them with their bayoneted rifles, their guards ordered the shocked and terror-stricken group of women to march out of the village. They were made to walk along a road – in reality little more than a track – through the jungle. Mothers carried their small children until they could no longer do so, when other willing hands took over despite their own exhaustion. Although they'd been allowed to keep their suitcases with them, many had lost their shoes and had tied strips of cloth around their feet to protect them. Some had nothing but the clothes they stood in; no suitcases, no shoes, no hat. Without shade, the heat was excruciating and there was no offer of water.

Sick with horror and disbelief, Georgina clung to the fact that she and Edith still lived. Unable to assimilate what had happened she concentrated on putting one foot in front of the other. Her feet were already blistered from the previous day's walk and each step she took felt as if she were walking on needles, yet the pain was a welcome distraction from the images filling her head. The sun was so hot her skin felt on fire. With

348

her red hair and pale complexion, she burned easily and the scarf she had taken from the suitcase and wrapped around her head offered little protection. Edith was only slightly better off. Her skin was more of a golden shade, but light enough to burn too. Everyone's did. Already most of their lips were a mass of blisters, their skin beginning to peel. Others clearly suffering the effects of sunstroke and traumatised by the events of the last hours, had to be supported. If a woman collapsed the soldiers would prod them with the points of their bayonets, screaming at them to get up.

There were five children in their group ranging in ages from a toddler to a seven-year-old. Out of the sixteen women, there were six Australian nurses, Edith and Linda, a doctor who had trained in Britain and worked in one of the hospitals in the north, two planters' wives, a missionary, and three other women who were the wives of government officials or businessmen. Most of them, including herself, had been petted and spoiled, their merest whim catered to by scores of servants, and had rarely had to walk more than a few hundred yards.

It was almost sunset when, dead on their feet, they arrived at what seemed to be their final destination, a cluster of wooden huts surrounded by a fence in a clearing in the jungle. They were so relieved to have reached somewhere, to know that the marching would stop, that they cheered with what little energy they had left.

They hobbled through the gates and towards the huts, desperate to sit down and get out of the sun.

On closer inspection, the huts were barely standing, with holes in the roofs and gaps in the walls and had nothing inside them except two rows of sloping concrete on either side of a long passage. Some of the women prisoners sat on the edge, exhausted, rubbing their aching, swollen feet, while the others, Georgina and Edith included, went to investigate further.

To the rear, they found a smaller hut with the remains of an open fire that had once clearly been used as a kitchen, along

349

with a couple of pans, and several rusty tins – stuff deemed too worthless to be taken by whoever had occupied the camp before them. Along one wall was a concrete plinth with a tapless sink embedded in it. Beyond it, close to the perimeter fence, was a well that appeared to be the only source of water. There were no bathrooms or showers, just outside latrines and the single kitchen sink to wash.

'They can't expect us to live here,' Gladys, one of the Australian nurses, protested.

'I'm very much afraid they do,' Georgina replied.

'Come on, let's get organised,' Edith said. She hadn't said a word since they'd left the village, but now, with the prospect of something to do, she seemed to have regained her composure. 'We should set up a nurses' station and have a look at everyone. Georgina, could you fetch some water? As much as you can?'

That first night they were fed, if you could call it that, watery rice and a cup of brackish water that passed for tea. If they weren't so hungry Georgina doubted any of them would have been able to swallow a mouthful. They lay down on their rock-hard beds, there was no space to have more than an inch or two between each body, and tried to make themselves as comfortable as best they could.

Lying sleepless, the hot, humid night filled with the whine of mosquitoes, the cries of children and the screeching of the monkeys in the jungle, with what had happened in the village playing over and over in her head, Georgina wondered how long they'd be there and how many of them would live to see home again. But, she promised herself, she would do anything and everything in her power to make sure she and Edith would be amongst those who did.

They were woken at dawn by the shouting of guards and the banging of rifle butts against the soles of their already tender feet.

'*Tenko! Tenko!*' the guards kept screaming at them as they were prodded and pushed and made to line up in the centre of the camp. Anyone who didn't bow low enough to the guards was beaten to the ground.

They stood there for the best part of the morning; long after the sun came up and for hours after, with nothing to eat or drink. There was no shade and the heat of the sun was remorseless. If a woman collapsed she was beaten and those standing next to her quickly learned to support anyone who looked in danger of falling.

The guards counted them over and over again. Finally, when Georgina thought they were going to be made to stand there all day, the camp commandant came out of his hut to address them.

He was youngish with a clean-shaven face and glasses. Georgina could imagine him as a clerk or librarian except for the coldness of his eyes and his clipped, hostile tone. In broken English he made no bones of the fact that they were the lowest of the low. Women and prisoners. To be either was bad enough but to be both clearly made them beyond contempt. If they worked hard and showed respect, he said, they would be all right. There was more stuff about the Japanese military might and rubbish like that. Georgina suspected she wasn't the only one who barely heard a word he said, they were all concentrating too hard on staying upright.

They waited in the sun until finally, when they were all swaying on their feet, they were allowed to return to their huts.

Inside, the suffocating heat was almost as bad as outside. Some women flopped onto their hard beds, while others sat around listlessly. The mothers didn't have the luxury of rest – their children needed to be looked after, reassured and fed. A few hours later the cry of '*tenko*' went up again and once more they were shoved and pushed into the yard and made to stand in the burning sun while the guards counted them over and over again. How they came to hate the call to *tenko*.

Over the next few days the camp filled as survivors of other shipwrecks, along with the Dutch women who had been living nearby, were brought to the camp. Soon every hut was crammed to overflowing with stunned and exhausted women and children.

And so the first week passed, the women growing more listless with each hour. For Georgina, almost the worst thing was never having a moment to herself. All day and every day she was forced to share her waking moments with her fellow prisoners, who with their constant squabbles and petty arguments set her teeth on edge.

It was easier in some ways for the nurses, Edith amongst them. They had their nursing duties to keep them occupied, were used to hard conditions, used to being on their feet until they dropped with fatigue and used to putting the needs of others before their own. The other women, with nothing to keep them from thinking of their own misery, sniped at each other constantly.

Following a particular bitter quarrel between two women as to who was getting a larger portion of rice, it finally dawned on them all that help wasn't likely to come for months and that they should make the best of the situation in which they found themselves. Everyone was called together, and a leader, Mrs Barber, appointed.

After that meeting the camp arranged itself into some sort of order. Chores were divided between them. One of the women had been a teacher and she, along with a couple of the mothers, established a makeshift school at one end of the compound. Some of the women were given cooking duties and the nurses held their clinics, helping out with chores when they had some free time.

The rest, Georgina included, shared the remainder of the tasks. They scavenged for what little wood there was and chopped it with whatever they could find, fetched water from the well and collected the heavy bags of rice that were their rations and cooked it, adding whatever they could find to make it taste better.

Not everyone was able to contribute to camp life. Mrs McCutcheon, the wife of a planter, came down with fever and was confined to bed, and Cecilia Fairweather sat all day, knees tucked into her chest, not moving and not saying anything. They took it in turns to spoon the thin gruel that passed for food into her mouth.

Nights were worst; the huts unbearably hot and humid, the strange sounds from the jungle and the never-ending cries of children, the rats nibbling at their toes, the fleas making them itch and perhaps worst of all, the mosquitoes. Georgina slept in a kimono she'd taken from one of the abandoned suitcases, the long sleeves helping a little to keep the mosquitoes at bay, but almost everyone was covered in bites which became infected, turning into boils that required lancing.

Day after day followed the same relentless pattern. After a restless sleep, Georgina would rise at first light along with several of the more able women and walk to the well to fetch water. It was a thankless task. With very little suitable to carry it in except for some leaky tins they'd scavenged, they had to make several trips just to supply sufficient to drink let alone cook or wash with.

Bathing was a euphemism for stripping down in front of the kitchen sink and washing as best they could. Those who had soap and a towel were the lucky ones, those without had to make do with whatever they could find to dry themselves. Shy and embarrassed at first, they soon got used to being naked in front of each other.

In those early weeks there was enough rice to eat, if little else, and hours of free time to fill. Georgina gave French lessons to the children and to those adults who were interested. In the evenings there was bridge with homemade cards, mah-jong with bits of wood they found and once a week they held a camp concert, everyone, even the children, taking a turn to tell a joke, or sing.

353

Despite the horrific conditions and the occasional spat, a camaraderie developed amongst the prisoners. The Australian nurses in particular were quick to find humour wherever they could. Georgina was to look back on these days in the years to come with something akin to longing.

They had been in the camp for over two weeks before Georgina and Edith were alone. So far they hadn't had the opportunity to speak in private. Either Edith was busy, or she was in the company of the other nurses. Georgina was using a piece of broken glass she'd found to extract the flesh from a coconut after which the husk could be used as a bowl, when Edith came to sit on the rock beside her.

'How are you?' Edith asked.

Edith had lost weight, as all of them had, and if she'd looked exhausted before she seemed even more so now.

'As well as I imagine most of us are. It's good to see you. You look tired.'

Edith grimaced. 'No more tired than everyone else.'

'I wish we saw more of each other.' Georgina laid the now clean coconut shell aside and picked up another. It was odd how this simple, mundane task soothed her.

'We see a great deal of one another.'

'But never alone. Always with other people.'

Shielding her eyes with her hand, Edith looked towards a hut where children played in the dust. 'Is there something you especially want to talk to me about?'

'I . . . You're my sister. Isn't that enough reason?' Georgina hated the pleading note that had crept into her voice. She sucked in a breath. 'I need to know you're all right.'

'I'm fine. As you can see.'

Georgina blinked away the traitorous tears that formed behind her lids. It was only lack of food that made one so emotional. But oh, how she missed the easy atmosphere that used to exist between them.

'Can't we put everything behind us? You saved my life. You can't pretend you don't care,' she whispered.

'You're so melodramatic, Georgina! Of course I care.'

'But you haven't forgiven me, have you?'

Edith sighed. 'Please, Georgina. Let's not open up old wounds. Let's just agree never to speak of it.'

'But if it still causes such a rift?'

Edith took her hand away from her eyes and turned to face Georgina. 'If you keep bringing it up then matters will only get worse. You did what you did. What happened, happened.' She stood. 'I have work to do. I need to get back.'

Georgina reached for her hand and clasped it. 'Stay for a few minutes more. I promise I won't speak of it again.'

Reluctantly Edith sat back down. 'For a few moments then.'

'How are your patients?' Georgina asked. Amongst all the things she wanted to say it was the only thing she could think of.

'We are going to lose Madeleine Simpson. Why won't they give us some quinine? Mrs Barber has been to see the commandant several times about it.' She pursed her lips. 'Silly question. They don't care if we die. We are nothing to them except a nuisance.'

'Would people live if they had quinine?'

'Not everyone, but most would. Those who don't have dysentery as well as malaria.' Edith ground her heel into the rock-hard ground as if she were imagining crushing a Jap underneath. 'Any one of the things we put up with would be bad enough – the mosquitoes, the dirt, the bug-infested rice, the heat, the lack of water, not having medical supplies . . .' She bit her lip and shook her head. 'But there is no point in thinking like that. We just have to do our best. Chin up and all that.' A brief smile crossed her face. 'Never let them think we're beaten.'

Georgina squeezed her hand hard. 'We're not beaten. We'll never be beaten. I don't care what they do but I promise you and I are going to survive this.'

This time Edith did stand. 'I hope you're right. I for one have no desire to die in this godforsaken dump.'

As the weeks passed, their already meagre rations were cut and they became weaker and weaker. The only vegetables they were given were brought in on the back of a truck, dumped and left to rot on the ground before the women were allowed to collect them. They ate anything they could get their hands on, rotting banana skins, even the roots of the few plants that grew in the sun-baked earth. Their clothes turned to rags, their arms and legs were covered in sores and insect bites. Unable to stop themselves scratching, these often became infected and turned into suppurating ulcers. They buried Madeline and a pregnant mother who'd succumbed to malaria in a small graveyard.

Georgina kept a close eye on her sister, worrying as she watched her get ever thinner. In those early months, a Malay trader was permitted to come to the camp once a week and the lucky few who had anything to trade or sell were able to buy cigarettes, or an orange or even some sugar. But anything Georgina might have traded for extra food was long gone. The Japs had taken her ruby ring before she'd had a chance to hide it.

Those prisoners who did have money, in particular the Dutch who'd lived on Sumatra and because they hadn't lost everything in a shipwreck, were relatively well off and pre-pared to buy services from those who didn't. Those without earned money by sewing cloth – or more precisely rags – into clothes, or made straw hats to sell. Georgina couldn't sew, was useless at making hats and her French lessons were considered part of her contribution to the daily running of the camp so there was no money to be gained that way.

But there were a few dollars on offer for anyone prepared to clean the latrines. The latrines, no more than long planks with holes cut into the wood, and far too few to service the number in the camp, especially when at any time a number of the women had dysentery, were always getting clogged up with effluent, to the point they overflowed.

Georgina would earn less than two dollars a day, but when one had nothing and no other means of earning money to buy food, when hunger was a constant gnawing pain, when the odd purchasing of a piece of fruit might be enough to keep her and Edith alive for one more day, she couldn't see any other way. However, the thought revolted her and she gagged when she saw the task in front of her. The ditch was heaving with maggots, the smell utterly unbearable. How on earth was she going to do this?

But do it she would. She had no choice. First, she had to find something to scoop out the stinking mess – but what? She could hardly use her bare hands and the only pans they had were used for cooking and fetching water and there were few enough of them. It was then she remembered the coconut husks she'd hollowed out to make eating bowls. She returned to the hut kitchen, collected two and made her way back to the latrines.

She'd solved one problem, now she had another. Where to put the stuff when she'd scooped it out?

She was hunkered on her heels, considering the question, when a shadow fell across her.

'Pass me one of those husks,' a familiar voice said.

Georgina gaped up at her sister, stunned. Edith was the last person she'd expected to offer to help. Georgina smiled, a glow forming in the pit of her stomach. 'Don't you have enough to do?'

'I'm off duty for the rest of the afternoon.' Edith squatted beside Georgina. ' So what are we going to do with this stuff? We can't just pile it up.'

'Dump it in the jungle?'

Edith stared across the compound. The jungle was a good mile away from the latrines.

357

'In that case, we'd better get started.' She handed Georgina a bandana from her pocket. 'Tie this over your mouth. It will help with the stench.'

Georgina did as she suggested. 'What about you?'

'I'm a nurse. I'm used to revolting smells.' Edith dug her coconut into the seething mess. 'Let's just get on with it.'

They spent the rest of the afternoon working to clear the ditch. They used the coconut husks to scoop up what they could and carried it at arm's length over to the jungle where they poured it out. Then they would go back to the ditch and repeat the whole procedure over and over again. The Japanese guards lounged against the post of the huts watching them and laughing. Georgina would have liked to have thrown a filled husk into their faces and she was certain Edith felt the same.

Even after hours of back-breaking work they'd barely made a dent. All the time they were removing the excreta the toilets were still being used.

'Now I know what Sisyphus felt like,' Georgina said, stretching her back.

'Who?'

'You know. In Greek mythology. The chap who was made to roll the boulder up the hill only to have it roll back down, so he'd have to start over again.'

Edith rested on her haunches. 'I'm going to have to go back to work. I'll need to scrub before then.'

'Thanks, Edith.'

Edith gave the faintest glimmer of a smile. 'Whatever you've done, you're still my sister.'

It seemed, finally, Edith had forgiven her.

Chapter Forty

After two years, and without warning, they were told they were being moved to a different camp. At first they were pleased. The conditions in the new camp could only be an improvement.

They were only given enough time to grab what they could, before they were lined up and forced to march. Anyone who still had any strength took turns carrying the stretchers of those who were too weak to walk even though they were hardly in better health, suffering as they all were from the effects of malnutrition and repeated bouts of dysentery. After marching for a whole day, they were forced into a small boat and left in the stinking cargo hold without food or water for the night and the best part of the next day. Several died and the others had to share the tiny, suffocating space with their corpses.

The next afternoon they were taken out and told to wait in the pouring rain. There were some trucks standing by and Mrs Barber asked the guards to allow the sick and dying to take shelter inside. The guards agreed, and some of the nurses were allowed in with them. But their captors locked them in without food or water and by morning, only the nurses emerged. Georgina had thought it was impossible to hate the Japanese more; they'd proved her wrong.

Eventually, those who had survived that horrific journey made it to the new camp. At first glance, it did appear to be an improvement. It was near water, higher up than their old camp, and therefore cooler.

Although they could barely stand, they were lined up for *tenko* and after the usual waiting around, the new camp commandant came to address them. To Georgina's horror, she recognised him immediately. It was the officer who'd ordered the massacre at the village. She ducked her head. What if he recognised her or one of the others? What would he do? Would he be prepared to leave witnesses alive that someday in the future might testify to what he'd done?

He stood on his makeshift podium to address them, staring at some point above their heads. All the while thoughts spun around Georgina's head. There were only five of them, including her and Edith, left from the group that had been at the village that day, the rest having died. In addition, those who remained had lost weight and as a consequence looked different – drawn, gaunt and glassy-eyed. All of them had cut their hair in a hopeless attempt to keep the lice at bay, but in an act of defiance, Georgina had refused to cut hers. They'd taken everything else from her and her long auburn hair was the only physical reminder of the woman she'd once been.

Thank God, her head had been covered by a scarf the day of the massacre. Furthermore, she recalled, he'd hardly glanced their way. There was still a chance he wouldn't recognise them. Even if he did, they were obviously only hanging on to life by the merest thread.

To her relief he showed no recognition. He continued to address the air above their heads, before retreating to the comfort of his hut. When they were finally released from *tenko*, Georgina hurried across to Edith.

'Did you recognise him?' she said.

'I doubt any of us will ever forget him.'

'We must never say anything to anyone that it's him. Tell the others they mustn't say anything.'

Edith shrugged her shoulders. 'What more can they do to

us? Frankly I'm beyond caring what happens. We're all going to die anyway.'

Georgina grabbed her by the hand. 'You mustn't say that! You mustn't even think it! I told you, we are going to live. We'll leave here and live the rest of our lives. You have to believe it. You must never give up, do you hear me? Just concentrate on making it through one day at a time.'

Edith glanced over to the straggly row of women waiting to see a nurse and shrugged Georgina's hands away. 'I'll do my best.' She sighed. 'As long as there are patients who need me, I'll try to keep going.'

Conditions at the camp turned out to be far worse than they could have imagined, their rations were cut again and people came down with a new disease – one they hadn't seen before and didn't know how to treat, the source of which they suspected was the river water and people began to die in earnest. Soon the little patch of jungle they used as a burial ground was almost filled with graves.

Georgina forced herself not to think about the next day, or the day after that. Instead she let herself remember the past; recreating happier moments in her head. Games of tennis where she replayed every point, dances where she imagined every footstep of a foxtrot or a two-step, midnight picnics where she mentally savoured every mouthful she'd eaten.

It wasn't long before Georgina noticed that the commandant was watching her. She would hobble past with her tins of water, bowing as she passed him, aware that his eyes were following her until she'd disappeared from sight. It worried her. More, it gave her the creeps.

Today she'd placed her tins of water on the ground and paused to stretch her aching back. The thin, high voices of the children as they recited a poem one of the teachers had taught them drifted across the camp. On the whole they were in better health than the remaining adult prisoners. Their mothers had kept them alive by giving them the bulk of their rations, but as a consequence the women with children were even thinner and weaker than the others, although that was only a matter of degree.

The commandant was standing in the shade of the balcony of his hut. He glanced around and walked over to her. She bowed low, hating that she had to.

'Prisoner Guthrie,' he said. 'You are well?'

So he knew her name.

If she'd learned anything it was that their guards were completely unpredictable. She picked up her tins. 'Quite well. Permission to go?' She kept her eyes downcast, so he wouldn't see the hate in them.

Instead of replying, he stretched out a hand and touched a lock of her hair that had come loose from the bandana she wore. 'I have never seen such colour.'

It took all her self-control not to slap his hand away. She made herself stand rigid in front of him, keeping her head bowed.

'You have enough to eat?'

Her head shot up. 'No. Of course we don't.' She forced the anger from her voice. 'We could do with some vegetables. People are getting sick because we don't have enough. Could you find your way to giving us more?'

'I give you more,' he said. 'Vegetables, rice. Meat.'

'You could? That would be wonderful! The other prisoners would be so grateful.'

'Not for other prisoners. For you. Only you.'

Despite the suffocating heat her blood ran cold.

'You come my quarters,' he continued. 'Wash first. You eat.'

She almost laughed. How desperate did he think she was? She'd rather starve than eat with him. And to tell her to wash first! Really. That took the biscuit.

'I'll eat with my friends,' she said stiffly.

'Not just to eat, stupid woman. You will come to me. Japanese officer is not like ordinary soldier. He does not force

362

women. She must submit willingly. If you wish to survive, one day you will submit to me, Prisoner Guthrie.'

She would die before she would submit to him, as he put it. If she hated the Japanese she hated him most of all. Any man who could kill women and children without a flicker of conscience was no better than an animal.

Repelled, without waiting to be dismissed, she bowed again to hide her disgust, and walked past him.

She didn't tell anyone, least of all Edith, about the conversation with the commandant, but she worried constantly. She hated that he had noticed her. She had no way of being sure that he hadn't recognised her and the other women from the village and was biding his time until he could get rid of them. He didn't have to do much – just let the conditions in the camp continue to take their course.

Alternatively furious that he thought she would sleep with him and terrified he'd even noticed her, she tried to put the conversation out of her mind. So far the Japanese had been content to take the women who were prepared to sleep with them. No one had been forced. However, the memory of what she'd learned about the way the Japanese troops had behaved when they'd invaded Hong Kong wouldn't leave her. She tried to tell herself they had been troops drunk on stolen alcohol and fired up from the heat of battle, but she also knew that the Japanese considered rape to be the natural spoils of war.

The commandant could have raped her had he wished. There was no one to stop him if he took it into his head. But to refuse him was also dangerous. Face was everything to the Japanese and she was glad there had been no other Japs around to witness his proposal. Georgina wondered whether she should cut her hair. The commandant clearly found it attractive. But the Japs had control of almost every bit of her life and she refused to let them take this last bit of who she was away from her. She did ensure, however, that her hair was always hidden under a bandana.

She kept an eye out for him after that day, dashing past his hut whenever she had to pass in his direction, keeping her head lowered when he was around. Thankfully, he rarely appeared for *tenko* or out on his balcony.

They'd been at the new camp for almost nine months and almost every day now someone died. Under the new commandant, no trader was allowed within the gates and even those few women who had money left were unable to buy food.

So when the Japanese asked for volunteers to work in the native hospital in the village (the Australian nurses said no, a wise move on their part, as it turned out), Georgina wasn't at all surprised when Edith and Linda, the other QA, volunteered to go.

To begin with, it seemed that they had made a good decision. The hospital was run by a Dutch doctor and his wife, and security there was much more relaxed. After finishing their shift, Edith and Linda were able to walk to the village and, using the money the women had agreed to pool, were able to buy some fruit or vegetables that helped supplement rations back at the camp. Every evening when they returned the women would fall upon them to see what scraps they had managed to bring with them.

Edith and Linda had been working at the hospital for a few months when one evening they didn't come back.

When, by the next evening they still hadn't returned, Georgina was frantic. As usual the rumour mill was working overtime. Edith and Linda had been tortured and killed. They were being used as comfort women – it had all been a ruse to separate them from the others.

Georgina couldn't bear not knowing. She marched up to the commandant's office and requested to see him.

She bowed low at the waist and waited for him to acknowledge her.

'I have come to ask about my sister, Sister Guthrie. She and her colleague did not return to camp last night.'

364

'What do you want me to do?'

She raised her head. 'I'd like you to find out where they are. What's happening to them. Surely you can do that?'

He left his desk and came to stand in front of her. 'You make demands? Of me?'

'I'm only . . .' She didn't manage to get the rest of the words out before one of the guards stepped towards her and smashed her in her face with the butt of his rifle.

She tried to get to her feet but she was knocked to the ground and hit again and again, until there was only darkness.

She came to in a hut, although hut was too grand a word for it, cupboard would have been closer to the truth. There was only just enough room for her to sit if she drew her knees up to her chest. Her cheek throbbed where the guard had hit her and feeling her back tooth with her tongue she felt certain it was loose.

What had happened to Edith? Was she having to service the Japanese soldiers? Would they kill her when they were finished with her? Georgina had promised to keep her sister alive. Had she failed her once more? Would she ever see her again?

The sun beat down relentlessly through the gaps in the wooden slats, the walls of her small prison trapping the heat and making it almost impossible to breathe. For a moment she almost panicked. Did the commandant intend to leave her here to die either from the heat or from lack of water? She wouldn't put a slow, tortuous death past him. But screaming and crying wouldn't help. She had to conserve her energy. Had to believe that when he was satisfied he'd punished her enough he would release her. Had to believe Edith was still alive.

Every morning she was hauled out of her prison. Her legs, cramped from hours in the same position, refused to hold her weight, and she was dragged across the dust to a wooden post where her hands were tied behind her back and she was left without water in the full glare of the midday sun. She squinted through swollen eyes, trying to catch a glimpse of Edith but to no avail. If her sister had returned, Georgina knew she would have made sure Georgina was aware of it.

At dusk she was untied and dragged back to her prison where she would force herself to take small sips from the bowl of dirty, warm water that had been left for her along with a bowl of rank rice. In the darkness she couldn't distinguish the weevils from the rice and she ate them too, telling herself that they were protein and eating them might possibly save her life. She lost count of the days and the nights. When she was tied to her stake during the day, the women would pass by talking loudly, wondering aloud about Edith's whereabouts.

The thought that she might have lost Edith forever tormented her. They had been through so much. It was the worst thirty days of captivity so far. She almost gave up, but kept telling herself that she had to survive, had to hold on in case Edith returned.

One morning she was dragged out of her prison and instead of being tied to the stake, was left lying on the ground. The other women rushed to her, gathered her up and carried her into the sickbay. By the time she recovered, two weeks later, there was still no sign of Edith.

Two months limped by and Georgina was working, hacking earth to make a garden, when the gates swung open. She almost didn't recognise Edith at first. Thin to the point of emaciation when she'd last seen her, now she and Linda looked like two walking skeletons. But it was the look on their faces that terrified Georgina. No emotion, no relief or pleasure at seeing everyone again – nothing but blankness.

Georgina threw down her hoe and ran towards them, stopping only to make the loathed bow to the two guards accompanying the women. Close on her heels were the Australian nurses and the camp doctor. Between them they half-carried the two women into the sickbay and laid them

366

on the pallets, the rest of the women crowding behind them.

Accepting a bowl of water one of the women brought, Georgina bathed Edith's brow, murmuring to her that she was safe now. Her sister stared up at her with her vacant eyes and said nothing.

It took a few days for the full story to emerge. Edith still wouldn't speak and it was left to Linda to relate what had happened in short, faltering sentences. They'd been working as normal when one day, without warning, the doctor and his wife had been arrested. Shortly after, the Kempeitai – the Japanese secret police – came for Edith and Linda as well as the civilian nurses and took them to prison. They never saw the doctor or his wife, or the other nurses again.

Edith and Linda were locked in a windowless cell, so tiny they could barely take two paces before they had to turn around again. There was no toilet, only a bucket, and no way of washing themselves. In cells on either side were Malayan criminals without whose kindness, risking their lives to pass the women the odd bowl of rice and piece of fruit, they probably wouldn't have survived.

No one would tell them why they were there. They lived in fear of being executed every day and often had to listen to the sound of other prisoners being tortured, not knowing if they'd be next. At first they were only allowed outside for five minutes every day, but over time that increased to an hour twice a day. Then just as suddenly as they'd been arrested, they were released. When the guards had come for them the two women had been certain they were to be executed, but instead they were thrown inside a truck and driven back to camp.

As soon as Edith was back on her feet she returned to her nursing duties, but she was more an automaton than a person. She jumped if anyone spoke too loud, flinched if someone made a sudden movement. She was particularly frightened of the guards. When Georgina wasn't working, she would go and sit next to Edith, to try and draw her out of herself

367

by talking about the lives they had left behind, how one day they'd be home again and all this would seem like a nightmare. But Edith would shake her head and stare blankly in front of her. She had retreated inside herself, seemed to have lost the will to live and it terrified Georgina. She'd seen it happen too many times in the years they'd been in captivity. Women would lie down and turn their faces to the wall, and just give up, refusing food when it was offered. Sooner or later, they died. It couldn't happen to Edith. Not when they had made it this far. Georgina wouldn't let it happen. She had to keep her sister alive.

Inevitably Georgina caught malaria too. Her head had been pounding since the night before and all of a sudden she was overcome by a fit of shivers. Edith was released from her nursing duties and stayed by her side night and day. Georgina was conscious of waking and Edith being there, although occasionally it was Harriet – or their mother – sometimes even Findlay. At times she believed she was back in Paris or in her chummery in Singapore or in the cool comfort of Greyfriars.

Georgina was only just back on her feet and working in the gardens, hacking at the dry rock-hard earth with the other women, when one of the nurses came to tell her that Edith was unwell.

'She was all right yesterday,' Georgina said, as they hurried towards the sickbay hut. The commandant was watching so they had to stop and bow until he went back inside.

'You know how quickly malaria can come on.' Doris paused. 'The doctor thinks she has beriberi too.'

'No!' Malaria was bad enough but to have it along with beriberi was serious. Several women had already died from one or the other – what chance did Edith have with both – especially with how she was now?

'If only we had some quinine left – and some vitamin B,' Doris said.

'She's not going to die?' When Doris didn't respond, Georgina repeated, more firmly this time, 'She's not going to die. She can have my rations for the next few days. I'll ask others to give up theirs too. They know how much the nurses are needed.'

'Our rations have no vitamin B, Georgina. An extra couple of bowlfuls of rice won't help. And you can't ask the others to give up what little they have. It wouldn't be fair.'

'Then she can have all of mine. It will be better than nothing.' But her mind was racing. She meant what she said. Edith was not going to die. And there was a way to get both quinine and vitamin B, although the thought of what she'd have to do to get it made her want to retch.

Arriving at the sickbay she found Edith on a pallet almost submerged beneath the blankets that had been piled on top of her. Her hair was sticking to her scalp and she was so thin her bones protruded through the worn cotton of her dress.

Malaria followed a pattern. First the victim would get shivers and feel unbearably cold. Then almost as suddenly her temperature would rise and she would need to be sponged to bring the fever down. Georgina knew how awful it felt to go from one extreme to the next and how much reality faded – the nightmares – the ghastly feeling – the utter wretchedness. She dropped to her knees beside the pallet. 'I'm here, Edith,' she whispered. 'You have to fight this, do you hear me?'

But it was clear Edith could hear nothing. Georgina squeezed her hand and went in search of the doctor. She found her bending over another patient who, judging by the smell enveloping her, had dysentery as well as malaria.

'Could I have a word, Doctor?' she asked.

The doctor straightened. Her blouse and skirt was as patched and as grubby as everyone else's clothes, but while they wore the minimum in the heat, she refused to rip off her sleeves or do anything to make herself cooler. Georgina knew that the doctor was hanging on to what little dignity she had left for the sake of the patients. 'You've been told about Edith.'

'You must have some quinine squirrelled away for emergencies,' Georgina said desperately.

'If I had, don't you think I would have used it for one of my nurses? I haven't had any for months.'

'Then we need to get some.'

'And how do you propose we do that? Ask the commandant? We've tried. As everyone knows.'

'If I managed to get some for her, can you save her?'

The doctor gave her a long, slow look. 'There's none to be found on the black market either, if you're thinking of going under the fence.'

The thought had crossed her mind. Dangerous though it was, it was still preferable to the alternative.

'Are you sure?'

'My dear, I couldn't be more certain of anything.'

'Perhaps someone has something they've been keeping back?'

'You can ask. But I doubt it. The only women who might – and I'm only saying might – have something are those who have taken up with the Japs.' The doctor's mouth twisted in a moue of distaste. 'But we've asked them before to get us medicine and they've never come through. God help their wickedness.'

The women in the camp were divided on many things, but collaboration with the Japs was one thing they agreed on; decent women simply didn't do it. Not for anything. Georgina had been just as disgusted as everyone else when some had taken up with the guards but that had been when she still had the luxury of having Edith in reasonable health. She knew what she was considering – if it worked – would mean her certain alienation from the others in the camp – possibly even Edith.

There was no time to waste. Every minute could mean the difference between life and death for Edith. She left the doctor and returned to Edith's side. 'Hold on, dearest,' she begged. 'Hold on.'

Chapter Forty-One

Charlotte

1984

Georgina faltered to a stop. The only sound in the room was the ticking of the clock and the intermittent whines from Tiger as she lay on the rug chasing rabbits in her sleep.

Georgina's eyes looked haunted and I suspected she was gathering her courage to tell me about whatever came next. I left my chair and went to sit next to her on the sofa, taking one of her hands in mine. Hers was deathly cold. I rubbed it, trying to bring back some warmth.

'Perhaps you should stop for a while,' I suggested gently. 'Remembering all you and Edith went through must be very difficult.'

Georgina clasped my hand as if trying to anchor herself. 'No. I need to go on before I lose my courage completely. The next part is important for you to understand . . . ' She fixed her eyes on the carpet in front of the fireplace.

When she looked up her eyes were drenched. 'I had to save Edith. Whatever it took I had to save her.'

Chapter Forty-Two

Georgina

1944

She wouldn't think too much about it, she decided. She went to the kitchen sink and washed herself as best she could with the muddy water, scrubbing at the dirt under her fingernails until her fingertips almost bled. If she was going to do this, she had to make the best job of it she could. She couldn't risk him turning her away. She had one spare blouse that was reasonably clean although it had, like the skirt and dresses she'd acquired from the suitcases on the beach, been repeatedly patched. She couldn't help a wry smile. She would never have imagined in a hundred years setting off and seducing a man dressed as she was, let alone a man she despised.

As a finishing touch to her toilette she used her finger to brush her teeth with charcoal, pinched her cheeks and bit her lips to provide colour.

She walked over to the main hut and told the guard she wished to see the commandant. A few moments later the guard returned and shoved her in.

He was sitting at a table, writing. She bowed stiffly and waited for him to acknowledge her. He ignored her for a long while. His personal quarters were spartan and meticulous. Apart from a desk, on top of which there was a neat stack of papers, a picture of the emperor on the wall, and a small door leading off through which she could see a single bed, it was bare.

Eventually he looked up. 'Prisoner Guthrie. What is it you wish to see me about?'

She ran her tongue over her dry and cracked lips. 'You said I should come if ever I changed my mind.' Now she was here she couldn't bring herself to try and seduce him. He would see right through her anyway.

She saw the leap of desire fighting with contempt in his eyes. Almost immediately, the usual inscrutable mask snapped back down.

'Why have you changed your mind?'

'My sister is very sick. I need food and medicine for her.'

He came out from behind his desk and stood in front of her. He lifted a lock of her hair, laying a finger along her cheek. 'Your hair. I have never seen anything like it. It is the colour of the sun on the Japanese flag.'

It took every ounce of willpower not to shrink from his touch. Everything about him revolted her. Even looking at him made her skin crawl. He could have saved the lives of many of the women who'd died had he chosen to do so. He had no humanity or compassion. He didn't see her, or any of them, as a human being. Her mind flashed back to the villagers, the way he'd slaughtered them without mercy, the swish of his sword as he'd brought it down on the sailor's neck. She forced the images away. If she dwelt on what he'd done she could never make herself go through with it.

He let her hair fall and shouted for the guard and, when he scurried in, barked something at him. Her heart thumped painfully. Was he going to throw her out? Put her into solitary again? Worse, had he changed his mind about wanting her?

To her relief the guard bowed and hurried away.

'I am not so alone that I can have a woman who is not clean. The soldier will bring water and something for you to put on after you have bathed. Then we will eat.'

Even if it hadn't been an additional humiliation to be made

to bathe in front of him – time was of the essence. Every minute that passed brought Edith closer to death.

'Before I bathe, may I have some quinine to take to my sister? I will return immediately.'

'No. After. No more talk of medicine.'

The guard he had spoken to came back in carrying a tin tub which he laid on the floor before hurrying out again. A short while later he and another guard appeared with pails of water. They emptied them into the tub, bowed to their superior officer and retreated.

The commandant sat back down, stiff-backed and impassive. She remained where she was, refusing to bow her head.

'Take off your clothes.'

She unbuttoned her blouse, trying to hide the fact her fingers were trembling. Shut out everything, she told herself. Imagine, instead, that she was back in Singapore preparing herself for an evening out at Raffles hotel. Tsing Tsing had run her bath and Georgina was about to loll in it before slipping on her evening dress. The heat was the same – even if there was no swirling overhead fan.

She slipped her blouse off her shoulders, letting it fall to the floor, and stepped out of her skirt. Her brassiere and slip were tattered from a thousand washes yet still stained with sweat. They joined the rest of her clothes in a heap on the floor.

Almost naked now and aware of the greedy eyes sweeping her body, she thought of Edith lying on the bed, sweating and crying out with fever. She thought of that day down by the shore, the feel of Findlay's hands on her shoulders, the dark hairs on his arms, his broad chest, the hard muscles of his biceps, the intensity of his gaze – the green flecks in his eyes. No, no, no, she would not think of Findlay in the same room as this man. Instead she thought of the bleakness in her sister's eyes, of the promise she had made to protect her. She stepped out of her panties and into the tub.

A bar of soap had been set to the side and with her knees

374

drawn up to her chest she began to wash herself. Despite her horror a small part of her revelled in the water, exulted as the grime was soaped away. Remembering again the disinterested look on his face, the sickening sound of his sword as he'd decapitated the sailor, the implacable look on his face as his soldiers had murdered the villagers, bile rushed to her throat. She closed her eyes in an attempt to make the images go away.

'You must look at me,' he demanded. 'Not behave like a peasant woman. You must behave like an English lady.'

She raised her head and lifted her chin. She still didn't know for certain that even if she did as he asked whether he would give her what she needed.

When she'd scrubbed every inch of herself and washed her hair, and could no longer put off the inevitable, she stepped out of the bath. He tossed her a piece of fabric to dry herself. The heat was so intense that a film of sweat began to form on her skin almost as soon as she was out of the water. She wrapped herself in the cloth, tying it just above her breasts as the native women did.

He shouted for the guards and they came to remove the tub, keeping their eyes averted. He barked a few more commands at them and then gestured to a chair in front of the table. 'Sit. They will bring food. While we wait, I wish you to talk to me – as if I were one of the men you dined with. Japanese women know how to please a man. You must too.'

She scrambled around for something to say, but her mind was a blank. If she were at Raffles having dinner with Lawrence what would they have talked about? Tennis, people they knew, coming dances and outings, the war back home. But if she said the wrong thing, whatever fantasy the commandant was trying to create would be blown. He wanted her to behave as he imagined white women did, so that's what he'd get.

'Isn't this heat quite wretched?' she said.

Swish, swish went his sword in her head.

'Quite so.'

'Perhaps it will rain soon?'

He inclined his head. It was only when his jaw relaxed slightly that she saw that he was almost as ill at ease with proceedings as she was.

'Tell me about your family.' If she knew anything about men it was that the more arrogant they were and the more important they considered themselves, the more they liked to talk about themselves.

'Are you married?' she continued.

'You will not talk about my wife!' His expression had darkened and she knew she mustn't slip up again.

'Do you care for classical music?'

He nodded.

'Which composer do you like best?'

'Schumann and Bach. Bach is more serious. More like the Japanese way.'

Without meaning to she smiled. 'I'm not entirely sure that Schumann would agree.'

'You are an ignorant woman. You know nothing about music. Japanese women never disagree with man. Japanese man always knows best.'

For Heaven's sake was there anything she was allowed to say?

Happily, at that moment, the same two guards came back in carrying trays of food. The smell made her stomach contract sharply.

They set the bowls of steaming rice, roasted chicken and vegetables down on the table. He indicated to her that she should eat.

She shook her head. How could she swallow a mouthful, when her fellow prisoners, her sister, were dying of starvation? 'May I take it with me to have later?' she asked.

'No. You must eat now. You are too thin. I do not like women to be so thin.'

In which case, you bloody idiot, she thought, lowering her eyes, you should have given us more food.

'Eat and your sister eats. I will give you food to take with you. After.'

They ate in silence but she could only make the meal last for so long. Fear and nausea clawing at her throat, she pushed her bowl away.

Chapter Forty-Three

Charlotte

1984

'I don't imagine I need to go into the details as to what happened next,' Georgina said, her voice barely above a whisper. 'Suffice to say I did what the commandant wanted.'

She was pale and only the way in which she clasped her hands together gave away her distress. 'Let's just say it was rather unpleasant.'

'What he did was rape!' I said viciously.

She shook her head. 'Not by the way we measured such things back then.'

'When a man forces a woman to have sex with him, it is rape.'

She shook her head again. 'He didn't force me.'

'He had a hold over you. You did it to save your sister's life. If you hadn't done what you did he might have killed you.'

'He wouldn't have harmed me if I hadn't gone to him – we must be perfectly clear on that. He did many terrible things but he did not rape me.'

Although I ached for my aunt, and was sickened by everything I'd learned about the commandant, now was not the time to argue with her.

She took another shuddering breath.

'I had to keep going back,' she continued. 'He only gave me just enough quinine and food each time and it was many

378

days before Edith recovered. I tried to keep what I'd done from her, but of course it came out. There was no chance of keeping secrets in the camp. Everyone witnessed you using the lavatory, for Heaven's sake! There was nowhere to go where one wasn't under somebody's eyes.

'I kept more and more to myself. I didn't want their pity or their approbation, or even their understanding. I didn't want to lean on them – I had to rely on myself; it was the only way I knew how to be. The only person I could afford to care about – the only person other than myself I had the energy to care about – was Edith. No one who hasn't been in those circumstances can understand.'

'You loved Edith very much. It was the only way to save her.'

She gave a small, despairing shake of her head. 'What happened with the commandant ate away at my soul. Not just because of the sex – I coped with that by detaching my mind from my body. But in time it wasn't just sex he wanted from me. He still expected sex every time I went to his hut – it's important you understand that – but we spent longer and longer talking beforehand and often I would have one conversation in my head at the same time I was having one out loud.

'At first our conversations were as awkward as they had been that first time and the longer he took before the actual act the more excruciating it was for me. The anticipation of what was about to happen was almost worse than the act itself.

'Over time he began to talk of his family. He was married with two children – boys – and clearly very proud of them all. He even showed me photographs. I often wondered how he could reconcile what he was doing with me with loving his wife but I learned that sex for the Japanese was a much more practical affair than for us in the west. Prostitution wasn't looked down upon – no one thought it irregular in the slightest that men used prostitutes – not even the wives.

379

'He was, despite his brutality, an educated man and while overtly dismissive of the western way of life, deeply curious about it too. At times, for short periods, I was able to forget who and what he was. And to my shame I enjoyed the baths and being able to wear something clean even for a short time. I also lost my guilty conscience about the food and ate as much as I could. For years I felt more guilty about that than almost everything else. I think I still do.'

I gave her hand another squeeze. I could only guess how much recalling all this was costing her but the flat look she gave me warned me that she neither wanted nor needed my pity.

'Even after Edith was well again, he continued to give me small amounts of quinine – often left on the table for me to take as if he couldn't bring himself to actually give it to me. And as for the food – I realised early on that he knew I was taking more than I was supposed to, but he pretended not to notice.'

'Why didn't he just give it to you?'

'I suspect it was something to do with loss of face which was very important to the Japanese soldier. If he gave me what I needed overtly, it was an admission – even if only to himself – that he could and should have been giving us more food and medicine all along.' She pinned me with her deep blue eyes. 'I never stopped hating him – never.

'I put on weight with the food. My hair regained some of the sheen. I looked different to the other women and I knew they despised me for it. I think they would have forgiven me – not that I sought or wanted their forgiveness – if I had stopped going to the commandant but I was determined to ensure Edith had enough to eat and that she wouldn't get sick again. She begged me over and over to stop going to him, told me she'd rather starve to death, but I wouldn't listen to her. I couldn't take the chance she wouldn't get sick again.

'Then there was a change in the atmosphere of the camp

and in his demeanour. I could tell something was happening that worried him – this was late in 1945 and although we didn't know it then the war in Europe was over and the Japs were on the run.

'The rations increased slightly although it seemed to everyone that the soldiers were looking thinner and more bedraggled with every passing day. There was always a great deal of speculation in the camps,' she gave me a wry smile, 'not that I was included in that speculation – not since my continuing "relationship" with the camp commandant had become general knowledge, but Edith kept me informed. She made no secret she abhorred what I was doing but she still talked to me. She was the only one in the camp who still did.

'We didn't really understand what was happening at first. You have to remember we had no newspapers, no radios, no way at all of finding out what was going on. All we were ever told was what the commandant chose to tell us at morning *tenko* and judging by what he said the Japs were in control of most of the Far East as well as Europe. Not once, in all the time I spent with him, did he ever let on to the true state of affairs – that the war in Europe was over and the Japanese all but beaten. By that time only around half of us who had started off in the camp were still alive and many of us who remained had given up hope of ever seeing home or our loved ones again.

'The first inkling we had that things might not be going the Japs' way was when we received our first Red Cross parcels. You can imagine how we fell upon them. There was chocolate – stale but completely delicious – and even lipstick.

'It was then that we realised that the camp commandant had the food and medicines that have could saved many lives all along and if possible, the women hated him even more – and by association me. But I was in a dilemma. I didn't know whether these would be the last parcels we would ever get so I couldn't risk telling the commandant our arrangement was over. Apart from the risk to our supplies, I had no idea what he would do to me. I wouldn't have put it past him to have me publicly flogged or even killed on some made-up pretext. So although my skin crawled at the thought of his touch, I continued to go to him.

'Then one night the Japs simply disappeared. We woke up to find them gone. We didn't know what else to do so we carried on as normal. There was no extra food, no sudden change in our living conditions, except there was no call to *tenko*; no standing in the sun for hours and no fear of being hit in the face with a rifle butt if one didn't bow low enough.'

'With our guards gone, the women were free to vent their disapproval of me and the other women who'd sold themselves to the Japs and who could blame them? There was talk, always when I was in earshot, of reporting me as a collaborator.'

'They must have known why you did what you did.' I raged inside at the way the other women had treated my aunt. 'You could have made them understand.'

'My dear, I couldn't. My pride wouldn't let me. It was all I had left and I had to hold on to that.'

For a moment I was tempted to confide in her about Lucy and the difficulty I found myself in. But I quickly decided against it. How would a woman who'd been raped feel about another woman who'd defended a rapist? Her good opinion had come to matter to me.

'A short while after that our soldiers arrived,' Georgina continued. 'We were given food and treated, flown to Singapore and told we were free to make our way home. There was only one place Edith and I wanted to be. Here at Greyfriars.'

Georgina sighed and gently released my hand. 'I need to go and see if Edith's all right . . . '

I took Tiger outside. Low cloud hung over the island, obscuring the sky, and night would fall soon. But feeling the need to get rid of some of the restless energy inside me, I headed up the hill at the back of the house. I'd walked here before and although the path was overgrown it was distinct enough for me to follow. The path was steep but I walked quickly, only stopping to draw breath when I reached the top. From here I could see Balcreen and even closer, Jamie's cottage. I stood for a while thinking about what Georgina had told me. I was about to turn and retrace my steps, when out of nowhere a mist came down, blanketing me and making it impossible to see. I'd been too absorbed in my thoughts to notice.

I turned back in the direction I'd thought I'd come but I'd only taken a few steps when I realised I couldn't even see the path. Even Tiger seemed unsure of where to go. She sat at my feet and looked at me as if she trusted me to find the way back down. But I'd lost all sense of direction. I stood stock-still. What I did remember was up here, the hill fell away sharply and if I carried on without being able to see, there was every chance I'd go over the cliff – a fall that might well kill me. I took a breath to still my rising panic. All I had to do was remain where I was – hopefully the cloud would lift and I could make my way back then. But it would be dark soon and I was cold.

I heard a crack and snap from somewhere to my right and I squinted in an attempt to see what had made the noise. Tiger growled low in her throat and sprang to her feet, staring in the direction from where the sound had come.

Something moved in the mist and I held my breath, straining to see.

As it moved closer I could see it was a figure wearing a cloak that covered her head, obscuring her face as well as her body.

I was rooted to the spot. Although I couldn't see her face, I was certain it wasn't Georgina or Edith.

The figure beckoned, clearly wanting me to come closer. I could feel Tiger shivering through the thin material of my trousers as she pressed against me. Once again I flashed back to the dream Mum had told me about – the one where Lady Elizabeth had come for her.

I shook my head at my foolishness. Apart from the cloak, what reason did I have to think the figure I was seeing wasn't real? People wore cloaks, albeit I hadn't seen many do so, apart from in a play. Nurses did – although weren't theirs shorter? I was allowing, like my mother before me, the primeval atmosphere of the house and the island to get to me. God knew there were enough strangely dressed people in London – goths and punks amongst them – there could have been a hundred people wearing cloaks and I wouldn't have noticed. And there was nothing to prevent a sightseer from coming over to the island if they had their own boat.

Yet the hairs on the back of my neck stood to attention.

Hello!' I called. 'Are you lost too?' There was no reply – not even a raised hand. My voice was muffled by the thick mist, which to my dismay, had become thicker instead of lighter, so perhaps they hadn't heard.

The figure beckoned again, more urgently.

I had a choice. I could stay here and probably freeze, or I could follow the woman as she clearly wanted me to. Whoever it was turned away and I picked up Tiger and followed. She kept in front of me, turning occasionally to ensure I was still following. As we descended the mist began to clear and looking down I could see the path again. When I glanced up, the figure was gone.

Chapter Forty-Four

The next morning, as soon as breakfast was over and Edith had retreated to her room, Georgina asked if I would spend time with her in the library so she could continue with her story. I had said nothing of my experience on the hill, unsure now, in the cold light of day if I'd imagined it all. When we were settled, she plunged straight in as if her need to tell me what she needed to was growing stronger with every passing hour.

'I'm coming to the crux of my story,' she began. 'As I told you yesterday, being back at Greyfriars was both wonderful and painful for Edith and me. There were so many memories of happier times but it was also a reminder that those times were gone and could never be brought back. We had no plan, no thought of the future, all we wanted to do was recover in private, away from prying eyes. There were no servants any longer. Donald and his wife had vacated the farm cottage in 1939 and gone to live in Balcreen. Mrs MacKay did come to ask if we would like help but we refused her offer. All we wanted was to be left alone.'

She dipped her head, for once refusing to meet my eyes. 'You see, shortly after we returned, I discovered I was pregnant.'

As the silence stretched between us, I dreaded what she was about to tell me next. Had they killed the child was the thought that ran through my mind – ridiculous though it was.

Or had it conveniently died, either during childbirth or after? If that were the case, I didn't want to know. As a member of the law I would be obliged to inform the police if I suspected a crime had been committed. I gave myself a mental shake. I was getting way ahead of myself. There were other, more logical and therefore more likely things that could have happened to the child. Adoption, to begin with. Was that why I had been asked to come? To help them search for the child who would be ... what, by now? Ten years older than me. My – what would it be? – cousin.

'Georgina, I'll do everything in my power to help you, but you mustn't tell me something that as a lawyer I have to report.' The warning was automatic but even as the words left my lips I knew I'd do whatever I could to protect them.

'It's a chance we are prepared to take. You will be free to take any action you feel fit. I promise.'

It wasn't the firm rebuttal I'd hoped for.

'What did you do?'

'Something,' she said slowly, 'that I imagine you'll find difficult to understand.'

She paused and I braced myself for what was to come.

'We thought we had plenty of time to decide what to do about the baby. Edith and I never spoke of it. Perhaps we both hoped it would die and then we could pick up the pieces of our lives.

'It was a blessing that there were no servants at Greyfriars any longer and no one could see the house, not without coming to the front door, and although one or two did visit at first, we wouldn't invite them in, instead making it clear we wished to be left alone. We still had a milking cow, the hens, the vegetable garden and the shop in Balcreen was happy to send groceries over once a week the way they'd always done. Of course there was still rationing but compared to the camp, it was a bounty. Besides, we had more than we needed. Edith had always been decent at sewing – she made us clothes from patterns we sent away for – not that there was a need for anything fancy (and I had left trunks of my clothes behind so there was plenty that could be altered) and she could knit after a fashion. We rented out the house in Edinburgh and the income was sufficient for us to manage quite well on as long as we were careful. We sent some of it to your mother. That was only fair. And for the next few months we lived quietly, letting the comfort and peace of Greyfriars heal some of our mental wounds.

'The child was born just after Christmas. The moment I held her in my arms, I fell in love with her. Even though she was most definitely her father's child. She had a shock of dark hair and almond-shaped eyes. We decided on a name together – Mary. It was a happy time. We didn't think of the future. While she was a baby there was no need to decide anything. All babies require is enough to eat and plenty of love. And Mary got both. At least from me. For the first few weeks Edith wouldn't even look at her.'

She paused and glanced away, and once again I had the feeling she was keeping something from me. 'Eventually she couldn't help loving Mary as much as I did.

'It wasn't long before I began to realise that something about her bothered Edith. We no longer thought of her as being the child of a Japanese brute, so I knew it wasn't that. I pressed Edith and she admitted she was worried about the way Mary looked and her development. We'd thought she looked different when she was born but we put that down to her Japanese heritage. However, as she grew we knew there was more to it. She wasn't supporting her own head when she should have, or flipping herself over when placed on the ground. Edith thought at first that it was because she was premature and that she would catch up sooner or later, but eventually it became clear to us that Mary wasn't going to catch up and finally Edith told me she was certain that Mary had Down's syndrome. She had seen many such children when she had nursed. In the

387

forties most of them were put in institutions and left there. No one thought they could ever live normal lives.'

'Why didn't you take her to be seen by a doctor?'

'He would only have told us what we already knew and he would have asked questions. Anyone looking at Mary would know she was half Japanese. You have to realise that back then and for a long time afterwards people hated the Japanese and everything to do with them. Stories had come out about their cruelty to the prisoners, the way they had starved and worked thousands of men to their deaths – I learned later that Lawrence had been one of them – and the massacres at the hospitals and elsewhere. But it wasn't just that. What if they tried to take Mary away from us? Put her in one of those dreadful institutions? We couldn't take the chance. We both loved Mary dearly by then. She might not have been like other children but she was such so loving and happy. And she wasn't to blame for what her father or mother had done.

'Edith and I told ourselves over the years that there was no need to do anything. That Mary was fine with just the two of us. Edith could take care of any childhood ailments although there weren't many of those and if Mary did become seriously unwell of course then we would call the doctor. Although we had no idea what we would say. The longer we kept her a secret the more impossible it was to share her existence with the rest of the world. Not only was Mary half Japanese and disabled, she was also the child of an unmarried mother. Any one of these would have made her the object of derision, even hate, but all together? The outside world would have been a very cruel place for her. We might have started off wanting to protect ourselves but in the end we stayed here and kept her with us to protect her.

'Despite her difficulties, maybe even because of them, Mary grew up a happy, contented child. She was the centre of Edith's and my world. We had plenty of books to read to her and your mother's old toys as well as ours were still in the nursery. A child who has never known any other sort of life doesn't find it strange.

'We schooled her ourselves. We made sure she only played in the part of the grounds that no one could ever see, supposing they came right up to the door, and that she kept to our side of the house.

'But when Mary was six, your mother arrived on our doorstep. As you can imagine, it was a dreadful shock. Then Olivia collapsed. We might have been able to take care of her ourselves but Duncan sent for the doctor and it would have looked strange if we'd refused to let him attend. It was bad luck for all concerned that your mother turned out to have a potentially life-threatening condition. The doctor insisted that she be confined to bed – that she couldn't be allowed to travel – not even to Balcreen. We did manage to persuade him that Edith was capable of looking after Olivia and we promised that if your mother's condition deteriorated we would send for him.

'Mary was aware of your mother's arrival so we made up a story to keep her away from Olivia. We said she was very sick – which was true – but had to be kept away from Mary in case she made her sick too. Of course Mary accepted what we told her – she was always very obedient. But naturally she was intensely curious about your mother; the only people she'd seen up until that point were Edith and me. Because your mother was confined to bed there was little chance of her stumbling across Mary, but of course we couldn't stop her being aware at times of Mary's presence. Mary was used to running free at Greyfriars when she liked and when Olivia almost came across Mary in the nursery, I'm afraid we locked Olivia's bedroom door after that.

'Mary was here all the time Mum was?' It was scarcely believable.

'Yes.'

So Mum hadn't been losing her mind as she'd thought. Everything she'd seen and heard had been real.

389

'We discussed often whether we should tell Olivia the truth but we had no way of knowing how she would react. We would have told her had it been necessary and thrown ourselves on her mercy. As it happened, Olivia took you and left.'

'But why didn't you just tell Mum about Mary? She would have understood. Particularly when you told her what had happened to you and Edith during the war. She might even have been able to help.'

Georgina gave a quick, dismissive shake of her head. 'We couldn't risk telling her. At first it was because Olivia was unwell. We didn't want to add any more stress to her situation. We would also have put her in an impossible position. She would have either had to keep our secret and thereby implicated herself, or she would have felt duty bound to tell the authorities. I didn't know what they would do to us. I had some idea that concealing a pregnancy and birth was against the law. Mary's birth of course hadn't been registered. If they put me in prison, or charged me, I would have had to stand up in court and go through everything that had happened in the camp all over again. I couldn't bear to. I couldn't bear the shame. And if they did put me in prison, then what would happen to Mary and Edith?'

This part of her story didn't ring altogether true and once more I had the uneasy sensation Georgina wasn't being entirely honest with me. Everything I had learned about her so far had led me to believe that if there was a woman who was prepared to face her accusers, hold up her head and stare them down, who couldn't care less about what other people thought of her, it was Georgina.

'Is there anything else?' I prodded gently. 'It's best you tell me everything.'

'I'm telling you what you need to know,' she retorted. 'And that's difficult enough.'

'I'm sorry. I didn't mean to imply—'

She patted my hand in apology. 'Let me finish. I promise

390

there's not much more. 'Edith was never the same after the war. I thought that the seclusion of Greyfriars and plenty of wholesome food would heal the damage eventually, that all she needed was time. When we returned to Greyfriars she would barely speak, had no interest in anything and she had these terrible nightmares. Sometimes her screams would wake me in the middle of the night. I'd run to her and hold her. She thought she was back in the camp, that rats were chewing on her toes, or that the Japs had put her back in that dreadful prison. The nightmares were never identical, but they were always to do with that awful time.

'It was when Edith started sleepwalking I became really concerned. One night, shortly after we returned to Greyfriars, I found her down at the shore, at Sarah's rocks, balancing on the rocks and about to step in the sea. If I'd been moments later, I believe I would have been too late. I was terrified I was going to lose her, after everything we'd been through. I tried locking her bedroom door at night but when she discovered this she became so agitated she screamed the house down. It made her believe she was back in prison. I wanted her to see a doctor but she begged me not to make her. She said they'd lock her up and then she'd truly go mad. All I could do was try and keep her safe and hope that the peace and solitude of Greyfriars would heal her in time. In the meantime I waited until she was asleep before locking the outside doors, making sure I was awake before her so I could unlock them before she realised. You see, we had never locked the doors of Greyfriars before. There was never any need. After a while things did improve and I let myself hope that she might even return to nursing. She always loved it so much. I tried to talk her into it, I thought it would be good for her, but she kept saying she wasn't ready, wasn't strong enough – that maybe one day . . .'
A few beats of silence passed. That day never came.

'Over time Edith seemed to get better although she still had bad spells. When your mother came to stay Edith started sleepwalking again. I don't know if it was your mother's arrival that triggered it all off again. It must have been. I think Olivia was a reminder of the outside world and Edith didn't want to be reminded of it. In addition, Olivia being pregnant made Edith think about Mary and how she'd come in to the world. That's when I proposed to Olivia that she take our share of the house we owned jointly in Edinburgh in exchange for her share of Greyfriars. It seemed the safest and fairest solution. Unfortunately, Olivia seemed equally determined to stay. Until, that is, she found you'd been taken from her room.'

So that was why they'd come to the arrangement about the houses.

'Your cries woke me up,' Georgina continued. 'My first thought was that Edith had started sleepwalking again and had taken the baby. I ran to where the noise was coming from to Mary in the nursery holding you. When Mary saw me she hugged you tighter. I was terrified that you wouldn't be able to breathe. I knew I only had moments before Olivia woke to find her baby missing but I was frightened of scaring Mary.

'Edith had woken too by this time and had come up after me. She took the scene in in a moment. She persuaded Mary to hand you to her, promising her that she would be able to play with you another time. Mary didn't want to hand you back, but we could hear your mother calling. Edith grabbed you while I took Mary back to her room. There is a secret staircase that runs down past the nursery – we were able to leave that way, without your mother seeing us.

'Your mother came bursting in only moments before I returned after leaving Mary in her room. She was understandably frantic. She calmed down a little when she had you safe in her arms but then she became really angry. I told her that Edith had heard you crying and not wanting to disturb her rest, had taken you for a walk around the house to try and pacify you. I knew it wasn't a good explanation, but it was the only one I could come up with. And your mother didn't believe me either.

'After Olivia returned to her room, Edith came to me. She suggested we keep Olivia and you here, as a playmate and friend for Mary. She even suggested we tell Olivia that her baby had died and send her away. She came up with increasingly wild ideas. I knew then that Edith could never be trusted around you. Fortunately your mother decided she'd had enough of Greyfriars and agreed to the house exchange.'

So Mum had been right to feel threatened.

Georgina twisted her fingers together. 'Everything settled down again after you and your mother left but the sleepwalking started again when you arrived.'

'I thought I saw someone in the nursery one night, but they seemed to vanish,' I said. 'I remembered Mum telling me about the door at the back of the wardrobe that led to the secret staircase but when I tried it, I couldn't see a way to open it. Was that Edith or Mary?'

Georgina nodded. 'It must have been Mary. She uses the staircase often, although she knows she has to keep the door locked in case Edith sleepwalks. It was her in the garden that first night too.'

Finally, it all made sense. The shadows, the sound of feet, the figure in the corridor, the sensation of being watched – the beckoning figure on the hill. My first reaction was one of relief. I hadn't been imagining things. My second was one of disbelief.

'But Mary must be a grown woman! You can't have kept her here all these years.'

'We had no choice. As the years went on we thought about moving back to Edinburgh with her, introducing her to society, but it was too late. She's never been exposed to a virus of any sort – and how would we explain to others and to her why we'd done what we'd done? Could I really tell her that her father was a murderer? Was that fair? No, she was safer

393

and far happier here than she would have ever been in the outside world.'

There was so much wrong with her way of thinking I couldn't even think where to start.

My unease deepened. I had been here the best part of a week and apart from hearing her and those brief glimpses I now knew was Mary, I had never met her.

'Are you telling me you keep Mary locked up during the day?'

Georgina looked horrified. 'Oh, no! Of course not. We use part of the ballroom on the first floor as another sitting room. We've only kept her upstairs while you've been here. Edith spends most of her day there with her. Whenever you weren't here we went for walks or Mary helped Edith in the garden as she usually does.' She gave me a wry smile. 'Keeping you and Mary apart has been made easier as you've spent so much time off the island, although you came close to stumbling across her more than once. She knows you're here but that she can't meet you just yet. We didn't want that to happen until we'd come to know you better. It's why we asked Olivia to come. I realised we're getting on. What if I died? Who would care for Edith and Mary then? What if we both died? What would happen to Mary? Where would she live? How would she live? That's when we decided to write to your mother. We hoped she would agree to look after Mary if anything happened to Edith and me. We got quite a shock when we learned of her death and that you were coming in her place, and an even bigger shock when we discovered you were a lawyer. We didn't know if that was a good or a bad thing. Good if you'd help us, bad if you reported us to the police.' She leaned forward. 'It's why I needed to tell you our story. I hoped you might understand better why we did what we did when you knew everything.'

So this, finally, was the reason they'd asked for help. But what were they expecting *me* to do?

'Mary can't manage on her own. She will always need

someone to take care of her.' Georgina smiled sadly. 'She has as much right to her share of Greyfriars as you do, but more importantly we need to know that in the event of our deaths she will be cared for.'

I was still finding it all difficult to take in. Mary had lived here all her life and now the aunts wanted some sort of guarantee I would look after her. Where? Here? In London? I shook my head to clear it. Hopefully my aunts would live for a very long time and there would be years to help Mary adjust to a normal life. One thing was clear to me. She couldn't be kept here for another forty years.

Georgina stood, smoothing down her skirt, her expression lighter than I'd seen it for a while. 'Mary is looking forward to meeting you. I'll let Edith know she can bring her down. But remember, Mary isn't like other young women. She is very much a child in a woman's body. Please be very gentle with her.'

'Of course.'

Georgina disappeared into the hall while I remained, still too stunned to move, in my chair.

I did my best to hide my astonishment when Edith appeared, leading a young woman by the hand. A pale, moon-shaped face was framed by thick black, plaited hair, a braid of which hung over a shoulder. Her almond eyes were a deep brown, her full, beautifully shaped mouth red-lipped. She was shorter than Georgina and Edith and a little overweight. She wore a skirt that came to her knee and a white blouse. Heartbreakingly, she clutched a clearly well-loved teddy to her chest. There was no mistaking her Japanese heritage. Or the fact she had Down's.

She gave me a hesitant smile, half-hiding behind Georgina and Edith.

'This is Charlotte, Mary,' Georgina said with a reassuring smile. 'Remember I told you about her?' She gave her daughter a gentle shove in my direction. 'Shake hands. Just as I showed you.'

I had risen to my feet when I heard them coming and I smiled, trying my best to reassure the child-woman in front of me. I held out my hand. 'I am very pleased to meet you, Mary. Aunt Georgina has told me a lot about you.'

My head was still spinning. If what Georgina had told me was true, and although I was finding it difficult to accept I saw no reason why it wouldn't be, I was the first person Mary had ever met apart from her mother and her aunt.

Mary took my hand and held it briefly. 'How do you do?' Her voice sounded exactly like Edith's and Georgina's albeit a little thick and slurred.

'Sit over here, my dear,' Georgina said to Mary, leading her towards the sofa. My aunts sat on either side of her.

I sank back into the chair, hardly able to take my eyes off the three of them.

We spent the next hour together, the four of us. I still wasn't sure what they expected of me, what help could I possibly offer them, or assurances? If something happened to Georgina and Edith did they really intend for me to take Mary to live with me in London?

As we chatted I looked at my aunts, seated on either side of Mary like two fierce, but loving guardian angels. They had done the best they could to salvage some sort of life for themselves and Mary. Whatever the rights and wrongs of the situation, I had no doubt that the life Mary had at Greyfriars would have been far happier than if she'd been raised in Edinburgh, possibly confined to some institution and staring at bleak hospital walls. Here at least she had had fresh air, freedom and, most importantly, the love and protection of Georgina and Edith.

I thought about love in all its forms. The love of a mother for her daughter – of a daughter for a mother – sister for brother – a father for his child – and that fierce need to protect those we love. I thought of Lucy and her father's fury and despair that he couldn't protect her – of Susan Curtis – what she did to protect

396

her child. I thought of the women in the camp, the selfless acts of love and sacrifice, most of all the love of my two great-aunts who'd sacrificed so much for each other and for their child – for Mary was as much Edith's as she was Georgina's. Whatever wrong I'd imagined they'd done to Mum had been explained and what they were asking of me was so little. Surely I could find room in my life for Mary? And Edith and Georgina too.

Finally I thought about Jamie. Although I'd only known him a short while I knew everything about him I needed to. I had been scared of getting hurt, I could admit that now, and even more frightened of having my life turned upside down. Yet, despite my best attempts to resist, it *had* been turned upside down and would likely become more so over the next months and years. I wanted him to be part of that new life. Whatever there was between us might not last but I had to take that chance.

When Edith stood to take Mary back upstairs, I turned to Georgina. 'I'm going to go over to Balcreen for a little while. I'll be back later this evening.'

Alarm flashed in Georgina's eyes.

'Don't worry.' I laid a hand on her arm. 'I won't do anything to harm any of you. You have trusted me so far, please keep that trust.' I couldn't promise her I would keep their secret – how could I? But I needed time to think.

Most of all, I needed to see Jamie.

Chapter Forty-Five

I rowed over to Balcreen with Tiger in her familiar place in the prow. The sun was warm on my face yet I felt chilled to the bone. I walked quickly towards Jamie's house, Tiger at my heels, for once not running off to explore as if she sensed my driving need to reach our destination.

Jamie looked surprised when he opened the door but before he could say anything, I stepped into his arms.

'What is it?' he murmured into my hair. 'You're shaking.' He led me across to the sofa and, without saying any more, simply held me for a long time.

'What I'm going to tell you, you must promise to keep to yourself – for now,' I said eventually. 'At least until I've thought about how to make things right.'

I told him everything, about the camps, about the Japanese officer, what Georgina did for Edith, and finally I told him about Mary. He listened in silence.

'She's been living with them all this time? All these years and no one knew?'

'As far as I'm aware.'

'What are you going to do?'

'There has to be a way of sorting it out. I can't be sure whether they committed a crime or not. Even if they did, I can't imagine it's in anyone's interests to prosecute two elderly ladies. What would happen to Mary then? She's completely used to living at Greyfriars with no contact with the outside world.' I drew back so I could see his face. 'I'm sure I can speak to someone at the Fisc's office in Edinburgh and come to some arrangement.'

'What about the commandant? Do you think he's still alive? Do you think he was ever made to answer for what he did?' Jamie asked.

I was silent for a while. 'Do you think it matters? Do you think it's better if the truth is always exposed? Or, could there be instances where it is better that the truth is allowed to remain buried?'

He frowned. 'Are we still talking about Mary here?'

'I'm not altogether sure. Perhaps I shouldn't have told you. Now I've made you complicit.'

'You can trust me.' He pulled me close again. 'You can trust me with anything – even your life.' He laughed self-consciously. 'God, for a Scottish man to say something so sickly sweet.'

'I rather like it.' My voice was hoarse.

'I meant it. I have never met anyone since Gillian died who makes me feel the way you do.'

'You must have loved her very much.'

'I did. For years she was my world and part of me will always love her. I never imagined I'd fall in love again.' He grinned suddenly. 'Least of all with a defence barrister.'

'Don't . . . ' I covered his lips with my fingertips. The need to talk about Lucy was suddenly intense, maybe because of what Georgina had told me, or because I didn't know whether Jamie could still love me after he knew what I had done to Lucy. And perhaps because of the Guthrie family motto. "We Stand for Truth." If our relationship was to go anywhere, it had to start and continue with the truth.

'There's something I need to tell you.'

'I'm listening.' He took my hand. 'What is it?' The wind had risen while we'd been talking and rattled the window panes. I took a deep breath.

'As I told you the other day, when I was first called to the bar I took on more than my fair share of rape cases – although I hated doing them. I loathed defending men accused of rape and as soon as I became popular with solicitors and began to get a stream of other cases, I refused to take them on.'

Jamie was watching me intently and I now knew how it must have felt for Georgina to confess her so-called sins to me. As if I were judge and jury.

'I wouldn't have accepted this case either if it weren't for two things. Firstly, the accused's father was a long-standing client of Lambert and Lambert and secondly, one of my cases had been delayed for a psychiatric assessment and I was the only barrister free in chambers. I was also the only woman. Solicitors always prefer women barristers to defend their clients when they're accused of rape.

'I didn't take to Simon. I knew his type. There were plenty of older versions of him in chambers. Men who thought their privileged background gave them the right to do as they pleased. Who thought women like Lucy should be grateful to be noticed by them. But I don't expect to like my clients, I don't even have to believe in their innocence; my job is to defend them and to ensure they get a fair trial. It's the prosecutor's job to prove guilt and mine to ensure that they do.

'Lucy Corrigle was a first-year student at Imperial College in London. She'd come there from a small village in Northern Ireland and had been the first of her family to go to university. Her father was an electrician and her mother a clerkess in a hospital and Lucy, their middle child, was their only daughter. She was exceptionally bright. The family believed wholeheartedly in Thatcher's Britain. Lucy would go to university to study politics – get a first and go on to make her family even prouder. It hadn't worked out like that. Lucy had felt awkward at university, and socially out of her depth. It wasn't just that; her strong northern Irish accent, her clothes, everything had felt wrong, made her feel conspicuous and

uncomfortable. As you know, the IRA have made a proportion of the population suspicious of the Irish and their
allegiance to the Union. But she was determined to make
the most of the opportunity she'd been given. She put her
head down and studied. Nevertheless, she'd looked on the
social life her fellow undergrads were leading with envy and
a deep-rooted belief that if only she tried harder they'd accept
her. So when Simon had invited her to a party she'd decided
to go. She'd seen him with his sister, Cassie, who was in one
of her tutorials. Cassie was everything Lucy wanted to be;
confident, popular and wealthy.

'Lucy had drunk some cider before she'd left her rooms –
something God help me, I made much of during the trial.

'In the course of the party, feeling increasingly awkward,
she'd drunk more and was just about to leave when Simon
approached her. They'd ending up kissing and Simon had
suggested they go somewhere quieter. She'd thought he meant
outside, but instead he'd taken her to his room. She knew
Cassie, not well, but enough to make her feel safe with Simon.'

An image of the court room came flooding back. Lucy, her
face pale and drawn in the witness box, never looking at Simon
as the prosecuting counsel took her through her story. Despite
everything she'd remained composed. Or at least had up until
the point I'd stood to cross-examine her.

'Gone willingly,' I continued now. 'As I'd told the jury.
There was no coercion. She must have known what Simon
expected to happen.

'Except she claimed she hadn't. She said they'd only been
in his room a few minutes before he started kissing her and
making it clear that he wanted to have sex. She claimed she'd
said no but he wouldn't listen. That he forced himself on top
of her, and raped her. I could see the jury looking at Simon
and then at Lucy. He was handsome, obviously someone who
would have no difficulty attracting women, while Lucy was
plain and I hate to say, dowdy on the stand. Rape victims

often resort to making themselves look as unattractive as possible – I knew that but the jury didn't. He said it was consensual. That she was all over him. That it was only when it was all over and she'd sobered up that she'd felt ashamed and had cried rape.'

I fell silent and it was a while before I could speak again. 'I asked her if she'd been a virgin up to this point. She said yes. But I produced hospital records that showed that she'd had an abortion the year before. She was Catholic and her parents hadn't known about the pregnancy. It was as if I'd raped her all over again by forcing her to admit that. I found all this out and I used it against her. I kept telling myself she'd lied about being a virgin, why wouldn't she lie about everything else? It was her word against his. The forensics was inconclusive. There was some bruising around the vaginal area but that could be explained away by rough sex.'

I sighed and my voice caught. 'I was a triumph. I destroyed Lucy on the stand, Simon was found not guilty. Lucy never returned to university. A few weeks later Lucy tried to kill herself.'

Jamie didn't tell me that I was only doing my job, or that Simon could have been innocent, instead he slipped an arm around my shoulder and pulled me into him.

I took another deep breath. 'The day of the Curtis trial, Lucy's father was waiting for me when I left the Chambers. He hit me. He was furious and distraught. He shouted at me that Lucy had tried to take her own life – that I had made her feel that she'd nothing left to live for – and that Simon had raped before. The victim had reported it to the police but withdrawn her statement before it came to court. When she heard about Lucy she began to have second thoughts. She sat through Lucy's trial but when she saw what I put Lucy through, she decided her initial decision had been correct. She did however tell Lucy that Simon had raped her too.

'If I had been representing Lucy I would have delved

deeper into Simon's history. The abrasions of Lucy's vagina might have been caused by rough sex but they were more likely to have been the result of rape. I would have double checked to see whether there had ever been other allegations against Simon.

'I tried to make it right. When I discovered there was potentially another victim, I persuaded Sophie, my pupil, to approach a prosecutor friend of hers, and to ask whether a complaint had ever been made – even though I knew I was taking advantage of my position as her pupil master by asking her to do so. We both knew she'd be crossing a professional boundary by even asking – let alone getting a name from her colleague of the other, alleged victim. But Sophie did as I asked and there had been a complaint – but because the victim had withdrawn her statement, it had never been taken any further. Sophie gave me the name but refused, quite rightly, to do any more. I wasn't sure what to do with the information and besides, I was too caught up with Mum being ill.

'Giles, my head of chambers found out that I'd asked Sophie to look into this other allegation and was, quite rightly furious. He told me to take some time off and reconsider my position. If Simon's father discovered I was actively seeking evidence against his son, there was every chance he'd sue. At the very least he'd take his not inconsiderable business away from Lambert and Lambert. Moreover, if the Law Society finds out what I did I might lose the right to practice.' My voice hitched. 'I went into law because I wanted to defend the weak and the defenceless. Instead I destroyed a young woman and even worse, I allowed a man to go free who could and probably will, rape again and I'm powerless to stop him.'

Jamie brushed a lock of hair from my face. 'You're crying.' He gathered me into his arms and before I knew it I was in his lap, my cheek pressed to the rough wool of his pullover and I was crying in earnest. For Mum, for Georgina, Edith and Mary. For Lucy and for all I hadn't done.

403

When my sobs had eased he held me at arm's length and looked me in the eye. 'So, my love, what are you going to do about it?'

Later, as we lay in bed together, Jamie's arms around me, my head on his chest, listening to the steady beat of his heart, I knew something inside me had changed. I felt purged and vulnerable and embarrassed – all three. But most of all, I no longer felt alone. I'd exposed myself completely and he hadn't turned away from me. I didn't have to be perfect.

A splatter of rain hit the windows like tiny bullets. The weather had changed in that sudden way it was prone to do on the west coast and I knew I should return to Greyfriars before the storm took hold. But there was something I needed to do first. I'd been lily-livered, caring too much about my career. I knew what I had to do to make things right – although I would have to dig deep to find some of the courage my aunts had shown.

Reluctantly, I threw the covers aside. 'I need to go.'

He smiled sleepily and reached out for me. 'Stay the night.'

I kissed him quickly, tempted, but knowing there would be other nights. Hopefully many of them.

Leaving Jamie's, I noticed a familiar figure sitting on the bench, looking across the sea, apparently oblivious to the wind and drizzle. From where the bench was positioned I could see the top of Greyfriars turret. I recalled Jamie telling me that Findlay came here every day like clockwork. He had to still care for Edith. It was the only thing that made sense. Findlay didn't look at me when I sat down next to him. Not even when Baxter and Tiger greeted each other playfully. I had some half-baked notion that perhaps there was still a chance I could bring them back together. That some happiness was still possible for Edith.

'You're still here then,' he said without looking up. The air was so thick as the storm approached.

'Looks like it. As you are. I heard you come here every day, to sit on this bench. Is it anything to do with Edith?'

He gave me a steely look. 'Never met a woman yet who could resist poking her nose in other people's business.'

He dug his pipe out of his jacket pocket and lit a match to it. The pleasant tang of tobacco smoke tickled my nostrils, before it was whipped away by the wind.

'I want to talk to you about my aunts.'

His brow furrowed. 'Are they all right?'

'No, they are not all right! But why do you care? You just want to sit here day after day, pining for something or someone that you don't have the guts to do anything about!' I was almost shouting now but I couldn't help myself.

Findlay half-turned towards me, his eyes dark with fury. 'You don't know the first thing about me. What I feel. What I think.'

'I think you still love Edith. That's why you came back here, isn't it? It's why you are here every day, isn't it? Your lost love – yet you do nothing about it. That's not true love.'

'Love!' he roared back at me. 'What do you know about love?' He swept an arm out, pointing towards Jamie's cottage. 'You prance about with young Jamie as if you know one single thing about love, yet I can see the fear in your eyes. Don't you dare tell me that I don't know about loving someone so much that it hurts every second of every day not to be near them, to touch them, to hear their voice.'

All at once the anger drained out of me. He was right. Who was I to judge anyone? Lately I had done very little to be proud of.

'I thought I loved Edith. I wanted to love her,' he said, so softly I wasn't sure I'd heard him correctly. My heart sank.

'What do you mean – *thought* you loved Edith? Have you stopped?'

He dipped his head. 'Everyone thought it was Georgina who made a play for me. They were wrong. It was the opposite

405

way around. The moment I set eyes on Georgina, Edith might as well not have existed.'

He was in love with *Georgina*! So Mum's instincts had been right all along.

'Mum said you and Georgina came over on the boat together. That last summer when you were all together.' The penny was finally beginning to drop. 'You were already in love with Georgina, weren't you?'

He flicked me another, sharp-eyed look. 'I was supposed to meet Edith in Edinburgh but there was a delay – a meeting I had to go to about which regiment I was going to sign up with. When I came to the house Edith had left already and there was only Georgina.'

I waited for him to continue.

'I wanted her the moment I saw her.' He laughed harshly. 'I tried to tell myself that what I felt was no more than lust. She was the complete opposite to Edith; self-centred, vain, with the morals of a cat. Except when it came to her sister.' He stopped and looked off into the distance, a small, sad smile playing on his lips. 'She loved Edith. She would have done anything to make her sister happy.'

'But Georgina seduced you, or at least tried to, that night down at the shore. My mother saw everything. You must remember. That's what caused all the upset.'

He breathed out – a long deep sigh. 'Georgina never wanted to hurt Edith. So she let everyone believe that it was she who was trying to seduce me and that I rejected her. Her reputation – what had happened in Paris – what people *thought* had happened. Everyone was quick to believe the worst of Georgina. She thought Edith would accept that she'd been drunk and forgive her eventually.

'But it didn't work out that way, did it? Edith still broke off the engagement and never truly forgave Georgina anyway.'

He narrowed his eyes, unable to hide his surprise. 'Is that what she told you?'

'It's not true?'

He shook his head. 'Edith did come to me wanting to make things up but I said no. I told her I couldn't marry her because I was in love with Georgina. She was the only woman I could see myself spending my life with.'

It wasn't what Edith had told Georgina when they were in the camps. My memory was almost perfect when it came to recalling conversations verbatim. She'd said that Findlay had come to see her in Peebles, but to try and make amends, to persuade Edith to go back to him.

In which case, Edith had lied. And she'd known for years that Findlay had been in love with Georgina. Thoughts were tumbling around in my head. Georgina had always implied that what Mum had seen was no more than a clumsy attempt to kiss Findlay after she'd had too much to drink. I'd always suspected she was holding out on me.

'Did Georgina know how you felt about her?'

'Yes.'

Why hadn't Georgina shared this with me? When she'd shared so much.

'When the war was over, why didn't you go to Georgina then?'

'I tried. I rowed over one night. The war changed how people saw things. Old notions of wrong and right had gone out the window. Those of us lucky enough to have survived knew we had to grasp what happiness we could. If not for our own sakes, then for those who had died and were never given the chance. During the war it was the thought of Georgina that kept me sane. As soon as it was over all I wanted was to be with her again.'

'What did she say?'

'She said she couldn't leave Edith. She even tried to pretend she didn't love me any more, but I knew she was lying. When I pressed her she said that Edith wasn't well and she had to take care of her. I told her I'd wait. For as long as it took.'

407

He looked across the sea to where the turret of Greyfriars was disappearing behind thick cloud. 'I've waited almost forty years for her to come to me. And I'll wait as long again if I have to.'

On the way back to the village, I turned what Findlay had said over in my mind. He said he still loved Georgina, but was that even possible? By his own admission it was years since he'd spoken to her and he had no idea what had happened to her during the war. No notion she had a child. Was that the true reason she'd turned him away?

How would he feel about her now if he knew she'd been raped? I'd heard of men turning away from the women they loved when they learned what had happened. They knew it was wrong, yet some deep, primeval part of them could not accept that another man had been intimate with their wife or girlfriend – even though they knew she'd done nothing to provoke the attack and had been traumatised by it. Some of these women had been persuaded to tell their partners only to have them turn away in disgust. In many ways they had been hurt twice over. As always, Lucy leapt to my mind. Her father hadn't turned away from her, he'd done the opposite and blamed himself for not protecting her, and what I'd done in court was paramount to raping her all over again. Like Georgina I needed a way to make restitution, both to Lucy and Annette. If by so doing I ruined my chances of ever working as a lawyer again, it was a chance I was prepared to take.

I stopped at the kiosk, spoke to Directory of Enquiries and got the number I was looking for. My hands were shaking as I called Annette's number. There was no going back now, and I made the call.

Chapter Forty-Six

The clouds had completely obscured the sun and rain was falling steadily as I rowed back to Greyfriars, gusts of wind whipping the sea into waves and rocking the little boat. When I got to Kerista, I thought about pulling the boat ashore but in the end decided against it. It was one thing pushing the boat from the land into the sea, hauling it out required more strength than I had. I settled for tying it securely to the post at the end of the pier.

I ran up to my room and changed into dry clothes before looking for my aunts. I found Georgina in the library with Mary. Georgina was reading a book and Mary was bent over the needlework in her lap, her tongue poking out of the corner of her mouth as she concentrated.

Mary looked up at me and beamed. 'Hello, Charlotte,' she said carefully. 'Did you have a nice day?' Tiger, ever the dilettante when it came to her affections, was at Mary's feet, looking up at her with adoration.

'I did, Mary. Thank you. What about you?'

'I've been doing my needlework.' She held it out to me with a shy smile.

I recalled the embroidery I had seen lying on the table, the feeling the room had recently been vacated, and realised that Mary must have been there only moments before and been ushered away upstairs before I'd come in. No wonder Edith had wanted me to be more precise about my comings and goings.

I asked Georgina if we might talk in the sitting room. She rose to her feet and telling Mary she'd be back soon, followed me out.

'It was you Findlay loved all along,' I said as soon as we were seated.

She paled. 'What makes you say that?'

'He told me.'

'You've been speaking to him?' She leaned forward, clasping her hands between her knees. 'How? When?'

I explained how I had met him, his association with Jamie, his reluctant admission that it was Georgina he loved. That he'd told Edith. While I talked she just sat there growing paler, tears trembling like pearls on her lower lashes.

She reached across and clutched my wrist. 'You must never repeat any of this to Edith.'

'But she lied to you!'

'I can't blame her. She loved him so much.'

'I don't understand,' I said. 'If you and Findlay loved each other, why didn't you do something about it? I mean after the war. He would have understood about the baby and Edith would have had to come around eventually.'

'I didn't want his understanding!' Georgina cried. 'Perhaps if things had turned out differently. If Edith hadn't risked her life for me. If I hadn't . . . ' She broke off and gave a little shake of her head. 'What does it matter now? It's too late, too much has happened. You'll understand better when I finish my story. You can't judge Edith without knowing it all! My betrayal was so much worse than she knew.'

She was becoming increasingly distressed.

'I have no right to judge either you or Edith. What makes you think I would?'

Georgina took a deep breath, sat straighter and placed her hands in her lap. 'Very well. You want the truth. I'll give it to you.

'After the row with Edith, everyone left. I stayed behind at Greyfriars to oversee its closing. In truth, your grandmother was too fed up with me to have me in London and Edith was in the house in Edinburgh so I couldn't go there and there was still two weeks before my ship was due to sail. After the house was closed up, I dismissed the servants and settled down to indulge my misery and lick my wounds. Greyfriars was the only place I had peace to do that.'

Georgina's deep blue eyes glistened in the gathering dusk.

'A few days before I was due to leave for London and then Singapore he came. I should have known he would. Deep down I *knew* he would.'

'We just stood there looking at each other. My heart was pounding so hard I thought I might stop breathing at any moment. Once more I had the opportunity to do the right thing. To close the door. Send him back to Edith. But the way he was looking at me . . . I could no more have done that than I could have stopped breathing.'

Chapter Forty-Seven

Georgina

Greyfriars, 1939

'What are you doing here?' she whispered.

'I told myself it was to see Edith; to try and make things right.'

'She's not here.' Then his words sank in. 'Told yourself?'

'She's everything a man could want, you know.' He spat the words as if they were bullets. 'Kind, gentle, loyal.'

'I know.'

'And you are the most selfish woman I have ever come across.' He took a step towards her. 'But God help me, I want you more than any woman I have ever met.'

Suddenly, she wasn't quite sure how, she was in his arms.

She should have pushed him away then. She had one last chance to do the right thing. If she'd told him to go he might make it up with Edith and marry her. But she didn't do any of that.

She kissed him back.

When he released her they were both breathing hard.

'You should go,' she said, pushing him away, her lips still warm from his mouth, her body tingling from his touch. 'Now.'

'Do you really want me to?'

'You know I don't.' She removed a cigarette from the box on the table. Her hands were shaking so much he had to light it for her.

'I would have married her,' he said, still looking at Georgina as if he hated her. 'We might have been happy.'

'You could still marry her. If you go to her and beg she might forgive you. She can be stubborn, but she loves you very much.'

'It's too late for that now.'

'So you've come here. Seeking what? Compensation? If you can't have the one sister then you'll have the other?'

He took a step towards her, until he was so close she could feel the heat radiating from him. 'Don't pretend. It doesn't suit you. You know how I feel about you, just as I know how you feel about me.'

'And how is that?' Her voice was annoyingly unsteady.

'You and I were meant to be together. We deserve each other.'

She raised an eyebrow at him. 'Has anyone ever told you your love-making leaves something to be desired?'

'Don't pretend you don't know we're two of a kind. No matter how much we might wish it was different.'

'And what do you propose we do about it?'

He wrapped his hand in her hair and tugged gently, forcing her to look into his eyes. 'You know.'

Later, lying next to him in the big feather bed, she waited for the guilt to come, but all she felt was a deep sense of happiness. This is where she was meant to be. She turned on her side and, propping herself on her elbow, looked down at him. His eyes were closed, his breathing steady and rhythmic. Becoming aware of her eyes on him he opened his and smiled.

'Are we bad people?' she whispered.

'Very bad.' He rolled over on his side to face her and traced the outline of her jaw with the tip of his finger. 'How can this be wrong? I love you. I will always love you. Nothing will ever change that.' He said it with such conviction she had no choice but to believe him.

'What are we going to do?' she asked.

413

'We are going to get married. That's what people in love do, isn't it?'

'Get married? We can't. What about Edith?'

'What about us?'

'She'll never forgive me. Never.'

'She will. She's a good woman. And she cares about you.'

'You don't understand. She's my sister! She'd see it as the worst sort of betrayal. And it is. Much worse than what I did before – and she's furious enough with me for that.'

He pulled her close so that her head lay on his chest. 'I won't give you up,' he said, his voice vibrating through her.

She'd have to make him. But what if he were killed? This might be the last time she'd see him. How could she let him go? She only wanted a little time with him. Then she might be content to live the rest of her life without him.

'We'll have these few days,' she said. 'I'm going to Singapore as I planned. You'll be with your regiment. The war won't last long. We'll decide what to do then. Perhaps Edith will have met someone else.'

But she thought it unlikely. Edith was the type of person, always had been, who once she gave her heart and her loyalty would never be swayed from her path. And even if she did fall in love with someone else, she would never forgive Georgina for continuing her betrayal. She knew that in the same way she knew the sun would rise every morning. In the same way she knew *she* would never love anyone else.

The next days were a combination of agony and blissful, giddy happiness. They slept late, made love and slept some more. At some point Georgina would rise and make them eggs and coffee and bring it into the bedroom, climbing back in alongside Findlay. He ate in the same way he made love, with total concentration. Sometimes, if it rained, they stayed in bed, at others they would dress and sit in the library and she would read until Findlay would grow restless and come over to nibble her neck and tempt her back to bed.

He wasn't a man used to being cooped up, but she made him promise not to leave the island, not even to take the small yacht out for a sail. No one could be allowed to know he was here. If he was seen, it would cause no end of gossip in the village – some of which might get back to Edith. However, if the weather was fine, they would picnic outside hidden from prying eyes by the rhododendrons.

She tried not to think of Edith and how she was betraying her even more than she had done already, telling herself that as long as her sister didn't know she couldn't be hurt further.

They spent five days together, the clock relentlessly ticking off the minutes and she tried not to think about when they'd have to part. Inevitably the day came when he had to leave to rejoin his regiment.

And she spent the rest of her life paying for those precious, stolen days.

Chapter Forty-Eight

Charlotte

1984

Georgina's eyes were misty and she took a linen handkerchief from her pocket and dabbed at them, before giving me a shaky smile.

'What will you do now you know he still loves you?' I asked.

'What can I do? I still can't go to him. Not when Edith . . .'

'Don't you think you've paid your debt to her? After all, she lied to you.'

'I always suspected she had. But it didn't change anything. As long as she still loved him I could never be with him. And now there's Mary to think of – and everything else that happened. I'm not the woman he once loved.' She looked so sad when she said that, my heart ached for her.

'Don't you think you should let him decide?'

A floorboard creaked and I whirled around, certain that someone was in the doorway, listening, but there was no one there. I should be used to the strange noises the house made by now.

'Why don't you meet him at least?'

'No. I think it's better Findlay stays in the past.'

She stood, making it clear the subject was closed. 'I don't like the look of the weather. I think one of those dreadful storms we get sometimes is blowing in.' She crossed over to the window and fastened the shutters. 'You probably made it back just in time, although I suspect you won't be seeing your young man tomorrow. At least not until the gale blows out.'

A door banged somewhere and a sudden violent gust of wind screeched through a gap in one of the window frames. Tiger trotted towards the door and stood there, her ears pricked, before turning to me and whining softly.

'Here, Tiger,' I called. 'It's only the wind.' She remained at the door for a few moments before padding back to me and laying her head on my feet.

Georgina stretched. 'I'm ready for bed. I'll just say good-night to Mary and Edith first.'

I picked *Jane Eyre* from the bookshelf. 'I think I'll read for a while.'

I'd only read a few paragraphs when I heard Georgina shouting my name. She sounded terror-stricken. Immediately I was on my feet and running up the stairs, my heart in my throat.

I followed the sound of her voice into a room. The bed was neatly made, the corners of the sheets crisply, meticulously folded. Georgina was standing next to it, tears running down her face, a letter in her hand. 'Mary!' she cried and ran from the room. My heart still racing, I picked up the letter from where it had fluttered to the floor, and read it.

My dearest Georgina

Forgive me for what I am about to do.

I heard what Charlotte told you. That he is still waiting. That he still loves you. I have known for a long time that you love him. When you were ill in camp with malaria you kept calling for him. I should never have told you the

417

lie that he came to see me in Peebles asking to get back together. I went to him, to tell him I forgave him, but he told me that you loved each other and that he planned to marry you. It was this I couldn't forgive you for.

I meant to confess but somehow the time never seemed right. When we got back to greyfriars I was going to tell you then. Then I discovered I was pregnant and I had other things on my mind. I saw him come to you but you turned him away. I could have told you then but you might have left me and I couldn't bear for that to happen. So I said nothing.

I know you won't go to him as long as I still live. Any wrong you did me has been paid for in full. I am tired of this life. I will go into the sea - let it take me as it should have all those years ago. You saved my life at the camp, let me save you now. You have done so much for me, it is time I did something for you.

Don't be sad for me. I have had a good life with you and Mary at greyfriars. I know you will care for my daughter as if she were your own. As you always have.

go to him. It is not too late. Be happy. You deserve it.

Your loving sister
Edith.

Mary was *Edith's* child! Why had Georgina lied? Could I trust anything she'd told me? But there wasn't time to think about it now. I heard Georgina's footsteps running down the stairs. I dropped the letter and hurried after her, catching her at the door.

'Do you know where to look?' I asked.

'She told Mary she's gone to keep Lady Sarah company. She'll be down at the rocks.'

Grabbing torches, we ran together, the wind impeding our progress until we came to the rocks. There at the edge we saw a pile of neatly folded clothing. There was no other sign of Edith.

'We're too late!' Georgina cried.

'There's still a chance. You said she's a strong swimmer. You keep searching while I get help.'

I left her there and ran towards the pier. The rain was falling heavier now, the wind hurling it into my eyes, making it almost impossible to see. I stumbled on. I knew the chances of finding Edith alive were slim but we had to try. And I couldn't do it alone.

I tripped over the root of a tree and my torch tumbled to the ground and I lost more precious moments looking for it. Finally I located it half-hidden under a bush. I picked it up, banging it against my hand in an attempt to make the battery work for a little longer. My attempts succeeded and although the light was weak and not much help it was better than nothing.

At the pier I undid the rope attached to the boat and brought it closer in. I counted the waves, forcing myself to wait until one brought the little boat up against the pier and I sucked in a breath and stepped on board. The boat rocked under my weight, almost tipping me over the side, but I just managed to hold on.

As I rowed I was thankful for the times I had already crossed. My arms were stronger than they had been when I'd first arrived which was just as well as I needed all my strength to keep the combination of current and wind from pulling me out to sea. As it was, the trip that normally took me less than ten minutes took me twice that long.

I sobbed with relief when I finally reached the other side. Ignoring my sodden clothes I ran to my car and leapt inside. I drove to the kiosk and dialled 999. I asked to be put through to the coastguard and explained to the calm voice on the other end what had happened. I was told they would organise a search.

I slammed the phone down and ran towards Jamie's cottage. Who knew how long the coastguard would take. I remembered that Ian who'd taken me across to Greyfriars that first day was a volunteer with them but he hadn't said where they were based. Most likely Oban or Fort William. It would take time for them to gather the crew together and find their way to Kerista.

But Jamie wasn't in. There were no lights on and his door was locked. I thought frantically. Could he be visiting his family? Or be with Findlay?

There was one other place. The inn.

I ran again, my breath scratching my throat, my lungs beginning to scream, the short distance seeming like miles instead of yards. But finally, there it was; the lights of Balcreen Inn.

I flung the door open and several pairs of astonished eyes turned in my direction. My legs almost buckled when I saw Jamie's familiar dark head bent close to Findlay's at the table near the door. Jamie sprang to his feet and hurried towards me.

'Charlotte! What is it?' He took my freezing hands in his and started to rub them.

'It's Edith. She's in the sea,' I gasped. 'At Kerista.'

The room fell silent as everyone stopped speaking and turned to stare.

Findlay was already slipping his arms into an oilskin. If he'd been drinking there was no evidence of it in his steady gaze.

'Have you let the coastguard know?' Jamie asked, turning and picking up his jacket from the back of the chair he'd been sitting on.

'Yes. Where are they based? How long will they be?'

'Ian,' Findlay called out and a familiar figure stepped forward. 'Have you had the call yet?'

Ian shook his head. 'They'll be trying my house first. When they get no answer, they'll know to call here. Then they'll go on down the list.'

The other men in the bar were placing their pints on the counter and slipping into their jackets until there were four others beside Ian. 'We'll help,' one said and the others nodded.

'It's a wild night, lads,' Jamie said. 'But any help will be appreciated.'

Ian turned to the men standing beside him. 'My boat is tied up alongside my house. Willie, Jack, you come with me. Hamish and Stan, you go with the inspector here.'

'I'll be coming along too,' Findlay said.

Ian looked at him for a long moment, before nodding. He turned back to the barmaid who was standing behind the counter, a dishcloth in one hand, an empty pint glass in another. 'Get on to the coastguard. Tell them there's two boats going out. One skippered by me, the other by Jamie.'

As the men headed out the door, I grabbed Jamie's wrist. 'I want to come too.'

'You should stay here. Get into dry clothes and keep warm.'

I shook my head. 'I'm coming.'

Whatever he saw in my face appeared to convince him I meant what I said. 'Okay. But you have to promise to keep out of the way and to do exactly what I tell you.' A smile softened the grim line of his mouth and he brushed my damp hair from my face. 'I can't lose you too.'

We spent the next hour searching for her. Both boats had far stronger lights than the torch I held, more like search lights, but they were no match for the waves. It was like trying to find a needle in a haystack. When the sea-rescue boat turned up, Jamie went alongside Ian's boat, a fishing vessel that was far more stable than his, and transferred Findlay and the other men across to it. Then despite my protestations he headed towards the jetty at Kerista, tied up and deposited me on dry land.

'There's no more you can do. We'll stay out for as long as we can. But you should go back to the house.' He gave me an encouraging smile. 'You never know. There's a chance she didn't really go into the sea and is even now sitting by the fire drying off. '

I hadn't thought of that. But it was possible. He handed me a spare torch. 'If she is, go to one of the upstairs windows facing Balcreen and keep flashing the torch. I'll keep an eye out for it.'

I pulled him towards me and pressed my lips hard against his, tasting salt and rain. 'Please take care,' I begged him.

He tipped an imaginary hat and grinned before stepping back onto his boat and raising the sails to catch the wind again.

Georgina was in the kitchen, clutching a mug of tea, her face pale and her eyes red- rimmed. The look of hope in her eyes when she saw me told me everything I needed to know.

I sat down opposite her. 'She didn't come back?'

She shook her head and her eyes welled. 'She won't be coming back. Oh, dear God, Edith!'

'Where's Mary?'

'I put her to bed. She's asleep. I don't think she understands . . .' Georgina's voice caught.

I crouched by the side of her chair. 'You mustn't lose hope. Not yet. They're out there looking for her. The coastguard and two other boats. They won't stop until they find her.'

She shook her head. 'They won't find her alive.' The tears slipped down her face. 'All I ever wanted was to keep her safe.'

Now that the adrenalin was seeping away I realised I was

422

almost numb with cold. I should get out of my wet clothes but I couldn't leave Georgina.

'You did everything you could.'

'It wasn't enough.'

'Why did you tell me *you* were Mary's mother?'

Georgina closed her eyes and sighed. 'I'm as much Mary's mother as Edith was.' She was quiet for a long time. 'Remember I told you I found Edith down by the rocks not long after we returned to Greyfriars?'

'Yes.'

'It was then I found out she was pregnant. All I told you before was the truth. Edith being in prison, being unwell, my having sex with the commandant. But I switched the time scales around. She was taken prisoner *after* I slept with the commandant. Everything I told you about her being ill and needing quinine and food to survive is true. She did recover and when she found out what I had done to save her, what I was still doing, she was distraught. She begged me to stop going to the commandant but I wouldn't. Even with what he gave me, food and medicines in the camp were still almost non-existent. So many people were dying, that when the opportunity came for Edith to work at the village hospital she grabbed it with both hands. She told me then I would have no need to continue going to the commandant and what she and Linda brought back in terms of food and medicines did make a difference. So I stopped going to him. I think I said that he'd told me right from the beginning that he would never force me and he didn't. He was very angry, however, and I sometimes think it was he who arranged for Edith's arrest. To get back at me.'

'You can't know that.'

'Not for certain, no. But he was a cruel and proud man. People still died but many survived who wouldn't have stood a chance without the extra rations and medicines Edith and Linda stole from the hospital. Most of us put on a little weight

423

and because we were stronger those who had just about given up regained the will to survive. Between them, Edith and Linda are responsible for saving many lives. But all that came to an end when they were imprisoned. Either the commandant told the Japanese Kempeitai to arrest Edith and Linda or they found out about the thefts from the hospital, although Edith and Linda were careful. I did go to the commandant to beg him to intervene and he did put me in solitary, not just because I'd challenged him but because I'd stopped going to him.

'When Edith came back from the prison she was broken in spirit as well as body. She wouldn't speak, would barely eat and I was terrified all over again that she was going to die. I went back to the commandant then. I had no choice. But it was only a couple of weeks later that he distributed the Red Cross parcels and another couple of weeks after that when we were liberated. I wasn't pregnant and I didn't know that Edith was until I found her that night down by the rocks on the west side.'

Georgina shook her head. 'After everything we'd been through – after all we'd survived. When I thought, finally, that we could somehow get back to our lives.'

Her face was awash with tears and she dashed them away with an impatient hand.

'I still don't understand. Why did you tell me Mary was *your* child?'

'Because I promised Edith.'

She lifted her chin and took a shuddering breath before continuing.

'Just as I told you I found her down by the shore. In the same spot you found her and the same place she went into the sea tonight. She was balancing on the rock looking out to sea.'

Chapter Forty-Nine

Georgina

1945

She was terrified that if she called out, she would startle Edith and Edith would fall into the water.

She moved as quietly as she could until she was almost directly behind her sister and ready to grab her. However her approach wasn't as quiet as she'd hoped. Edith turned around and smiled. But her eyes were blank and as dead as the day she'd come back to the camp from prison.

'Oh, Georgina. You shouldn't be out of bed.'

'Neither should you, darling. Why don't we both go back inside? I'll warm up some milk for us.'

Edith shook her head. 'Warm milk isn't going to make this better. I'm pregnant.'

'Oh, Edith, no! How?'

'The usual way.'

'Are you sure?'

'I didn't want to believe it. I tried to pretend it couldn't be possible. That my swelling stomach was down to beriberi. But I was wrong.' Her mouth twisted into a moue of distaste. 'There is a baby – a Japanese baby – growing inside me. If I could slice my stomach open and cut it out, I would.' She grimaced. 'Ironic, isn't it? If you hadn't got the extra food for me I wouldn't have survived. I certainly would have never been able to get pregnant. Oh, I don't blame you,' she added quickly. 'I like to imagine I would have done the same for you.'

Although it was daylight the sea was grey, the light flat, the colours of the hills a muted brown.

'How did it happen?'

'One of the guards in the prison raped me. The day we were released. I thought he was taking me away to execute me, but instead he raped me. I wish he had killed me.'

'Why didn't you tell me?'

'I couldn't. I didn't want to think of it. I just wanted to shut it out. Pretend it never happened. Not even Linda knew.'

It explained so much. The imprisonment must have been traumatic, she and Linda not knowing from hour to hour whether they would be executed, hardly seeing daylight for days on end, and for it all to end in rape! No wonder Edith had barely spoken when she'd been released back to the camp.

'We can get through this,' Georgina pleaded.

'How? For God's sake, Georgina, how? How can I give birth to a child who is half Japanese? How could I bring myself to look at it! Every day I'll be faced with a reminder that I was raped! Every day I'll be reminded of what I suffered these last few years. Can you imagine what people will say? At the very least they'll believe I collaborated. No one will ever wish to have anything to do with me. I will never be able to show my face anywhere again.' She looked out towards the sea and all the animation drained out of her. 'Far better both it and I die. You at least can have some kind of life.'

'Hasn't there been enough death and dying?' Georgina cried.

'I don't care about my life any more. I thought being back here I would recover. I have such nightmares, Georgina. Every night. I can't go on.'

'I'll take it,' Georgina said quickly. 'I'll say it's mine. I was the one who really collaborated after all. Please, Edith. The child and I can stay here. You can go back to nursing. No one need ever know. The shame will be all mine!'

Edith hesitated. 'You promise to say it's yours?'

'Yes! Please, darling. Say you'll think about it. If you die now, after everything, I don't know if I can continue either.'

The last was said in desperation. If Edith couldn't bear to live for herself she had to be given a reason to want to stay alive.

Georgina stepped forward slowly until she was standing next to her sister. She took Edith's hand. 'If you go in, it won't be alone.'

Chapter Fifty

Charlotte

1984

'Edith came back to the house with me,' Georgina said. 'Everything that happened after was how I told you, except it was Edith who had the baby, not me.

'I kept my side of the bargain and when Mary was born I took on all the duties, responsibilities and,' she smiled slightly, 'the joys of being a mother. Edith helped care for us, but as I told you, at first she could hardly bring herself to look at Mary.'

'You gave up any chance of being with Findlay, not because you had a child but because Edith had? Why didn't you tell me right from the start Mary was Edith's? '

'Because I'd promised her I'd always claim Mary as mine. And Mary wasn't the only reason I couldn't go to Findlay. I had to look after them both.' Her voice quavered. 'One day, when Mary was only a few weeks old, I woke up to find her gone. I searched everywhere for her and Edith but they weren't anywhere in the house. I was so terrified I could barely breathe. Especially when I remembered finding Edith down at the shore. I ran there and sure enough, balancing on those same rocks, was Edith with Mary in her arms. Edith was asleep but I was petrified that this time she intended to go into the sea with Mary. It took a while but eventually I persuaded her to hand me Mary and she let me lead them both back to the house.

'I didn't know what to do. I knew Edith loved Mary, that when she was awake she would never hurt her, but I couldn't be sure what she was capable of when she was sleepwalking. All I could do was keep my eye on Mary all the time during the day and keep her in with me at night, locking my door to stop Edith coming in.'

'Why didn't you make her see a doctor?'

'I tried but she wouldn't have it. She said they'd lock her away and she couldn't bear to ever spend another single second behind a locked door. I just couldn't do it to her. Not after everything she'd been through. So I gave up on the doctor and kept as close an eye on her as I could. I locked all the outside doors as soon as she was asleep and unlocked them in the morning.

'Over time she came to love Mary as much as I do. The sleepwalking stopped, as did the nightmares, and the three of us were happy. But then your mother came and Edith started sleepwalking again and behaving oddly. I was terrified of what she might do. I had to make Olivia leave. I tried to do the best I could to keep everyone safe.' Her face crumpled. 'But in the end I wasn't able to save Edith.'

It was three days before Edith's body washed up. Tossed by the tide onto the rocks, her final return to Greyfriars. Jamie helped with the police investigation – not that there was much doubt that Edith had taken her own life. A week later, she was buried on Kerista, with Georgina, Mary, Jamie and me – and Findlay – her mourners.

After the service I walked outside and looked across the sea. I no longer found the silence oppressive – quite the opposite – there was a comfort in the shushing of the waves, of the wind in the trees. *I am a thousand winds that blow.* I turned around and looked back at Greyfriars and thought of the people its walls had sheltered over the years. I thought of ghosts and that you don't have to believe in their manifestation to know that they exist. Mum was there in my memories, in the love that I felt enveloping me, that I knew would always wrap around me. I thought that finally I was proud of myself and how now I could think of her without my heart breaking into a thousand pieces.

I sensed him behind me before I heard him. He wrapped his arms around me and I leaned into him. His breath was warm on my neck.

'What are you going to do?' he asked.

'Go back to London. Try to salvage what's left of my career.' After my phone call to her, Annette had agreed to go to the police and revive her complaint against Simon. The new accusation had made it into the papers and since then one more girl had come forward accusing Simon of raping her before Annette or Lucy. I hoped this time he'd go down. Horrified that his son did appear to be guilty, Simon's father had agreed not to make a complaint against me. Nevertheless, I was no longer welcome at Lambert and Lambert.

'Will you change sides?'

'I don't want to be on one side or the other. I don't want to prosecute the hopeless and the desperate. Someone else can do that. My heart has always been with defending. Even though I haven't always got it right—'

'No more rape cases then . . . ?'

'No. Even if I have to starve.'

He nuzzled my neck. 'I would never let you starve.'

'I know.' I guessed what was coming next.

He turned me around and lifted my chin with his finger so I was staring into his eyes. My heart was thudding.

'Come live with me in Glasgow?'

I thought of the people who needed me, Georgina and Mary, the Annettes and Lucys of this world.

'I won't give up being a barrister whatever happens. I'll probably carry on working horrendous hours. We'll hardly see each other – you haven't seen me when I'm involved in a case – I can think of nothing else . . .'

'Then I'll just have to get a job with the Metropolitan police and move to London.'

'Georgina won't live forever. I'll have to help her take care of Mary when Georgina gets too frail – and after – when Georgina dies.'

'I know. It's one of the reasons I love you.'

There was a lump in my throat. 'I will miss her when she goes.'

He placed his hands on either side of my face, brushing away my tears with the pad of his thumb. 'Anything else? Or are you telling me you don't love me? Because I won't believe it. Or are you telling me that you don't love me enough?'

I held his gaze. 'I'm telling you that I love you, more than I can say, but life with me won't be easy.'

He laughed again, unable to hide the relief in his eyes. 'Who said I like easy?'

Chapter Fifty-One

There was something I had to do before I returned to London and I told Jamie it was better I did it on my own.

I didn't know if what I was thinking would ever happen, but I had to try. I rowed across to the mainland and, with Tiger trotting by my side, took the steep, bare path to Findlay's house. Winter was coming in fast now and I stopped to inhale the sharp, crystal air, knowing I would miss it when I returned to London, but also knowing it wouldn't be long before I came back.

He was sitting outside mending creels, his long fingers surprisingly nimble in the cold. Although my steps made no noise on the soft earth, I knew he was aware of my presence.

'What do you want?' he asked gruffly without looking up. 'Why can't women leave men in peace?'

I sat next to him, my gloved hands thrust deep in my pockets. Tiger and Baxter sniffed each other before starting a game of tag. 'I've come to invite you to dinner at Greyfriars.'

'Now why would you do that?'

'Do you still love Georgina? Or did seeing her again change things?'

'What? Because you think she's old and old people can't fancy each other?' He rounded on me. 'She's as beautiful as the day I first saw her.' His voice softened. 'More beautiful even.'

'Then come to dinner.' I slid him a look. 'Or are you worried she might not fancy *you*?'

432

He laughed harshly. 'Now that is far more likely.' His eyes clouded. 'She didn't seem that keen to talk to me at the funeral.' I saw his anxiety for the first time.

'The funeral of Edith probably wasn't the best time for you to approach Georgina. She loved her sister very much. Everything she did was to protect Edith, to atone. All her life she's been paying for falling in love with you. Don't you think she deserves some happiness now? It's not too late.' Even as I said the words I wondered if that was true. Georgina had been changed in ways I could never fully appreciate by what had happened to her during the war. She, as much as Edith, was a victim of rape, and I knew her guilt about the commandant still tormented her. Was I right to interfere?

'She's been through some terrible experiences. Both of the sisters went through something so horrible it's almost impossible to imagine. I don't know if Georgina can ever shake that off, but I do know she wants to see you. However, I'm warning you, if you hurt my aunt . . . '

'I would never hurt her. That's why I don't think I should see her again. She's not the only person who has changed. I'm an old man.' He narrowed his eyes at me. 'One who has his own demons. Not exactly a catch.'

I stood. 'Jamie told me you were a hero in the war. You don't look much like one to me.'

I turned on my heel, whistled for Tiger and marched back down the hill.

Chapter Fifty-Two

I watch from the sitting room window as he strides towards the house – in the failing light he is tall, vigorous – the man Edith and Georgina loved. Dressed in a clean, pressed white shirt and clean–shaven, his wild hair tamed (or almost), and I am unbearably moved to see his neatly knotted tie. As he comes closer, his limbs appear to loosen and love blazes from his eyes. He has become a different man – his expression has lost that hunted look, his mouth the sarcastic lift. He stops for a moment as if doubtful and I hold my breath – he can't change his mind. But then his face breaks into a wide smile – the first I have seen – and she comes running towards him as if the years have fallen from her too and she is once more the young woman he fell in love with. A foot or two away and she pauses, uncertain. Then he holds out his arms and as she steps into them and he wraps his arms around her, I know it will be all right. Everything is going to be all right.

Chapter Fifty-Three

Eighteen months later

I have slipped upstairs to the turret from where I can see my wedding guests gathered on the lawn. I wanted these few minutes alone, to hug my happiness before I allow myself to be enfolded in the arms of my new family.

I find it difficult to believe that eighteen months ago, with the death of Mum I had thought myself alone – now I am surrounded by more family than I know what to do with.

These last months have sped by and it has not always been easy. I have spoken to the registrar of births, deaths and marriages and, not without difficulty, have had Mary's birth registered. She is now officially Mary Guthrie although in the space where a father's name should go, it says unknown. Not every loose end can, or should be, tied up. I think about my father, half-sister and -brother and sometimes wonder whether I should try to track them down. Perhaps I will one day.

The commandant, according to records, was executed for war crimes in 1946.

Mary is sitting on a wicker chair, with the ever-present Georgina protectively by her side. My great-aunt has since recovered the sparkle my mother spoke of, along with her love of champagne, and is waving her glass around as she talks animatedly to my new husband, who appears to be as under her spell as he is mine. Close by Georgina is Findlay, who, I

435

have discovered, polishes up rather well. He is handsome in his morning coat, and has, I have also learned, a roguish sense of humour. He still enjoys his whisky but his wife keeps a close but loving eye on the amount he drinks.

Mary is slowly becoming used to company and although still painfully shy has ventured as far as Edinburgh in recent weeks. At first it was brief trips to Balcreen, the villagers agog when they learned of her existence, but they have become accustomed to seeing her dark-haired figure arm in arm with Georgina. She has let it be known that Mary is her daughter, although not the circumstances of her birth.

'Let them think what they like!' she says. 'Mary is mine in every way.'

My aunt and I have come to a rather complicated arrangement about the houses, which although the lawyer in me is more than a little aghast at its lack of precision, suits us both. I think Mum would have been pleased and that makes her absence easier to bear. The house in Edinburgh has been sold and a portion of the proceeds used to buy a small flat in Mary's name in Edinburgh. Whether she will ever feel able to live there on her own, only time will tell. Certainly Georgina likes to have her daughter with her at Greyfriars although she is looking to a time when she might not be there. She doesn't like to think of Mary living alone at Greyfriars, which I will inherit in full when Georgina and Findlay die. I desperately hope that won't be for a long time.

The remainder of the proceeds of the house in Edinburgh, along with that from the sale of Findlay's house, has been spent on restoring Greyfriars to its former glory. The ivy has been cut back, the garden tamed. Every window has been repaired or replaced, likewise every rotten floorboard. It has been painted and polished until it gleams and shines like the old dowager lady she is and a large chunk of the money has been spent on building a simple stone causeway from the road across to the pier. Findlay, Georgina and Mary often sally forth on trips to Oban and Fort William, and Georgina has rediscovered the joys of shopping for herself. She's still to be found in trousers and wellington boots, but delights in dressing up for dinner. Should she, Findlay and Mary decide to make the flat in Edinburgh their home, Georgina and I have discussed turning Greyfriars into a refuge for women who need a sanctuary for whatever reason. I think Mum would approve of that too.

Agnes is here as well. Although she is a little bemused at the turn my life has taken, she is happy for me. She and her family have spent the week here at Greyfriars and together have revisited her childhood home in Balcreen.

Shouts of laughter fly through the air and Jamie's nieces and nephews scamper across the lawn, watched by the proud eyes of their parents. I have a whole other family too now.

I press my hand to my stomach, still flat but surely not for much longer, as my husband comes to stand behind me. He wraps his arms around me and nuzzles my neck. 'Happy?' he asks.

It won't always be easy for us. Jamie and I have equally strong views on justice and they don't always align. I no longer work for Lambert and Lambert, but have set up on my own, in a small office in a less salubrious part of London. Sophie is my partner and we focus on human rights cases. My practice took some time to recover – reputations are forgotten as quickly as they are made, but recover it did – and although there is little money in our new line of work, it is enough. We win some and lose some. The losses I still find painful.

I continue to work long hours, although I try to leave one evening a week and a day at the weekend free just for Jamie. It doesn't always pan out the way we'd want – the evenings I am free, he is often working.

I love my husband with an intensity that takes my breath away. It seems the Guthrie women might not have always loved wisely but they love deeply.

'We should go downstairs,' Jamie says. 'If you are ready?'

I lean into him. Just for a moment I think I see a figure – a woman – although I can't be sure of how she looks or what she is wearing – standing in the trees looking directly at me. I blink and the image is gone. Edith? Mum? Mum's child ghost all grown up? Who knows? I want to believe that Mum knows I am not alone or lonely any more, and will never be. This child will almost certainly be an only one – a visit to the doctor suggested I am about to go into early menopause – so Jamie and I decided not to wait until we tried for a baby. We were surprised but delighted when I fell pregnant within a couple of months. But only child or not, he or she will, like me, be watched over by good people, will know right from wrong, and be overwhelmed with love. All I care about is that everyone I love and who loves me is here at Greyfriars and that it is, once again, a happy place.

Acknowledgements

It is said that it takes a village to raise a child – the same could be said for writing a book. With that in mind, my heartfelt thanks to my husband Stewart, sisters Flora and Mairi, sister-in-law Lesley and daughter Rachel, for their insightful, if at times ruthless, feedback; to my agent Judith Murdoch for her advice and support; to my editor, Manpreet Grewal for her enthusiasm for the book and to the rest of the amazing team at Sphere – you are all part of my village!

For anyone interested in learning more about the women's experience while captives of the Japanese I can recommend the following books:

Sisters in Arms by Nicola Tyrer, *The Real Tenko* by Mark Felton, *Quiet Heroines* by Brenda McBryde and *White Coolies* by Betty Jeffrey.